Interior Designed By

1st Edition

ISBN: 978-1-964324-01-2

# Soul'd

By:  J. L. Christie

# Chapter 1: "Real" Real Estate

Sissy strummed the steering wheel of her silver '82 Honda Civic and stared at the infamously fogged windows of the empty brick fortress known as "The Rawlins Mansion." Tuning out the soundtrack to "Lovely in Pink" in the background, Sissy muttered to herself, "March madness killed somebody. Sure, whatever, Mr. Taylor. Just because I'm not from around here doesn't make me stupid . . ."

***Earlier That Day***

At the young age of twenty-five in the spring of 1985, Melissa "Sissy" Clayton felt she had arrived. Sissy, who felt average in almost every way - - from her average height, average to heavy-ish weight, average mouse brown hair (though it was cut in an a-symmetrical cut because she saw it in a magazine and thought it was so progressive), down to her bitten fingernails with chipped neon polish - - felt she finally achieved something unique.

In 1979, she graduated high school and went as far away from home in Atlanta to go to college in Deep South Georgia. After getting a "useless" degree in psychology, she decided to be "practical" and also earned her real estate license "just in case." Her "just in case" immediately landed her a job in Even Deeper South Georgia, making her "gainfully employed" as her father unabashedly proclaimed to anyone willing to listen.

Yes, impressing her father was perhaps the greatest feat of all. Never mind he had predicted she would follow in the family footsteps, and not become the next Freud, Jung, or Pearls as she had jubilantly proclaimed one semester from the other end of a long-distance phone call, only to be reduced to tears when her father loudly "humphed" and laughed, "No, no my dear, making money is far too important to you. Focus on that license in real estate. Your mother can't wait to show you how to take over her accounts."

At this moment, Sissy comforted herself with the knowledge she had not ridden on her family's coattails to do it. Despite the prediction, Sissy was proud of one thing - - she had not gone home but had stayed far, far away and in three years time, had progressed from being a greenhorn associate whose experience in real estate consisted of managing paperwork between slum lord to slum lord, to selling dozens of shoe-box-sized ranch houses to first time home owners, to becoming the youngest realtor at *First Team Realty* to handle The Rawlins Mansion. A mansion. Not a ranch house. Not a condemnable crack den. A bona fide mansion. "Real" real estate with all the nice things that come with it: Big commission. Prestige. Resume building . . .

Sure, the house had just been sold three years prior when Sissy first started working for *First Team* and no one else at *First Team Realty* wanted to take it, but she was ready and willing. This was to be her first big commission sale with wealthy buyers. She had hit "the big time" at the age of twenty-five.

Giddy with excitement, Sissy awoke particularly early on the third of March, ready to start her day cleaning and scouring the unoccupied Rawlins Mansion. One giant cardboard box of cleansers and cleaning supplies filled the back of her silver hatch-back '82 Honda Civic when she pulled into work that morning. Even though the Rawlins had only been empty for a few months, Sissy was determined to make the prestigious old home sparkle and shine. After all, it reminded her of her Gammy Clayton's house where she visited several magical summers in her youth. Visions of being personally responsible for bringing the Rawlins back to its former glory bounced in her head.

Of course, when she told her boss, Mr. Taylor, about her plans to put a little elbow grease into the house's notoriously famous fogged windows and dusty crown moldings, the man just sardonically huffed, instantly reducing Sissy back to her status of greenhorn associate with no experience in "real" real estate.

Such verbal exchanges made Sissy feel very self-conscious and she began to wish she had worn something more conservative to work that morning. In the name of comfort and eighties fashion, Sissy wore some cut off blue jeans with the cuffs rolled, two tank tops layered on top of each other - - one pink, the other turquoise, with her fashion forward matching Converse: one hot pink and one turquoise. She had multiple ear piercings and was wearing the solar system in them: a sun earring in the left, moon in the right, and dangling, tinkling star earrings cascading down. Even without the outfit, Taylor had a way of making her feel as if she were twelve and had sneezed during his mother's eulogy.

Mr. Taylor, a white-haired man with decades of experience and alcohol-nicotine induced lines in his face stared at Sissy as he spat tobacco juice into a tar stained laxative bottle/make shift spittoon, "You want to waste your time and risk ruining your perty little outfit trying to clean up the place, fine by me, but I am not reimbursing you for cleaners and whatever."

Sissy tried to hide her self-consciousness at his remark and her revulsion at his nasty habit, which made inconspicuously untangling her long spiral earring from the loosened hem of one of her various layered tank tops very difficult. Trying not to struggle,

Sissy remarked, "But, you're supposed to clean the house. I always clean the houses."

Taylor moved his flicked his tongue over his tobacco stained teeth, "Yeah?"

Sissy felt challenged as if he were questioning her integrity, "Of course. That's what the manual says you're supposed to do. So I always have."

Mr. Taylor chuckled and rearranged his chaw to the other cheek, "Maybe. But it's a waste of time on that house." He spat and put the laxative bottle on the desk in front of him beside his coffee thermos. Sissy wondered if he had ever accidentally gotten the two confused, spitting into his coffee and drinking his spit.

Sissy visibly shivered but turned her head as if her ear itched and she was scratching it on her shoulder in a feeble attempt to dislodge the dangle. *Yep, this earring is definitely caught.* Still trying to remain inconspicuous, Sissy gave up trying to untangle the earring and just stood with her head cocked to the side, "Why?"

Taylor pulled out a pair of large, silver scissors from his drawer and walked toward Sissy's head with them wide open. Sissy stared back at the man in confusion, but he just huffed stale cigarette breath in her face and clipped the hem in one small snip - - and like that she was free. Taylor stepped back from Sissy as if nothing had happened, shrugged his shoulders, and replied, "March madness."

Sissy straightened her back and turned her head in freedom, "Thank you. Now, what were you saying?"

Taylor sat down at his desk and spat into the laxative bottle, "They say that's what killed Judge Rawlins and that's why it's up

4

for sale now. March madness. House'll sell because it's a great house, not because you practically *kill yourself* trying to clean it. Trust me. Put your sign out front and call it a day. Hell, take the rest of the day off and tell me you spent it cleaning."

Sissy cocked her left eyebrow and said with sarcasm, "March madness . . . what's that supposed to mean?"

Taylor let out a ragged sigh, "It's just a catch phrase."

Sissy shook her head and held out her hand, "So, this 'catch phrase' killed somebody?"

Taylor shifted his chaw and looked up at Sissy, "The honorable Judge Rawlins was the man who had the house built for his 'child-bride' back in the early 1900s. Then he killed himself in the month of March while she was away visiting relatives or some crap. Just about everybody's heard the story and tells it different: he hung himself, he shot himself, he killed himself in the house, at his mother's, out in the woods, the damn butler did it. Who knows, who cares. The thing is, the house has been the 'three year rental' ever since. The Vaughan's are selling it so damn cheap, somebody'll snag it, sink money into it, and leave after another three years. Then you can sell it all over again, if you want to. You could really profit from March madness."

Sissy found the entire conversation strange. Even though that was the first time she had ever really spoken to or interacted with Mr. Taylor, her initial impression of him was not the caring boss who allowed his employees to play hooky, much less tell them to do so. If anything, his discouraging words were fuel for Sissy's young determination to rebel against authority and prove him wrong.

## Chapter 2: Pools of Memories

Therefore, March the third of 1985 found Sissy pulling up into the open carport of the illustrious Rawlins Mansion, her "New Wave" music blaring and faulty Civic brakes squealing her arrival. The house had beautiful "curb appeal" with lush landscaping made of ancient boxwood topiaries and bright perennials lined the driveway in precise layers and depth like a robed choir. Sissy got out of her car and walked around to the back of the house, pushing open the rusty gate to the pool. The gate's groan seemed to ripple the pool, but it was just the newly hatched spring insects flitting and skirting above the surface of the water.

*Ahhh, the pool. Just like Gammy's.* Sissy closed her eyes and breathed in the fresh chlorine, opened them, and allowed her mind to dive into the luscious sparkling clear water. *I haven't thought about Gammy's since I was there last . . . feels like forever ago, but this makes it feel like yesterday. Fresh cookies, milk, learning to dive. Tipper, the pool man, letting me help him skim the water. My first crush, a blonde twenty-year-old bum called "Tipper." With his pink oxide nose. Shirtless tan, chiseled abs I could have sharpened knives on. Faded cutoffs and ripped Converse. I was twelve? Thirteen? Old enough to know he was hot with or without Florida in July.*

More memories . . . memories of staying at Gammy's house in Florida while her parents "worked through it." Sissy snickered. In the beginning, Sissy thought that "it" was the summer that her parents were merely working through the summer and couldn't vacation with her at Gammy's. After a few years, Sissy realized "it" was each other. She took a deep breath, *Thank*

*God they worked through it.* Sissy let out a deep sigh, *God, how
many summers did it take them to work through it? Four? Five?*

Slowly, Sissy's thoughts went back to Tipper. Her first
kiss was Tipper when she was sixteen. Well, it was sort of a kiss.
Sissy was trying to impress Tipper by doing a back flip off of
Gammy's springboard and hit her head, knocking herself out cold
in the water. Tipper dove in, pulled her out of the water, and gave
her CPR for ten minutes on the side of the pool.

Tipper told her later that she came to crying, "Tell him he
can't have me! Tell him he's wrong! He can't take me! I won't
go!"

Tipper and Gammy said they both thought Sissy was
arguing with God as if she were trying not to cross over . . . into
the light . . . die. Gammy was so scared, she wanted to send Sissy
home the next day, but Sissy begged her not to and promised she
would not do anything else to scare her.

And then the noises started, and the nights became long,
and the house became scary. Voices asking muffled questions
indiscernible to her ears that echoed in her brain without clarity or
definition until they became nothing more than humanoid sounds
that she couldn't drown out. Cobwebs wafting on Sissy's face,
waking her just in time to see shadows darker than the night dart to
the far corners of her room.

Fingertips constantly poking her on the backs of her arms
as if to check to see if she were alive, thereby rousing the sleeping
teenager, who fussily waved off whom she believed could only be
her gammy and grouched, "I'm okay! Leave me alone, Gammy."
To make matters worse in those confusing moments between
waking and sleeping, Sissy always flung her arm into the darkness,

expecting to feel her gammy's silken robe for resistance as if she were pushing the woman back to bed, only to feel the startling weight of an empty void filled by gravity as her hand cascaded back to the bed rail with a painful "thud." The angry muttering and loud whacking of the bed rail, belonging to an antique and fairly unstable bed, always resulted in a real appearance from Gammy . . . followed by a feeble excuse from Sissy then warm milk and "nervous pills" from Gammy.

Nervous pill after nervous pill never got rid of that damned sudden, piercing coldness in July in Florida in a house whose thermostat was controlled by Gammy - - a woman with the world's thinnest blood and least ran air conditioner. Never got rid of that terrifying darkness so dark it seemed eternal and omniscient . . . malicious. Never stopped her favorite toys constantly going missing to be found outside, getting her in trouble for things she didn't do. Never made anyone believe her.

Which, was probably the reason phone calls home became coached by a very nervous Gammy. And poor Gammy. Always rocking Sissy to sleep with the repetition of silly mantras like a priest over liturgy, "You're okay. There's nothing there. It's just your imagination. You'll grow out of it." Gammy nervously giggling with guests, "She doesn't know what she's saying. She's just a very precocious child with a very vivid imagination." Gammy scolding her for telling the truth, "Believe me, it does no good to say these things. Do you want to be taken away from me and locked up for being crazy?" Gammy threatening her with being sent home if she didn't stop getting out of bed and begging to sleep with her at night.

But the worst of "it?" Nightmares she couldn't remember

that left her screaming for reasons she couldn't remember, only to awaken to Gammy screaming back in her face, "Wake-up Sissy, baby! You're waking the neighbors! You gotta stop it! Please, Pumpkin!"

That magical house ended up scaring the hell out of Sissy. But, there was only amnesia to answer exactly, "why?" Why did those voices choose *her* brain to echo, those shadows *her* room to dart against the night, those cold spots *her* body to chill under preposterous circumstances? And why couldn't *she* remember *her* nightmares or who the elusive "him" was that wanted her that day by the pool?

More importantly, why worry about "it?" Over the years everyone had rationalized those tough years for Sissy: "it" was the stress of her parents potentially divorcing (even though she was clueless), "it" was her imagination, she was a forgetful child, she had very sensitive skin, pre-teens are prone to nightmares due to hormonal fluctuations. But, her favorite? "It" runs in the family . . . just like her grandfather who had such an active imagination.

Eventually Sissy bought into "it," too. And, why not? This particular version of "it" made life easier, "Oh, I forgot I left my bike behind the car," "I may have left my radio on with the volume low," "a car probably went by and made those shadows," "remind me never to eat spicy food before bed," and the list of excuses went on and on until there was no longer a need for them. No longer a need for those painful memories. No longer an "it." Just the bliss of forgetfulness until her very active imagination honed in on more important things over the years: getting into college, graduating college, getting a job, making money, and now . . . selling a large house to make enough money to call home with bragging rights.

Still . . . just glancing at the pool brought back those teenage years with the sudden impact of a door kicked open. Almost a decade had passed since these memories surfaced and here they were, coming up for air, breathing new life into her mind's eye with the ferocity of a drowning victim grasping at a life raft. The child in Sissy wanted to run away and find comfort in the folds of Gammy's silken robe. The young adult version of Sissy felt confident, cocky even.

Lost in the memories, words detached from thoughts slipped past her tongue, "I will dominate this house and make a name for myself."

The words were so strange and foreign, Sissy immediately came out of her stupor. Quickly looking all around, she looked to see if anyone were there to hear her talk to herself. No one was, but she felt like people were laughing at her anyway. More teenage feelings crept in: awkwardness, embarrassment, insecurity, and that damned paranoia.

Not liking these emotions, Sissy turned her thoughts to someone who always caught her talking to herself and had the rare talent of making her feel normal about it: Tipper. Tipper's uncanny ability to say the right things always left Sissy laughing. His ability to self-deprecate and change the subject. His ability to pick on her so that she felt she was in the company of a big brother who understood her when no one else did. Yes, Tipper. Perpetually pink nosed Tipper with the perfect abs, perfect tan, and perfect smile. If he were here, he'd know what to say.

Slowly, the teenager in Sissy left until the confident young adult came back to take the helm. Still, she couldn't help but feel an odd combination of comfort and fear, leaving her dreamily grinning through one of her "creepy-feeling" shivers as she thought to herself, *Thank God I outgrew bad dreams and pink nosed pool guys.*

## Chapter 3: Hard Work Never Killed Anybody

Having enough of the pool and the memories it dredged up, Sissy made her way to the front of the house, looking for a good angle to take a picture for *Glasser's House Finder*, the tri-state area's premier printed catalogue of available upscale housing. After all, Sissy had never thought back on those horrible things in years, why dwell on it all now? Ever the pragmatist, Sissy felt she had more pressing concerns: making money.

Taylor said she needn't bother putting an ad up for the place, but she wanted the practice. Sissy took one good look at the three story, red brick Colonial and felt as if she had been kicked in the stomach. Sissy thought to herself, *I can't clean this place by myself! Those windows look like they've been spray painted white! I bet there's mildew older than me, which means I gotta go Betty Crocker on the place, bake some pies, and hope no one notices.*

The cumbersome weight and size of the large cardboard box full of cleaners made for a difficult journey from the carport, which was over ten feet behind the house. Sissy thought this to be a flawed, inconvenient design plan, until it dawned on her, *If you can afford the house, you can probably afford the servants to go with it. I bet Judge Rawlins' child-bride never toted a single box inside this monster.*

Walking toward the door and trying not to drop the big box that was slowly slipping under her grip, Sissy looked at the magnificent landscaping with its neat little topiaries, freshly cut lawn, and the grass edged perfectly from the outer parameters of the walkway. *Thank God they're still paying the yard guy.*

The March wind sent a gust of pebbled white sand across

Sissy's shoulders and onto the aesthetic, curving driveway, dusting it lightly. *Like the beach, shiny and white, pristine. A ha!* Sissy envisioned the title for her *Glasser's* ad, "Rawlins Mansion, Pristine and Perfect." Sissy dusted off her shoulders and walked toward the neat little black door on the side of the house labeled "Servant's Entrance." Sissy giggled. Tinkle, tinkle went her earrings. Clank, slosh, clank, slosh went her cleaners. Crunch, click went her shoes.

*Click?* As Sissy walked, the sound her sneakers made upon the pavement was a distinct "click." Her sneakers were soft tread and had more of a tendency to squeak than "click." The sound was so uncharacteristic of her beloved Converse, Sissy lifted her feet to look for pebbles lodged in the tread. Seeing nothing except the bottoms covered in a sandy dust that reminded her of powdered sugar, Sissy vividly imagined one of the "servants" escorting her into the house in his hard soled shoes, clicking the way bravely ahead. In fact, her imagination was so vivid, she thought she could see a white gloved black man grinning at her as if it amused him to see her coming in to clean the house.

Sissy tightly closed her eyes and thought she could hear Gammy say, "No one's there, Baby. It's just your active imagination playing tricks on you. Now take a nervous pill."

With a child-like eagerness, Sissy pulled her first lockbox out of the cardboard box and fished the lockbox key out of her shorts pocket. A giddy Sissy said beneath her breath, "Let's try out the lockbox!" She danced a little jig in front of the door with sheer excitement. *This is really happening! This is my first real-deal gig!*

The squeaky side door led into a small foyer filled with

custom built, gilded cabinets. *Is that real gold? How friggin' rich can you get? Gammy didn't have gold in her kitchen.* A beautiful marble floor that had once been shiny and perfect but was now so worn it had an indentation in the middle from decades of foot traffic seemed to sprawl forever in every direction. *If heaven has a floor, I bet it never had this much traffic.*

Sissy tried to think of a cute way to present the indention, *Love scrub? Wear and tear? Ummm . . . Walk in the footsteps of history. Uh-huh. That is so awesome.*

"The footsteps of history" led the way to an enormous kitchen. Dingy white enamel appliances large enough to start a restaurant waited to sparkle. Wall-to-wall black marble countertops were covered in dead roaches, moths, flies, and behemoth mosquitoes. Glass paned cabinet doors displayed cobwebs. A strange scraping noise by the refrigerator caught Sissy's ear. When she investigated, she found, to her dismay, a dying gray mouse with a rattrap's arm tight around its neck. Constellations of dried blood spatters on the floor and baseboards proved this spot to be frequented by unlucky mice and competent rattraps alike. The sight made Sissy shudder. *Gross.* Sissy knew she could not just leave it.

The realtor fished a large pair of orange plastic gloves from her big cardboard box and tried to figure out what to do. Having no prior experience with traps or dead animals, Sissy threw the trap and mouse into one of her many heavy duty garbage bags she brought and threw trap, mouse, bag and all onto the side door stoop.

Being "totally grossed out" by the dead mouse, the realtor optimistically decided to explore the rest of the house. First, she went through what she guessed to be the formal living room. There were no curtains on any of the windows, but the room was dark because an opaque white coating covered the panes.

Sissy scratched at a windowpane with her neon green fingernail, but all she could feel was clean glass. *Is this white crap on the outside?*

Sissy spat on the window and tried rubbing some of it off, but nothing. The window felt smooth and polished. A draft wafted past her face, leaving a chill on her cheek and cigarette smoke in her nostrils. Sissy coughed and went back to inspecting the windows, squinting to see if she could determine if it were inside the house or outside the house.

Sissy coughed again and remembered, *I'm allergic to cigarette smoke. Damn there's probably a century's worth of nicotine staining those panes.*

Sissy walked through each room, scratching the windowpanes. *This house could be so much brighter if that white crap weren't all over the windows.*

The more she scratched the panes, the more a secondary smell began to innocuously seep into her nostrils. At first it was not that noticeable, at least not as much as the cigarette smoke. Cruising the halls, Sissy discovered the dining room. Going deeper into the house, she found the men's parlor, the women's parlor, a family room, and deeper down there was yet another room for who knew what.

The deeper she went into the house, the stronger the smell became. When she stood at the extra room's window, she realized the stench was coming from the window sashes. The realtor rubbed her hand down the wood sash. A slick moisture covered her hand. Sissy looked at her hand and thought, *Like fresh tears.* To her surprise, though, the plaster walls around the sashes were dry. Sissy worried that the sashes might mold and mildew while the house sat empty. She inspected the area to find another negative selling point - - the general area around the windows was drafty. Sissy made a mental note that she would steer clients toward the far wall away from the windows and focus on something else.

Sissy began practicing her pitch with pretend clients, "If you'll feel the walls, they're quite sturdy." *They're not first time homeowners approved for a small loan. Somebody wants this house doesn't care about how sturdy it is. Place already looks like a fortress.*

Sissy looked around as if there were someone standing there, laughing at her and began again, "Original marble imported from Italy throughout the entire house. If you'll feel the walls, they're absolutely fabulous. Original plaster. Wide wood moldings and these ornamental chair rails give a texture that lifeless sheetrock in newer homes never will." *Bingo. Appeal to their emotions and they'll fall in love with the place even with a draft that smells like a pool hall. And Dad thought that BA in psychology would never come in handy.*

Sissy walked along the hall, repeating those three simple lines, working on her finesse and style. "If you'll feel . . . original . . . lifeless sheetrock . . ." Sissy went downstairs into a hall that dead ended into what she thought to be the study. *It is cold down here! Lighting is worse down here than it was upstairs! Friggin' scaredy-ville.*

Before stepping inside, she peeped inside and saw that

wall-to-wall custom dark cherry cabinetry covered the walls, except for the window, which was, again, covered in the unknown white substance/maybe-nicotine-stains. Sissy looked overhead at the entrance.

Here, unlike the rest of the house, the walls were less than perfect. Above the study's entrance was a spot of uneven plaster that didn't match the rest. The patch was sizeable, about the size of a fully inflated beach ball. A broken line in the "wide wood molding" on the ceiling gave the flaw away. Small holes in the plaster patch showed that attempts had been made to cover it up with pictures or plaques.

*Maybe buyers won't notice or care about the patches. After all, a house this old is supposed to have imperfections.* Sissy looked at the wall and feared it may portend structural damage. *Maybe I could cover it with something from home.* Sissy looked around at the stature of the room and realized her *The Answer* band poster wouldn't exactly blend. *Maybe I can just buy a mirror.*

"Just part of its charm," Sissy practiced telling a pretend client with a big, fat, fake smile. Her stomach turned when she saw her reflection in the perfectly polished cabinets beside her - - it was that of her mother's staring right back at her.

Sissy walked into the study, which was quite spacious with a lovely coal burning stove "snuggled" inside the fireplace in the room. Around the fireplace sat a twelve foot tall mantel, carved in a hideously detailed baroque fashion. Columns six feet in height held hand carved swooping eagles with snakes in their talons. Above the top of the three shelves in the mantle was an etched mirror, which was also marred by the same white coating as the windows.

*What if it's not nicotine? What if it's mold? Should I be wearing hazmat stuff or something?* Sissy looked around at the combination of heavy wood moldings, the overly ornate carvings, the dark wall-to-wall wooden shelves and the etched mirror in the top of the mantle. *It's gross. Just big . . . and too much. Nothing like Gammy's house.*

Sissy shut her eyes and envisioned the wealthy people who would be standing beside her, patiently waiting for her words of wisdom regarding the finer points of the house to then breathlessly wait in high anticipation to sign on the proverbial "dotted line."

Sissy cleared her throat and held out her arms in a modeling pose saying out loud, "An antique. Hand carved on site. A famous French artisan was flown in just to make this. A Pierre Bonaparte." Sissy giggled at herself, entertained by her own lie, "That thing is so damned ugly! My God! You have to be insane to have something like that in your house!"

Sissy walked around with her hands on her hips and took a deep breath. *No giggling in front of the buyers. Again from the top (inhale, exhale),* "An antique. Hand carved on site. A famous French artisan was flown in just to make this for Judge Rawlins' wife." *Come on, you can do better.* "Hand carved on site. An original. A famous French artisan made this as a wedding present for the Rawlins. He signed his name on the back." *Jeez, okay. If they seem uninterested, throw in a fake appraisal.* "Grotesque, you say? At last appraisal, this alone was worth at least ten thousand dollars. And we haven't seen the rest of the assets this home has to offer." Sissy jigged and yelled out loud, "I am so freakin' awesome! I've got my mother's smile *and* her knack for bald faced lying!"

A clattering sound from the recesses of the house made Sissy shriek and jump in surprise. Sissy muttered in embarrassment, "Damn, rodents! I've got to call an exterminator."

*Why did I just say that out loud?* Sissy looked around for an excuse and could not find one, which made her come to terms with herself: she could not shake the sensation of having an audience. One that found her comical and silly. Child-like. *A wandering fool in a snoozing palace where the princess sleeps, waiting for her prince. This is Gammy's house in a Southern-fried hellish nightmare. God, what I wouldn't give for one of those nervous pills RIGHT now.*

After regaining her composure, Sissy scanned the room and decided that the plaster patch was the least of her worries. In the middle of the empty room sat a dark, long stain in the seemingly freshly buffed marble floor. The stain was black and copper colored, shaped like a long smear, as if it were absorbed paint. Unlike upstairs in which the marble was frequented to such an extent that it had become worn and somewhat pocked, the floor in the study was so shiny she could see her fluorescent outfit beam back at her in full detail. *Guess this isn't the most popular room in the place.* Sissy peered over at the mantle and sarcastically thought to herself, *Wonder why.*

Sissy put her hand up to her mouth and muttered to the marble floor, "I gotta hide that." Sissy looked around and stepped back, "And I don't have a rug nice enough to cover this stain! What am I gonna do?" The realtor walked over to the stain and irreverently scuffed her sneaker over the stain, when she heard a door creak open in the hall. With wide eyes, she looked down the hall and saw that a wooden panel in the hall by the stairs had swung open. Curious, Sissy went to investigate.

The panel was actually the door to a hidden broom closet. Sissy inspected the door and saw that the catching mechanism was loose, allowing the panel to swing open from the least amount of jarring. Sissy indignantly huffed, "The lengths rich people go to hide the fact that that their houses get dirty, too. God! Carports so far away from the house you need a servant to drop you off at the front door, park your car, and carry your groceries for you. And now, a closet that's used, but not seen."

Sissy snickered, "Probably like his wife." Sissy put her fingers up to her lips after hearing words that sounded irreverent and mean, unlike herself. In a louder voice she said, "Sorry! I really didn't mean that." *Oh my God, this house is making me freaking paranoid!*

In the closet, Sissy found dusty old bottles of cleaner brands she didn't recognize and a rusty floor sweeper. When she reached out to grab the handle, it conveniently fell with a loud "Bang!" upon the floor that made her heart go into her throat. Sissy put her hand to her heart and thought, *For a moment there, I thought I'd been shot at point blank in the face.* Sissy stooped over to pick up the handle and spied the tasseled end of a rolled rug tucked neatly into the far corner of the narrow closet. Sissy smiled at her good luck, "Hell, yes!"

The realtor slid the sweeper out into the hall and, getting down on her hands and knees, pulled the rug out into the hall. Dust stirred as dense as cigar smoke. The rug was thick, long and heavy. Sissy dropped the rug on the way back to the study, sending huge puffs of dust spattering out of the carpet fibers like tiny explosions. She choked, coughed, and sneezed her way back to the study.  With a big kick, she unrolled the carpet neatly over the stain.  To her relief, the rug was absolutely beautiful, made with a traditional floral pattern and large enough to cover the spot on the floor.  It suited the room to perfection.

*This is so nice.  I bet this thing is worth a small fortune. Who'd leave something like this?*  Sissy bent over and inspected the rug, *Needs a little cleaning.*  Sissy straightened up and stared at the open closet door down the hall, *Huh, that's what the sweeper's for.  Duh!*

When Sissy pushed the sweeper across the carpet, the dust trap disintegrated, dumping fist-sized dust bunnies and fine powdered rust on the rug.  Sissy was mortified, *Shit! Now, I gotta go home and get my crappy vacuum cleaner.  Of all the things I didn't bring!  Who knew I'd need a vacuum cleaner in a house with friggin wall-to-wall marble floors?*

Sissy went outside, tossed the broken sweeper beside the trash bag, and reluctantly started up her trusty Civic.  After a quick dash to her duplex, Sissy lugged Gammy's ancient hand-me-down upright vacuum into the trunk of her car.  Once she arrived back at the Rawlins, Sissy again lugged the thirty pound machine across the yard and through the house to the down stairs study.  Once downstairs, Sissy caught her breath and wiped her sweaty brow, letting out a sigh of relief at having the strength to walk the vacuum across the yard and through the house.  *Now if I can just find the energy to vacuum.*

However, when the eager realtor plugged the vacuum into the cracked electric cover and hit the power button, she didn't hear the sound of the loud motor rev, but a shotgun blast.  Everything went black for a moment.  Then a sensation, as of a numbing, overwhelmed the young woman, who got down on her knees and started wiping away the dirt and bits of vacuum belt with her hands until she had pushed all of the debris to the outer edges of the rug.

Next, Sissy sank her left index finger into the thick, compacted wool fibers and began drawing an outline. However, the outline didn't follow the rug's pattern or spell out "I WUZ HERE" or similar nonsense, as Sissy was prone to do. Instead, the outline made a permanent indention in the shape of a body, much like a chalk line. Without hesitation, or even realizing what she was doing, Sissy sat in the middle of the outline and began to feel dizzy, much like in a dream that was beyond her control.

## Chapter 4: That Fateful Day

Another place, another time. Dreaming while awake. Watching. Hearing. Sensing all there was in a forgotten moment. Removed from now. Taken to then. The moments before Judge Rawlins decided to end his life.

A middle aged black butler in white gloves and a snug fitting formal black suit with matching bowtie entered the lavishly decorated study, where the aging Judge Rawlins sat in a deep brown leather wing backed chair, reading a thick book, swirling a large piece of ice in an empty snifter, "Mr. Judge Rawlins, sir, there's a man here to see you."

"Thank you, Henry. See him in. And get me another, would you, Son?"

"Yes, sir." Henry took the snifter, disappearing into the foyer. He promptly returned with "the guest" and showed him to a leather loveseat across from the judge.

A diminutive man with a clean shaven face and neatly trimmed little mustache in a loose fitting brown suit walked into the study, holding his hat in one hand and a briefcase in the other. The judge did not budge or address him, instead he just stared at his book, as if it were mesmerizing. Even though they were only eight feet away from each other, the separation between them seemed to be expansive and enormous, accentuated by a large, floral printed wool rug.

Henry put his white gloved hand to his mouth and cleared his throat, "Can I get something for your guest, Mr. Judge Rawlins, sir?"

The judge put his book down and turned to the man as if it

were an inconvenience, "What'll you have, Mr. Lovette?"

Mr. Lovette just motioned with his hand that he didn't want anything.

The judge shifted in his chair, the leather creaking beneath his legs, "Mr. Lovette will have a glass of brandy on the rocks."

Henry nodded and disappeared down the hall.

Judge Rawlins turned back toward his desk and pulled open a drawer. From it he grabbed two fat cigars and a cigar snip. Rawlins snipped both cigars and offered one to Mr. Lovette. "Well, now, normally, we'd retire into the men's parlor and have a good smoke with a good drink like gentlemen are supposed to do. But, I don't think I have to worry about the missus getting upset, do I?"

Mr. Lovette took the cigar with trembling fingers from Rawlins while shaking his head "no." The judge pulled a golden flip top lighter from his coat pocket and lit Mr. Lovette's cigar before lighting his own. Mr. Lovette puffed on his cigar and seemed hesitant to release the second hand smoke into the dark study, so he blew the smoke slowly from the side of his mouth toward the curtain-less window, as if he wanted the smoke to go through the glass and not into the same atmosphere as the judge. The exhaled cigar smoke did not miraculously go out the closed window as Lovette had hoped but clung to the window and fogged it. The window held onto the smoke, turning opaque and white.

Mr. Lovette noticed the smoke on the window and thought it looked as if the smoke were being held prisoner against its will by this unyielding, tyrannical window, sealed so tight the smoke may never escape. Then the thought that the judge might notice his social ineptitude struck him, so Lovette coughed to try to call attention to himself and away from the window. Clinching the cigar between his fingers, Lovette sat his briefcase on the loveseat, "Mister, I mean, Judge Rawlins, can't we just say you were right? I don't see the importance of

having to . . ."

The judge interrupted Mr. Lovette and let out a sad chuckle, "I am a judge after all. So, I hope I'm right most of the time. How right was I?"

Mr. Lovette quickly spattered out, "Your wife is being unfaithful."

The judge swallowed hard at this bit of information, "And there's no nephew?"

Lovette looked down at the thick wool rug and shook his head, "No."

In a calm voice the judge asked, "So, who is he?"

Mr. Lovette conscientiously rubbed the tip of his black dress shoe over the rug's thick fibers, "An actor."

The judge grinned at the man's nervous actions, "She gives him money? My money?"

Lovette realized the judge was watching him, so he sat up straighter and planted his feet firmly on the rug, "It appears so." Lovette stared at the window he covered in white cigar smoke and tried with all his being to will it to dissipate. Still, the smoke clung to the window as if the smoke intended to choke the window, blanket it in an unashamed dirtiness.

"How old is he?"

Lovette shifted in his seat, making it squeak, "Judge, it doesn't matter. He's an actor, who you know are all reprobates. You're an honorable man with an illustrious career."

The judge unintentionally ran his hand through his thinning, gray hair, "Lovette, a few minutes ago, I was 'an honorable man with an illustrious career.' Right now, I'm just an old man with a young wife, a pretty, young wife, who stole my heart and my money, making a fool of me in front of the entire town."

"But . . ."

The judge rubbed the back of his hand, circling his liver spots, "At least I'm not a paranoid old man, am I right?"

Lovette tightened his grip on the cigar and nodded, "No one would think you're a fool or paranoid. You're too respected."

Henry entered the room with two brandies on a silver tray.

Mr. Lovette took the brandy and a sip that ended in an audible gulp, "Thank you, Mister uh?"

Henry paused a moment before realizing he was being addressed, "Who me? Henry, sir."

Lovette grinned at the butler, "Thank you, Mister Henry."

Henry broke out into amused laughter as he walked toward the judge, "You hear that Mr. Judge Rawlins? He call me 'Mister.' He ain't from around here, is he, sir?"

The judge raised his snifter at the bemused butler, "No, Henry, Mr. Lovette is not. Could you check on something in the kitchen for me?"

"Yes, sir. I'll check for you. Half hour or so?"

The calm voice said, "A good half hour."

"Yes, sir." Henry took his tray and disappeared down the hall.

The judge took a puff from his cigar and blew the smoke into the room, which swirled and danced above the middle of the rug between him and Lovette, "Henry's a faithful, loyal servant. More faithful than that wife of mine ever was, it seems. If I didn't think it'd turn this town on its ear, I'd leave everything I have to that man." Judge Rawlins took a drink and stared at the wool rug beneath their feet.

Mr. Lovette looked down at the rug, too, when he lost his grip on the cigar and dropped it onto his briefcase. Lovette let out a deep breath and swept the charred tobacco with his hand, getting smut on the side of it, "Do you really need to see these?"

"I'll take'em. I've got decisions to make. Delicate situation."

Lovette went back to staring at the rug, "Yes, I understand."

Rawlins squinted his eyes at the rug, "Not just for me. I got the community to think of. Reputation. If I could be wrong about her, I could be wrong about anything."

Lovette tried to inconspicuously rub his hand onto the side of his jacket, "I'd say she'll come back. It's only been an extra week. She's come back every time before."

Rawlins took a swig of his brandy, "I don't want her back. Not after the shame she's brought me."

Lovette took a swig of his brandy, "No one has to know. You were happy before you ever suspected anything. Maybe you could reach an agreement, or . . ."

Rawlins looked up at Lovette upon hearing his proposal, "An 'agreement?' That's called wedding vows! Next you'll tell me to get a divorce." Rawlins puffed on his cigar several times and deeply exhaled. Another puff of smoke danced and dissipated above the rug between the men, "And be the only ones in town to get such a detestable thing? I'd never be able to show my face again."

Lovette shrugged his shoulders and offered a sympathetic, "You could move somewhere and start over."

Rawlins glared at Lovette, "Have the shame of being run out of town by a woman? And at my age? No. This shouldn't be happening to me."

Lovette opened his briefcase and took a large, fattened folder from it. He handed it and the glass of brandy to the judge. He placed the snuffed cigar into a pocket in his briefcase, "Well, Judge, I hate when these investigations go this way. I wonder if it's even worth knowing sometimes."

Rawlins shrugged his left shoulder and nonchalantly sipped his snifter, "The truth. It's about finding the truth." Rawlins turned his back to the man and picked up his book.

Lovette rubbed his neck, "I'll just see myself out. Good bye, Judge."

When Lovette left the study, Judge Rawlins put the book down and opened the folder. However he did not bother to pull out its contents but began staring at the rug, "Henry! Henry! Get in here!"

Henry came into the study with a dry dish towel on his shoulder, "Yes, sir?"

Judge Rawlins never looked at Henry, but remained intently staring at the rug, "Henry, I want to give you something."

"Sir?"

"Take that rug, Henry."

Henry took the towel from his shoulder and rung it, "I'm not sure I feel comfortable taking that there rug, sir. I believe that was the first thing Miss Mary Beth got for the house, just for you in here."

"But I'm the one who paid for the Goddamned thing. She said it was quite a nice rug, handmade in Persia, India, er someplace. She said it was the 'finest quality.' She said it would last forever, even after you constantly walk all over it."

Henry had a confused look on his face, "Now, maybe I'm just confused. Where you want me to take that rug, sir?"

The judge exhaled a billow of smoke through his mouth, "No, Henry, I want you to roll it up right now and take it with you when you leave today. I'm giving you the rest of the day off, so go ahead and get it right now."

Henry slapped the dish towel back over his shoulder, walked over to the rug and began rolling it up, "All right, sir, since you insist. Now, I don't think it'll look as nice in my house as it does in here, but I know the missus will sure appreciate you."

Judge Rawlins looked up at Henry, "Take the rest of the day off, Henry. You deserve it."

Henry laughed a nervous laugh, "You right, Mr. Judge Rawlins. You right."

Rawlins gave Henry the two brandy snifters, "Not always, Henry."

"If you say so. You want me to do anything for you before I go?"

The judge stared at the folder on the table, "No, Henry. I can do it myself."

Henry didn't wait for Rawlins to change his mind about giving him the rug or the day off. He took the rug and walked out the door.

The good judge sat in his chair, staring at the floor where the rug once was, while the folder sat on the desk, unexplored. Time passed and he just sat, starring at the bare floor, looking for evidence that the rug was ever there to begin with. When the sun started to go down, and the room darkened, Judge Rawlins got up from his chair and walked over to a panel adjacent the desk. There he opened a secret compartment that hid a gun safe and pulled out a perfectly polished shotgun that had a wooden stock etched with eagle heads, mouths agape. When Rawlins sat back down in his chair, he opened a desk drawer and pulled out his cleaning kit. Then he started cleaning his shotgun and thinking. *Make a mockery of me. Object of pity. I'll not be run out of town over a whore for a wife. I'd rather die than have everyone I know look at me with pity. We'll just see if your actor will be so obliged to entertain you after I'm gone. After my money's gone.*

The judge put the shotgun down and opened his drawer for a sheet of paper. Then he began to write. After finishing his writing, he put a notary seal on it and said out loud, "Well, Henry, you can have the rug and somewhere nice to put it, right here where it belongs. I'll be damned in hell before I make some actor and his whore rich off of my 'illustrious career.'" The judge laughed, loaded the shotgun, and stared at the mantle with the matching eagles and snakes carved in intricate, excruciating detail. Then the judge placed the shotgun in his mouth and squeezed the trigger. Some of the buckshot hit its target, other pieces landed in the plaster above the entry way, which promptly fell out in chunks onto the floor below.

## Chapter 5: Self-Medication

The room was finished whispering its secrets to Sissy, who awoke to find herself face down on the rug in an uncomfortable position that left her right arm numb and tingly. After sitting up and popping her neck, Sissy realized it was nighttime. Suddenly, an extreme fatigue came over Sissy's entire being, body and soul. The memories of the house's secrets lingered in her mind, swirling like sand caught in a March breeze. The entire experience was too intense for Sissy, who left the rug dirty, her vacuum plugged into the wall, and all of her cleaners in the kitchen to drive off as quickly as she could.

Once home, Sissy found sleep impossible. Never before had she wished Gammy could rock her to sleep and give her those pills that knocked her into miniature comas. Feeling panicky and anxious, she resorted to her other favorite tranquilizer: alcohol. After downing an entire large bottle of red wine, Sissy gladly passed out in the safety of her bed with the television left on to give her familiar noises and to drown out any that may not have been so familiar. When the light of noon rudely awoke Sissy, a sense of dread infiltrated the last shreds of sleep inducing inebriation. A slight hangover pinged in Sissy's brain as she made herself get out of bed and prepare for her return to the Rawlins Mansion.

### Chapter 6: Told Ya' So

When Sissy arrived, she sat in her car with her head resting on the steering wheel, holding back tears. Even though the realtor tried to tell herself that she had imagined the details of the judges' last moments, or fallen asleep and dreamed them, she couldn't entirely convince herself. Finally, she left the comfort of her car and entered the mystery of the house.

Once inside, Sissy discovered that nothing much had really changed about the house at all. Her cleaners were as she left them - - all in their box, undisturbed. The acrid smell of the rotting sashes still made its presence known. And the white smog still covered the windowpanes, refusing to let the sunshine in. *Maybe it was just a . . . case of mild heat stroke. I imagined it all. Let's go grab Gammy's vacuum.*

But one thing did change. When Sissy entered the hall, she noticed that the closet door was shut, which she did not remember shutting. When she looked into the study, the nasty stain glared back at her because the rug was gone, as was her vacuum. Sissy tiptoed to the hidden closet and hit the barely noticeable door with her fist. The closet door swung open, revealing her vacuum in the exact place the rusted roller was the day before. Sissy did not touch anything, but stood there with her hands to her sides, looking for the rug to be in its corner. And there it was, rolled as tightly as it had been the day before. Sissy shut the door without making a sound and tiptoed up the stairs to the kitchen to retrieve her box of cleaners. She grabbed the box and lumbered out the "Servants Entrance" as quickly and noiselessly as she could.

Sissy pushed the box into the back seat of her hatchback

and pulled out the "For Sale" sign. Next, the realtor walked down the winding driveway and pushed the sign into the neatly manicured lawn as hard as she could, as if she were harpooning it to death. Then Sissy turned and walked up the driveway, got in her car, started the ignition, and said at her reflection in her rearview mirror, "Forget this shit!" and drove to work.

***

Mr. Taylor stopped in Sissy's office for a quick harangue, "I see you survived cleaning the Rawlins Mansion."

Sissy turned from her computer screen and forced a smile at her boss, "Yep. Sure did."

"Spent the whole day trying to clean the place?"

Sissy turned back around and stared intently at her computer, "You were right. Complete waste of time trying to tidy it up, so I gave up about halfway through, went home and took a nap. But the sign's out front. One question, though."

Taylor lifted his head, "Mmm?"

"Who got the mansion after the judge's demise?"

Taylor chuckled, "Oh, yes. That would be the 'rest of the story.' Well, The Honorable Judge Rawlins gave it all, and I mean everything, to his butler. It was a rather big scandal. The wife tried to fight the butler for the house and money, but that ended abruptly. She moved out west to tend to some sick cousin or nephew or something. Ironically, the butler's wife left him, too, after only a few years."

Sissy furled her brow in confusion, "What happened to the butler?"

Taylor took a deep breath, "Well, that's something we don't like to advertise."

Sissy shook her head, "What?"

Taylor chuckled, "He's still there. Buried somewhere on the property." A knowing grin lifted the man's chaw bulging from his cheek, "Think you'll be ready to sell it again in another three years?"

Sissy threw her hands up in the air, trying to play along with Taylor's stint at ego bashing, "Sure, all you gotta do is let it sit there and sell itself."

Taylor spat tobacco juice into his coffee cup, "Good girl."

\*\*\*

The mansion sat on the market for only a few months, when Lee Bozeman, a young judge from New York with his new wife, fell in love with the house. Flemming, Georgia seemed like a bargain basement seconds sale, compared to the higher cost of living in New York, explaining why the judge did not haggle over the price, which was inflated by over fifty thousand dollars. (Everyone thought Sissy was crazy for marking the price up so much and would NEVER move that money pit, but her instincts told her otherwise.) Within a month, the paperwork was all signed and closing costs completely negotiated.

Making an all-time record, the Bozemans lived in the house for close to a decade, after which they moved back to New York, claiming that they never wanted to live so close to rednecks ever again. Mrs. Bozeman was quoted as saying, "The neighbors shooting a shotgun in the night, almost every night in March is too much for civilized people. And the police never do anything about it, no matter how much you call. And that money pit, putting more and more money into those damned fogged windows and sagging, rotten sashes is just stupid. As is living in Flemming."

Mr. Bozeman specifically asked for Sissy to be his realtor, but she didn't care. In the tradition of *First Team Realty*, she let the greenhorn associate who had "worked so hard and deserved to get out of slum peddling" get his hands on "real" real estate. The greenhorn, Rob Heimmerman, was more than happy to oblige.

## Chapter 7:  Turn onto the Dirt Road

For nearly a decade after selling the Rawlins Mansion,
Sissy went back to selling whatever houses and businesses came
her way in the sleepy town of Flemming.  Slowly, memories of
what happened to her that strange day faded the same way
memories at her grandmother's house did:  denial and excuses
mixed with time and avoidance.  Life had returned to normal.

Then one day, Mr. Taylor had a new assignment for Sissy .
. .

"But Mr. Taylor, I don't know that much about the area!
I'm a city girl from Atlanta.  I don't know anything about
farmland, plantations . . . and it's out in the woods *with those types
of people*!  You hate me.  That's what this is."

Mr. Taylor laughed through his dip, "I'm telling you,
you're perfect.  Trust me, it's no different than selling the Rawlins
Mansion - - if you'll take my advice and just let it sit there.
Besides, Gal, you're good with pricing things.  You can make even
more money.  This is a feast and famine business.  You gave the
only 'mansion' this town has to offer to Heimmerman and there's
only so many small ranchers going around."

Sissy cocked her eyebrow at Taylor and said sarcastically,
"Lemme guess - - nobody else wants to work the property so
you're left with just me.  And if I don't do this, you're not gonna
throw me another bone for quite some time, so I'll be asking to sell
this backwoods hellhole anyway."  Sissy changed her tone and said
in a fake, perky manner, "Sure, what's the worst that could
happen?"

Taylor grinned with his hands on his hips, "You and your

sassy mouth. So, be nice. This is an old, old family. They're stuck in their ways and, yes, a little . . . backwoods compared to a modern woman such as yourself. You'll just have to overlook some things, but nothing I'm sure you can't handle for the money."

Sissy let out a deep sigh, "Fine. If it's as bad as I think it is, I hope the ignorance is contagious because I'm bringing it back to you."

Taylor winked and chuckled at Sissy, "Too late. Unlike you, I was born and raised in this here briar patch. Remember . . . Be. Nice."

***Later That Day***

A typical South Georgia June deluge fell from the sky, making travel hazardous and prolonged on the Friday that Sissy set off to meet Mrs. Abigail Greer, who, oddly, was not the owner, but the niece and power of attorney over the owner of the remaining acreage to a long since defunct plantation in the middle of a country town called McDonnell. Sissy already knew she was in for a treat when Mrs. Greer told her the directions to the plantation, which ended with, "go past the two cemeteries . . . turn off the main highway onto the dirt road . . . cross the railroad tracks . . . follow the crepe myrtles." The grey-out rainstorm just added to the seemingly sadistic fun.

An hour commute turned into an hour and forty-five minutes. Several times Sissy had to turn on her hazards and wait for the rain to lessen enough for her to see the road in front of her. Eighteen wheelers whizzed by her with a tremendous force, rocking her Volvo station wagon like a domestic compact.

During these moments, Sissy flashbacked to conversations she had with Mrs. Greer on the phone, her voice and thick accent churning in Sissy's brain, "*Yap, yap, yap. Nag, nag, nag. Yeah, yeah, yeah, I get it. Ewww, poor me, ma' brother tore the place up when he found out we was gonna ta sell it . . . Whut? Clean it up? Come out and tell me what we oughtta do 'bout it . . . I cain't describe it on tha phone . . . I haven't seen it ma'self in yars . . . Aunt Catherine says it's still niiice . . . We don't know how much it's worth.*" Sissy twisted her neck, "God that accent! It's so thick, it's like another freaking language."

By the time Sissy found the dirt road, she wished she had not let Taylor intimidate her into taking on the isolated property. The saturated dirt road was so muddy that her tires left giant ruts behind the narrow vehicle. Her wheels spun out and then caught the road in spurts, making her worry whether she was going to bog down or land in the deep ditch that lined the narrow dirt road.

To make matters worse, there was a giant gulch in the bend of the road that led to the plantation house. The gulch was flooding with water and made the dauntless (foolish?) realtor's stomach knot. But she trudged on with thoughts of making five percent, thereby motivating her to dismiss her uneasy feeling as merely lunch not agreeing with her.

When Sissy finally completed the obstacle course, the rain miraculously stopped, leaving a warm haze of white fog sitting just above the ground in every direction. Sissy parked her car underneath a cascading, large oak. Beyond her parked car, Sissy found a sight that only the artistic would appreciate, perhaps a photographer who loves to capture the last remnants of the Antebellum South . . . earlier than that . . . pre-Civil War South.

Sissy quickly assessed the exterior of the house - - it was an old one story house with a porch on the front and the right side, but not the preferred wraparound. The windows were covered in plastic, which was torn and wind whipped. The plastic shreds flapped against the house like a horse swishing its tail.

The front steps were concrete, but not original to the house. They slanted to the side and were not aligned with the porch's landing. A bare steal pipe improvised as a handrail. *Not the safest structure for welcoming guests, especially buyers who might want to have a look inside . . . before they burn it to the ground. God, I hope nobody asks for an inspection!*

A mangled mess caught Sissy's eye. Just ten feet from the front porch was a tangle of wadded steel wire that looked as if it had been run over with a car and assaulted by over-grown weeds. *That would be the "fenced off" outdoor water well Mrs. Greer warned me not to get too close to, or I'll fall in. Ok, so liability is definitely an issue I'll have to discuss with her. Jesus.*

Sissy stepped back and examined the tree under which she had parked her car. The ancient oak towered across both her car and the largest portion of the front yard, which was surrounded by a hand built stick fence that was made of old wood, laid horizontally in a zigzag pattern around the front yard.

Sissy thought to herself, *How quaint, picturesque, even.*

But, Sissy was not an artist looking for beauty in the moldering remains of dwindling inheritances. Rather, Sissy had come to make the ever important dollar. With no one present to show her around, Sissy's curiosity led her around by her nose, which she followed while shooing gnats from her mouth, slapping pissed off fire ants from her ankles, and wiping smut grass seeds from her tan trousers.

While walking around, Sissy began to imagine what Mrs.

Greer might look like based on her impressions of the property and the woman's voice on the phone. Feeling a bit lonely and exposed walking around out in the open, Sissy verbalized her thoughts out loud to herself, "I bet she's a fat, pasty woman with teased hair . . . heavy make-up . . . fat, saggy breasts in a bra that doesn't fit. She's wearing a plain cotton top with matching shorts, and no-name, blown-out, dirty-white, canvas tennis shoes. Possibly holding a lipstick stained cigarette with a three inch ash hanging off of the end. Long red nails. A double chin with goat hairs. Just a modern day witch. Or just a bitch. Or a witchy bitch." Sissy laughed and pulled her hair off of the back of her neck because it was sticking from the humidity. *Be nice. Whatever. No shame in my judging game.* And with that, a horsefly landed and bit her on the back of her neck like a harbinger of instant karma. Sissy rubbed her neck and thought, *I can't wait to blow this popsicle stand.*

Sissy walked along the front yard, avoided the barns and sheds, watched her watch, and walked some more until she became bored with walking and went toward the house. Tucked almost invisibly into the door jam, Sissy found a note made from the back of a gas receipt , *Waited as long as I could. Can't stand rain no more. Feel free to have look inside. STAY AWAY from barns there dangeroos. Be ware of snakes there every were. Key under mat.*

Sissy laughed to herself, "Okay, you wrote a note saying you hid the key under the doormat?" The realtor took a step away from the front door and looked down at the dry-rotted, plastic doormat that was half missing, beckoning visitors to simply, "COME." Sissy shoved the note in her pocket and thought to herself, *Okay, so Mrs. Greer has the power of attorney, but not the*

*English language.*

With key in hand, Sissy decided to make the trip worthwhile - - see, appraise, leave. After opening what she thought was the world's rustiest screen door, Sissy flipped the nearest light switch and saw that the inside lights were all naked, flickering and buzzing. The light was yellowish and pale, barely revealing a room that appeared to be the kitchen. *Probably 40 watt bulbs, wonder if the circuitry can handle 100 watt bulbs.* Dead moths littered the floor.

Inside the house was dank, smelly, creaky, leaky, and slanted, making the realtor feel off kilter. *Spooky, like a real-to-life "Shooby-Shoob" cartoon. Maybe Mrs. Greer is here after all, hiding in a mask to scare that "pesky realtor from the gold."* Sissy snickered at her own silliness. *I ought a write that lady a note of my own and leave it on the door, "Help, I fell down the well, come save me." I can't believe she left me in this death trap by myself in the middle of nowhere.*

Flies flew all about the kitchen, which smelled of rancid grease. *There's probably some ancient grease trap underneath the house, festering and bubbling - - all gooey and gross.* Sissy shivered, so she deliberately started looking at the "assets" the house had to offer. All of the appliances were gone, even the kitchen sink had been ripped out of the wall and an exposed pipe jutted out with a filthy rag thrust in its jagged end. A dried black puddle sat beneath it. The ugly faux brick linoleum floor was torn, and the sheen had long since worn off. Deep indentations of where a large "something" once sat were filled with permanent stains of soot and decades of rust.

Visions of a large, angry man grunting, hefting, and pulling the sink from the wall with sheer brute power flashed before Sissy's eyes and her imagination ran wild. *The man was related to Mrs. Greer, her . . . brother. I think I'll call him Gary. Legal problems - - power of attorney over the aunt. Arguments and anger over whether or not to sell the plantation. Hence . . . the ripped out kitchen.* Sissy laughed at the classic southern dilemma. That is, if her imagination proved right. *Gammy, I think I'm gonna need a "nervous" pill to get through this one.*

Sissy walked out of the kitchen and into the dining room, a large room that was just as empty and in as much disrepair as the kitchen. To her right, there was a broken windowpane with a piece of cardboard replacing the missing glass. *A woman in a worn flannel nightgown holding a shotgun poked through the pane, shooting into the darkness at trespassers in the night. A real life western, but southern. The woman was . . . Gary's wife.*

Blurry visuals of nonexistent heavy antiques cluttered Sissy's sight, making her feel confused: large banquet dining tables, monolithic buffets, a couple of cluttered curios, littered desks, and a rusty chest freezer large enough to store an entire cow. *Pieces inherited, fixed, sold.* There was not a happy feeling emanating from the room. Sissy could feel a surge of emotions touch the palms of her hands. *Frustration. Anxiety. Intense need for money.* Sissy closed her hands and balled them into tight fists until she could not feel anything but the pressure of her fingers smashing into her palms.

Walking quickly through the dining room, Sissy entered the living room, which, to her amazement, had an air conditioning unit stuck in a windowpane that appeared to be fully intact. *No central air.* She looked to her left and saw a large gas heater. *No central heat.* In the center of the living room floor was a faux painted rug made from material that appeared to be a giant piece of cardboard, which was ripped and missing pieces.

*Damn, I could have made up a wonderful story about "unsung southern folk artists."* Sissy coughed and looked up, seeing another blurred image of something that was not there - - *a little girl playing on the painted rug. Face covered in dirt. Dirt rings around her neck. Barbie dolls with melted hair. Melted hair?* Sissy sniffed. The grease smell had been expunged by a leaking gas smell. *I think that stuff can make you hallucinate. Shit, I gotta get the hell outta here.*

Sissy walked down the hall where the floorboards creaked and buckled beneath her weight. She looked to her left, revealing that a bathroom had been installed. *No outhouse? I feel cheated.* Sissy went into the bathroom and thought to herself, *If hell were in the market for a bathroom, I'd be in heaven.*

A toilet sat with a cracked lid, the bowl full of rust colored stains from, paradoxically, years of use and neglect. The shower stall was tiny and unbearably dirty looking. Rusted stall walls cascaded leprous bubbles of ancient melting iron. There was a wharf rat hole at the bottom of the shower. *That rat's probably cleaner than this damned bathroom.* Twisted metal hung out of the wall where the showerhead used to be.

The floor was bare in places and covered in beige linoleum in others. The walls were painted beige, too, but there were places where missing shelving revealed unpainted clapboards. A rust covered space heater sat against a wall. Sissy sniffed. *Gas. Again. Remember to tell Greer to turn off the damned gas in case any smokers are interested in the place.*

Sissy put her hand over her mouth and nose and left the bathroom to look into the room across the hall, which turned out to be the washroom. *Ugh, it smells like shit in here!* An old washing machine lay on its side with a load of dirty towels covered in motor grease and dung spilling out of the basin and onto the floor. *Vandalism, that's gotta be cleared out before we show the place.* The small window in the room was cracked, making a spider web-like pattern. A child's drawings covered the floor. Sissy looked closer at the art, which was titled *Love Sara* and irreverently covered in shoe prints. Sissy let out a disapproving grunt and left the room.

Down the hall was another room off to the right. Inside the room were many windows covered by dry rotted, scalloped blinds with stained fringe and tassels. Holes and cracks let some light through, but not much. Sissy sniffed. *No gas. Is that burnt cedar?* Sissy looked across the room and saw a crumbling brick fireplace that still had charred pieces of wood in it. A blocky, plain, hand-made-bed sat against the adjacent wall. Sissy wanted to have a closer look at the bed, so she flicked the light switch, but the lights did not turn on. She tried to pull one of the blinds up, but instead tore it in half all together. Sissy made a mental check list: *Clear out old blinds. Let light in.* Sissy walked closer to the bed to inspect it. *Or not.*

The bed was massive, made from oak with the natural knots left intact on the footboard and headboard. Notches carved semi-discreetly into the right running board revealed someone's sexual exploits - - three wavy lines to be exact. Sissy snickered. *Ya' mean they had sex back then?* On the mattress were dry rotted linens hanging in shredded fragments. A sweat stained and mildewed lumpy pillow sat on the right side of the bed. *Is that a head indent in the middle of the pillow?* Sissy walked closer to the pillow to inspect it and saw the corner of a note sticking out from beneath the pillow. Sissy held out her index finger and lightly scooted the note from beneath the pillow without touching it.

Sissy walked out into the hall to read the note, which said, *Do not move. This stays.* She pulled Mrs. Greer's note from her trouser pocket and compared the two. *Handwriting's different.* Sissy shoved both notes in her pocket and continued her inspection. *"This stays." Whatever. When the place is sold, they can do whatever the hell they wanna do with it. What an ass.*

Across the hall was the only other bedroom, but it was completely devoid of furniture. However, the windows were covered in the same style of rotted, torn, once-new-and-expensive blinds as the other room. A wood burning stove sat against the far wall with dents kicked into the sides. The sliding door of the closet had been pulled out of its tracks, kicked or punched through, and left leaning against the wall like a murder victim. The closet itself was empty, except for a haggard gaggle of bent wire hangers. This room proved to be the master bedroom, as it had direct access to the only bathroom. *I dunno if that's a plus or a minus.*

The hallway dead ended to a semi-collapsed side porch. Wasp nests covered the eaves and their tenants buzzed around the rusted screen door. Sissy mused that the wasps overlooked the fallen porch like evil striped faeries. One buzzed right up to Sissy's face through the brittle protection of the warped screen, staring her down with those wicked giant eyes and a drop of water in its mouth. Sissy spoke to the wasp, "So Little Mamma, paper house getting too wet for comfort? I bet I could sell your home easier than I can this one." The wasp audibly buzzed outside the screen, making a circular path that outlined Sissy's face until dropping its water droplet and flying away.

Sissy exhaled and stepped out onto the porch. The left side of the porch was screened in with a warped wooden door. *Wonder what's in there. Forgotten antiques I can buy on the cheap?* Inside the screened in porch were broken cardboard boxes that spilled out stacks upon stacks of mildewed college books. Sissy read some of the titles, *statistics, government, modern psychology, pre-calculus. You mean somebody around here was educated? What the hell happened between modern psychology and "dangeroos"? Bunch of random crap.* Sissy left the screened in porch and stood in front of the backdoor with her hands on her hips.

The side yard contained what was left of a stack of wood for the wood burning stove and fireplaces. A black snake slithered from out of the pile and toward the drier conditions of the sunken porch. Seeing the snake gave Sissy goose bumps and made her realize that she was, indeed, in the bowels of the country. Just because she was inside the house, didn't mean she was safe from anything outside. At least the roof wasn't leaking . . . that she knew of.

Sissy had seen all she needed to and more than she wanted. Besides, the rain was starting up, again. The realtor walked carefully back through the dilapidated old home and out the front door. Once outside, she put a lockbox on the front door. As if it mattered this time. Squatters would turn their noses up at this place. Still, she was getting a fat percentage, so she could at least act as if she cared.

## Chapter 8: I'm Tired, and I Wanna Go Home

As Sissy walked to her car, another heavy downpour fell to earth. Not even the thick sprawling oak could absorb the droplets before Sissy got into her car. Within seconds Sissy was miserably soaked. Her hair stuck to her face in fat rivulets. Looking into the rearview, Sissy saw that her mascara was running and her foundation was dripping off of her chin, staining her blouse.

Sissy closed her eyes and began yelling in the privacy of her car, "That stupid bitch couldn't even stay out here to show me through that hellhole or call to cancel before I drove all the way out to the freakin' boonies! God! As if I needed to see that house! Nobody wants . . . that!"

Sissy drove down the sandy drive and slowly approached the impending bend in the road. The gulch was completely filled with water. Both sides of the mud hole were covered in brambles that stood at least three feet deep. The only way to get across was to wade through the mucky water. As if that were a choice. A long black snake darted out of the brambles and across the miniature pond to another set of brambles on the other side. Sissy slammed her car into reverse and headed backwards to the house.

Sissy knew there was a ninety-nine point nine percent chance that the house was never modernized enough to have phones. If it were, there was a ninety-nine point nine percent chance that all of the lines had been snatched from the walls and the remaining jacks kicked, or blow torched, or filled with motor oil covered cloths and ignited. Sissy didn't remember seeing a phone, but she didn't look for one, either, allowing for that point one percent chance in hell. Then again, the odds of her bogging down in the middle of a snake infested wet weather pond were one hundred percent, so she knew she was making the right decision by heading back to the shack at the end of the road.

The rain fell even harder, and the wind picked up. Twice Sissy ran off of the road and into the brambles, which let out a shriek of woody spines clawing against the clear coat and paint. Leaves and spindly pine branches flew across the road. The sky overhead darkened and lightning struck in streaks like claw marks. Sissy turned on the radio and heard the deejay warn of a lightning storm, pebble sized hail, and flash flooding in some low lying areas. Judging the distance of the gap in the stick fence in front of the house, Sissy drove through the opening and right up to the porch. When she stepped out of the car, water several inches deep covered Sissy's loafers and soaked her stockings above her ankles. Lightning crackled across the sky in narrowing intervals.

Despite the chaos outside, the house was still and quiet inside. Instinctively, Sissy flicked on the lights, which, surprisingly, came on this time without so much as a flicker. Sissy looked for a phone jack in the main living areas. As expected, there were no phones in the house, just empty jacks. The realtor went back to her car, and wondered what to do, as the sky darkened and hail the size of ping-pong balls fell, loudly hitting the car. The hail hit the windshield, making tiny spider veins. Even the hood was beginning to visibly dent.

Sissy sat in her weather battered car, "Was that mud hole really 'filled' with snakes?" Sissy sat and thought, strumming her fingers on the steering wheel. Each time she thought about wading through the muck to hitchhike a ride to town, she saw the shiny black eyes of the snake peering at her and the smooth, clean "S" the snake made as it wriggled across the miniature pond.

"Forget it, I'm not staying here," and the frustrated realtor slammed her key into the ignition and stepped on the gas, only to spin her wheels and go nowhere. Sissy popped the car in drive, still only the back wheel spun. Determined not to get out into the rain and hail, Sissy tried again and again to get the car to move forward. A rolling sound caught Sissy's ear and she watched her ink pen roll across the dash into the crevice between the window and the dash. Then she realized what she had done: she bogged herself down so deeply she had tilted the car.

Suddenly, a large ball of hail landed on a spider vein in the car's front windshield. The impact knocked the top lining of the windshield out of the frame, allowing the freezing summer rain to pelt Sissy like miniature spears. Sissy crawled into the back seat to avoid being hit by any incoming hail and heard, or more accurately felt, lightning strike the giant oak, which sat about ten feet from her incapacitated car.

Sparks and limbs flew in all directions, covering the diminutive Volvo. Sissy popped open the right back door and heard wood loudly creaking and crackling. Then a sound, wooden, hollow, and loud, as of a ship lurching in the ocean, issued from the old oak tree. A massive tree limb, which had stood majestically into the sky, was now leaning dangerously close to the house and her car.

Without second thoughts, the realtor ran out of her car and onto the front porch. Then she realized she had left her purse and the house key in the car. More afraid of going back into her car than the house, Sissy tugged and tugged on the lockbox. Nothing. Sissy kicked the door and it cracked down the middle. *It's completely dry rotted!* Sissy kicked and kicked at the door. She rammed her body against the door until it gave way in pieces, the lockbox still securely on the doorknob.

Immediately Sissy stepped into the kitchen and hugged her arms around herself. From the bowels of the dark kitchen, Sissy watched as the tree limb separated from the trunk in slow motion, wood fibers like stiff sinews, snapping and breaking as the great wooden arm crashed to earth, or more accurately, her car.

Glass shattered and metal groaned as acorns plinked and plunked in skips across the metal of her car. The car was totaled. "Oh, God!" Sissy exclaimed with her hands over her face.

The sky was as dark as night, even though it was only five in the afternoon. The air was still, or perhaps just seemed so in comparison to the previous events. Sissy stared out at the purple, sweltering sky, "Does this mean I'm going to get to describe what 'the tornady' sounded like?" Sissy looked around herself and huffed beneath her breath, "Only if I'm lucky. There's no way this tinder box can make it to Oz."

No leaks came through the rusted tin roof, astonishingly. What was Sissy going to do? She couldn't spend the night in her car and there was no furniture in the house, except the creepy bed down the hall. Because of the lightning, Sissy couldn't walk down the road and look for a way to get to the highway and flag down help. However, there was also the threat of snakes, which had thus far proven to be large and black. Water moccasins? Sissy wasn't sure if she even knew what a rattlesnake sounded like, and she didn't want to find out by getting too close to one. It'd be morning before anyone knew she was missing and go looking for her. Sissy found a corner in the kitchen where she had a full view of the front yard, sat with her legs in front of her and waited.

## Chapter 9: And Then Night Came

Sissy wasn't sure when she fell asleep with her head propped against the wall. But, she was sure she had fallen asleep against the kitchen wall, and NOT in the creepy bed, which was where she found herself. Sissy was sure she didn't sleepwalk, and in terms of "firsts," she did not want the creepy bed to be her first sleepwalking experience. But the bed was comfy despite its age. Crickets, cicadas, rain frogs all bleeped, blurped, chirped, and whirred in an undulating, peaceful chorus somewhere in the world outside the room with the big, comfy bed. Scraps of plastic lazily flapped the windows.

The rain had stopped and there was a full moon out, which let in a bright iridescent light around the perimeter of the pulled blinds, none of which appeared to be torn. The house settled and creaked. Overhead a slithering sound emanated from the fifteen foot high ceiling, which was probably just an attic - - with a varied assortment of creatures in it. Sissy rolled over and tried not to think about wharf rats large enough to eat through rusted shower stalls.

The sheets felt silky and solid, even though they were visibly frayed in the daylight. The pillow seemed larger and fluffy. Instead of smelling the musty scent of dirt and rot, Sissy thought she smelled a fresh fire, a pleasant smoky mesquite, mingled with a homey cedar. The words "Momma's cedar chests" echoed through Sissy's sleepy brain as she drifted pleasantly back to sleep.

From the blank darkness of solid slumber, Sissy woke up with all of her senses alive. There was no noise. None at all. Earlier in the night, she had barely noticed the constant white noise of crickets, cicadas, and rain frogs. Their constant drone had been subconsciously comforting, as they breathed life into an otherwise dead house and helped lull her to sleep. Now that the sound was gone and the air did not stir, Sissy felt as if she had been sucked into a vacuum.

The light coming through the windows seemed to intensify in brightness. Then her ears involuntarily pricked at the sound of her bedroom door creaking open. For a fleeting moment, Sissy hoped that someone discovered she was missing and had come to the house looking for her. With this comforting thought in mind, Sissy calmly turned her head toward the open door and saw nothing but heard the distinctive sound of footsteps lightly padding across the floor, which gave "it" away via creaks and squeaks. Sissy followed the sound with her eyes because she was too scared to move.

When the sound approached the right side of the bed, the realtor found her paralysis was all consuming as she was unable to move, scream, or inhale. The footsteps were beside her bed, but she could see nothing, only hear loud, muffled breathing not her own.

Then, against the background of the glowing shades, Sissy made out the darkened outline of a thin hand holding a large, pointed dagger aimed at her side of the bed. Fear so overwhelming took over and short circuited her will to live. In an instant she just accepted death without question. Sissy closed her eyes and felt every muscle in her body quiver. What she heard next absolutely amazed her.

Sissy felt nothing, but heard a physical struggle play out, seemingly on top of her. Voices grunted in the night and a light shuffle ensued as fabric audibly ripped and people struggled, rolling around the bed. Fingernails scraped the wooden bed railing beneath her. The last sound was that of a watermelon splitting open and air escaping out of an untied, pulled balloon. Then the footsteps retreated, and Sissy opened her eyes to see a hunched, dark figure limp back and forth in front of the bed where her feet were. There was no face, just black darkness. Unable to swallow, Sissy involuntarily choked on her spit and coughed so hard she felt it burn the back of her throat.

In an instant, the crickets, cicadas, and rain frogs returned to Sissy's ears and the wind blew the tattered fragments of plastic against the window. Beneath her barely breathing body, Sissy felt the soaked shreds of brittle cotton sheets and smelled the dank age of the lumpy, tiny pillow beneath her head. Sleep left her. Throughout the entire night, Sissy could not sleep nor move. When the morning sun rose, Sissy let out an audible sigh of relief and left the house.

# Chapter 10: Meet the Family

After glancing momentarily at the mangled mess, Sissy couldn't help but to deliriously giggle at her Volvo's tree toupee. *Now I have two cars*, she thought sarcastically to herself. Sissy made footprints in the sand as she walked to the crepe myrtles. On the near horizon, she saw a large four-wheeled drive Ford sloshing its way through the large puddle that threatened to swallow her Volvo the day before. Mud sprayed and water flew in a redneck display of machismo. Sissy was never so grateful for rednecks before in her life.

Sissy waved at the large grizzly bear driving the over-sized truck. He was wearing a "Native Son" cap on his full-bearded head. The man stopped the truck and yelled at the stranded woman, "Git in."

The realtor uneasily grinned and went against every code of conduct her mother had taught her since childhood. However, the truck was very tall and very dirty so swinging herself up into the truck without a step stool was in itself a tall order. Sissy contorted her body as she got into the truck without getting mud all over herself. The man's only reaction was to spit tobacco juice out of the window. Merle Haggard hung precariously out of the eight track deck, covered in a thick layer of dirt. More dirt and empty crushed soda cans littered the floor and jumped around Sissy's feet.

"So she left ya' here all night, huh?"

"What? Oh, yes. But she left a note."

"Ain't no need to say somethin' nice. I know she's a slam bitch. Been a slam bitch ma' whole life. She know'd better n' ta' have ya' come all the way out here in tha' rain. You be sure and charge her greedy ass extry for whatever it is she's got you doing." The man emphatically spat a fat wad of tobacco juice out of the swiftly moving Ford.

"Oh, yes." Sissy was too afraid to ask the man his name or say anything and hoped the scene that played out in the bedroom was not a premonition. *Be nice, Sissy. Don't let your Atlanta show.*

Once at the house, the man let out a deep chuckle, "I'll be damned. Tree fell on your car like somethin' out a' tha Wizard'a Oz. I hope it's totaled. Sue that heifer fer all she's worth, get you a real car made in 'Merica. None of that slave labor shit."

"Oh, yes," Sissy said with a bloodless smile.

"Welp, I best get ta' work and get that thar tree off your car." The man got out of his truck, lifted his hat off of his head and scratched his scalp, "Ain't ya' wonderin' what I'm doin' out here?"

Sissy felt a large lump in her throat, but forced out, "You used to live here?"

"Yeah, but I's got a 'strainin' order out on me not to come out here. Didn't Abbey tell ya'?"

"Oh, no," Sissy said again, with the fearful, forced smile.

"Name's Harry. Harry McDonnell. I'm Abbey's brother. Called ma' momma this mornin' to find out what that damn Abbey's doin' in town, and she told me she's fin'lly gettin' around ta' sellin' the old place out from under Aunt Cat. She's supposed to meet some realtor yesterdee, but left 'fore the hole filled up with water. I fig'red I'd git in and git out whilst I still can. I know'd Abby'd wait 'till affer noon to get her sorry ass out of bed and see about the place. I'll be damned if I didn't find you out here with a tree landed on your Nahtzi car."

And with that, Harry pulled a smutty chainsaw from his pick-up bed and began cutting the tree off of Sissy's "Nazi car," while she sat on the most stable of the concrete steps and helplessly watched. Sweat poured off of the man's body and stained through his cotton t-shirt. Tiny particles of chipped wood stuck to his skin. Once he finished cutting the giant tree, he pulled the limbs off of the smashed and bent car, "Keys?" Sissy pointed at the car. Harry cleared the remainder of the broken glass from the driver side window with a tree limb, reached his thick arm through, and turned the ignition. The car started, but the engine clanked against the bent hood. Harry chuckled, "I bet you wish't you'd never seen this place, huh?"

Sissy just shook her head in the affirmative. Held-back-tears were burning the lump in her throat.

Harry walked up to the house and saw the kicked in door. "Now why in the hell did you have to go and do that for?" Sissy's voice crackled through the snot and tears, "I found it like that." Harry stomped on a piece of the door and held up a fragment that had the doorknob with the lockbox on it, "So you put this thang on it when you found it like this?"

Sissy just shrugged her shoulders, "Habit, I guess."

Harry shook his head and threw down the piece of door. Despite his large size, he quickly disappeared into the house. After some grunting and rummaging noises, Harry appeared with the gas heater from the living room. He threw it into the back of the truck with the chainsaw. Harry motioned for Sissy to get in the truck, "I'll take you to Momma's. Make Abbey take you somewhere and get you a rental. Ya'll settle this. I ain't even s'posed to be here, and ain't none of this my problem. Tell her to fix yer shit and make it right. She got Aunt Cat in the settlement. She's the one you sue. Got it?"

Sissy just nodded and got in the truck, tears filled her eyes, but she tried not to show them.

Harry revved his engine, "And I weren't here. You ain't never seen me."

At first, the ride was silent, and Sissy would shudder out a stifled whimper ever so often.

"Look. Don't cry. I know I'm a scary guy, 'specially to you pro-fessional women. But I'm tryin' to make thangs right. Guess ya' had a rough time, tree fallin' on yer car, sleepin' on the floor. You awright?"

Sissy smiled and sniffed back a thick run of "crying" snot, "Well, at first, but I made it to the bed and slept . . . some."

Harry got quiet and his face turned pale, "They's only one bed left in that house. How'd you get in tha room?"

"It was open when I came in. Abbey left a note not to move the bed."

"That's horseshit. I nailed that door shut and boarded it from the inside after we moved out last month. I left the note fer whoever buys this place. And I know, Abbey's fat ass ain't gawn in there."

"Maybe she paid somebody to go in and open the door."

"Well, I jess checked it and it's still nailed tight."

"I don't know. I just know I woke up in that big, creepy bed and felt silky sheets and smelled wood burning. Not like a house fire, but like a . . . fireplace with scented wood."

"Well, that explains it. You dreamed it. Ain't no silk sheets on that bed, I know. Well, good."

"Why did you nail the door shut?"

"House and every thang in it was meant to be fer family, the McDonnell family and nobody else. Except that bed. Damn bed has hist'ry. Ain't right movin' it. Folks jess need to leave it be."

Sissy just turned her head and looked out the window. The rest of the ride was silent, and thankfully, uneventful.

"Momma" lived in a fixed income neighborhood that consisted of small two bedroom, one bath ranch homes built in the '60s. Harry dropped Sissy off at the end of his mother's dirt driveway after honking his horn and waiving at the confused looking elderly woman, who waved him away like he was not her son, but a stray goat in her garden. Sissy dropped out of the tall truck and slowly walked up the dirt driveway, the sound of tires screeching away and Harry's hemi revving behind her.

A short, elderly woman greeted the haggard realtor, "Well, Lady, who'n the hell are you?"

"I'm Mrs. Greer's realtor. Harry found me at your aunt's house this morning after a tree fell on my car yesterday."

"Good Gawd. Well, Abbey ain't here and she's got the . . . custody or whatever it's called over Aunt Cat. She'll be back in a little bit. Gone to visit Cat at the home. Come on inside and I'll fix ya' some cawfee."

Sissy went inside and was immediately assaulted by an almost palpable wall of smoke and nicotine residue. Momma walked over to the kitchen counter, picked up her smoldering cigarette, and began pouring the coffee. The woman was suffering from the beginnings of osteoporosis and the long-time abuse of smoking: yellow skin, thick wrinkles, and a voice that sounded like a tin can being dragged behind a newlywed's car.

Momma took a bite from some jam covered toast while she gave Sissy a cup, but offered no cream or sugar. The woman forced a sweet smile at the bedraggled realtor, "I told Harry not to go out to that house. But, now I'm glad he did. He's always had a knack for knowin' stuff like that. Kinda' like women's intuition, but for men. Who knows what would've happened to you out there all alone. I can tell you're not used to bein' out in the country."

Sissy was beginning to grow weary of her misadventure, "No."

"I reckon Abbey's got insurance, but who knows about the house with Cat's condition. Abbey's been working on things, even from up in Tacoma. You got car insurance, right?"

"Yes."

"Mrs.?"

"Miss Clayton."

"Abbey's too proud to tell you what's goin' on, but in light of your bad experience, I think you outta know. Look, Abbey's already got a buyer who's been wantin' to buy that shack and the hundred somethin' acres it's sittin' on for years. He's loaded and is willin' to pay whatever Abbey asks - - no matter how much he tries to poor mouth us. Problem is, she ain't got a clue what numbers to start at. How's about you appraise the place and a little extra, just fer you? I mean, the whole family's already been to court once, right? Aunt Cat stands to make a lot of money off of that sale. And I'd hate for the judge to find out Harry went nosin' 'round that dump after the 'strainin' order. Who knows how his wife and kids would fare while he's in jail, and after all the good he did to try and help you."

Sissy was furious. "He went looking for me because he knew your daughter, his sister, put me through a little thing called 'endangerment' due to her 'neglect.' Being as you knew I was potentially out at that shack, and you discouraged Harry from coming to look for me, I'd say that makes you an accomplice." Sissy hoped her use of common legal jargon, no matter how misused, would be enough to intimidate the horrible little troll-like woman, who was trying to use her own son as bargaining material.

Momma didn't flinch but tapped her long ash into the sink and blew a wide, long puff of smoke that had been patiently waiting from the lowest regions of her trachea, "Humph. You're already gettin' five percent. Abbey ain't got no damn money. All's Abbey's gettin' is Aunt Cat, who's deaf and blind with bad teeth. Eighty years old. If she was a horse, we'd a'done shot her by now. Hell, it'll be another five, ten, fifteen years 'fore Abbey gets anything from that old bitch. You . . . can get a good amount right up front. No court. No lawyers eatin' up any money you make off of this little unfortunate mishap. A big misunderstandin' and lack of communication, I'd say."

Sissy took a swig of coffee, which, too, had somehow been tainted with the flavor of Momma's cheap cigarettes, "I want a new car."

"Get you one. I don't give a shit how you spend your damn money. You'll be better off 'n Abbey. Aunt Cat's too mean to die. Told Abbey. Mess always happens to that damn bunch of kids."

"Goes with the territory, I'd say."

"Watch it, Girlie. You're still in my house."

"I'm just curious. Why did Harry board up that door?"

"What door?"

"To the bedroom with the big bed?"

"Hell, if I know. He's got some sort of sentimental crap stuck in his head over that house, the land, everything. Why?"

"I wish he had been more thoughtful and boarded up the front door. The house is a death trap. I'd say you're getting any asking price in spite of the house."

"I told Abbey that. She won't listen. She grew up there with Aunt Cat as a little girl and thinks it's like it was over thirty something years ago with fresh paint and fat, green ferns lining the porch. Not the rotten down ramshackle it is. You're lucky you didn't fall through the floor, much less sleep in a bed. Even if it was on the other side of a barricade. All sounds kinda suspicious if you ask me."

"But I did sleep in that bed," Sissy leaned toward Momma, whisper yelling, "*and I saw things*. I want you to tell me who was stabbed in that bed and when it happened because it scared the hell out of me last night."

Momma picked up the closest butter knife and pointed it at Sissy's face, "I don't know what you're talking about, but you best keep your damn mouth shut. Ain't nothin' happened in that bed or in that house. Nothin.' You're a damn liar."

A large middle-aged woman flung the kitchen door open as Sissy was backing out of it with Momma's butter knife pointed squarely between the realtor's eyes. Unbeknownst to the dark haired, middle aged woman, she got there in the nick of time; her realtor was being assaulted at dull knife point.

Sissy lost her footing as she tripped over the door stoop. Abbey called out, "Hey, Momma," but Sissy's stumbling took Abbey off guard before she could finish her greeting. Once Abbey's eyes adjusted from the midday sun to the dusky kitchen light, she exclaimed, "Damn! I can't leave you alone for fifteen minutes before you got somebody cornered."

Abbey pushed Sissy back into the kitchen and secured her footing with one hand while reaching around Sissy and grabbing Momma's butter knife with the other. Sissy turned to see Abbey lean toward her with her eyes rolled and hands on her wide jiggly hips, "You gotta leave Momma's cig'rettes alone. She's a damn fiend when it comes to those things." The obese woman laughed, "You get used to it." Without social cue, body language or other cue, Abbey aggressively shoved Sissy out of her way to the coffee pot and began pouring herself a cup. With her back still turned away from Sissy and her mother, Abbey asked, "Who's your little friend, Momma? What's *she* need? Fifty dollars? Groceries? A ride to town?"

Momma exhaled another long puff of smoke, another butter knife in hand, "This is your realtor. She had to spend the night at the old house last night when a tree fell on her car. We come to an understandin' on it, though. She's gonna ask a real good price on the place and drive away in her brand new car. Right, Miss Clayton?"

"Momma! Put the damn knife down, now! Gawd! You're as bad a redneck as Harry. Now I know where he gets it from," Abbey took the second butter knife out of the old woman's hand, who disdainfully walked out of the kitchen and into the living room, muttering and waving her hand. Primal fear seared through

Abbey's eyes as she began her interrogation, "A tree fell on your car? You thinkin' 'bout suing me?"

Sissy realized her unkempt appearance and suddenly worried that the women could smell fear on her. Trying to soothe her nerves, the realtor smoothed out the sides of her hair and nonchalantly answered, "No."

"How'd you get here, then?"

"A redneck found me off of the road."

"It wasn't Harry, was it? He's dangerous when it comes to that house. Crazy."

"No. It was another redneck. In a big truck. With a chainsaw. Knew your family."

Abbey took a sip from her coffee cup and nodded her head, "Coulda' been anybody, then."

"Yeah." Sissy felt nothing but disgust at the strange family she had temporarily gotten involved with. Mrs. Abigail Greer was everything she thought she'd be but wearing a blue and white checked Sunday dress that was two sizes too small, pearl earrings, and stretched pumps that made the top of her feet look like muffins. Her hair was black in a tight home perm. She had a giant mole on the corner of her thin lips, which were painted a bright pink.

Mrs. Greer was trying to play the best reaction against Sissy. No poker player, the fat woman's face suddenly looked fit for a cockfight, which would have been her, "*I'm trying to intimidate you into submission*" face. When that didn't move Sissy, she tried on her, "*Poor pitiful me; I'm so unlucky,*" demeanor. Even better, the next expression passed like a chameleon's colors, the: "*I'm calm, pensive, and very concerned* *for **your** well-being.*" So, which would Abbey choose?

"I'm just glad you made it out of that house in one piece. That storm had *me* scared. If I'd a' honestly thought for one minute that you'd a' have driven through that rain, I'd've waited at the end of that road and sent you away. This is just . . . terrible. Really awful. I bet you're sore from sleepin' on the floor all night, aside from bein' upset about yer car and all."

Sissy wryly smiled, "Actually, I spent the night in the guest bedroom. The one with the gigantic bed. Apparently, the only way I could've gotten in was through the window. Any ideas?"

Abbey just shrugged and looked around Sissy to her mother, who was turned around in her recliner, glaring at the back of Sissy's head. Momma yelled from the living room, "Nope. You're, uh, mistaken. Must've been dreamin'."

Abbey waved Momma away and asked Sissy, "So, what's your trouble gonna cost me?"

Sissy took a sip of nicotine, "Five percent more under the table and you take me on a guided tour of the old family plantation."

Abbey just smiled, "What, you got anything in particular you want ta' find?"

Sissy reproached the woman with a glare, "Hospitality."

## Chapter 11: This Wasn't In the Brochure

Sissy woke up early that Sunday morning to another beautiful day. Unlike Friday, Sunday was excessively hot and the only moisture in the air was from the thick humidity.

Great day to go snooping around for . . . unmarked graves? A masked villain hiding in the attic? Buried treasure hidden from the carpetbaggers? Of course, the theme song to "Jillian's Inlet" rang through Sissy's head. Still, what was there to be afraid of in broad daylight? Well, other than snakes.

That Sunday afternoon, Sissy picked up Abbey in the flashy red convertible Mustang they picked out from *U Rentz* the day before. Sissy had been contemplating getting a sportier car after her Volvo, and the "accident" proved to be an opportune time to try one out. Of course, the rental had a slipping five speed gear shift and a faulty radio. The trunk would only pop after turning the key rapidly from side to side, removing the key, and then punching the empty key hole with your fist. These inconveniences allowed Abbey to bargain for a lower price, which Sissy didn't care about. The car was sporty, fast, and mobile, unlike her Volvo which was currently crunched, immobile, and scrapped.

Abbey actually looked cute when she got into the convertible: bright yellow cotton shorts set, a clean pair of Nikes, and tennis socks. She kind of looked like a well fed, cleaned up two hundred pound ten year old with a menopausal disposition. Her make-up was consistent with her deeply southern up-bringing. Despite the fact she would be in sweltering heat that could melt ceramic tile in seconds, Abbey wore the classic southern staples: lipstick and mascara.

Abbey's purse was a giant purple monstrosity that clanked loudly when she got in the car, "Hey, gal. How's your sports car doin' fer ya'?"

Sissy smiled widely, "Lovin' it."

Abbey sniffed her approval, "Not gonna let the top down?"

Sissy shrugged, "We can . . . if you want lovebugs in your teeth."

Abbey flicked a set of lovebugs that were hovering near her face in full coitus, "At least the bastards die doing what they love the most."

Sissy squeezed the padded steering wheel, blinking as she came to a realization, "That's why those ugly little alien things are called 'lovebugs?'"

Abbey looked incredulously at Sissy, "You're not from around here, huh? No accent, not married, got that 'I'm-better-than-you' look on your uppity little professional face. Lemme guess, you're from Atlanta. Well, let me tell you how not tuh die in the country: if it makes a noise, go in the other direction. Snakes are everywhere and in everythang out here. Do not pick up, inspect, open, or poke your fingers into anything you cannot fully see. Why? Because there's a snake in it, and most likely the kind that can kill you dead. Stick with me. Do not wander off and do not go in the barns."

Sissy revved the engine and giggled, "You got me a convertible."

Abbey held her purple purse tight, "You get us killed, I will never forgive you. Us McDonnell's might hate each other, but we stick together. And, I'm pretty sure there's plenty of us in hell already, so prepare for that eternity, Miss Prissy Britches."

The ride over to the plantation was quiet, except for the constant splattering of lovebugs on the windshield and grill, making a milky, puss like film all over the car's front end. Sissy secretly grinned at Abbey, who held her purse clutched tightly in her lap like a child for the entire trip. Sissy couldn't help it. She found the abrasive woman endearing.

Once at the plantation, Abbey took one look at the "damage" left in the bugs' wake, "If those bastards at the rental place think I'm payin' to have these bugs scraped off the car, they're crazier than I am for bein' out here with you."

Sissy just inhaled the hot country air, "Think of it as getting a tan without the beach, ocean, or tourists."

Abbey put her humongous purse on the bespeckled car hood, "Get your butt over here. I need to spray ya' down."

Sissy turned and looked at Abbey untrustingly, "What are you talking about?"

"Horse flies? No see'ums? Deer ticks? Lyme's disease? Insect repellent. I know you had some romantic idea in your head of running around in the country and smelling the flowers and visiting old crap while I tell you some family secret about 'that shit and this here shit.' But, you gotta wear your insect repellent *and* your sunscreen. Damn Scotch-Irish skin makes me burn like a pig."

"Pigs burn?"

Abbey fished out a cigarette from her bag, "Why do you think they waller in mud?"

Sissy watched Abbey light her cigarette. The realtor was utterly amazed at how someone could complain about the heat, and then light a fire, "Because they're filthy, yet amazingly, tasty animals?"

The big woman mumbled through her cigarette, "Humph, that, too, I suppose."

Sissy obediently allowed Abbey to spray her from head to toe in some highly offensive, ozone depleting, oily, itchy insect repellent, while Abbey's lit cigarette threatened to turn the can into a flame thrower and torch the realtor alive. Abbey turned out to be a touch sadistic, as she was careful to spray the poison particularly dense in Sissy's face. The suntan lotion didn't want to mix or absorb in the presence of the repellent and left a milky smear that smeared and dripped on Sissy's body, making her wonder if that was the same magical substance inside lovebugs.

Standing like a drying egret, Sissy dripped with her arms out by her sides, "Abbey, what are your thoughts on the plantation?"

Abbey rubbed suntan lotion into her marshmellowy soft, white arms, "Whatda' ya' mean?"

"It's been in your family for so long; how do you think you'll feel about selling it to somebody else? What's the rest of the family think?"

Next, the large woman violently shook the can of repellent. In a fog of poison, the woman asked Sissy, "Selling the place? More like, gettin' out while the gettin's good, I'd say. Taxes to pay. Repairs. Up keep. I bet Adam and Eve had an easier time in The Garden than my family's ever had trying to keep this place alive."

The fog didn't seem to bother Abbey, but the wind shifted it into Sissy's face. Sissy let out a cough, "So, it'd be okay? With everybody?"

The can let out a faint whiff, until there was no more. Abbey shook the can, which let out a hollow rattle. "Can's empty, I guess," was all she said before throwing it into a clump of weeds. "No. Harry keeps saying, 'The house won't take it' as if it's the heart and soul of the whole family. Truth is, he thinks it's haunted. Crazy bastard. That's why he boarded up that damn room. I didn't want to say anything in front of Momma. She's crazy in the head, too."

"What happened in the room to make it haunted?"

Abbey wiped a fat drop of sweat from her wide brow, "How should I know? I spent the night there with Aunt Cat most of my childhood, and I don't know why everybody's so upset."

Sissy swiped gnats away from her face, "Not even Harry's said anything?"

Abbey tapped the ash from her cigarette. The cinders fell to the ground, burning the dry grass to curled ribbons. Taking a drag of smoke, Abbey said, "He's always been a sissy. Sorry, Sissy. Just scared of the place. In love with it, too. Big on the whole 'family tradition' idea. Considerin' our family, that's just damn delusional."

Sweat was dripping down Sissy's brow. The sweat saturated spray stung her eyes, "What's he afraid of?"

Abbey chuckled, "The dark."

Sissy smiled at Abbey. She got the impression that the fat woman wasn't going to tell her what she wanted to know and that the day may turn out to be a complete waste of time.

Abbey inhaled a deep asthmatic breath, "Let's go over to the barn and get the buggy."

Sissy rubbed her eyes, which only made them sting worse, "Buggy?"

"Dune buggy. Belonged to Harry, but Aunt Cat got it in court somehow. I say we use it. I ain't walkin' all over creation so you can go bird watching or whatever you're wantin' to do."

The dune buggy was, in fact, a dune buggy; a fully operational vehicle with a thin, open frame big enough to hold two people. Sissy frowned when she saw that Harry had built a wooden box, much like a pickup truck's bed, over the exposed engine, creating a potential fire hazard. Inside the wooden bed were gloves, a cut off shovel, and a dog collar with blood spatters on it. Sissy shivered.

Sissy thought to herself, *The man lost the ancestral estate, his buggy, and his dog. At least he had a truck, an eight track, and a chainsaw. But is a redneck without his dog and dune buggy, really a true redneck?*

The vehicle was dusty but cranked on the first try. The seat belts were for display only; they didn't work from the fabric being too brittle, the belt length too short, and the clasps mismatched. There was even a CB radio hazardously rigged to the shell, rivaling the hazard caused by Harry's handy-man-special wooden truck bed rigged over the exposed engine. From the chimneys, cigarettes, flammable materials, faulty wiring, and wood over exposed motors, Sissy was convinced that the McDonnells were part of some strange government conspiracy involving asbestos mixed with human DNA.

*Are they just trying to set the world on fire?* Sissy wondered, trying to seem unaffected by everything around her.

Abbey rolled the buggy out of the barn with a mischievous

grin on her face, "Harry'd die if he saw me on his buggy. You got a camera on ya'?"

Sissy solemnly shook her head, "No."

"Damn. He's worth more dead than alive. Be the best present I ever gave his welfare wife and raggedy ass kids."

Sissy was appalled, "You're evil."

Abbey was unphased, "Runs in the family. Git in."

Sissy stepped into the car and got a firm hold of the sides of the vinyl passenger seat, and braced herself by digging the tread of her tennis shoes into the bare metal floorboard.

"First, I'm gonna take you to see the pond, then we'll loop around to the family cemetery, come in the back way to the swamp, and end off back here."

"That's it?"

"What'd you expect? A three hour tour?"

## Chapter 12:  You Call It Creepy, We Call It Tradition

The ride to the pond was less than a quarter of a mile over thick, tall weeds.  It wouldn't have been pleasant to walk over, but it hardly seemed to warrant the use of a dune buggy.  The pond proved to be nothing more than another wet weather mud hole, about the size of two king size beds, not unlike the one that formed in the bend of the dirt road leading up to the house.

Abbey took a deep drag from the small remainder of her cigarette, "It's small, but deep.  Probably where all those damn snakes come from.  Best we can guess, it's fed by a spring or something.  Farm could have a drought that kills everything, but that pond will always be here."

Sissy was disappointed.  The pond was quite anti-climactic, "So?"

Abbey flicked her cigarette butt into the pond, "It's no good for drinking.  Won't keep fish.  Certain times of the year the water turns red."

Sissy shook her head, "Red bloom?"

Abbey lit another cigarette and mumbled through it, "No, not algae.  The water.  From the top to wherever the bottom ends."

"Any ideas why?"

"Great Grandpa told me that this pond used to be a whole lot bigger.  He said not when he was a little boy, but when his father was little.  Anyway, story goes that Old Man McDonnell got himself a Haitian slave woman who was supposed to be good at using weeds and stuff to cure ailments.  He set her up a house off in the woods back behind this pond where she lived . . . and he'd visit, so to speak.  Until he drowned her.  Maybe Old Lady

McDonnell did it herself. Anyway, the slaves found that Haitian woman floating face down in this pond, bleeding from her eyes, nose, and mouth. Old Man McDonnell had her buried by the pond, which was when the thing started to shrink and all of the fish died. Want to see the grave?"

"Yes, of course!" Sissy was ashamed of her childish enthusiasm and outward delight in the macabre.

"This is what we think is it. Feel that stone," Abbey showed Sissy a thick clump of tall smut grass, which had all but hidden a worn white piece of marble that was shaped like a large, worn tooth. "This here headstone is supposedly what was left over from carving Old Man's headstone. Hear it told correctly, he feared a curse and went on ahead and had his headstone built right after that Haitian witch was found floating face down in the pond. Turned out, he was right. Anyhow, you gotta see Old Man's headstone. A great big pillar." Abbey snickered, "Reminds me of a pointy pecker." Abbey watched Sissy touch the stone. Abbey slouched over Sissy and blew a big puff of smoke out of the side of her mouth. Abbey huffed at Sissy, "It's hot, real hot, huh?"

"Yeah. But it's like over a hundred degrees out here. Everything's hot."

"But it feels like that in the wintertime, too. Pull your hand back."

Sissy did as she was told and looked up at Abbey, who had blocked the sun with her wide bulky body.

"See that light flickering on the stone?"

Sissy looked and saw a barely perceptible white light in the shape of a ragged line flicker on the stone like a miniature strike of lightning, "Okay. I found it. Maybe your shadow's not completely covering this thing."

"Put your hand over it, so's you can still see behind your hand."

Sissy put her right hand a few inches above the rock and looked up at Abbey, "Like this?"

"Yep. Look at your hand. See anything?"

"No. The light's still flickering on the stone. So?"

Abbey tapped her ash with disdain, "If your hand's covering the marble, shouldn't the light flicker on your hand?"

Sissy pulled her hand back quickly away and held it with her left hand, "Okay. That's a little weird."

Abbey pushed past Sissy and snuffed out her cigarette on the stone, "On to the cemetery, City Girl."

Sissy got up and dusted herself off, paying close attention to wipe her right hand on her blue jeans shorts a little harder as if the flickering light had been contagious, "I'm game."

The cemetery was about three miles from the homestead and contained the headstones of about a dozen men, three babies, and the only female - - the infamous "Old Lady" McDonnell, who began married life as Margaret McDonnell. Across the road from the cemetery was another plantation home. Different in design from Aunt Cat's house. This house was in better condition and covered in gingerbread trim. A young couple puttered around in their loosely manicured flower gardens. Sissy and Abbey waved at the couple before they fidgeted out of the low riding buggy and poked and prodded around the cemetery as if they were on a ghoulish Easter egg hunt.

Abbey lit another cigarette, "This is the cemetery the family used for the men the war got."

Sissy put her hand over her face to block some of the harsh afternoon sun, "Which war?"

Abbey chuckled, "'Which war.' I'm glad you didn't say that in front of Momma. The Civil War!" Abbey deeply coughed, "But, I still don't know why the babies are here."

"What about Mrs. McDonnell?"

"She put up a big fuss to be buried out here with her husband and her sons."

"These can't all be her sons."

"Grandsons, too. Some are only twelve or so."

"Well, the place is in good shape. Who keeps it up?"

"County. It's a place of pride for the whole community. We're all still related on down the line one way or another. That and Harry got it registered as a federal monument."

"I think I know which one is Mr. McDonnell's." Sissy walked over to the giant obelisk and felt the cool marble in the bright sunlight. She stared at the tall pillar and examined its blue and gray marble veins, when she stubbed her toe on the base.

"Notice anything strange about it, yet?"

"It's cool, despite this heat."

"Nah. That ain't it."

"What?"

"Look at the base a little closer."

"It's been cut. The base is a lot wider than the next segment. It's not symmetrical at all."

"Look at this picture I brought. It's of Daddy when he came out here 'fore goin' off ta war. See how tall the column is?"

Sissy assumed this "war" meant either World War II or Korea, but thought it better not to ask, "It seems a little taller, but I don't know how tall he was."

"Lemme tell you, this pillar has gotten shorter and shorter since the time Old Man died and it was put up out here. And you know what?"

"What?"

"That stone you touched out by the pond has gotten bigger and bigger."

"If you say so. It's just a hunk of rock, not clay."

Abbey put her hands on her hips and pursed her lips, "You're no fun. Don't tell me you're not havin' any fun anymore."

"I just expected, I don't know. I really don't know what to think. But you seem to believe. You don't find any of this weird?"

"Grew up with it, I guess."

"Maybe. Is this all?"

"What do you mean?"

"No scandal about any of the people buried out here? No family rivalries? No family secrets buried out here with the dead?"

"I guess I could've hired a couple of my cousins to chase us with chainsaws in white bed sheets. Sorry you're not entertained like you thought you would be."

Sissy let out a big sigh, "Where to next?"

"The swamp."

Sissy chuckled, "Isn't there always a swamp?"

Abbey looked confused, "I don't know. What're you talking about?"

***

Sissy and Abbey rode in the loud white noise of the rushing wind, which made Sissy's eyes tear up. She held on tight to the sides of her seat with her eyes shut even tighter.

The lovebugs spattered and bombarded the women like flecks of juicy shrapnel. The bugs only hurt when they hit her face. Otherwise, they'd hit, squash, and fly away as empty carcasses, leaving behind a white smear on clothing and exposed skin. Occasionally, large bugs, such as dragonflies, would hit Sissy in the chest and sting from the impact. The wind from the buggy made Sissy's hair a dangerous weapon and petulant mess, slapping her face and slicing into her eyes despite how tightly they were shut. To make matters worse, her face was wind burned. Sissy began to rethink the merits of a dune buggy.

Abbey made a large loop, speeding down gravel paved roads and dirt roads with the gusto of a race car driver. Unfortunately, Abbey did not seem to understand that she had the advantage of holding onto the steering wheel; her passenger did not. Sissy's rear slid all over the slick vinyl. Had she not worn her tennis shoes with the thick treads, she may have been tossed out of the swiftly moving vehicle all together. But she locked her knees and pushed as deeply into the back of the seat as possible.

Curiosity got the better of Sissy, who found that she could see a little if she squinted her eyes. As best she could tell, they passed various side roads and dirt roads all named after dead McDonnells. Sissy recognized some of the names from the cemetery.

Miscellaneous broken down shacks dotted the landscape. Even though she couldn't see it, she could smell a hog farm somewhere close by. That, and the acrid stagnant smell of the swamp baking in the midday heat. Abbey turned left and Sissy gladly took the moment to catch her breath. She had not realized how hard it was to breathe with all of that wind racing at her face and chest.

Abbey turned back in the direction of the plantation and went straight for about a mile before turning onto a long, unmarked dirt road that crossed the railroad tracks. A clump of trees in the distance proved to house about twenty Mexican workers, who were all sitting in the shade outside of their dilapidated single wide trailers, eating freshly opened watermelon straight from the tips of their pocketknives, and napping. Inside the trailers, children peeped out from behind thin sheets, which improvised as curtains. A single, orange, beat-down, seventies model Ford truck with a cracked camper shell seemed to be their only mode of transportation. Laundry, hung on a myriad of clotheslines, blew in the breeze. The men half waved, until they realized they didn't know the people in the buggy. Cold stares and the general cease of movement proved they didn't like the intrusion.

Still the women drove on where the road led away from a large dusty field to a forest of dense vegetation. The road ended, but a skinny set of tire tracks marked a narrow path into the woods. Kudzu engulfed every branch, every shrub, every blade of grass. Poison ivy, or sumac, or oak (Sissy always got confused over the number of leaves) stuck heroically through the choking vines. Large pterodactyl-like mosquitoes buzzed and whined loudly in Sissy's ears.

The path was uneven and rocky, shaking the buggy and bumping its passengers. That familiar smell of stagnant water and prolific algae assaulted Sissy's nostrils. Mud so thick and sour it smelled almost like excrement. Moldering leaves and tannic acid. Now that Abbey had slowed to a creep along the almost hidden tracks, Sissy took the moment to take in the swampy sights.

Abbey asked through her cigarette, "Ain't you glad I made you wear all of that bug screen?"

"Yes, yes, I am. Thank you. That was thoughtful."

"So thoughtful you'll reconsider the ten percent?"

"Only if you throw in this magnificent piece of fine machinery as part of the deal. I always wanted my very own dune buggy complete with CB radio and fire hazard."

"Nope. City girl like you would never take it off the pavement and get it dirty. Be a waste."

"This is true. So, I take it we're going to the swamp, are we not?"

"Almost there, if memory serves me correctly."

"So, what's the story on the swamp?"

"Oh, it's just a neat place. During The Depression Uncle Herman found some human bones out here when a real bad drought passed through. The family was trying to dredge the thing to get more water out of it when they unearthed all sorts of bones. At first they tried to say it might've been deer bones from old alligator dens. But, you can't quite get around a human skull, now can you?"

"No, I guess not."

"Aunt Cat hadn't been married into the family long enough to know stuff and she pitched a fit."

"Aunt Catherine married into the family?"

"Yeah. Anyway, she wasn't used to living out in the country and the way the family did things, so she notified the police."

Sissy listened, wanting to hear more, "Mmm-hmm."

"The po-lice was out here every day for a long time. They'd come out here and stay and eat Aunt Cat's cooking and drink Uncle Herman's 'shine for free. Everybody was so mad at Aunt Cat."

"I bet. Taking a man's moonshine, that's a shame."

Abbey cocked a brow at Sissy and continued, "They all thought that the bones might've belonged to a couple of missing persons from a few years back and that'd be case solved. But, they weren't. They were too old for all of that. Best they could figure, they were the remains of some slaves. But, the family already knew that."

"Why didn't your family just tell your aunt?"

"She was new."

Sissy wanted to laugh, but refrained and sarcastically said, "Makes sense."

"It made the papers and what not."

"Why were the slaves in the swamp? And how was it better to get the secret out in the papers than to tell your aunt?"

"Family figured the po-lice would be too well fed and drunk to figure it out, call it missing persons, and sleep it all off."

"A risk that didn't pay off."

"Who knew? A coupla' generations before, po-lice didn't make their way into our land. They knew they'd a' gone missin', too. Just thank everything gettin' civilized, I reckon."

Sissy sank back in the sweaty vinyl seat, "Why would anybody want to do something like that to other human beings?"

"Harry said it was an epidemic that hit the slaves particularly hard one summer way back then. It was too hot to burn anything, so the family threw the dead bodies in the swamp.

Wasn't against the law back then."

"Must've made a terrible stinch."

"I guess."

Sissy looked around and swatted hummingbird sized mosquitoes, "What are all those rock mounds over there?"

"That's Harry's doin's. I told you he was crazy. Family kept those bones on display for years. During the Depression, folks didn't get out much so they'd travel all the way out here to see the bones they read about in the papers. Uncle Herman started chargin' admission and had real nice displays set up. Take folks on tours of the place. Then somebody got snake bit and wound that all up."

"So, the place could have been a redneck amusement park?"

"Anyway. When we was little, Henry told me that the bones talked to him and they wanted to be buried. Ain't that just some craziness?"

Sissy raised both of her eyebrows and shook off a shiver, "Yeah."

"When he moved into the old house to help take care of Cat, he took the bones and buried them out here with rocks for headstones and wooden crosses. Spooky. The man's a nut. Certifiable."

"You never heard anything or felt anything?"

Abbey's face turned red, and the woman fluffed up in anger, "No, never. I'm not crazy like *them*. There's nothing here but old shit and dry land that cain't be farmed."

Sissy just nodded and swatted.

Abbey shot a look at Sissy, "Thinking of Harry made me

remember. That room. The one you say you woke up in? Harry never did like that room. When we were kids, we'd stay with Aunt Cat. He'd wake me up in the middle of the night with his cryin' because of some woman walking back and forth in front of the bed, wearing all black. Black dress, black headdress, bent over with a cane. Momma said it was Old Lady McDonnell in her Civil War widow's mournin' dress. She wore it to Old Man's funeral and never took it off. Buried in it. Wore it to her own funeral, you might say. I never saw a thing. Not a single, solitary thing. I kinda wanted to, but then I figured if they was something to see, I'd've seen it by now."

Sissy looked down at her lap, "That must've been what I saw."

"What are you talking about, what you 'saw?'"

"I don't know, Abbey. You don't really seem to be into the paranormal."

"I watch the Discovery Channel. Bet I caught you off guard, knowing what you was talkin' about with 'red bloom,' huh? I've seen stuff on TV about the paranormal. It's just not true is all."

Sissy was not convinced of Abbey's open-mindedness, "Mm-hmm. Never mind."

"You seen all you wanna see?"

"Let me get one more look around and take it all in." Sitting firmly in her sweat covered seat, Sissy looked at the cypress trees and small mud hole. From the best she could tell, the swamp was shrinking, and Friday's deluge did little to revive it. Algae sat in the middle of the puddle surrounded by deep indentions of deer tracks. Monolithic, ancient oak trees sat a few feet from the cypress line. Kudzu was encroaching to the heart of the swamp, threatening to choke the last remnants of what it once was. Nothing prodded her imagination, not as the house had, so maybe Harry had put the once restless spirits to rest, "Does your gentleman buyer know there's a swamp here?"

"Goddammit, Momma!" Abbey slammed the palm of her hand into the steering wheel so hard it vibrated. "Yes," Abbey replied almost too calmly. In a sarcastic tone, she asked Sissy, "Does he know? Know? He's crazy about it. He's gonna turn the whole thing into a huntin' plantation and says this place is perfect for fowl. He's even gonna restore the house and turn it into a lodge for Yankees to stay, eat country cookin', and hunt for weeks at a time."

"That should be a real treat for them."

"The guy's got more money than sense. But, he knows what he's doin', I reckon."

Sissy took a deep breath and motioned to Abbey, "I'm ready when you are."

Abbey drove the buggy straight across the bog and over one of Harry's unmarked graves. Sissy's skin crawled. It was hard, but she made herself quit staring at Abbey for such calloused behavior.

The swamp, it turned out, sat just about thirty feet from the house. After maneuvering around fallen in shacks, tobacco barns, and old rusted fence wire, Abbey got Sissy back to her car in one piece.

"Have you had the land surveyed lately?"

"Not since Aunt Cat moved in, say the 1920s, I think."

"I'll see if that will suffice."

Abbey swatted gnats with her chubby hand, "Got a number, yet? A price in your head?"

"I'm afraid I'm going to need a calculator and a little bit of time to come up with some adjectives for Mister...?"

"Laudenmire."

"Okay. He wants the place. Been several years now, right?"

"Yeah. It'd be long sold by now, 'cept Harry wouldn't leave without a court order. Bastard."

"Anyway. Lauderwhatever is a highly motivated buyer, who's already told you some of his plans."

"Which are going to cost him a lot, he says. So, I don't think he wants to spend a whole lot on the land itself."

"I'm a realtor. I don't care what he does with the place once he's got it. If we know he wants it and he's so 'loaded' as everybody keeps telling me, how much he pays for the place 'as-is' is less important to him than he says. Make sense?"

Abbey was not convinced, "I guess. You better not turn him off is all I have to say or there's likely to be one more pile of rocks out in the ol' swamp, got me?"

"Of course. Trust me." Sissy put her key in the trunk and racked her key back and forth as hard as she could without breaking the key and gave the keyhole a good whack. The trunk popped open and the realtor pulled out a couple of towels. "So I didn't count on mosquitoes the size of pigs with wings, but I did think we might get hot and thirsty. Take a towel and dab off. I've got soda and bottled water in my cooler back here."

Abbey was definitely interested, and as expected, wanted a soda, a "Coke" more precisely, and propped against the car with the towel draped across her flabby broad shoulders. Sissy rubbed her hands and repositioned her college ring on her right middle finger, "Heat's making me swell. Even my old college ring is bothering me."

Abbey held out her hand to motion for a towel, "Yeah, South Georgia heat's a real pisser. No wonder southern women are known for bathing all the time. Hey, want to go inside and see the door? The breezeway in the hall is a lot cooler than out here."

"No, that's quite all right. I don't need to go inside that house ever again. I'd rather swell up like a balloon . . . and pop."

"So, something gave you a good scare, huh?"

Sissy thought it best to play her real emotions down and shrugged as she swallowed her water.

"Something spooked Harry's oldest one time. That room, Aunt Cat's guest room, was the girl's bedroom when they moved in after Cat got the trailer." Abbey pointed over to a patch of missing weeds behind the property, showing the outline of where the trailer once sat. "One night, the lil' girl refused to sleep in that room and slept on the couch in the den for a couple of years. Something about how she didn't want to 'get stuck.' Pissed Harry off so bad. Harry even took out that old ass bed and bought her a used canopy bed from a woman he worked with. His girl only slept in it once and wouldn't go back. That kid told him to sleep in it! Harry did one night just to prove to her wasn't nothing there. I don't know what happened, but he got rid of the canopy bed and moved the old one back in. Took him four guys and a case of beer to get help movin' that thang the second time. Bubba got a herniated disc and Harry threw out his back. Laid out of work for a whole week over that old bed. Lot of trouble over nothin', if you ask me."

"How old was she?"

"Nine, ten. I don't know."

"But why would he expect her to sleep in the room when he used to complain about the thing when he stayed there as a boy?"

"You grow up and believe it when folks tell you it was all just bad dreams, I reckon. He had bad dreams, then his daughter did, was all. He'd say, 'Just part of the family curse, we all outgrow it.' He was always muttering on and on about us bein' cursed. Stupid man."

"Were you guys ever close? You and Harry?"

"Sort of. We had a falling out over this place and we're not gettin' over it anytime soon, if you know what I mean."

"I suppose." Sissy finished her water and was going to offer Abbey another Coke, when she saw an emaciated mother cat carrying a little kitten in her mouth. "Here, kitty, kitty, kitty!" Sissy called. The cat came toward Sissy, but when Abbey turned to look at it, the cat ran away. Sissy was frustrated by the woman's presence, "I think you scared it, Abbey."

"It's just one of Harry's abandoned mongrels."

"Abandoned? That's awful. So, it's tame? That's why she's so skinny! Look, she's pitiful. Abbey, we can't leave it here; she'll starve, and her kittens will starve. We gotta get her."

## Chapter 13: No Good Deed Goes Unpunished

"Sissy, that cat'd eat you up over those kittens. Either she'll catch a mouse, or she won't. Leave her. I'm tellin' you, she's used to living like this."

Sissy felt her heartbeat in some sort of maternal panic over the pitiful kitties, "Give me a minute to try. Okay?"

Abbey took a hard gulp of her soda, "Knock off that extra five percent and I might break a sweat helping you."

Sissy cut her eyes at Abbey, "Don't take this the wrong way, but I don't see you breaking a sweat over anything."

Abbey grinned, "You're not as dumb as you look, City Girl."

Sissy called to the cat, which vacillated between stopping and going toward Sissy and running away. The direction in which she was headed led to a patch of briars and a shack that sat alone in the far left side of the yard. For every three scurries backward, the cat teasingly took two small steps toward Sissy, who followed, knelt and twiddled her fingers, and called with Abbey distantly in tow.

Sissy yelled over to Abbey, "Dang it, Abbey, if I only had some food, or a can of tuna."

Finally, the kitten, which had been so quiet and limp in its mother's mouth, began to squirm. The kitten's distress panicked the mother cat, who darted straight away through a narrow gap in the briars to the broken down shack.

Sissy stared at the shack and pointed, "I bet her kittens are in there."

"Yeah, I bet they're all cozied up in there with a den of

rattlesnakes. Sissy, you get bit, it'd take us a good half hour to get you to the hospital. I'm not responsible, I'll have you know. So, don't you go takin' your sorry ass anywhere near that shack."

"I get bit and I'll say you're not responsible."

Abbey rolled her eyes and huffed before lighting another cigarette.

Sissy shrugged, "I promise! But I'm going to see if I can hear the kittens mewing in that building."

"Frogs gettin' ate by snakes can sound like kittens, too. It's true. Had one stuck in my chimney once. Opened the flue to get the little critter out, and out popped a skinny old oak snake with a poor little rain frog in its mouth. I'd 'a bet good money it was a kitten stuck in my chimney."

"Quit trying to scare me, Abbey."

"You gotta have sense to be scared, City Girl."

Sissy walked ahead into the briars. At first, Sissy could navigate through the briars, which barely put any pressure on her legs. But the deeper Sissy went, the denser the briars became and the harder they tore into her legs. In just a matter of moments, Sissy had deep, bleeding scratches. Not wanting to give Abbey any satisfaction, Sissy kept the pain to herself. Just when she thought she couldn't take it anymore and she'd have to beg Abbey to go get a lawn mower and a set of shears, Sissy made her way to the front door of the shack.

The door was eaten through at the bottom by what looked like to be the same beast that had eaten through the shower stall in the plantation house bathroom. There was an old, rusted lock on the door, which originally required a skeleton key, but now was so rusted as to necessitate bolt cutters. Sissy called to the cat from the outside of the shack and listened. At first, she didn't hear anything and was about to turn around and brave the briars, when she heard the deep mew of a grown cat from inside of the shack. Sissy eyed the door and saw that it was weathered and rough. The hinges were rusted, and the wood was thin and brittle. When she attempted to put her palms flat upon the door, fat splinters loosely dug into her skin. After she picked out the shards of wood, Sissy decided to give the door a solid whack with her foot.

No graceful full round karate kick, more like a cancan kick with a charley horse cramp, Sissy's foot knocked the door off of its hinges. Immediately Sissy heard a barrage of rattles, from deep holes in the shack's dirt floor, reverberated off of the tin roof and the confines of the cramped quarters.

Once inside, Sissy saw light filter through the widened cracks between the shrunken boards. A large trunk sat squarely in the middle of the room . . . waiting. Sissy looked but couldn't see the snakes that were making the noise and hoped they were somewhat shy. After all, that trunk was just too interesting not to explore. How could a snake get inside of a closed trunk, anyway?

Sissy carefully tiptoed across the floor, her heart beating hard inside her chest, head threatening to swoon as her nervousness made her eyesight blur. After what felt like forever, the nosy woman finally made her way to the trunk, which turned out to be a cedar chest. Much to Sissy's delight, the pad lock on the chest was rusted so badly that the thin clasp disintegrated in her hand. The top proved to be heavy due to the heavy brass and lead ornamentation. By pressing her shoulder into the lid, Sissy was able to lift the top. The rusted hinges soon dissolved under the unaccustomed pressure, making the lid fall heavily to the dirt floor.

The rattling only intensified and a cloud of fine, orange, powdered dust flew up and infiltrated the beams of light that lit the tiny shack.

After several sneezes, Sissy rubbed her eyes into focus and saw a pile of cut rags and moldered bones. Oddly, she wasn't the least bit surprised, until she saw the morbid deep scratches that raggedly seared the lining of the lid. Sissy looked around and saw that she was completely alone. There were no cats. There were no frogs. Just the ominous rattling of little scaly tails in parts unknown.

Sissy muttered out loud, "What am I supposed to do now?"

A swirl of wind made miniature dirt devils spin around the dirt floor. The sound of the startled rattlesnakes died away and was replaced by grunts and groans of unseen men dropping a large object squarely on the floor. The box blurred, as if time were layering upon itself like a double exposed picture. An unseen hand grabbed Sissy by her arm and placed her hand upon the stained rags in the improvised coffin. Immediately, Sissy felt a strange sensation, reminiscent of her experience in The Rawlins Mansion. Blurring details of the bones, once human existence, fogged Sissy's mind. A story unfolded like a fast forwarded and extremely edited film. Words, just words, loosely connected words. Sensations . . .

*A bad storm, family, and a few close friends. One friend of a friend, a stranger from South Carolina. Never let in strangers. Drinking. South Carolina drunkly asking to buy the farm, has cash on the spot. Challenged to prove it. A chest, this chest full of money. Old Man McDonnell letting the man stay. Sleeping in the guest bedroom. Never let in strangers. Stabbed by Old Lady*

*McDonnell. Held down in the box, bleeding to death, lung
collapsing. Lantern light, some scared faces. Some angry. All
darkness. The smell of wood, cedar. The sting of splinters in
arched fingers. Never let strangers leave, especially when they're
worth more dead than alive.*

***

Sissy lifted her hand and knew she found the secret to the
guest bedroom. However, her feverish curiosity made her neglect
to notice the small elliptical hole dug beneath the front of the
trunk. At one point it was a gopher tortoise hole. But as every
Southerner knows, an abandoned gopher tortoise hole is
synonymous with rattlesnake hole. When Sissy came out of her
psychic swoon, she found two large fang marks imbedded in the
side of her middle finger. The same finger she was currently
wearing her tight college ring.

The holes entered the top side of her finger and exited the
bottom, grazing the middle bone. Poison seeped out of the holes in
dangling droplets. Shock prevented the realtor from entirely
realizing what the holes, the pain, and the swelling meant. Sissy
carelessly walked out of the shack and forced her way through the
briars, which tore into her face, bare legs, and arms like barbed
wire, but Sissy felt no pain.

Abbey had a giant grin on her face as she jangled Sissy's
keys, "You ain't gonna believe what I got in your trunk, City
Girl!"

Sissy just stared blankly at the large yellow figure in front
of her, "I think I got bit."

"Damn cats. Scratched me all to hell, but I didn't get bit.
Lemme see it."

Sissy limply held out her hand.

"You *did* get snake bit! Damn, Momma told me not to let you out of my sight."

Abbey walked Sissy over to the passenger seat of the convertible and tore one of the towels into thin strips with her bare hands. Next the frantic woman tied off the finger before wrapping it tightly with the terrycloth. Abbey jammed the keys into the ignition and nervously put the five speed in gear.

"Don't worry, Sissy. Don't worry. Jess don't panic. It ain't that bad. You're okay." Abbey shoved the stick, mashed the clutch, and revved the engine. Gears grinded. "If you can't find'em, grind'em, goddammit!" Abbey yelled with a forced laugh in Sissy's direction. The car spun out on the rich black dirt, but the tire caught with a sudden lurch followed by the sound of several objects rolling in the trunk ending with several thuds hitting the back of the trunk with a snarl and several mews.

Sissy's head pounded as she instinctively held her wrist limply on her shoulder.

"Hold your hand above your head. Try to keep the circulation down." Abbey tried to take a cigarette from the carton, but her hands shook too much. "What the hell were you doin' back there?"

"I found someone."

"What? You were supposed to be lookin' for cats. What'd you do, stick your hand down an old gopher turtle hole? Rattlesnakes live in gopher turtle holes. Whole place is ate up with 'em. Didn't you read my note about the snakes? Didn't I tell you about the damn snakes? Damn, damn, damn. You promised!"

"No. Abbey. I found someone."

"After this, I'm gonna go find Jesus."

"A man in a box. The one that got stabbed in the bedroom. Cedar trunk."

"Stabbed? You mean somebody got stuck in the guest bedroom?"

"Yeah. Your great, great . . ." Sissy let out a deep sigh.

"Old Man McDonnell. He didn't get stuck. He died of consumption after that witch died. You're as crazy as Harry. Runnin' after stuff, nosin' 'round the place."

"Your great, great, great, great . . . granddad's friends. There was a . . . stranger with money who offered to buy the place. So she killed him and put him in a cedar chest. In the shack."

"How do you know, Sissy? Was there a book? Did he write his memoirs before he died? You're dreaming. Most folks hurt when they get bit. You just run your mouth about craziness."

"I saw it. I just saw it. Not my eyes, but my mind. I know."

Abbey's eyes welled up with tears and she bit her trembling lip, "It's not fair! It's just not fair! I'd kick you out of this car right now and leave you for dead if I knew you'd die. That house showed Harry everything. He knew everything. It didn't never tell me shit. I couldn't see 'em. I couldn't talk to 'em. He just . . . knew . . . saw. Once he stopped being afraid, it just showed him more and more. He found the stone by the pond. He saw Old Lady McDonnell. He felt things . . . was a part of things. Now you, too."

Abbey had to literally catch her breath before continuing, "You're not even family! Why the hell can you do it and I can't? Why the hell do you get to know and I don't? Why . . . why wouldn't it let me be a part of something?" Abbey wiped away a tear and sardonically chuckled, "At least you got snake bit. I hope your damn dirty cat and her kittens die in that trunk on the way to the hospital; it'd serve you right." The words were angry, frustrated and sad. Abbey floored the gas pedal; the cats scurried and bumped in the trunk, hissing and spitting their disapproval. Sissy stared aimlessly out the car window.

## Chapter 14: Losing It

Within ten minutes, they were at the emergency room door. Abbey threw Sissy's purse at the admittance secretary, who asked for identification and insurance and was told gruffly, "Find it your damn self!"

Doctors and nurses walked by, ignoring the two women until Abbey grabbed the nearest person in baby blue scrubs by the scruff of his neck, "She's been bitten by a rattlesnake on her finger and she's spouting off gibberish. If you don't get somebody right now, I'll take that hairnet of yours and strangle ya' with it. I got one ugly cat and her scrawny ass kittens in the trunk of my rental, so I'm kinda in a hurry. Do you understand me, Son?"

The man just nodded with a confused look on his face and ran to the back of the E.R. Within minutes, a security cop came running toward Abbey with mace and a baton. Abbey ran away from the security cop with her purple purse flapping each side of her jiggly body. Nurses in cartoon print scrubs put Sissy in a wheelchair and ran her to a lab where her blood was taken and her blue-black finger examined. Anti-venom was administered, but Sissy's finger had suffered extensive damage. In a scurry of IVs and tubes, she was taken to surgery to have it removed.

After what felt like only minutes later, Sissy awoke to a numb pain, a heavy hand, and a loud TV set. The noise was coming from a program about cheating spouses, who were yelling at each other with a boisterous studio audience egging them all on. Abbey's laughter ran off the last bit of anesthetic fog.

Abbey chuckled with the remote in her hand and looked genuinely happy at Sissy's revival, "Hey, Stephanie's awake!

How're you feeling?"

"Huh? Who's Stephanie?"

"You solved the mystery of the haunted guest bedroom. Or have you forgotten?"

"No. What happened?"

Abbey turned her attention back to the TV program, chuckled, and turned back to Sissy. Abbey mockingly held out her hand to count upon her fingers, "For one thing, you got snake bitten. Two, I got chased by damn security. And three, your cats got away in the parking lot. Oh, yeah, and four, the doctors had to cut off your finger, but I got your class ring in my pocket. That ring saved your life. Something about too much adrenaline and other doctor type mumbo-jumbo. I dunno. I'm sure they'll give you a big ol' bill." Abbey immediately became re-absorbed in her television program, "I swear, this stuff is so funny. I oughta get me, Harry, and Momma on one of these. I hear they pay money for you to yell at each other. Hell, we do that for free all the time."

Sissy tried to lift her head, but let it drop heavily back onto the pillow, "The cats ran away?"

Abbey turned her head toward Sissy, but kept her eyes glued to the TV, "Oh, yeah. I never got the chance to tell you. I caught'em on the other side of the shack while you were gettin' bit. The momma cat was pitiful, living in a knocked over pig trough. Her kittens were big enough to hiss and spit, but they didn't run. I got'em all in the trunk. Momma cat scratched me all to hell all over my arms."

Sissy mumbled out, "Why'd you take the cats out of the trunk in the parking lot?"

Abbey was quite pleased with herself and wiggled with

delight, "Oh, you missed it. It was good. It was reeeeeeeal good. Remember when security came after me?"

Sissy tried to rub her head with her left hand, "No, but tell me anyway."

"All I know is I was trying to take care of you, when security came after me for no good reason. They chased me down and put me in handcuffs. Then they wanted to see what was in the trunk. I told 'em it was just a bunch of cats, but they said that was animal cruelty and I'd have to pay a fine. I said I wasn't planning on leaving them in there. I mean, come on now, the car's a rental. They had to have the damn trunk open. But, the dumb sommabitches couldn't get your trunk open, so they had to uncuff me so's I could open it. I opened it and the cats sprang out of there like something out of a cartoon. Scratched those security guys all to pieces. I ran off and hid in the ladies bathroom. They's cat shit all in the trunk, for your information. I laughed my ass off. End of story."

Sissy smiled at the imagery of pissed off cats springing out of the trunk, "Aren't you worried they'll find you?

Abbey self-satisfactorily shuffled in her seat like a hen over freshly laid eggs, "I still know people in town. Just a couple of nobody security cops. Family name still carries weight around here."

Sissy laid back and stared at the ceiling, "So, why'd you hire me, if you're still so connected to this town?"

"You're from out of town. Not supposed to know anybody or anything, ask too many questions or try to make me feel guilty about selling the place. Shoulda' known I'd get somebody like you."

"Fifty percent commission."

"Fine. Take it all. Every damn thang. Aunt Cat'll just end up in some shit retirement home, live forever, drain the family fortune, and we'll just have to stuff her old ass in a cedar box in the middle of nowhere."

"Laudenmire could put her on display and charge admission to the Yankees."

"Everybody gets money, but the McDonnells. All is right with the world, again."

"Abbey?"

Abbey lifted her chin toward the TV, fully absorbed by her program, "Yuh-huh."

"When the painkiller wears off, I think I'm going to be real pissed about my finger."

Abbey turned completely from the TV and pursed her lips with an eyebrow cocked, "Only after I make you clean out the trunk of that damn car."

***

Negotiations ran with Laudenmire, who acted appalled at the price Sissy set for the plantation. In a weak attempt at blind man's bluff, the self-made millionaire held out on the sale for two months. Sissy and Abbey agreed on her commission as five percent of the sale price . . . with money under the table to cover her Volvo and her hospital bills.

# Chapter 15: All's Well . . .

Sissy replaced her beloved Volvo with a sturdy, American-made SUV and was the talk of Flemming for being the only single woman to have a V8 with four-wheel drive, a wraparound chrome brush guard, and matching rear guard.

As for the commission? Sissy took Taylor's "feast or famine" comment to heart and put as much of the commission away for a rainy day, and continued to contentedly sell all the little ranch houses he sent her way. No big commissions, but no more psychic moments.

Several months passed in the small, sleepy town of Flemming when Sissy received a letter at the office. It was from Abbey with her typical misspellings and bad punctuation.

Turned out, Abbey was selling the dune buggy and wanted to know if Sissy wanted it. Laudenmire turned the plantation house into a "rustic" hunting lodge, which was becoming quite successful after clearing out the swamp, cutting down the pecan orchard, and knocking down all structures excluding the house itself, which was already gutted and redecorated. Of course, the McDonnells were not allowed anywhere near the property and all of the groundskeepers were on constant look out to "shew us off."

Abbey ended the letter in a most sentimental manner:

*"I hope your finger is doing all right and you bought yourself an American made car. As for me, I'm moving out west. Went there on vacation right after selling the plantashun. Can't stop thanking about it so I'm taking mom and were going to New Mexico. No offence but you can't come along cuz they got real rattlesnakes out their! Anyhow, call me if youd like the dune*

*buggy but dont go buying it just to sell it back to Harry!*

  *Holler Back,*

  *Abbey.*"

Sissy laughed out loud, wadded up the paper and threw it in the wastebasket. Then she looked around and realized that years in the countryside left her wanting to move on as well.

## Chapter 16: New Places, New Faces

Originally from Atlanta, Sissy was more than aware that the market there was open and highly competitive. Highly lucrative, but too demanding. Getting back into that traffic and working all hours of the day, night, and weekends was unsavory, especially since she had become accustomed to such a slow pace of life living in Flemming. Plus, she had never fully adapted to being a finger short on her right hand and was more than a little self-conscious about it. Atlantians tend to be somewhat vain, and explaining that she lost her finger to a rattlesnake on an old southern plantation would potentially make her a pitiful laughing stock. Not to mention, having her father go on and on about his "predictions" and how he "just knew" she'd "come home to the family business." Instead, Sissy set her sights on a town she felt would be a good compromise between the city life of Atlanta and the country life of Flemming: Athens.

Athens was home of the state's university. In the '90s, real estate there changed hands faster than a dollar at a rummage sale. College kids were always moving in, moving out, and therefore the locals were always moving in and moving out. Rich college kids. Rich college professors. Families sick of the next door potheads, grown folks tired of missing sleep to loud drunken parties that lasted into the wee hours of the night, and landlords losing money to replacing sheet rock, broken windows, and lawsuits over drunks who fell off the roof. Or worse, fat drunks who fell through the roof, which was not uncommon. No matter the state of the economy, business around such a large campus was always booming. After all, it was a town supported by plebian commerce,

Mommy and Daddy, and subsidized and unsubsidized college loans. And, the town was a veritable ghost town during holidays, the summer, and away football games. Some may have feared feast or famine, but Sissy considered it all vacation, vacation, vacation.

If Athens were a boomtown for real estate, downtown Athens was the goldmine. The upstairs portion of downtown Athens was filled with bohemian, simplified, overpriced lofts where the "cool" people would lose their cool just to get the next available one. Ground level was filled with everything a carefree, just-out-of-the-house, experimental, newly liberal, and highly opinionated person with plenty of time and beautiful youth could imagine: head shops, independently owned clothing boutiques, coffee shops, newspaper stands, fast food of every ethnicity, junk shops, tattoo and piercing parlors, night clubs, 24 hour cafes, and pubs, clubs, and more pubs, all within walking distance of the liberal arts campus. Everything tomorrow's leaders could imagine, yes. But afford?

Well . . . if they had Mommy's and Daddy's money to spend. Or a new credit card. Or two or three new credit cards. Or the maximum amount of loans the government would allow. It'd all get paid back later, when the little geniuses become rich for finally being recognized for being geniuses. The hopeful business major who is so grown up for having his own subscription to *The Wall Street Journal*, even if it only sits on the floor by the commode and lines his live-in girlfriend's cat litter box. The aspiring law student, who tells everyone everyday she's really going to be a lawyer, while biding her time as the dreaded, but lofty, undergraduate English major. The philosophy major who will . . . will . . . figure it all out later, but is having a very meaningful, mind expanding, educated, if not altogether spiritual college experience. Ah . . . the experience.

Sitting out in the open air, smelling the trash cans that never get emptied because they were all locked into receptacles, attached to concrete because the highly civilized students would kick them or throw them during less civilized times of compromised sobriety. The pollution of about a dozen buses following five separate routes about the behemoth campuses, transporting the university's thirty thousand promising students who will someday become tomorrow's responsible adults. Drinking cappuccino, ordering a latte and pronouncing it correctly, and finally, becoming so sophisticated as to sip a nonfat double espresso mocha latte with skimmed froth, while smoking and chatting with friends or Greek siblings over very important, meaningful, perhaps even political topics. Eating out every day, because you'll have a maid or personal chef later anyway. Studying over a pitcher of beer or two (adults can handle their alcohol, after all). Failing tests and wondering why you must fit your high and individual intelligence into their formulaic and standardized tests, which only allows for more conversation over smokes and anything but just, plain coffee.

However, not to neglect the freedoms of youth, there are tattoos, because you can. Piercings because they're sexually scandalous and a true marker of independence and individuality, just ask your friends. Outrageously dyed hair because you laugh in the face of conformity. "Vintage" jeans because you value the past. Sex toys because you're young, beautiful, and still finding yourself. Incense because you like the way it smells, really, no really, you like it. The pubs because you have a license to drink, legal or not. The feather covered picture frames, the plastic blow-up furniture, the strobe lights, and the very unique yet quite popular giant light-up Budweiser picture set in a cafe with Marilyn Monroe, James Dean, Humphrey Bogart and some dead celebrities you don't know the names of, because you've never seen them, but heard they were cool because . . . it's your house and your rules and you like it! Plus, you deserve it all because you were only overdrawn by a hundred dollars this month.

So, kids will be kids. Lose their scholarships. Piss off their parents, who cut the purse strings. Career students who have to either get a real career or go to another school because they've majored in everything at this one already. Girlfriends unexpectedly get pregnant. Addictions accidentally develop. Classes get harder. Some professors are "just mean." Jobs turn into dead end jobs because that degree will always be there "someday." But, more importantly, people move on and others move in. It's a beautiful thing, if you're a realtor.

Sissy arrived in Athens on a blustery winter day in November of 1993. The ensuing Thanksgiving and Christmas holidays would allow her time to explore and become acquainted with the general layout of the town and temperament of her co-workers and customers.

The first thing Sissy's boss, Mrs. Barb Roth, told her was, "No one likes to deal with the young, but it must be done in a town overrun with them. Get used to it. Contracts and agreements smeared with pizza sauce, blurry pen and beer signatures. Touring houses with car-sick, hung-over students. Idiotic, idealistic parents, and their idiotic, idealistic kids. Frustrated locals.

Absent-minded professors. But, you can all but pick your price and get it. Remember that."

That advice came in handy just a few days later. Sissy was bored, writing out her grocery list for the third time, when a young twenty-something entrepreneur named Talon Gilfry entered the Roth Realty Agency wanting to unload his downtown pub, "Talon's," before Christmas. He was moving to California because Georgia was "just restricting his lifestyle too much." That, and his dad wanted him to start repaying the loan for the bar.

The young man had on a poncho made of thick, coarse fabric over a torn and stained pea green t-shirt with khaki cargo shorts and partially buckled Birkenstocks, even though it was sleeting outside. A fat nose ring with a giant ball in the middle, resembling a prize bull, scrawny dirty blond dreadlocks, and a smell as if he hadn't bathed in months completed his attire. The "hippy scent" phenomenon and was going above and beyond the calling of "eau naturale." It was winter for goodness sakes! For that matter, thank goodness. His demeanor was none too sweet, either. A quiet, judgmental sort. The boy coolly gave Sissy a copy of his keys and told her to go in and have a look at the place as flippantly as he could muster, "I live above the bar, so I'm there with my girlfriend most of the time. Unless I'm out."

Sissy fakely smiled, with her eyebrows raised, nodding.

"I gotta go. So. . ."

Sissy continued to smile and waved the key, "Well, I've got the key. Can we set up an appointment to meet?"

Talon rubbed his face with his hands and inhaled deeply, "Uhhh, ya' know? I'm not good with appointments. Just drop by. The guys'll let you in and just walk around and whatever. Get a free drink or something."

"That's not typically how I like to do things, Talon."

"Sorry, I'm not typical. So . . ."

In a forced fake tone, Sissy managed to keep smiling, "I'll just drop by, then. Nice to meet you, Talon. Bye-bye, now."

The man shrugged his shoulders and spun around on his heel, sandal straps flapping, and exited Sissy's office, his stink wagging its tail behind him.

Sissy added air deodorizer to her shopping list and tried not to think of how much she hated people who thought the word "so" was a definitive statement.

# Chapter 17: Filthy

Two days later, Young Gilfry welcomed Sissy into his dark pub. About three other young men, who could have been Talon decoys, were in the bar, cleaning, setting up tables, beating bongos and strumming on an acoustic guitar. The place had an ancient soured smell of rot, cigarette smoke, and urine. The ceiling was covered in acoustic tile and the walls were painted black. The white tiles in the black and white checkered floor were scuffed and ground into a dingy gray. A large, cracked mirror behind the bar suggested that the place could get rowdy from time to time.

All variety of liquor sat in brilliant, shiny bottles and lent the only tint of color to the place. There was a profusion of wells, midgrade, and premium grade liquors from every background. Beer kegs leaked into large mugs, which were frequently emptied by one of the young Talon clones. Drinking on the job was not a requirement, but apparently being able to hold one's alcohol was. Angry alternative music with strong male vocals fazing through poorly recorded sound played in the background. Immediately Sissy could see why the place was so successful, a blackboard with fluorescent writing read:

*Ladies night, FREE mugs of beer for hot chix.*

*Talon Show: Amateur pole dancing $75.00 first prize!!!*

*$0.25 beer shots*

*Free slice pizza at happy hour 2-5 pm*

Sissy pulled her "realtor bag of goodies" higher onto her shoulder. Talon watched Sissy look over the place. Talon bobbed his head, crossed his arms, and pushed his hands under each opposite arm pit, "It's been real popular with the students. We're a bar, but we mainly focus on unknown bands and local talent. A lot of left over grunge and neo-punk. Moshing. Pole dancing for the ladies 'cause the testosterone can be too much for 'em. Cheap drinks. Place for the freaks to come and be free-kay."

Sissy caught a whiff of Talon's funk, which was stronger than she had remembered, and forced a smiled, "Any ideas on selling the place?" Her cupped hand caught an involuntary gag.

Talon just threw his arms up in the air and huffed, "All I know is, it'd suck to sell this place to some yokel who'd turn it into some cheesy Irish pub with green shit everywhere."
The young man grabbed a handful of beer nuts off of the counter and popped them into his mouth like pills, one at a time.

"Well, you know we can't discriminate," the animation intensified the smell and Sissy's eyes began to water.

"Yeah. Sucks." Talon popped back another nut with an inappropriate giggle.

"Would one of your . . . associates be interested in buying it?" Sissy's nose was running and becoming stuffy.

"Yeah, but they ain't got no money . . . can't get no money." Another silly giggle ensued, producing beer nut spit.

After the cold first impression in her office, Sissy was confused by Talon's ghetto-surfer accent and had to sequester a sarcastic snicker, "We'll just have to advertise and try our luck."

"I want, like, a wad of money. This place is prime. Location. Cool looks. It's got everything and you haven't even seen 'the pad' yet." Finally, Talon finished his snack, smacking and spitting. A goofy grin adorned his skinny face as he bobbed his head in rhythm with the pounding cacophonous background music.

"Well, let's go," Sissy held her breath and followed Talon up the almost pitch-black stairway.

Sissy and Talon walked up a set of stairs so dark, she feared she'd miss a step and fall into a monster filled moat, "I feel as if I need echo tracking to navigate these stairs."

"I know. It's so cool. The bathroom is up here," Talon pointed to the landing, "So many drunk guys have rolled down these stairs going to take a piss. It's so funny! Man, I'm gonna miss this place!" The boy laughed out loud, heard his echo, and forced a laugh just to hear it echo in the stairs again.

"What about when the girls fall?" Sissy felt Talon had completely misrepresented himself at her office, but why?

"Girls don't have accidents around here. Just big goofy guys and skinny freaks like me." Talon's nodding became full blown shaking of his dreads, animated with air drums.

Sissy's ears perked up at that last bit of information, "You've gotten hurt in here?"

"All the time. Place is haunted by a chic and she don't like men." Suddenly Talon yelled out through the cavernous black tunnel of stairs, "But I like pain, Baby! You can give it to me anytime!" Talon laughed a noxious laugh.

Sissy fell as far back behind Talon as she could and put her hand to her face. Sissy asked the boy, "Do you think it's good to taunt it like that?" Talon's body funk began to stifle Sissy in the tight quarters of the banister.

"'It?' You mean Betty Deadbabe? Hell, yeah. She's good for a laugh. Attracts lots of people wantin' to see our ghost gal and get all, like, 'Whah?'. . . Freaked out."

Sissy and Talon reached the landing where the bathroom was. A single strand of white Christmas lights outlined the door to the unisex bathroom, which opened to a large room with three stalls. Sweet smelling feminine perfume, roses, suddenly permeated the air. It wasn't Talon.

And it certainly wasn't the bathroom, which was filthy from the toilet paper that littered the floor. Stall walls were covered with phone numbers, comments, and libel written in thick permanent marker on every available space. The once white tiled walls had brownish, dried urine splatters running down them. There were used condoms thrown on the floor around the overflowing trashcan. The soap dispenser had a steady leak, so a pink puddle of soap sat in a wide wash along the cracked countertop. The mirror was not glass, but a once shiny, flat, reflective piece of metal, which had been scratched with keys and rendered useless.

Fat flies buzzed around the stalls but made no attempt to leave. The last fly to remember the feel of fresh air on its wings probably died generations ago. The sight was an atrocity that decried the advances of modern civilization.

"We don't do bathrooms around here. It's safer to go take a leak in the back alley. I got my own private bathroom upstairs, but if I had to use that one in there, I'd get a full round of shots at the health department, man. That's nah-stee." After an overly animated squinch of his arms around his stomach and sour puss on his face, Talon went back to shaking his head.

"If you want to sell by Christmas, you might want to hire a cleaning crew to clean it up," Sissy said a little quieter, "Clean you up."

"Nah. It's ambiance." The boy walked on in his own world.

Sissy just raised her eyebrows and crooked her mouth, nodding her head, "Oh. Okay." Sissy held out her right hand to steady herself amidst the all encompassing darkness; her white skin glowed against the black wall. Unexpectedly, Talon reached his hand back to help steady her by taking her right hand. Unfortunately, his moment of kindness was short lived, as the man repulsively pulled his hand back.

"Oh, nah-stee, man, what happened to your hand?"

"I lost my finger to a rattlesnake," Sissy said with a most unpleasant tone in her voice.

"Cool. Hiking?" Talon seemed a little embarrassed by his reaction.

"Something like that." Sissy could only concentrate on how much money the tavern was worth but was beginning to find that difficult as the pungent scent of Talon's filthy body, bathroom, and bar were making her nauseous.

"It's cool, but it sucks. One night I thought about cutting off my middle toe on my left foot 'cause me and my bros got one of Mimi's toe rings stuck on it and I knew she'd be pissed if she knew we were messin' with her stuff. I was high, real high on this sticky shit my cuz brought. Went to the kitchen to, like, get a butcher knife and whack that big fat fucker off, but when we got into the kitchen, forgot all about it. Ya' know . . . 'till I saw your hand."

"That's interesting. Perhaps a little too much information, Talon." By this point, Sissy was tired of her visit and wanted to leave. Go home and bathe, no, scour her body.

"Huh? Oh, okay. Whatever." Talon seemed mad at Sissy's hint of conformity and general disdain for his pothead ramblings.

The two completed the last set of dark stairs to find a door, spatter-painted in fluorescent black light paint. Talon pointed to the door in the darkness, "Isn't that the coolest door you've ever seen in your whole life? My girlfriend is an artist and she painted it for me. In fact, she's the one who decorated the place."

Sarcasm clawed its way out of Sissy's mouth, "She's very creative." Sissy was no longer pretending to smile, and neither was her voice.

Talon was not phased, "Oh, no you've never seen her work. Her real work. She had an exhibition down in the bar. Made some serious cash."

The inside of Talon's studio apartment was an odd mixture of skater punk, intellectual, and suicidal artist. Skateboards and skater propaganda hung over windows and lampshades and stuck out from beneath the bed, which was covered by a red satin comforter and black satin pillows with tassels and fringe. The bed itself was kempt and made, oddly enough. Several three foot high stacks of hardback books and creased paperbacks stood like random upright dominos across the floor. Black tasseled curtains were pulled to the side of the enormous windows, lighting the apartment. An incense cloud lazily drifted from a vanity covered in antique stained lace, feathery Mardi Gras masks, and a gothic black leather bustier covered in silver studs. The room smelled musty like dust, dirt, earthy incense and arm pits.

Across the room was a dart board that had several silver darts in it and one large knife dug deep into the bulls eye.

Cattycornered and below, a purple futon shoved against the far wall awkwardly stared at a large screen TV, upon which sat a fat white cat with bright blue eyes staring stupidly at Sissy and her high host. Posters of Gandhi, Einstein, Bach, and Shakespeare contrasted the lumpy oil paintings of what looked to be impressionistic bug smears in varying shades of black with tiny glints of red and purple seeping through the canvas like open veins.

An open closet revealed black clothing hanging limply from padded antique white hangers covered in lace and pearls. A thick pile of khaki shorts, muted t-shirts, ponchos and Bajas made of that coarse, itchy looking material were scrambled together like a broken omelet and festering in the oils of unwashed cloth and unbathed body funk.

But, much to Sissy's relief, the walls were not black. Instead, they were left untouched in an old white-wash that allowed the brick walls to show through. The floors were bare wood with that worn-in homey scuffed look to them. The kitchen appeared to have been updated with new black appliances. The counters were not cluttered, but sparkling and tidy, revealing beautiful black and silver flecked marble countertops.

Sissy's imagination began to run away with her as she imagined herself saying, *"Okay, you wanna make some serious cash? Ditch the wanna be Goth shit in the alley with the piss puddles and clean your damn bar you little punk!*

Suddenly, Talon held out his arm for Sissy to not walk further. Then the young man yelled out, "Hey, Mimi! Realtor's here. Put some clothes on, okay?"

Mimi came walking out of a steaming bathroom to Sissy's right. Mimi's hair was wet, but she was wearing a red velvet robe tied loosely in the middle, "Is this good enough?" A girl with died black-blue hair sat down in a huff upon the low sitting futon and pulled a pack of cigarettes from beneath the cushion.

"Lady, my girlfriend's a witch *and* a nudist. How cool is that, huh?" Talon let out a stifled giggle.

Mimi lit a cigarette and rolled her eyes, "Oh, God. You're high."

Talon wiped his nose and shrugged, "Yeah, so?"

From out of the fumes of a black cigarette, Mimi muttered, "You know it makes you act like a total rube."

Talon glanced at Sissy quickly, blushed, and puffed up his scrawny physique, "Yeah, well, at least I don't act like some holier-than-though Goth queen-bitch."

Mimi looked at Sissy for affirmation, "Let me guess. He's been talking trash, telling stupid pot stories, and acting like a loud loser." The woman coolly exhaled a steady, slow stream of smoke from her mouth, "Am I right?"

Despite the smoke, Talon's stink was still overwhelming. Sissy walked over to the window in the kitchen area, "Does this open?"

Mimi shrugged and looked away in disdain. Sissy tried the sash and found that the window needed a good push to open. Once the window was open, the realtor stuck her face out of it and inhaled deeply without shame. As if a part of the before mentioned "ambience," even the outside air was dank, moist, and acrid.

Talon was quiet, having been scolded. But his mood suddenly shifted and he accusingly asked Sissy, "Uh, Lady, what're you doing?"

Sissy inhaled and exhaled and with her head still out of the window, she exclaimed, "My name is Sissy Clayton!" Looking down to the alley below, she saw one of Talon's employees taking a piss against the wall.

The employee saw her and looked up at her, grinning through a lit cigarette and giving her the bird finger. The pisser exclaimed, "Sissy Clayton, quit staring at my dick, Bitch!" Sissy reluctantly pulled her head back inside the apartment.

"Uh, *Sissy*, what in the hell are you doing hanging out of my window like that?" Talon asked, having definitely sobered since Mimi's entrance.

Sissy balled her fists as a consuming anger took over her better judgment and controlled, perhaps, forced composure, "I was trying to breathe the fresh downtown stink because it stinks less than you do! I've been trying to avoid a confrontation, but I'll be honest, if I'm going to work for you, you've got to do something to get rid of that god awful smell! Bathe, wash your clothes, sit in bleach, but do *something*. No one will buy this place if it smells like this!"

Mimi laughed and picked an "Abnormal Psychology" textbook off of the floor and began reading, "Talon's helping me with an experiment in my psychology class. I'm studying pheromones."

Talon walked in front of his girlfriend and took his shirt off, "Damn it Mimi, I told you that crap you smear on me stinks! You wear it and be your own damn experiment." Talon was breathing heavily.

Mimi grunted, "I told you, you can't smell yourself. Thus far, you've proven part of my theory. Finish the experiment, and (Mimi smiled) you remember what you get."

Talon banged his shirt into his closed fist, "Fine. But, I don't wear it until the place is sold. We gotta get out of here."

Mimi smiled with her face squinched up like a little girl, "Thank you, Talon."

Talon turned to Sissy with his white concave chest glowing like an ember. There was a yellow smudge like ear wax smeared in an arc from his left nipple to his belly button. A gnarled, circular scar bulged from recent healing below his nipple. Talon had yet another mood shift when he turned to Sissy and said, "I'm sorry. I didn't think I stank that bad. When you come over and bring clients to look at the place, I won't wear the pheromone shit."

Sissy's professional demeanor took over, "Actually, Talon, it'd be much better if you and Mimi were both gone. Prospective clients tend to feel uneasy looking over a place and making comments with the current owners around. But, if you promise not to . . . stink, I will get this place sold for you by Christmas. And hire somebody to clean up the bathroom. Put more lighting on the stairs because we might have older people or folks with poor eyesight coming up these stairs, okay?"

Talon smiled and opened his arms as if to hug. Sissy shrank away and held out her hand in the "stop" sign. Mimi was already oblivious to the situation, absorbed in her book.

To Talon's outreached arm, Sissy handed a bag of brochures and tips on selling a home, along with various magnets, cards, and a free calendar, all of which advertised her business. "Um, I think I've seen everything I need to see today, so I'll just leave you with this literature. It should help you figure out a few things to get the place in shape for the sale. It was interesting meeting you."

Talon lifted the opened bag to his head and said into it, "So, you think we can make a lot of money?" The boy rummaged through the bag as if it were a Christmas present.

Sissy rubbed her neck, which had become stiff, "Surely we can get a good bit more than enough. Let me check the current listings for comparison and I'll have you a price drawn out in a couple of days."

Talon turned to Mimi, "Can you see her out, I gotta take a piss."

Mimi looked up from her book and sardonically smiled at Sissy, "Sure, I wasn't doing anything important."

Talon turned the corner behind a partition and disappeared into their private bathroom. Sitting low on the futon, Mimi reached out her hand, which Sissy took with her right hand open and her eyes closed. The last thing she wanted was to give Mimi some sort of lewd thrill over flashing the uptight realtor. Mimi walked Sissy the five feet to the door and stopped her, "You know, you give off a strange energy. I read energy, I bet you do, too. So . . . did *you* smell roses on the stairs?"

Sissy cocked her brow, "Yes. Isn't that supposed to be Betty?"

Standing, Mimi rolled her eyes, "Her name is Edith. That's what Talon calls her to piss off both of us. Edith is so unhappy with us, but Talon thinks that's her problem. It's sad. I think we should look for new owners who might make her happier."

Sissy wrinkled her brow, "You advertise, you can't discriminate. Whoever steps up with the cash first, wins."

Mimi looked down at Sissy and reached out for Sissy's right hand, who put her hand in her pants pocket and gave Mimi her "eat shit and die" look.

Mimi opened her eyes widely and stretched her neck forward toward Sissy's face, "Don't look at me like that. I already know how you lost your finger."

Sissy took a step out of the foyer, "Good for you, honey. I've got to go." Sissy pivoted on her right foot and walked down the stairs.

Mimi loosened her robe behind the realtor's back and said, "Good bye, Miss Clayton." Sissy didn't respond and she did not look back, either.

# Chapter 18: No Vegan

The very next day Sissy received a phone call; it was Mimi. Mimi almost sounded normal when she said, "I want to talk to you more about the bar. And other things."

Sissy tapped her pen against the desktop, "I'm sorry Mimi, but I'm very busy. I don't have time to chat. Could you just leave me a list and I'll get back to you?"

"Lunch, then. Realtors have to eat. Your pick, my treat."

"I don't do vegan."

Mimi made a guttural noise as if pleased, "Good. I like to use my teeth."

***

Sissy met Mimi downtown at three o'clock in a downtown coffee shop that just opened. Sipping an overly priced cup of cappuccino in a porcelain cup inside a trendy coffee shop while watching a thirty-something homeless man sit on the pavement with a French bulldog on a new leash and a "Feed Us" sign, Sissy thought that the rainy cold day was perfect for meeting with a contrived and mysterious character such as the elusive Mimi who would undoubtedly be dressed all in black, perhaps with a red or purple accessory.

Had the day been sunny and warm, Sissy may have considered canceling because the setting would not have fit the character. Like an actress trying to find her motivation, Sissy played possible scenarios in her mind of what Mimi would have to say, what her demeanor would be, what exactly her purpose was, and the appropriate responses to not be made fun of by the Vixen of Darkness. Embarrassed by her own childish curiosity, Sissy cleared her mind as Mimi, who was dressed all in black, waltzed into the cafe like a dancer upon a stage. Mimi's movement appeared somehow choreographed and practiced to Sissy, who pretended not to pay too much attention as the Goth girl approached their table.

Mimi pointed at Sissy's cup, "I know I asked you to meet me here, but I am not in the mood for that overpriced crap. Gave me the worst stomachache all night last night. Whatdaya say we eat at The Grate? It's only, like, ten steps from here."

Sissy put down the oversized cup and wiped the foam from her upper lip, "Okay. Is it good?"

"Good? It's 'real' Athens. Less touristy than The Fraternity, but Athens. Eat there once and you've done your duty."

"Well, if it's my duty, I'll try to manage the ten steps from here to there."

Mimi's teeth gleamed against her crimson smiling lips, "Good, and no vegan."

## Chapter 19: Lunch Bites

Mimi picked a table in a far corner. The clientele was dirty and less than savory. Sissy couldn't tell if they were homeless, students, or homeless students. The girl's pale face with dark make-up and crimson lipstick with matching crimson nails, black dress, fishnets, and Doc Martens made her look like a semi-technicolor "Morticia" set against the back drop of a grimy 50s diner.

The Grate could have been the set for a happy teen daytime series, except the black and white checkered floor was covered in dropped, stepped-on, and smeared food; the display case was filled with eerie wind-up toys with macabre expressions on their faces. The air was visibly filled with grease vapors, and the white washed walls were seared in dirty beige water stains, reminiscent of Talon's ear-wax covered tummy. Even the waitresses were anorexic, pierced, and tattooed while carrying contemptuous hangovers, not food. All of the elements combined, created a fractured sense of unwholesomeness. Despite the sickly atmosphere of the restaurant, Mimi looked as if she were a little kid who refused to undress from Halloween.

Sissy picked up her plastic-coated, stained menu, "So, what's good?"

Mimi said, "Nothing," as she read over the menu intently, "I'm getting the chicken fried steak with gravy and onion rings."

Sissy nodded her head, "Uh-huh. Sounds too fattening for me."

Mimi looked up from the menu and smiled with that blinding white grin, "I'm not going to eat it. It's for Gene."

"Who's Gene?"

"The homeless man outside. He said that's what he wants."

Sissy decided to be friendly, "Well, if that's what he wants, it's probably really good." Mimi raised her eyebrows in acknowledgement of Sissy's repartee. Sissy felt stupid and rejected for being friendly. "Well, what *are* you going to eat, if the steak and rings are for . . . what's his name?"

"Gene? Yeah. Mmmm, I'm going to have their hamburger, rare, with everything and mashed potatoes. God! If it weren't so cold, I'd have a strawberry malt. At least their sweet tea's good." Mimi sat her menu down and folded her arms on the table with her chin almost rested on her hands, grinning but no teeth showing.

Sissy flared her nostrils, "Wait. Rare hamburger? Isn't that dangerous for ground meat? That could make you really sick."

"But, I really like rare. Anymore cooked and it doesn't taste right. Not as . . . sweet." Mimi rubbed her bloodless tongue across her glossy crimson lips, looking somewhere between a seductive dominatrix and an uncoordinated toddler.

Sissy raised her brows and twitched her mouth. Mimi made her feel uncomfortable and old. Sissy tried to sound unaffected, "Well, I'm going to have the turkey burger and steamed vegetables."

Mimi sat back and lit a cigarette, talking with the stem in her mouth, "Don't get the vegetables. You don't come here for fresh vegetables. Go frozen and fried. Much safer."
After she finished speaking, she dramatically took the cigarette out of her lips and slowly blew smoke above her head.

"And yet, you'll order rare burgers?" Sissy was miffed that Mimi had not asked her if she could smoke. But, Sissy felt she should have known better, so it was her own fault for not setting the rules beforehand.

"I also smoke," Mimi smiled at Sissy as if she were challenging her.

"But the vegetables, don't go there. Okay." Sissy rolled her eyes and felt old . . . er.

One waitress wearing a nametag that jaggedly spelled out "Britt," emerged from the darkness and took the two women's orders without making any eye contact with either of them. When the order was over, "Britt" scuffed her Mary Jane style Doc Martens heavily across the floor and mysteriously melted into the grease vapor like a Viking ship into the fog.

Awkward silence followed. Mimi smoked her cigarette and seemed to hold it in a choreographed, practiced manner, but her face looked as if she were enjoying herself.

Sissy pulled a small mirror out of her purse and flipped her hair just to do something to avoid sitting clumsily, waiting for Mimi to reveal why she invited her to lunch. Her curiosity was killing her, but she felt that letting on would compromise her maturity.

Finally, Mimi seemed to come out of her euphoric haze and acknowledged Sissy's presence.

"Miss Clayton, can I just call you Sissy?"

"Please. The whole 'Miss' thing makes me feel old."

Sissy put her mirror back in her purse and leaned toward the table to give Mimi her undivided attention.

Mimi held out her cold, pellucid right hand for a shake, "Well, Sissy, I want to congratulate you for choosing to go to lunch with me."

Sissy awkwardly shook the dry, skinny hand, "Thank you, I guess. Ya' know, three o'clock isn't the traditional lunch hour, but I think I kind of like it. Disgruntled, smoking, creepy people with no obvious means of employment. Being served by tired, under zealous waitresses at the end of their shift. Waiting forever for your food because the grease is cold. It's great." Sissy felt that her time spent in Flemming had been well spent, after all. That was a classic passive-aggressive southern belle snippy comment, which Mimi certainly deserved for prolonging the mystery.

However, Mimi seemed unconcerned, "I had weird hours this semester. It takes me awhile to get on a normal schedule, *again*. (Inhale of smoke) And (exhale of smoke) . . . I figured you wouldn't want to talk about personal matters in front of an audience."

Sissy shifted in her seat and felt very uncomfortable, but it wasn't the booth's fault, "What makes you so sure I'll talk about personal matters with you? No offense."

"S'okay. You can't help being personal." Mimi put her cigarette between her fingers and pointed at Sissy, "It's really who you are."

Sissy cocked her brow and sat back against the booth, "I'm going to go ahead and apologize for my sarcasm in advance."

"Does your missing finger ever bother you? Feel the need to wiggle it?" Mimi put her cigarette back in her mouth and made "I love you" signs with her fingers and intently examined them, comparing them to Sissy's hand.

"Am I part of some sort of study for your psychology class?" Sissy authoritatively squinched her eyes and stared at

Mimi. Even though she knew she looked silly, she was quite serious.

"No. Why?" Mimi laughed out a puff of smoke.

"Talon may enjoy being toyed with, but I do not. I have other things I could be doing."

Mimi bit her lip and smudged the crimson lipstick onto her front tooth, "Poor Talon? Humph. He loves it. I'm the dominant one. He's my . . ."

Sissy held out her hands in the "stop" signal and interrupted Mimi, "That's okay. I can look at you and imagine."

Mimi laughed and let out a big smile, "Free rent. What did you think I was going to say?" The Goth's smudged tooth created a clumsy flaw in an otherwise stark appearance, "If you're into stereotypes, you're going to be more wrong than right. I hope that doesn't bother you."

"Not as much as being right in this instance."

Mimi sat her cigarette down into a chipped ashtray and sat up close to Sissy across the table, "You think I'm strange?"

Sissy huffed, "That's the idea, isn't it? I mean, that's your shtick, right?"

Mimi cocked her head to the side and rolled her eyes like a scolded teenager.

Sissy let out a laugh, "Well, isn't it? You don't dress like that to blend with 'the masses.' You're 'special' . . . 'different' . . . 'misunderstood' . . . uh . . . 'undefinable,' etcetera, etcetera."

Mimi regained her I'm-in-control composure. Pointing her cigarette at Sissy, she said, "I like that. I'm going to have you write that down so I can add it to my alter." Mimi tapped her cigarette, took a puff, and crossed her arms.

Sissy flicked her menu and strummed her fingers across the top in an angry tone, "Will our food be here soon?"

"Sissy, you know you're psychic. So why do you act like you would have nothing in common with someone like me?"

"Psychic? Humph." Sissy popped an ice cube into her mouth and sucked on it, pushing her back further into the booth, crossing her arms.

Mimi consciously unfolded her arms and leaned forward. In a softer tone, "It's nothing to be ashamed of. What you need to do is be more careful, though. Losing a finger in a psychic daze is not good. (Tapping ash) You know what else you need?"

Sissy leaned her head to the side and consciously kept her arms folded, "Please tell me it's not something sexual or deviant."

Mimi laughed, "No. Practice. You need practice to hone your skills. And I have the perfect, safe, environment."

"Your bar and rose girl?" Sissy maintained her crossed arms, but held up her right arm and waved her pointer finger in the "whoopty-do" sign.

Mimi smiled and exhaled smoke, "Yep."

Sissy tightened her crossed arms and cocked her head to the other side. She could feel her neck tightening into a bulging knot. In a hushed, angry tone, "So what did you have in mind? Wear a blindfold while you lead me around in the dark? We play with tarot cards and hold a séance?"

Mimi reached out her cold hand in a reassuring manner, "All you need is yourself. Your vibes are really strong." Pulling her hand back, an idea seemed to pop into her head, "Are you menstruating?"

Sissy squinched her face with her mouth agape, "Excuse

me?"

"Some women do best when they're on the rag."

To avoid Mimi's touch again, Sissy uncrossed her arms and pretended to chew on a hangnail, "Do 'what' best?"

"Psychic readings, knowing things that happened in the past."

Sissy talked with her finger in her mouth, "What am I supposed to read for you?"

"Not me. I already know about Edith. I want you to read for yourself. You could be a decent psychic if you weren't afraid."

"And what do you get out of helping me become Super Psychic?"

Mimi shrugged, "Nothing. But that whole 'no discriminating' thing is bullshit. I want you to help Edith find an owner for that building who won't piss her off. She likes to hurt men, and I'm afraid it'll only get worse over time, if we don't do something."

Sissy dropped her hands in a "you gotta be kidding me" pose, "This is for Edith, a dead woman who likes to trip men down the stairs after they defile the john?" Sissy started pouring salt out onto the table, crushing the miniscule cubes with the bottom of the shaker.

"Angry spirits can grow stronger over time. People like us with the gift should use it . . ." Mimi reached over to the salt pile and threw a pinch over her right shoulder.

"For good, not evil? Yeah, right." Sissy dipped her finger into the dry powder and made swirls.

"To make a difference. Dead or not, it's still a cognizant energy."

Sissy looked up from her salty artwork and let out a chuckle, "Cognizant energy?"

Mimi picked at her crimson nails and then sat on her fingers, leaning toward Sissy, "Cognizant energy means it's a thing that's acting of its own volition. Then there's residual energy, which is just trapped energy like a memory that's playing itself out. Cognizant energy reacts to or acts on you. Residual energy doesn't even know you're there. It's like a movie playing at a theater. But Edith. Edith is definitely cognizant. If I could give her Prozac and therapy, I would."

Sissy sat back and tried to absorb everything, "I'm sorry, I just didn't take you for the philanthropic sort."

With a hint of disdain in her voice, Mimi said, "You'll find out that the dead can be a lot better company than the living," and snuffed her cigarette.

"Hence, the reason you look like death?" Sissy couldn't help herself. Someone as self-absorbed and dramatic as Mimi wanting to appease a distraught spirit was a bit too much.

Mimi pulled out a hand from beneath herself and then pointed a finger at Sissy, "Now you're just being mean. I'm serious. Completely serious. This is personal and I don't share this with just anybody. You want to help or just make money for yourself?"

"I like money," Sissy looked over at Mimi's smushed cigarette and the black-red lipstick stain on the bent, tar filled filter.

Mimi pushed her back against the booth and began lighting another cigarette, trying to play down a nervous tick that made her head twitch toward her left shoulder.

Sissy didn't want to stare, so she made herself clean up her salty mess by scooping it into her palm before dumping it on the floor, "But, if I could make money and do some good, I guess that'd be even better." Sissy thought she may be losing a lucrative sale, so it may be best for her to play along. "Tell me what you want me to do."

Before Mimi could answer, the food arrived. Cold. Sissy decided to test Mimi's sincerity. Mimi was about to take Gene's to-go-box outside, when Sissy stopped her, "Why don't we bring Eugene in to eat with us?"

Mimi wrinkled her brow at the realtor, "Aren't you afraid he'll stink?"

"Worse than Talon? I could inhale a ripe trashcan while eating a ham sandwich after smellin' that boy. Bring the man in out of the cold, Miss Philanthropy. Or is he too alive for you?" Sissy giggled and wiped her hands on her sweating water glass.

Mimi just huffed and walked out of the restaurant.

Gene came in out of the cold with his dog and sat uneasily next to Mimi, smiling shyly at Sissy, "It's nice to meet you. I'm Gene and (pointing at the dog) he is Papillion. If you don't mind, I might better take this outside. Pap-Pap makes a mess when he eats."

Sissy smiled, "Well, Gene, it was nice to meet you and Papillion."

Mimi cleared her throat, "Gene, before you go, you want to tell Sissy about your experience in Talon's bar?"

Gene looked at Mimi strangely and shook his head no, but Mimi urged him on, putting her hand firmly on the to-go box with a smile. Gene inhaled deeply and coughed politely into his hand,

"I was taking a piss, oh sorry, we're eating. I was taking a leak in the bathroom. All of a sudden, the stall door flew open, like, WHAM! I turned, like, 'I know you didn't!' and there was this woman standing there. Except she didn't look normal. You know? Her clothes were a real old style and she stared at me, looking through me, not really at . . . me. Anyway. She looked behind herself like somebody was coming in and she whimpered . . . like a scared puppy. Then she was hit in the face, very hard, but I didn't see a hand. I just saw her just being beaten by someone. Then she let out this scream and suddenly stopped, like mid-scream. Then there was this nasty gurgling, like somebody was just crushing her throat. I heard her body fall, but I didn't see her fall. For that matter, I didn't see *her*. She just . . . poof . . . disappeared."

Sissy felt that something wasn't quite right, but she sat and ate her bland turkey burger with a slight sense of amusement. Mimi nudged Gene with her elbow and took a squishy bite out of her rare burger. The bright pink meat burst through the gray scab and contrasted starkly to the flaccid green lettuce. With a full mouth Mimi told Gene, "And?"

Gene continued, "I slipped in my own piss and knocked my ass out cold on the toilet bowl. I guess I was so freaked out by the whole experience I pissed again, on myself. I woke up on that nasty ass floor, covered in my own piss." Gene shivered all over as if he had heebie-jeebies.

Mimi knocked into Gene with a giggle, "Yeah, the only reason he woke up was because some drunk sorority girl tripped over him and screamed her head off! She made everybody think he was dead."

"Oh, yeah. I cracked my molar right out of the socket. It was so bad, I had to have surgery." Papillion yawned and sat panting on the floor next to Gene.

Sissy put her sandwich down, "I hope Talon picked up the bill."

Gene laughed, "Of course! Honey, I was gonna sue." Gene cleared his throat and quit laughing.

Sissy stared down Gene and looked at his sparkling white teeth and nine o'clock shadow. His clothing was unstylish, but clean. His hair was messy, but not altogether unkempt. Mimi's altruism toward a dead person was more believable than toward a supposedly homeless person. Finally, Sissy felt compelled to ask, "So, Gene, how much did you earn with your sign and unthreatening hobo look?"

Gene grinned, "You're good."

Sissy nodded and felt her face burn with anger, "And you're little story. Is this all a part of some elaborate joke?"

Gene looked at Mimi, "I thought she already knew Edith. She's not one of your friends?"

Mimi put her arm around Gene, "No, not yet. I'm working on her. She doesn't fully believe. Yet."

Gene turned red and motioned that he was ready to leave. Mimi pinched Gene's pink cheek and giggled at Sissy, "Sissy, Gene is working on his Master's thesis, too. *I'm* doing a qualitative blind study on the psychological effects of odors; *he's* doing a quantitative blind study on people's reactions to various degrees of homelessness. I didn't want to tell you, because we try not to compromise each other's work."

Through a sequestered laugh, the shy man said in a lowered

133

tone, "I still haven't told Talon the real reason he smells like a bag of ass!" Mimi and Gene shared a moment of wildly flashing a look into each other's eyes. Not like lovers, but like kindred spirits that fed on meanness.

Sissy chewed her turkey burger, feeling more confused than before. She eyeballed the pair and muttered to them, "I just know I'm part of some study. Talon's hiding, taking notes."

Gene put his hand on top of Mimi's to-go order and strummed his fingers on the back of her hand, "Oh, really? What's the study?"

Sissy, having her own undergraduate degree in psychology, decided to put it to use, "Something to do with peer pressure, shared psychosis, power of suggestion, maybe even mass hysteria if we can involve some more people."

Gene turned his chin into his collar bone, "Psht, as if Talon could spell 'psychosis' or 'hysteria'."

Mimi joined in, "As if Talon had the attention span to hide, much less write. No, we're serious about all of this and we're not trying to trick you or put you into a study."

Gene petted Papillion on the head, "I don't tell just anybody that story. It's too embarrassing, but I swear to *God* it was real. I hadn't had but two martinis at that point, so I wasn't even drunk. But there she was, this little flapper girl with the cutest bob and a tall ass feather in her hair."

Sissy put her tasteless burger down and pushed the plate away. Turning around in her seat, the realtor surveyed the restaurant and found it virtually empty. Sissy put her hands on the table and said, "Okay. So you've seen things, Gene. I'd say that despite the initial deception, you were, in fact, being sincere about your supernatural experience. So, I'll be open about my own. I have seen some strange things over the past several years. Not a lot, but enough."

Sissy held up her right hand to show off the missing middle finger. Gene gasped and put one hand over his mouth and the other over his heart. "Since Morticia over there wants me to develop 'my gifts,' I gotta know, honestly, what is your take on Edith?"

Gene shrugged, "I think she was killed at the bar, when it was, like, a speak easy or something. If you were a man, honey, I'd tell you to stay away from that bar. She's really mean."

Sissy shrugged, "So? She's not the one who hurt you. You slipped in your own pee and hit your head. That wasn't her fault."

Gene leaned in close and said under his breath, "Yeah, but I was in drag that night. I think I *confused her*."

Sissy shut her eyes and blinked them, "Talon lives with her. Why hasn't he had any mishaps?"

Mimi took the check from the waitress, "Oh, he did. You saw that scar below his nipple. He was working on a leaky pipe in the bar's bathroom sink, when the sink popped out of the wall and fell on top of him. It cracked his ribs and punctured a lung."

Sissy raised a brow, "Yes, I saw his scar and that smear of ear wax crap you sadistically smear across his chest. More importantly, and this affects selling the place with or without Edith's blessing, I've seen the bathroom. If the whole thing collapsed on itself, I wouldn't be surprised."

Mimi pulled out her debit card and waved the waitress away like a fly, "Oh, we need Edith's blessing. The sink had two metal posts holding it up. Those were twisted like . . . pretzels. Nobody was there with him. He almost died. Why do you think the bathroom looks like that? He can't pay those guys enough to clean it."

"Why don't you clean it for him?"

Mimi waved her hands at Sissy, "No thank you. I don't clean our bathroom enough. You think I'm gonna clean somebody else's piss? No. NO."

Gene saw the bill and coughed, "Speaking of piss. I gotta go . . . research to conduct and . . . It was nice meeting you, Sissy. You've got this, right, Mimi?"

Mimi nodded the man away, as he made his way to the bathroom with his dog. After watching the dog prance through the restaurant without saying a word, Waitress Britt walked over to the table and pre-bussed it as a cue for the two remaining to leave. Mimi pushed the to-go order to the side of the cleared table and said, "I think you should spend one night in the bar. Touch everything. Fine tune. Nothing will hurt you. Once you get to know her, you'll want to help her feel better."

Sissy shook her head, the knot in her neck tightened, "This is . . . weird. Favor or no favor, this is taking up my precious time and time is money."

"No problem. Take Talon for a bigger commission. His dad is loaded. If he lost money on the place, he'd get a tax break. Why else would anybody let Talon own anything?"

"So, I can name my percentage?"

"Why not? Talon won't know any better."

Sissy chewed her lip, "Okay. When?"

Mimi uncharacteristically clapped her hands with a glint in her eyes, "This weekend."

Sissy leaned her head on the back of the booth and

exaggeratedly exhaled, "Okay. That gives me time to go to the library and do some research."

A scuttling of toenails and an offbeat hum announced the sudden appearance, swipe of the to-go order, a quick, "See ya' later, ladies!" and a swift departure of Gene and Papillion, who walked across the street and set up camp. Sign reading, "Feed Us," and Papillion eating chicken fried steak, licking gravy off of his chops. Gene spread out a mat and waved at people as they tossed coins onto the mat and kept walking. Sissy looked at the slowly collecting coins and thought to herself, *Quantitative.*

## Chapter 20: See You at Noon

Sissy met a dressed up Mimi in the low lit bar at ten
o'clock Saturday night. The gothic woman was wearing black
glitter make-up. Her lips were still red-black, but they sparkled.
Her eyeliner was too thick, but her lids sparkled. Her foundation
was too light, but it made her face sparkle. She was still wearing
dark clothes, but they, too, sparkled, with black sequins and
beadwork. Her fingers were covered in gaudy black costume
jewelry and sparkly black fingernail polish. But, the inside of the
bar was not sparkly.

Aside from the chairs that were resting on their prospective
tables, the bar was completely empty. All of the signs advertising
free this and that, as well as the "this and that" were all gone,
leaving the place darker and more barren than before. The shelves
that held the beautiful bottles of sparkling liquor were completely
empty and dusted. But, the acrid smell of rot and urine still
pervaded the premises. The floor had been swept, but not
polished. One wall was completely painted in primer, the one
adjacent to it was partially painted. Apparently the couple read the
real estate literature and thought the bar could benefit from a more
conventional hue. That was promising.

Mimi gave Sissy the keys and hurriedly explained, "I'm
going out, but I'll be in sometime around . . . before noon. So I
won't bother you. You've got the key already, but you can turn
the lock so you can lock people out, but you can't lock yourself in.
The key unlocks everything. The alarms are off. Any questions?"

Sissy just nodded, "Have fun."

Mimi grinned, showing that her canines were now shaped

like fangs. Temporary caps. Sissy laughed and rolled her eyes. The girl disappeared across the street, running maniacally to a small group of ghouls who had been waiting for her.

The realtor carried her bag up the dark stairwell. On the landing, Sissy smelled a fleeting waft of roses and felt a cold breeze blow past her, heading toward the bottom of the stairs. Talon's things were all gone, meaning his pile of t-shirts and Baja jackets and the dart board. Mimi's belongings were all there, except the large screen TV, which was replaced with a small screen. Sissy sighed relief. There was no sign of the moronic looking white cat. Sissy smelled vanilla scented plug-ins, but no kitty litter. Good, no cat going bump in the night, sneaking up on her, scaring her.

Sissy had no intention of staying the night, but was going to walk about the bar and go home. If Edith were such a tormented soul, she could make it known as well in one hour as she could in ten.

Meanwhile, downtown was alive. Despite the fact that it was only ten, already girls were yelling what the ladies at the realty office called "the sorority girl mating call," also known as, "I'm *so* drunk!" Young men were yelping their approval, "Whoo-HOO!" People were laughing, talking, and yelling to one another all over downtown and it was coming in as clear as audio through the loft's brick walls. Sissy checked the windows to see if they were open or missing panes, but the windows were fine. In fact, some were painted shut.

The downtown loft apartments were definitely for the young and sleepless. Of course, if you live above a bar that encourages moshing and pole dancing before closing the next morning, you should either be deaf or a part of the action. Mimi was the latter, probably sitting with her friends in some dark dungeon of a night club, drinking trendy drinks that would've been free at Talon's, but more fun elsewhere, listening to emotional, highly synthesized alternative music, while people made out and others watched.

Sissy tried not to think of her years at Southern College spent with a tight knit group of friends from her dorm, all sharing a common fascination with the "brat pack," but lacking their money and innate drama. Hanging out, making out, drinking, smoking, going to the club and listening to shallow, highly synthesized pop music. Same scene. Different clothes. Neon nail polish traded for black. Sissy felt old and was mad that she couldn't take Talon up on his offer of a free drink.

Even though Sissy had not planned to spend the night, she was a firm believer in Murphy's Law, which she lovingly renamed "McDonnell's Law," which had prodded her to bring a bag filled with a change of clothes and essential toiletries. Sissy plopped her bag upon Mimi's bed, when a police car went blaring down one of the numerous side streets. It was coming toward, rather than going away from, the direction of Talon's. Somewhere in the bar a door shut, but that did not completely register in Sissy's mind.

Sissy gave the loft a quick scan and walked immediately to the closet. She felt around inside the closet, pushing Mimi's clothes out of the way and looked for any sign that it was hiding a passageway. Then she saw what she was looking for - - two metal contacts jutting out on the right side at the top of the narrow closet. With a triumphant squeal, Sissy jumped up and clapped, "Just like in the books at the library! Let's see if the research was right."

## Chapter 21: Speak Easy Does It

As if by second nature, Sissy grabbed one of the few metal hangers in Mimi's possession, flattened it, and touched each elongated end to the knobs that sat up so high in the closet, she had to stand on her tip toes and reach until she felt her neck tense. The wall opened like a creaky old door. Sissy put her left hand on her forehead and stared for a moment at the hanger in her right, "Oh, my God! It really worked! Just like the illustrations said it used to, er, does. Good God, how much fun!"

The metal knobs were actually contacts, part of a hidden electrical device that created a complete circuit through the conductive metal of the elongated hanger, whose sole purpose was to make the closet's back wall swing open. Carrying the hanger in her hand, Sissy pushed the door all the way open and stepped through the closet. Bulbs flickered on as if they were stricken with Alzheimer's and couldn't quite remember how to work.

A long white corridor, reflecting several bulbs' yellow lights, beckoned Sissy like Dorothy down her yellow brick road. The walls were covered in condensation and sweating in tears that fell in tight puddles against the wall, seeping beneath them. Flecks of black mold lightly outlined the painted brick like magnified snowflakes. No doubt, this was the source of the damp, acrid smell. Sissy was more than a little satisfied with her accidental discovery.

"The place *was* a speak easy!" she triumphantly said to herself.

The secret tunnel whispered back the word, "easy, easy, easy."

Sissy examined her clothes hanger and found that it was just a simple, modern hanger, nothing special. Still, she had walked through the closet with it in her hand, so she decided it may come in handy later.

The tunnel wound itself down through the building, coming to a flat wall from which a lever prominently stuck out like a metallic erection. Sissy looked around and remembered Mimi's words, that nothing could hurt her, and to touch everything. Like a little kid taking two cookies when only one was offered, Sissy snickered and pulled the lever. White metal slats in the wall opened, showing that she was right behind the broken mirror in the bar itself, and was in fact, looking through it, with a clear view of the pub and the street via other cleverly angled mirrors. Of course, the lever was not entirely lowered, and had more room to spare. Like an optimistic game show contestant, Sissy lowered the lever even more, finding that it lowered the shelves against the wall, dumping their contents, which, in this case, were memories. Sissy mused, *Had Mimi foreseen that I would throw the switch, so she packed the liquor in anticipation, preventing a large mess, or had the bottles simply been cleared for packing and painting?*

"Wow," Sissy lowered the lever as far as it would go. A mechanism ticked in the wall, the shutters closed, and the shelves audibly popped back into place on the wall, "This is so neat!"

Next Sissy decided to tackle the solid wall that stood to her right. She felt the wall and discovered a tiny hole that was almost covered by a dried paint drip. Taking her clothes hanger, the clever realtor pushed the narrowed end into the hole and jiggled the wire back and forth in a rapid motion, hoping to trip some other sort of electrical mechanism. After a clicking noise, the door jolted slightly open. Sissy pushed on the wall, but it did not want to budge. Still, the thing could move, so Sissy pressed her back against it and heaved it open, holding her breath and straining so hard she saw the backsides of her retinas.

Once the door swung back enough to allow entrance, Sissy discovered a vault. In the dark, bottles reflected light from the hall. *That's where Talon put the liquor and glasses from the bar.* At least, now, she could have her free drink. Some dusty bottles of alcohol and dusty snifters were resting patiently in a helter-skelter pattern in the shelves of the hidden tomb. *That's way too much dust to be Talon's stuff. Wonder if this is from the original bar. Yum, vintage liquor!* Sissy was more than a little excited.

The vault was once a wine cellar; the empty catacombs that once held fine vintages were now filled with ragged webs, aged darkness, and forgotten bottles of spirits. Sissy sat at the small table in the large vault and helped herself to a shot of gin and toasted the room with a satisfied grin on her face. "I'm older, but I can hold my liquor and pay my own way home!" After saying so, Sissy still didn't feel much better about the prospect of aging in a town defined by its youth.

An exciting thought occurred to the realtor - - if there were one tunnel, there may be others, leading to some interesting place beneath the city through a forgotten door across the street, or out at the public cemetery about a mile away. Sissy thought about her studies at the library. She looked over the room, the corridor, and thought about what she had learned of places that required inebriation be coupled with secrecy and silence. *Prohibition.* A completely different day and age from the present, in which overt alcoholism, ironically, became a social requirement for the young and reckless.

Walking around the room, the realtor threw back her fifth shot, touching the worm eaten posts, and inhaling the acrid, damp wood, "Prohibition. 1920s?, '30s?, '40s?, '80s?" Sissy tried to think through the swirling drunken jumble in her brain. Sissy tried to talk through the alcohol induced, drowsy thickness of her tongue. Slowly thought and words combined in a slurred, slow cohesiveness, "Yesss. Lesss see, ummm, flapperss . . . gangsterss . . . speak easiess . . . jazzss, gambling, secret wordss . . . secret knocksss."

Exhaling the drink's heat, Sissy tapped an odd beat on one of the beams . . . only to hear it unrhythmically tapped back somewhere from the bowels of the bar. Sissy was shocked and felt somewhat frightened. Momentary sobriety zapped her fun little buzz like a fly in a South Georgia bug zapper. *What did Mimi call it? "Cognizant energy."*

"Edith?" Sissy asked out loud. She was about to ask, "is that you?" but felt silly and stopped. Sissy thought to herself, *What if Mimi is doing this somehow. Not really studying psychology. Paranormal bullshit. More like paranoia. Video recording my fat ass. Great. Too much gin. Not enough tonic. I'm old and I can't handle my liquor like I used to. Great, great, great, great, great.*

The tipsy realtor walked to the back of the vault and wrapped her right hand around the post, *feeling* her missing finger wrap around the post as well. Sissy stared at her hand and didn't see the finger, until she waved it in front of her face. When she waved her hand, it looked as if it were there.

*Drunk. I need to leave. Go home.*

There appeared to be no way other way out of the vault, but through the heavy door, which she entered. The realtor felt along the back wall, which seemed to be a dead end. If there was another trap door or secret passage, she couldn't find it. Perhaps if she hadn't drank so much so quickly . . . then she smelled the smoke of a nice, expensive cigar, and possibly a pipe. Aromatic. It was a welcomed improvement to the pervasive smell of rot. Sissy turned around and tripped over a champagne bottle, a full champagne bottle and to her far right in a dark corner, she heard a couple . . . grunting.

*Beast with two backs? Get a room.* By now, she figured that what she was hearing was just residual noise, no one was actually there.

Walking toward the noise, Sissy held out her right hand and pushed one of the wine racks, which swiveled like a rotating door. The inebriated realtor stumbled into a dark unlit room on the other side of the wine rack. Sissy could see nothing, so she drunkenly felt her way around. The walls here were smoothed over with paint, and invisible pictures were knocked aside by her hand. The smell of roses, spilled liquor, leather. The noise stopped, the pleasant smoke dissipated, and Sissy found she had several large splinters in the side of her hand.

Sissy walked out of the vault and examined the hall, which appeared to dead end at the vault's faux door. There were no holes to prod or nails sticking out, hiding broken electrical currents. No levers. Just a flat, solid wall sitting upon a flat, solid floor.

Once back out in the main hall, Sissy decided to go back the way she came. In the hall, Sissy noticed that fuse boxes lined the winding hall every five feet or so, which seemed profuse considering that the overhead lights were spaced every six feet or so. Wondering if any of the fuse boxes were false, Sissy examined each one like a destructive toddler, poking, prodding, pulling at the face plates, flipping switches. Sissy wound her way up and up and up, around and around the hall, going from one fuse box and up the hall to the next, until she found the fuse box she was looking for. Upon flipping the switch inside the box, the back of the plate lifted, revealing a large orange button. Sissy punched the button and was rewarded with another secret door. The entire fuse box was attached to a painted brick veneer door that popped open in the same manner as the loft closet door. Behind the veneer was a blindingly dark narrow passage that led between the walls.

Without hesitation, Sissy entered the dark passage and hated herself for drinking so much. If she were not drunk, her senses would be heightened and more alert. But, as it turned out, she clumsily tripped over a large metal handle screwed into the floor and fell two feet against the plaster wall on the other side, absorbing most of the fall with her hard head. Feeling around in the dark, the resourceful realtor found the handle and lifted it, after which she discovered a ladder, which lowered onto a landing. Sissy uneasily climbed down the ladder, which led to another landing, and another ladder. The alcohol, the fall, or both, made her head swoon and her balance unsteady at best. When she arrived in a tiny space at the bottom of the last ladder, Sissy eagerly opened the door, burst through it, and then unexcitedly found herself in the side alley between Talon's and a fly-by-night trendy art store. Sissy was surrounded in complete darkness, but not completely alone.

Stepping out of the claustrophobic enclosure, Sissy absent

mindedly let the hidden door close behind her. A woman cooed and giggled from the darkness, followed by the scent of roses, gentle rustle of clothing and clinking of a belt buckle being unfastened. Sissy cringed and turned to say, "Get a room!" but no one was there. More importantly, a way back inside Talon's was not there. All of Sissy's keys were in the loft: keys to her home, keys to her car, and, as the moment necessitated, keys to the pub.

## Chapter 22: Under the Influence

The wall from which the realtor emerged felt solid. No holes. No fake fuse boxes. Just chipping painted brick and frozen trickles of water from the gutters. Out of frustration, Sissy scratched the hidden door with her clothes hanger. Nothing.

Walking around to the front of the building, Sissy encountered various inebriated twenty-somethings traveling in morose packs like oppressed dogs. Despite the freezing weather, the girls had chosen scantily clad fashion over warmth and had since deprived their more sensible male counterparts of their coats. The school of students swam past Sissy in huddling pairs, seemingly oblivious to her presence. The party was winding down, or was this merely a reprieve before the real fun? Who could tell? Quite frankly, the younger generation frightened her. How, she couldn't quite put her finger on, which only made her feel old, again.

The front door was locked tight and the stinging wind was beginning to penetrate the realtor's warm buzz. Sissy realized she wasn't wearing a coat, either, and she had no male friend handy from whom to borrow one. Inhaling the crisp, sulfur smelling air because the water treatment plant needed to be told they were producing too much stink, Sissy heard yet another siren blaring through one of the nearby downtown streets. As if on cue, the now very familiar scent of roses coolly breezed by with the sound of tassels swishing and heels clicking. The curious realtor followed for a lack of better options.

The invisible heels clicked on the pavement to the alley, continued around to the back of the bar, and up a precarious fire escape ladder where the clicks became metallic clanks. The ladder was freezing cold and creaked beneath Sissy's weight. Students walked by below and gave the realtor no notice.

Once on the landing, Sissy found a closed, metal door waiting silently. She stood in front of the giant iron door, which politely waited in return. Nothing. Then Sissy had an idea. Rubbing her hands to circulate the blood, the realtor tapped out the odd beat as she had done in the cellar. Waiting a moment, there was no return knock, so she finished the knock as the "cognizant energy" had. The door audibly unlocked from within and loudly creaked open.

Sissy stepped into an unlit, windowless apartment on the back of Talon's bar. The air inside of the dark foyer was cold, colder than the landing. Again, the scent of roses filled Sissy's nose and a woman's high heels clicked in her ears. At first, Sissy tried to reach in the darkness for a light switch, but the walls were cold and clammy, almost slimy to the touch. The sensation made Sissy shudder.

However, the heels clicked away into the darkness and Sissy obediently followed. Remembering the trapdoor, Sissy thought it best to slide her feet across the floor and hold her hands out for balance. The darkness held more sounds than Sissy's scraping feet and Edith's clicking heels. All around, there were hushed whispers, glasses clinking, women giggling, and men puffing on fragrant cigars. Cold spots sprinkled the surroundings and tired the realtor. Sissy smelled liquor and wanted some, too.

The dust tickled the back of Sissy's throat, making her cough. Lifting her right hand, the realtor scratched her throat and felt the fingernail of her middle finger deeply graze her skin.

Touching her throat with her index finger, Sissy felt a red whelp where the missing finger's nail scratched her. The scents, the sounds, the energies in the room became stronger, in spite of her alcohol induced dulled state, but her personal strength was weakening. Her breath was becoming difficult to catch. The room was growing colder; her hands and nose stung from the crisp air. Sissy wanted to sleep, but knew she had to make it back to the loft before she could pass out. However, she also realized this was not one of her typical drunken swoons, rather this feeling of intense lethargy was coming from somewhere in her . . . soul?

Sissy chuckled at the clicking heels as she clumsily followed, "Sweetheart, you're killin' me!"

Then Sissy bumped into what felt like a large, fat person, but, after the initial sensation, she walked right through it. Still, the energy had been so real, she slurred out, "Excussse me, uh, sir, sir. Ma'am? Sorry, sorry." The room's darkness seemed to swarm around her and follow her, right up to the heavy door at the far end of the foyer, which Sissy was unable to see.

The body processes information at different rates. Just as science explains that lightning and thunder occur at the same time, but the human body sees lightning before hearing thunder, Sissy saw the lights of sparkling pain, then heard the actual sound of her body coming to a noisy halt against the door, and last, but not least, felt the pain of running into the door along her face, chest, and abdomen where the doorknob punched her in the kidney. The surprise and overall pain knocked Sissy to her knees, where instead of feeling the gritty bare floor she had been walking across, she felt a thick wool rug pad her fall. The realtor fell back upon the carpet to catch her breath, which smelled like fragrant cigar smoke, cigarettes, and spilled alcohol.

There was no doubt in her mind that she was not the first woman to sprawl in an unlady-like fashion upon the floor. *The only question left is, were drunken flappers the originators of the sorority mating call? Or was it considered garish to yell out, "I'm soooo drunk!" in the 1920s?*

Once the pain subsided and the shock wore off, Sissy felt extremely embarrassed and knew that something was watching her. Then the entire scene became very funny. Even though she could not see it, Sissy felt the room spin. The first sign that she was nearing the passing out point.

"A little help here, people! A little help, please!" Sissy giggled and inadvertently slapped her own face. The noises and sensations stopped. The disappearance of the reverie had a sobering effect on the realtor, as the room somehow felt more eerie without ghosts. "Gotta get up and get the hell outta here," Sissy found the offending door knob and slowly pulled herself off of the floor by it.

Sissy thought to herself, *Forget beer guts, five shots of alcohol immediately adds thirty pounds to every body part. My entire body feels as if it needs a forklift.* Once on her feet, the realtor discovered that the door opened to the unisex bathroom from hell. Talon's unisex bathroom from hell to be exact. A safety light illuminated the wretchedness and Sissy reluctantly walked through the wall and around the running toilet. Condoms and toilet paper littered the floor several inches thick and made Sissy cringe as she walked through the litter.

"Dear Jesus, get me out of here without catching some weird disease, and I'll . . . I'll . . . do something really nice for somebody, someday," Sissy prayed out loud and didn't care if it showed up on a hidden video camera or was overheard by a hiding Mimi on the other side of the real bathroom door. "I wanna go home! Call me a cab! I've had enough!" Sissy called out. "Surely Mimi will take pity on me," Sissy muttered beneath her breath and added, "Probably look like I've been to a cockfight, banging into walls, falling over crap. Jesssussss."

Sissy passed by the scratched mirror and glanced at herself. However, her shadowy reflection was accompanied by another shadowy reflection in the background, hovering overhead, looking at her with heavy eye shadow, fake eyelashes, crimson pouty lips, and a blunt bob.

## Chapter 23:  Out of Body, Out of Mind

Sissy was so scared by the face she couldn't move.  Her face stared fixedly at the other's, which came nearer and nearer. Then there was a moment of darkness.  Sissy shook her head for a moment to clear her wooziness.  But she wasn't inebriated anymore.  Not sleepy anymore.  Not lethargic.  Looking back into the mirror to reconstitute herself, another face stared back at her. Now, the face in the background was Sissy's.  Like a dream in which you can randomly play any part and simultaneously watch yourself, Sissy looked upon and looked through the other woman, Edith.  Like a shadow, Sissy followed the possessor and became her.

The bathroom changed from the scene of disease and disrepair into a woman's dressing room.  Boas, sequined outfits, hats, fishnets, and silky lingerie hung from every available space in the small room.  Where the toilet from the pub sat, a large white vanity held bottles of perfume, feathery masks, bottles of make-up, and vases of long stemmed roses.  Beside the vanity, a long white shoe tree held rows and rows of flashy shoes with fancy ribbon laces.  Large feather fans hung from bare nails hammered into the hard plaster.

Edith straightened her sequined headband and the tall, white peacock plume that towered above it. Then she lazily put on yet another layer of crimson red lipstick and puckered her lips.  A nude colored, sequined and crystal bejeweled bodysuit covered her body.  A knock at the door sent the woman into a frenzy looking for a particular perfume.  At the back of a collection of about twenty bottles, Edith found a bejeweled bottle with a crotched bulb, and doused herself with its delicate rose scented contents. Sniffing her assortment of fresh roses, the flapper sprayed them, too, with an ironic giggle.

Running out of the door, Edith grabbed a large feather fan, dashed across the hall, and into an open narrow passage that led through the stairway to the back of the downstairs stage, where a single white chair waited for her. Taking position, the woman straddled the chair and fanned her feathers, lasciviously hiding her nude colored body suit covered in sequins and crystals. Any light that found its way past the feathers and to her body made her appear to sparkle and twinkle. Giving a quick nod, the curtain raised and smoking men in suits that ranged from tailored to zoot applauded and hooted as the sexy jazz music began.

The routine was decidedly tame by modern terms. Not once did Edith actually get out of the chair. Rather, her raised legs, suggestive lounging positions, and methodically placed feathers were enough to send the men into a frenzy. Not that Edith was particularly endowed by modern terms, either. Her willowy stick figure was all the rage and the men either could not see or did not want to see the body suit that concealed the illusion. Perhaps people had better imaginations back then. With masterful undulations and execution of the chair like a silent partner, Edith finished her act and received a standing ovation. The curtain dropped and the flapper ran back through the tunnel, across the stairwell, and into the safety of her dressing room.

Slamming the door behind her and catching her breath, Edith was shocked to find a large, muscular man sitting in the chair of her vanity. The massive man was the bar owner, and he looked extremely angry as he held a flower card with the name of another man on it.  Edith wiped the sweat from her brow and held out her hand, motioning for him to give the card back.  The man, "Robbie," threw it at her.

Robbie snorted, "I thought you got rid of him months ago."

Edith snatched the card out of Robbie's fat hand, "I did. He just can't get enough, I suppose."

Robbie closed his hand into a fist, "I'm already payin' him more than I do myself.  I can't afford no more bribes or shake downs.  Do you know what that man could do to my place, Edith? Do you have any idea what he's done already?  Do you?"

Edith unabashedly sniffed the cologne on the card and shrugged, "Robbie, he's just an admirer."

Robbie pointed a fat finger at Edith, "He's also the sheriff. He keeps comin' around, I keep losin' business.  Nobody wants to come here and just watch you, Sweets.  People want to drink.  Heh, makes you pretty."

Edith popped the neck of her bodysuit, "Sounded like to me they already think I'm gorgeous.  Maybe the drinks make you look like more of a man who can handle his business, even with big, bad Monroe in this lousy dump."

"Shut your trap, or I'll shut it for ya'," Robbie looked at himself in Edith's vanity mirror and rubbed his chin.  "Look, I told you and I told you, over and over again to get rid of that creep and all you can do is disrespect me, in my own place.  You know what happens to little girls who disrespect Robbie in his own place?  Or do you think I've gone soft?"

Edith glared at Robbie, "Lay a finger on me and I'll have this place crawling with Monroe and his guys.  Might even tell 'em about that little love nest down in that forgotten wine cellar.

Monroe might've shook you down for the booze but he ain't shook you down for your whores. Yet."

"Ain't nobody snitchin' out Robbie. Ain't nobody takin' nothing' away from me, not after it took me this long to make you into something somebody'd pay good money for."

Edith wrinkled her nose, "Oh, go back to hidin' in the alleys, you low life. Find some little girl who don't know nothin' so's you can sell her on the cheap to those dirty bastards. Think they might be too good for you after Monroe's done with you. But it won't bother me none; I'll be too busy bein' the next Mrs. J. W. Monroe."

At this remark, Robbie's face turned a deep shade of crimson and Edith's cool demeanor turned to pale fear. She opened the door to escape, but there was a bouncer, solid and immovable as a mountain, blocking her path. He reached out to grab her, but she slid out of his slow, clunky hands away from him and back toward Robbie. In desperation, Edith made a quick dash for the door on the other side of the bar owner, to the secret room on the other side of her dressing room, but Robbie grabbed her arm as she swung the door open to make her escape.

A quiet crowd of what looked to be the city's finest momentarily stopped chatting and drinking in a room filled with leather furniture and posh modern art, all of which gave off a warm, smoky glow. As if this were a regular occurrence, the revelers ignored the woman being dragged back into her dressing room, kicking and screaming, and continued whispering, sipping, and listening to music, which loudly filtered through the vents from downstairs.

Robbie hit Edith hard upon the face, bloodying her nose,

"You damn whore! You are not going to ruin me to become the wife of the biggest crook in town!"

Edith pleaded with Robbie, coughing up bubbles of bloody snot, "I didn't mean it, Robbie! I'll get rid of him! I was just teasin' ya' before!"

Pausing only momentarily, the man stopped his fist in midair, "No. The only

thing to do is get rid of you!" Edith screamed, but Robbie proceeded to crush Edith's bird sized throat with his beefy bare hands. In a matter of moments, the woman was dead.

Robbie dropped Edith's dead body on the floor. He motioned for the bouncer to come in, "Ed, wash her face up. If anybody asks, she passed out from too much cough medicine, again . . . uh . . . you know where to dump her."

The gargantuan bouncer silently walked into the room for the body. Robbie stepped over Edith as if she were a puddle. Ed cleaned her face up and then ripped the bloodied bodysuit with his bare hands. Sequins and crystals glittered in the lamp light as they hit the floor, making little tinkling noises.

Ed huffed in the dead woman's face, "I don't see what these guys want with ya'. No tits. No hips. No ass." The bouncer put his massive hand on Edith's face and squinched her lips into a pucker. He turned her head from side to side. "Must've had a pretty throat." He slipped his index finger into her mouth, pulling it back and forth several times before pulling it out. Ed grinned at himself for what he perceived as being witty. Pulling the remainder of the ripped bodysuit off of Edith, Ed threw it into the trash, put Edith's robe on her, slung her dead body over his boulder sized shoulder and exited the room.

Like a mindless ant carrying a crumb to the hive, Ed carried Edith's body out of the dressing room, up the stairs into the loft, through the closet, down the passageway, behind the faux fuse box, down the ladders to the final landing by the alley. Here, the path was different. Instead of going to the alley, Ed turned to his right and slid a portion of the wall to the right. "The wall" was a pocket door. Ed lifted a manhole covering on the opposite side of the wall and went down into the underground sewage system beneath the building. There the girl was dumped behind several trash bags full of empty liquor bottles. Silently, the man ascended the sewer stairs. Business as usual.

***

When Sissy came back into her own consciousness, she was standing in the closet in the loft apartment. Immediately, she ran to the "private" bathroom and threw up in the sink.
She smelled the liquor that came up and out of her guts and threw up again. Avoiding the mirror, Sissy wiped her mouth with toilet paper and walked to the bed. She plopped on the mattress with a dull thud and drifted into the safer depths of subconsciousness. Her last thought to herself was more like a silent prayer, "No dreams. No more dreaming, please."

## Chapter 24: Hair of the Dawg

Mimi walked through the doors of the pub around noon, just as she predicted she would. Sissy sat at the empty bar, eating a delivered pizza and drinking one tall glass of water with two empty shot glasses and a full bottle of gin sitting just to the left of her.

Sissy swallowed hard, "Mimi, you look like shit. I take it you had a good time last night?"

Mimi's red cracked eyes squinted out a smile through a painfully obvious hangover, "Yeah, I had a *real* good time." The young woman inhaled and wiped her face with a clumsy effort, "Question is . . . how was your night?"

Sissy slapped the bar, "Lemme pour you a drink."

Mimi lifted her brow, "Where'd you get that?"

"The pizza?"

"No, the gin. That's not Talons. Did you bring it with you last night?"

Sissy said sarcastically, "Well, yeah. I mean, I don't normally pack a large bottle of liquor. I prefer dainty flasks. . . No, it's not mine! It's from the speak easy."

"God, how old is it? Is it even safe to drink?" Mimi asked. Sissy held the opened bottle over to Mimi, who sniffed the bottle and immediately grabbed her head, "Owww. My head! Well, good. I was about to get pissed. Talon said he gave all of the liquor away to his employees as severance pay. God, you know how much I spent on booze last night? Stupid little prick." Mimi pulled up a stool next to Sissy and delicately picked at a slice of pizza, "This smells good, but I think it'd make me puke. Gimme a shot."

"Maybe you don't need any more alcohol, after all. You think?"

"God, how do you think I function in this godforsaken town? Hell, why do you think I'm even with Talon? Stupid little prick." Mimi reached over Sissy and poured her own shot. Before throwing the shot to the back of her throat she made a toast into the air, "To the hair of the dog that tore me a new one."

Sissy put down her pizza, "So, you've never been in the vault downstairs?"

"Downstairs? There's the crawlspace, but Talon said it always smells like crap."

"Funny he would say that. You really wanna know how my night went?"
Sissy sardonically smiled and told the weary Goth about the secret passages in the building, saving the information about Edith for the end.

Mimi was intrigued, if not enthralled. "You mean to tell me this building is, like, covered in these, like, ant tunnels going to secret rooms? Talon never told me. Sneaky little prick."

"You wanna see?"

Mimi held her head and let out a soft burp with a gag at the end, "Maybe some other time, I feel like I have a fur coat on my tongue and a baboon sitting with its fat red ass in my face."

Sissy felt disappointed by Mimi's rather anticlimactic reaction. The realtor tried to pique her interest, "What about Edith?"

"What about her? Did you see her?"

"Yeah, you could say that."

"Good. I'm going to bed. I'll care more about this

tomorrow."

## Chapter 25:  Shop Therapy

Sissy went home and bathed in her clean bathroom, scrubbing away at her skin and memories of walking through the nastiest bathroom in Georgia. The loofah was too soft, and the pumice didn't work wet. Finally, Sissy turned off the cold water all together, and turned up the hot as high as it would go, and raked her legs with her fingernails. Dark red lines ran up and down her legs as if she were wearing red and pink striped Capri pants. The pain felt better than that uncomfortable "icky" feeling that made the hair on the back of her neck stand on end.

Every time she shut her eyes and rinsed her face in the hot stream of water, memories of Edith's face emptily staring back at her resurfaced, causing panic and fear. Sissy laughed at herself, but she still felt as if she were not alone. The only reason the realtor got out of the shower was because the hot water had run out and her soggy frame was more than a little scalded. Otherwise, she would have stayed there all day.

Every light in Sissy's small apartment was lit and both the TV in her bedroom and the living room were on. Sissy just wanted the noise. The presence of something that was *supposed* to be there. When Sissy blow dried her hair, she found herself not looking in the mirror, and once she realized she was avoiding the mirror, she found she had a hard time forcing herself to look. The day outside was gray and conducive to sleep, especially since Sissy had gotten so very little the night before, but she didn't want to sleep. She didn't want to watch TV. She didn't want a drink, oddly. The nub of her missing finger throbbed, probably some sort of arthritis or scarring, or deep healing that the doctor warned could take many years.

Sissy just felt . . . restless, not comfortable in her own skin. Her gait was off, making her walk clumsily through the one bedroom apartment. Her thoughts were foggy, as if they were being confiscated right from her brain. A strange numbness and a tinge of the same lethargy she felt in the abandoned secret lounge the night before was creeping upon her, or worse, into her.

The only time she had ever felt that confused and tired was when she tried a crash liquid diet in college. Her blood sugar was so low she passed out and her roommate made her eat a quarter pound Mondo Burger and extra large fries, which she threw up. Ever since, Sissy was a pizza kind of gal, which she had eaten plenty of only two hours before, so she knew her blood sugar was fine. What could possible make her feel better? Sissy decided she needed to go somewhere, perhaps the mall. *Yes, buy myself a cute outfit, treat myself to something deliciously sinful, and sleep through a two dollar movie.*

Throwing on a pair of jeans, a long sleeve t-shirt, a sweater from the clean pile, and a pair of sneakers, Sissy grabbed her purse and ran down the stairs to her SUV before any further complications stopped her. Sissy wasn't even sure if she were "with it" enough to actually pick out an outfit to fit her mood, because she didn't feel as if she really had one and was only vaguely aware that she needed a coat. For that matter, she was only vaguely aware that she was wearing clothing at all.

Her brain was not concentrating, so she sat in her loaded leather interior, staring at the familiar dials, steering wheel, gear column, and pedals like an astronaut in an alien mothership. None of it registered. Her keys sat in her hand, until they dropped on the thick beige carpet with an audible clinking. The noise made her somewhat aware she should pick them up, but then what? Slowly, the memory of what she was supposed to do came back to her. Sissy checked her side view mirrors, as always, but shuddered and tightly shut her eyes when she touched the rearview mirror. Keys turned the ignition, and a still unsure hand pushed the transmission into reverse.

The thought of driving scared her, but there was an away game and Athens without its thirty thousand college students was not unlike a western ghost town. In a fleeting moment of clarity, Sissy remembered that the locals didn't seem to get out much in dreary weather, so if she were to get in a wreck, it would most likely be with a foreign exchange student in an early eighties model foreign tin can, nothing her SUV couldn't handle. The thought bounced in her head and was sucked out of her mind before she was through pondering it. Sissy was driving on autopilot with a remote desire to go to . . . and the destination bounced in her brain, but would not stick. If the realtor were allowed to feel frustrated, she would have.

Slowly, against sheets of sporadic rain and strong gusts of wind, Sissy cruised down the narrow connecting streets, until she right turned the corner of Wesley and Covington, downtown. The realtor waited stupidly for the green light, even though no one was coming or going, either on the streets or the sidewalks. Sissy had no clue where she was until she passed the glaring store front of Talon's, and saw a scrawny woman dressed all in white standing behind the front glass window against the total darkness of the closed bar. The willowy woman lifted her arm and waved with a large smile on her face. Sissy blinked and she was gone.

For the first time since her shower, Sissy was able to have an independent thought.

She could smell the car freshener, feel the leather, and more importantly, the cold, and turn on the heat. Her breath made steamy streams like a fairytale dragon and her hands were so cold, they felt as if they were on fire and cracking against the frigid leather steering wheel. The clock in her dash showed an hour had passed, even though the trip should have only lasted ten minutes. The sluggishness subsided. Looking at her surroundings, Sissy could feel herself staring through her own eyes. Finally, she was *there* with herself, by herself.

*Damn it! I'm losing my damn mind. I need to go home and get my coat before I catch a cold. Then I'll go to the mall and hang around the living until I feel better. Wait until I see that damn Mimi and tell her a thing or two.*

Sissy sped up from her creep of ten miles an hour to fifty and squealed tires in the direction of her apartment. Once inside, she realized she had left all of the lights and both TVs on. Clothing wise, she had picked out her "working in the mud" tennis shoes with the holes over both big toes and had forgotten to put on socks and a bra. No make-up, and her hair was only partially dried. "My God! What was I thinking?" Sissy felt better than usual and was eager to get out and about; she didn't want to really tell herself what might come over her next.

The bathroom smelled like . . . deodorizer. Just deodorizer, no roses she told herself.

A little primping, lipstick, mascara, some base to cover up that stress induced pimple, a quick blast with the dryer, and a spritz of hairspray. Sissy rubbed her lips together and smiled at herself in the mirror one last time, just in case she had the dreaded smudge on the ivories.

Then the fog rolled in. Her breath was hard to catch and the room sporadically became dark, as if someone were flipping the light switch repetitively. But the lights weren't being turned off in the room.

Sissy tried to catch her breath and tightly grabbed the sink basin, "Stop it! Stop it!
Get out of my house! Get out of my head! Leave me . . . alone!"

## Chapter 26: Bar Hopping

When Sissy came to, several hours had passed, she was freezing, and standing in front of Talon's, but her beloved SUV was nowhere to be found. Her favorite pair of brown leather loafers were soaked through, completely ruined. The muscles in her legs ached. No doubt about it, Sissy had walked the six miles from her apartment to the bar in some sort of, what had Mimi called it, "psychic induced trance?" Having no better option, Sissy knocked on the door loudly and hoped the Queen of Darkness was home and could hear her knocking. Of course, the walls were made for carrying sound, so unless Mimi were passed out or in an alcoholic coma that should not be a problem.

Eventually, Queeny arose to find a shivering realtor hopping up and down, too cold to feel embarrassed. Mimi looked genuinely confused as she let Sissy into the chilly tavern. "Sissy. I thought I told you I'd see you tomorrow. Did you leave something?"

"Hell no! I'm . . . I'm having some serious problems. Oh, Jesus, my feet are cold!" Sissy invited herself up to Mimi's loft with the intention of taking off her socks and wrapping her feet in a blanket.

Mimi stood in front of Sissy like a guard dog, "Where are you going?"

Sissy spoke the best she could through chattering teeth and lips she could not feel, "This is all your fault, and you're going to fix this today! So either you turn on some freaking heat and bring me a blanket, or I'm going to waltz my fat cold ass up to your loft and snatch one off of your bed."

Mimi balled up both her fists as if infuriated, "What are you talking about *my fault*? I've been asleep all day, and what gives you the right to tell me what I'm going to do in my house?"

Sissy sneezed and visibly shivered all over, "This isn't even your house!" Sissy stamped her foot, sending searing pain up her numb leg, "All I want is for you to tell me how to get rid of Edith! I walked here from my apartment and I don't remember how I got here. Everything turned black and my head . . . I wasn't there in my own head! Roses. If I ever have to smell roses, I swear."

The look on Mimi's face softened, "I'll go turn on the heat. There's something I gotta take care of first. Wait here, okay?"

Sissy sneezed and snuffled, "Like I have a choice?"

Mimi came down the stairs with a down comforter cumbersomely scrunched in her arms. While Mimi wrapped Sissy in the comforter, a pale androgynous looking man dressed all in black with long, blue-black hair pushed his way past Mimi, tucked his shirt, and angrily bolted out the front door.

Mimi huffed, "You'll get over it, Nick! Asshole!"

With a genuine touch of tenderness, Mimi walked Sissy up to the loft and into her bed. Mimi wrapped the shivering woman in a crimson blanket on top of the comforter and tucked a black king sized pillow behind Sissy's back and fluffed the end to cradle her damp head. In a tone showing genuine concern, Mimi asked, "So, Edith went home with you?"

Sissy sneezed and coughed out, "You could say that. And I think I'm contagious. With a cold, not Edith."

Mimi walked over to the purple futon and pulled out a pack of cigarettes like the first time Sissy ever met her. Mimi tamped on the pack and asked with that same wild glint in her eyes as

168

when they were with Gene in the restaurant, "So what was it like?"

Sissy physically shivered, "It was the creepiest thing I've ever experienced in my life. Worse than the chest with the dead body in it."

Mimi walked over to the bed and sat on the end. She held a cigarette between her fingers and pointed at Sissy, "Ha! I knew it. I totally read that when I shook your hand that time!" Mimi lit the cigarette and inhaled deeply, "So now, (exhale) you're having problems with energy, thinking, and feelings of numbness?"

Sissy held her head in her hand and looked at Mimi with that "you've gotta be kidding me" look, "What is this, a list of side effects on a pill box?"

Mimi shook her head "no" and took her cigarette out of her mouth, "Just answer me."

"Well, yeah. Exactly." Sissy felt thirsty and chilled to her bones, "Do you have something I can drink? Maybe something hot?"

Mimi got up from the end of the bed and walked into the kitchen. There she pulled out several black storage canisters from beneath the marble countertop, "You want medicinal tea, herbal tea, green tea, chai, or some cheap instant shit Talon left?"

Sissy just shrugged, "Surprise me."

Mimi pulled up the smallest canister in the grouping, "Herbal. It'll help calm your nerves."

Sissy lifted her brow, "It's not anything that'll make me fail a pee test, is it?"

Mimi laughed, "No, it's my own mixture I make for my little coven after we do our little thing. It helps restore positive energy, which you need."

Sissy snuggled deeper into the blanket, "What I need is to stop all this 'psychic' fooling around mess. I'm afraid to even look in the mirror." Sissy stared out the window by the bed, "That's how I saw her. She was staring at me in the bar's bathroom mirror."

Mimi put a kettle on the gas stove, "Then?"

Sissy sat straight up in the bed and leaned toward Mimi, who was packing the herbal tea into a silver diffuser. The realtor held out her palm in front of her for added emphasis, "I was looking at me, but I didn't look like me, I looked like her, only I saw her and me. It's confusing. I can't explain it." Sissy put her hand on her face as if she were unsure about her current status.

Mimi took a drag on her cigarette and dangled the diffuser in front of herself like an amulet for hypnotism, "Damn. A full blown possession. That is so cool."

Sissy shook her head, "No, it's not. I've lost track of time. She won't go away. I keep coming here. This is my second time getting here and not remembering how. We got to take care of this, but I don't know what the hell she wants."

Mimi sat the diffuser on the counter and walked back over to the bed, resuming her place at the far end, "Well, she's been buried. The city found her bones when they were re-doing the sewers a long time ago. They even figured out who she was, somehow."

Sissy chewed the side of her lip and said, "So it's not an unmarked grave thing."

Mimi shrugged, "Everybody she could possibly be pissed at is dead. She's here. She wants something. I was hoping you'd find out so we could do something."

Sissy cocked her head to the side, "You can read my hand, but you can't figure out the Edith thing . . . and you live here?"

Mimi puffed on her cigarette and blew out a long stream toward the window, "Edith doesn't really care for me. We don't communicate. I've tried, but she . . . just ignores me." Mimi walked over to Sissy, reached over, and put her hand on Sissy's foot, "Lucky you, huh?" The kettle went off and Mimi made the tea. After it steeped for a few minutes, she brought Sissy a dainty little porcelain cup and saucer that were white with roses and gold gilding.

Sissy took a sip of her herbal tea and grimaced, "I don't understand. She hates men. Doesn't like you. Brings me here. I mean, I'm not the one buying the place. I have an idea, but . . . since you've told me about you two's dysfunctional relationship, I don't know."

Mimi leaned over the side of the bed and put her cigarette into an empty soda can that was under the bed, "What?"

Sissy leaned back against her pillow and said in a low, bashful tone, "I thought you should buy the bar and turn it into something just for women."

Mimi looked up from the side of the bed, "Like a lesbian bar?"

Sissy fluffed the covers around her neck, "I don't know. I don't care. Aren't you a witch?"

Mimi sat up straight and smoothed her hair with her hand, "Yeah. So?"

Sissy sat up with a burst of enthusiasm, "What about a meeting place? What about a place to buy magic stuff, like shops you see on those trendy horror movies?"

Mimi snickered, "That'd be really cool, but I have no money."

Sissy pretended to take another sip of her tea, "I thought about that, too. Any rich friends?"

Mimi turned away from Sissy and looked out the window, "Just Talon and his dad's money."

"So, you just need money?"

Mimi looked down at her hands and stared at her chipped sparkly black fingernail polish, "Yeah."

"What about Talon's dad? Couldn't he use you for another tax write off? Businesses trade hands, names on papers, but never real ownership all the time. S'how the mafia works."

Mimi started pushing back her cuticles, "Yeah, I know. His dad launders money for the mafia."

Sissy leaned over the bed and put her tea on the floor. She sat straight up and tucked her damp hair behind her ears, "Well, okay, then. We can definitely work this out. Do you want the place?"

Mimi looked around the room as if she were taking a mental inventory, "Take me on a full tour, first. Then, I'll make up my mind."

## Chapter 27: Catering to Ghosts and Goths

Armed to the hilt with flashlights, a box of matches, and a couple of white candles, Sissy took Mimi on a guided tour of the building, showing her the intricate ins and outs. They found all of the passages and rooms, as well as a couple extra that Sissy did not find during her previous night there. Mimi discovered two extra entrances to the second story secret room where Sissy fell on the floor and felt a rug beneath her. Sissy regaled Mimi with stories of seeing Edith perform, and the "gangsters" hanging out in the secret room smoking and drinking, while the local sheriff sat downstairs. Mimi was fascinated at the details of Edith's last moments and the tragedy of her success.

Sissy's business-side kicked in full swing, "Mimi, what if Edith really does like you? What if she never opened up to you because she has some sort of respect for you? You seem to be the only one who can co-exist in this place with her. Let's be honest, just because she doesn't mess with you, doesn't mean she doesn't like you. Can't you cast a spell over Talon's dad so he'll give you the money?"

Mimi gave Sissy a sarcastic look, "Cute. Very cute. You don't have to sell me, okay? I don't think I need Talon's dad, anyway. I definitely have the down payment, but I'll need a low monthly payment from the bank. Good interest rate, that sort of thing."

Sissy scrunched her eyebrows at the little gothic girl, "I thought you said you don't have any money."

Mimi took a deep breath and looked Sissy straight in her eyes, "Talon might've owned the bar, per se, but I handled the books. A bar in Athens is going to make money. Talon was never supposed to make money, well, not as much as money as he did. You know the whole tax write offs and laundering. So . . ."

Sissy sniffled and waited with her head bobbing, "And . . ."

"And it had to go somewhere. Some just went to the right person." Mimi smiled and that fiery glint glowed in her dark eyes.

"Impressive." Sissy tapped her finger to her chin and thought, "I can price the bar low. If anybody protests, the company's got a building inspector who'll help with all that. But, you are really gonna owe me."

Mimi laughed, "How? You get rid of Edith."

Sissy waved her finger at Mimi, "Who would never have been my problem if it weren't for you."

\*\*\*

Some opportunists have all the luck, and Mimi was one of them. She got a bank loan and made her down payment. Sissy made less in commission than she would have liked, but it didn't bother her. For that matter, neither did Edith. Mimi remodeled the bathroom to look more like a powder room and named her bar "Jade." Sissy visited the bar and her new friend, Mimi, at least once a week, mostly because she got free drinks. No, not from Mimi, but the female patrons, who gave Sissy lots of flattery along with the free drinks. Sissy loved the attention, but wished she were as popular in the straight male community as at the "lesbo bar." After enough shots though, Sissy shamelessly showed her appreciation by hitting the dance floor, where it was not uncommon for her to smell the wafting of roses.

## Chapter 28: Now Accepting Gifts

In just a short time, Sissy successfully settled into life in Athens and found the work to be as easy as knocking down bowling pins with a scoped rifle. Real estate moved at a dizzying pace, making the barren holiday months a God send. One thing Sissy soon realized about her new town was that despite the modern and hip influence of the university, Athens itself was a relatively old town with a strange history.

The cemeteries proved to be forbidden territory, especially the old campus cemetery where the out-of-state and foreign students were buried. Dating as far back as the late 1800s, these students had the misfortune of catching various contagious diseases and dying oftentimes painful deaths. Because of the contagions, they could not be shipped back home for burial in their native lands. Instead of respectful funerals, they were often given quick burials to try to prevent the spreading of the diseases. These sad souls spoiled the surrounding area with their lingering impressions of pain, loneliness, and frustration. The last thing Sissy wanted to do was experience another possession or have one of those troubled souls follow her home, so she would plan her route accordingly and stayed away the best she could.

Other creepy places Sissy encountered were just the blaring windows of various Greek houses, a few dorms and some campus classrooms. The energy seeping from these houses left passing images of suicides ranging back to the beginning of the school's history.

Drug overdoses, particularly around the sixties and seventies. Of course, those deaths were tame compared to the latest horror, which was the sudden onslaught of do-it-yourself home abortions.

A month after Sissy moved to Athens, a student who did not go home for the holidays, gave birth to a small baby, which she promptly killed with a pair of scissors and threw in a garbage can covered in blood stained sheets. For weeks, the news stations relayed the details, begging for anyone with more information to come forward. No one did. Sissy knew she could assist, but how would the police know to trust her? How did one go about being of assistance, when your only evidence is because "you know, you just know?" Furthermore, to potentially re-live the last few moments of an innocent's life or an unwilling mother's pain and insane desperation were more than Sissy could emotionally tolerate.

Marriage, domestication, and babies never crossed Sissy's mind. Until the afternoon she saw a car commercial starring two beautiful little cherubs sitting contentedly in car seats in the back seat of the newer model of Sissy's SUV. The announcer used such buzz words as "safety" and "fulfillment" and the realtor broke down into tears. Suddenly, her abdomen felt empty. Sissy felt a distinct pinging in her sides and could only guess it to be her ovaries aching, which seemed to be punishing her for not ever using them to their full potential. Oh, Lord, Sissy's biological clock was ticking and she didn't know how to hit the snooze button.

## Chapter 29:  Ticking Ovaries Get Personal


Every place Sissy went, from the grocery store to the clubs,
was a potential mating ground.  Men ranging from their late
twenties to mid-fifties were fair game.  Forget hair color.
If they had hair, that was just a bonus.  Wedding ring?  Maybe
there was a possible separation or divorce in the near future.
Handsomeness was preferred, but not required.  Body odor?
That, perhaps, was a big no-no, but if they were foreign and that
was just a minor part of their culture . . . Okay, so Sissy was
desperate.  Not that she had ever been hard up for a date or got
jilted for the prom, but something inside her was telling her to tie
the knot *now*.  But where was all of this coming from, and why
now?

Maybe it was the influence of all the horny youths walking
the streets, their pheromones and hormones and incessant flirting
infiltrating the air like chemical warfare.  Perhaps it was the
swarms of codependent females working on their "MRS" degrees
as diligently as salmon swimming upstream to spawn.  Perchance
it was the fact that Sissy was *getting older?*  Her own mother
started going through menopause at forty-five, which was "only"
ten years away for Sissy.  Fears of the stigmas plagued her
thoughts: "old maid," "homely," "self-absorbed," "difficult," "set-
in-her-ways."  The lowest point came when Sissy found herself
browsing in tobacco and fine cigar shops, and she didn't even
smoke.  What was she going to do?

The realtor couldn't sleep at night and her appetite was
decreasing.  Instead of feeling like a grown woman who had made
adult and responsible decisions regarding marriage and children,

Sissy began to second guess her life, herself. She felt like a lovelorn teen wallowing in self-pity. In fact, when she was a teenager, Sissy didn't care about dating that much.

Excluding ogling Tipper since she was a pre-teen, there were no monumental crushes or anything that would constitute a "first love." Although in college, there was that thing she had with one of her college professors. When he told her he was married and wanted to call it off, Sissy just shrugged it off and said, "Okay. I'll see you around." No one had ever broken her heart. Had *she* broken any hearts?

There was the guy she made cry in high school, but it had been so long ago, Sissy couldn't remember all of the details. Something about she kissed another guy playing truth-or-dare on a church trip. Still, it wasn't anything she found worth keeping in her memory. The boy was more upset than she had ever been. Unlike most girls growing up, Sissy had always loved herself and been, well, a little self-absorbed.

Now, all Sissy could do was focus on the opposite sex. Where were all of the "good ones?" What made for the proverbial "good one?" At least property had guidelines and clear standards written in books. There were real estate classes and papers to certify you worthy to play the field. Lately, it seemed that the only standard Sissy had was breathing. Coherent, on the other hand, optional.

Playing the field, she felt like a one person football team crying for attention against a fully staffed pro-team, who wanted to bowl her over to get to their pick of the cheerleaders. The odds were against her. The feeling made her sick. Sick of feeling lonely, sick of feeling old, sick of feeling like she had missed out on something, and, ironically, sick of not feeling like her old self.

Commercials upset her so badly, she quit watching TV altogether. Movie stores were also off limit, as Sissy always made her way to what she used to call the "sentimental slop" aisle. While waiting in line at the grocery store, she picked up a bridal magazine and imagined how her hair would look in a "romantic up-do with a princess tiara." The realization scared her so badly, she left her buggy in line and ran out of the store as if she were about to be tackled.

While staring off into space one day, Sissy's boss, Mrs. Barb Roth, walked into her office and chuckled at the oblivious realtor, "Oh, my God. I know that look. You've got it. You've got it *bad*." The announcement woke Sissy from her stupor.

"What? The flu? I feel . . . fine." Sissy stared up at her boss. Her impression of Barb was that she was the most got-it-together, blonde-headed, fifty-something year old woman she had ever met in her entire life. From the woman's throaty voice, to her bright, sparkly blue eyes that were rather large for her head, to her expensive Italian shoes and coordinating handbags, and never forget her perfect size six waist and impeccable matching cardigan sets with perfect jewelry. Sissy oftentimes wondered if she, herself, would age so gracefully.

Barb laughed her self-assured, rich woman laugh that Sissy had previously only heard on soap operas, until she met Barb. Barb genuinely laughed in that same fake manner. "The flu! A few more weeks of this and you'll wish you had the flu! You're what? In your early to mid thirties? Single, no kids?"

Sissy crossed her arms in front of herself, "Yeah. Do I win a prize or a pity party?"

Barb reached over to Sissy's crossed arms and touched her wrist, "Neither, unfortunately. If you are a winner, it's in the 'Oh-my-God-I'm-getting-old-and-I-need-a-husband-and-two-point-five-kids-by-tomorrow' lottery. Am I right?"

Sissy felt her shoulders droop in self-defeat, "I guess so. I can't concentrate . . .

I feel . . .," before Sissy could finish, her boss interrupted her.

"I know. Well, I don't know." Barb shook her hair and looked as if she were calculating math in her head. "I've been divorced three times. Love. Marriage. Prenuptials. Pretty much all the same to me. But my sister, Trisha." Barb touched her hand to her heart and sighed loudly, which was another soap opera gesture Sissy had never seen in real life until meeting Barb. "Ohhh, she was so bad off, it was funny. Started writing to men in prison. Well, that wasn't funny. But . . ."

Sissy winced. The disclosure of such sensitive information made Sissy feel sorry for Trisha, "Please, Barb, I promise not to write men in prison. Do you have an idea of how I can get rid of this . . ."

Barb "humped" and threw out her leg and put her hands on her hips, "Get rid of it? Honey, you've just got to go with it! Find a man, preferably one with a clean record, a nice, fat income, a house you want to re-decorate, and an ex-wife you can hate together. Then you can immediately have one or two of his ungrateful spawn. Then there's always two or three of his previous ungrateful spawn visiting on the weekends, and you're practically the modern day Blandy Brood."

Sissy put her head down on her desk, "I want to die."

"What did you expect? A twenty-something marriage in

your thirties? We're women, that's as good as it gets for us. Now, if we were men . . .," Barb threw out her index finger and squinched her right eye shut as if she were taking aim and shooting Sissy squarely in the face.

Sissy lifted her head and threw out her hand for emphasis, "I just want a good looking man!" Sissy put her head back down and groaned. Then she picked her head back up and took a deep breath. "This isn't me! This isn't what I care about! I have set goals and I don't have any time for this bunch of crap. I want my career and money. Lots of money."

Barb leaned into Sissy and asked in a hushed tone, "You had your hormones checked recently?"

Sissy sat straight up and felt invaded, "No. Why?"

Barb waved off Sissy's question, "Oh, nothing. Just don't start crying when the gals talk about their kids." Barb leaned back into Sissy with the same hushed tone as before, "Now, that's really pathetic."

Sissy's eyes immediately welled with tears as she fought back an audible sniffle, "Okay."

Barb put her hand to her chest, "Get your hormones checked, and quit staring into space." Barb waggled her hand at Sissy, "Look busy."

To Barb's surprise, Sissy uncharacteristically bowed her head and shook it in the affirmative. A tear escaped and rolled midway down Sissy's cheek before she could wipe it.

Barb's demeanor softened and she let out a sympathetic sigh, "Have you ever thought about putting a personal ad in the paper?"

Sissy looked up at her employer, wiped her eyes hard, and

cocked a suspicious eyebrow.

Barb laughed in a softer tone, "No, really. Worked for my sister. Lives on a farm, got four or five little brats running around. Picture person for 'the power of the personals'." Barb made quotation marks with her fingers in the air and chuckled at her own cleverness. Then she continued, "Woman makes me physically ill, but, what the hell do I know? I've been divorced three times."

The next day was slow, which allowed Sissy to work on her personal ad. She typed her rough drafts on the office computer to "look busy." Not knowing what to say, Sissy began typing, "SWF in early thirties looking for SWM in late twenties to early fifties for companionship and good time." Sissy huffed in frustration, "'Good time'? Like that doesn't scream, 'rape me.'"

Sissy started again, "SWF in early thirties looking for SWM in late twenties to early fifties for companionship. Enjoys shopping, making money. . . Desperate, Desperate, Desperate." Sissy stared at her computer screen, mentally begging it to tell her what to write, but it didn't. *What straight man wants to go shopping? Making money? Why don't I just call myself a call girl and avoid the confusion?*

"SWF in early thirties looking for SWM in early thirties to early fifties for a mature relationship. Enjoys Athens nightlife, movies, and occasional drink." *Why don't I just call myself an alcoholic?*

"SWF in early thirties looking for SWM in early thirties to early fifties for a mature relationship. Enjoys Athens nightlife, movies, and adventure. Prefers gentleman with independent nature and sense of humor." *Perfect.*

## Chapter 30: Let's Meet Over Drinks

Sissy submitted the ad in the newspaper and waited for a reply. And waited. And waited. And waited. And waited. Nearly a month later, Sissy got her first hit. A kind voice on her personal-ad-voicemail told her his name was Dave Howard and he looked forward to hearing from her. Sissy returned Dave's call and they made plans to meet at O'Harry's downtown at seven o'clock and to go to a movie before "the young'uns came out."

Arriving a few minutes late (Sissy was mortified at the thought of appearing desperate), the hopeful realtor found a patiently waiting Dave sitting in the cool spring evening, sipping a strong cup of black coffee, reading the comics, and tapping his foot nervously against the leg of the table. He was adorable. Brown hair, wide shoulders, neatly dressed, and the breeze provided a waft of his spicy cologne. Sissy loved spicy men's cologne and had been known to stop by the perfume counter at department stores and get samples for "her husband's birthday." Dave was slightly pudgy, but it made him seem that much more amiable. Approachable. *Daddy material.* Sissy was pleased and her heart beat hard in her chest, anticipating the rest of her date. *Oh, don't screw this up!*

Sissy walked up to the man and smoothed her hair behind her ear, "Hi. Are you Dave?"

Dave had been looking all around like a novice spy over his comics, but looked up at Sissy with gratitude, "Yes. Dave Howard. Are you Sissy?"

"Uh-huh." Dave got up to shake Sissy's hand and then he slid a chair out for her, which Sissy graciously took. Dave pushed her to the table.

Dave leaned into Sissy and said in a hushed tone, "How'd you guess I was Dave?"

A waitress came up to their table with menus, as if on cue.

Sissy casually opened her menu and peeked over to look demurely at Dave, "What do you mean?"

Dave quickly ordered a stout lager and went back to their conversation, "Well, I realized after we hung up we didn't describe ourselves and I didn't have your home number. So, I've been kind of sitting here worrying if that chick over there was you and if I should go and introduce myself."

It never dawned on Sissy that they forgot to describe themselves on the phone. She just assumed they would "know" each other. Rather than say that out loud for fear it might sound weird and turn him off, Sissy played dumb, "Hmmm. Maybe you just look like a Dave, you know?" Catching Dave's cue about the beer, Sissy ordered the same for herself. She was so glad he didn't order another coffee because she felt like she really needed a drink right now.

The waitress disappeared.

Dave shook his head and smiled, "I dunno. Glad you could figure it out. Otherwise, I would've made an ass out of myself, asking that lady if she were Sissy."

Sissy grinned teasingly, "Or made a new friend."

Dave huffed in disapproval, "In Athens? Not likely at this time of day. She looks like she's holding out for a long night. Like, her third free tequila shot and beer goggles. Oh, God. Do I sound cynical?"

Sissy unabashedly looked over at the brunette in the shades, reading a British classic, no doubt for an English class. She was wearing Greek colors, "No. By the looks of her, I'd say realistic."

The waitress promptly returned with their lagers. Dave gulped down a swig of his beer, "I know this town and these people. How long you been doing the personal ad thing?"

Sissy took a petite sip, trying to remember to be feminine, even though she felt comfortable enough around the guy to buy one more and swill the entire thing down, "Well, I just kind of got started. Been dedicated to my work, so to speak."

"Nothing wrong with that. How long you lived here?"

"Ummm, three, four months?"

Dave nodded and smiled, "Going back to school?"

Sissy shrugged, "I sell real estate."

Dave took another swig of his beer, which was now half finished. He seemed to choke a little at the end of his gulp, "No kidding. My cousin, Rob Heimmerman, sells real estate back home in Flemming."

Sissy put her hand over her head as if she were trying to avoid someone, "I totally used to live in Flemming. In fact, I sold a property that he sold, like, what, five years later?"

Dave burst out with, "No way! So, if we were to marry, I couldn't possibly talk you into moving back there, huh?" At this, Dave nervously chuckled and turned bright red, "Okay, that's a first. I've never mentioned the 'm' word, ever. My family calls me the perpetual bachelor."

Sissy shrugged it off and nonchalantly looked around their table to try to take some heat off of Dave. She thought to herself, *I haven't said anything weird or embarrassing to run you off, and I'll be damned if you're gonna run your own self off!* Sissy took a larger sip with more confidence from her mug, "I'm used to weird things that happen just around me for some strange reason. It's no big deal, really."

The waitress walked up to the couple with a notepad and a pink feather pen in her hand. Dave picked up his menu, "You ready to order?"

Sissy giggled, "Why? You ready to get rid of me?"

Dave put the menu back down, "No, no. We can wait."

Sissy said in a flirtatious manner, "It was a joke. Let's order. You know what's good here?"

"Yeah. I like the Philly cheese steak with fries. Their house beer is better than the lager, which is what I'm going to order next. You don't mind if I have a couple of drinks do ya'?"

Sissy put her menu down as if her search were over, "Nope, I'll have the same."

The waitress asked Dave if they wanted one ticket, which Dave affirmed. The man smiled as if he were impressed, "What? No salad, and then eating all of my food?"

Sissy turned and looked over her shoulder at Dave, "No. I want to be really immature and say I could probably drink you under the table, too."

Dave had a sudden glint in his eye, "I want to be really immature and say, 'Yeah, 'cause you're passed out.' Damn these college students. They're contagious, aren't they?"

Sissy leaned forward, "Imagine being a woman, surrounded by girls with eating disorders wearing clothes that I couldn't afford until I was in my thirties in sizes I haven't worn since elementary school."

Dave leaned in toward Sissy and then leaned back in his

chair, "I live in Basley Hall off of Yarbrough Street, and all I ever hear is 'Oh, I'm soooo drunk!' and the hooting. What is with that?"

Sissy mimicked his body language, "Rebel mating yell? Sorority girl mating call?"

Dave genuinely laughed, seeming to be surprised at Sissy's wit, "That's funny."

Sissy finished her lager with gusto, "Just wait 'till I get some food and a little beer in me. I'm a riot. Just remember to ask me and I'll tell you so."

Dave finished his lager and then rubbed his chin, "I thought you said you could hold your liquor."

Sissy pushed her empty mug toward the side of the table, "Mmm-hmmm, I hold it. A little tipsy. Relaxed, but adequately held."

Dave pushed his glass beside Sissy's until they touched, "Ah, I see."

Sissy held her hand to her chest to suppress a burp, but hoped it wasn't obvious, "So, why are you in Athens? I, mean, people from Flemming seem to think their town is the end-all-be-all or something."

Dave waved his hand at Sissy as if to shush her, "Ah, Camiella's okay. Small. I know everybody, which, gets old. I've been going to school here, taking time off to work on my PhD and get away."

Sissy waggled her head to flirt some more, "PhD in?"

Dave wiped a bead of sweat from his brow, "Oh, yeah. Agri-business. I was working in Flemming under a grant that ran out."

Sissy felt confused, "And, how will a PhD help you?"

Dave smiled a confident smile as if he had all the right answers, "I can write my own grants. Publish my own opinions. Be a college professor if I'm truly useless."

Sissy ticked her head to the side in approval, "Makes sense."

Dave maintained his confident grin at Sissy, "I've got this year and that's it. Then I have to figure it all out."

The waitress returned with their house beers and food. The food smelled hot and delicious. The beers were served in frosted mugs. The waitress asked in a professional tone, "Get you anything else?" The couple both shook their heads "no" and the waitress politely exited back into the bar.

Sissy sniffed the beer and noted that it had a crisp, clean scent to it and was excited that Dave may have introduced her to something she liked. She took a sip and let out an "mmm," and said "Sounds kind of anti-climactic."

Dave looked for Sissy's reaction to the beer. She seemed to like it, so he sipped some of his own, "Maybe. But, what am I gonna do with a PhD in agri-business in Athens?"

Sissy wrinkled her brow, "Does that mean you're going back to Flemming?"

Dave opened his palms, "I dunno. Think about it. S'where my network is, so it'd be the easiest place to get work."

Sissy sipped her beer and looked around their surroundings. The open air cafes, the annoying students, the beautiful architecture, and the mingling smells of cooking food. It was a nice scene and she didn't want it to end. She didn't know how she felt about meeting a man she'd either have to follow or let go in a year.  Sissy shrugged her shoulders, "I don't know what it'd take to make me move back.  I'm not originally from there.  I'm from Atlanta, so."

Dave never took his eyes off of Sissy and watched her look around.  He sipped his beer and nodded his head as if he were somehow suddenly enlightened, "So you never really got to be on the 'inside.'  Single, working woman, too.  You were just begging to be ostracized."

Sissy drifted to some old memories of Mr. Taylor with his dip in his cheek, "Yeah, but, I never really knew while I was there."

Dave looked down at his food with a little dismay, "That's actually as good as it gets.
If they didn't like you, you definitely would've known."  Then he picked up his cheese steak and took a bite.  After swallowing most of it he said, "Besides, this town has it all.  Even this little restaurant has its own microbrewery thing going on.  I'm gonna miss this."

Sissy sliced her sandwich into pieces to start eating hers, "Especially since Flemming's dry.  You ever drive to Newbury?"

Dave washed down his bite with some beer and motioned for the waitress.  When she came near, he pointed to their beer glasses and threw up two fingers.  The waitress nodded and went back inside the restaurant.  "What, to 'the-crappiest-little-liquor-store-in-America?'
It works in a pinch."

Sissy picked up a bite of her sandwich on her fork and pointed it at Dave before putting it in her mouth, "Damn straight."  She chewed, swallowed and snickered, "They stay open until twelve o'clock midnight on Saturday nights, too." Sissy felt really embarrassed.

Dave seemed to be a nice guy, and she didn't want the emphasis of their date to be about alcohol. What kind of a father would he make? Then again, what kind of a mother would she make? Why were her thoughts immediately going there? The questions made Sissy's chest tight and she began to feel self-conscious.

Dave steadily devoured his sandwich and said in between bites, "But you gotta look out for Newbury drunks. They'll run you off the road, turning their blue lights on and all."

Sissy laughed, "If it weren't for the liquor store, the roads through there would still be dirt!" Dave's retort put her mind at ease. If anything, he seemed to not mind the fact that he was on a date with a woman who had no real clue about dating. The waitress brought two mugs over to Dave. Dave gave the first mug to Sissy, who hadn't even finished her second mug. He took the last mug and thanked the waitress, who looked around the table and walked off.

Dave grinned from ear to ear, sat back in his chair and took a big swig of his third mug of beer, "Hold on, now. Don't forget the fine grocery establishment of Ruby's. Where else you gonna get W.C. Cola in a glass bottle, cold . . . on ice . . . in a metal tub?"

Sissy polished off her second mug of beer to begin her third, "This is true. I'd never pondered the scarcity of W.C. Cola before in my life."

Dave let out a soft burp into his closed fist, which Sissy would have thought to be gross from someone else. But he had a way of doing it that seemed almost regal, as if everything he did was genteel and correct, "Came up in one of my business history classes. I actually had to write a paper on the economic value of W.C. Cola and Astro Pies in relationship to southern agriculture."

Sissy finished her second beer to start on her third. She was feeling tipsy, warm, and very comfortable talking to this man she just met. She felt as if they were old childhood friends who never really lost touch with each other and were merely picking up an old conversation. She put both of her elbows on the table and crossed her arms. Then she dreamily put her head into her left hand. "Damn. You mean there is such a thing?"

Dave looked at Sissy's missing finger, but never batted an eye, "Yeah. Apparently, they helped fuel the small farm economy by supplying field hands with an economic meal, not to mention the caloric . . . never mind."

Sissy strummed her fingers on her cheek and thought Dave was looking into her eyes. She grinned, "I hope you got published for all of that."

Dave put his hands under the table and looked at his own right hand, wiggling the middle finger and looked back up at Sissy, "I got a 'B,' the bastard. He didn't like one of my references."

Sissy let out her trademark tipsy snicker, the same laugh that had been very popular with the gals at "Jade," who seemed to take it as a cue to start buying shots. She snickered out, "Why?"

Dave laughed into his beer mug, "It was my grandpa." Dave put his mug down and wiped his lips, "I was one source short, so I used him for an interview."

Sissy made her hand into a fist and waved it into the air, putting on a fake Spanish accent, "*Bay-stard!*" Then she sipped more of her beer and mused into the swirling suds, "Anyway, I'm impressed. It's not every day you meet a man who fully appreciates the value of a W.C. Cola and an Astro Pie."

Dave laughed and Sissy thought she caught that glimmer in his eye that told her he was really attracted to her. Sissy found him to be smart, and the fact that he laughed at her jokes sent her into a veritable euphoria.

Dave finished almost all of his sandwich and wiped his mouth, "I just don't know how this date can get any better. And, I don't know about you, but I am really enjoying myself."

Sissy took another bite, swallowed, and answered his question, "I'm enjoying myself, just sitting here with you, being myself. Ya' know, I never understood all of those dating rules and . . . polite feminine bullshit."

Dave just laughed, "God, you're refreshing!"

The realtor finished off her sandwich and cocked her eyebrow at Dave, "Thank you, I think."

Dave reached out and touched her hand on the table, "No, really. It's a compliment." Then he sat back in his chair and laughed. He paused with his eyes closed as if he were having funny flashbacks, "Most women I've dated at our age just try too hard. It's like they're in 'desperation mode,' which . . . is just damned creepy."

Sissy let out an audible huff, "My boss must've thought I was in 'desperation mode.' She's the one who suggested I place an ad."

Dave reached over to her hand again and touched it, "Well, I'm glad you did. We've been together all of an hour and I feel . . ."

Sissy sipped her third beer and held her breath in anticipation of Dave really being some sort of psychotic stalker.

"Comfortable with you."

Sissy let out an audible sigh of relief, "That's sweet."

Dave leaned toward Sissy, "You really want to go to a movie?"

Sissy looked around and said with a coquettish grin, "I have a friend who owns a bar where we could get some free drinks."

Dave laughed and clapped his hands together, "My God, you're a wonderful woman."

Sissy leaned in even closer and said in a hushed tone, "It's a lesbian bar."

Dave put his hands on his face, "My God, you're truly a wonderful woman."

Sissy sat back and grinned with her eyes closed and her face toward the dimming sunlight. Then she eyed Dave with only one eye open, "Then we could walk down the streets yelling about how drunk *we* are afterwards."

Dave got up, walked over to Sissy, motioned for her to get up, and slid her chair under for her, before taking her arm. She started walking in the direction of Jade. Dave leaned into Sissy in a playful manner and asked, "So, not that I have a problem with it or anything. In fact, it's kinda cool on you, but I was wondering. What happened to your finger?"

Sissy leaned back and whispered into Dave's ear, "Rattlesnake."

Dave laughed, "Hell, you are my kinda woman." He threw his free arm into the air as if to catch falling coins, "Can it get any better than this?"

## Chapter 31: Needs Some TLC

Apparently, it did get better. Dave asked for a second date. And another. And another. He called her just to see how her day went. He answered the phone when Sissy called. He was respectful to the waiters. He opened doors for her. He stayed over later and later, but never pushed himself on her. Sissy set boundaries the best she could, but she was ready to check off that kids-and-a-picket-fence list *now*. Finally, the day arrived. They made love. And it was amazing. Dave wasn't Sissy's boyfriend; he was her soul mate. They were inseparable.

Having so much in common, they naturally did everything together. Sissy wound up paying for a lot of it because Dave was temporarily a poor student, but she didn't mind. He was worth it.

Sissy loved Dave's attention. She started getting her nails and hair done, buying nicer clothes, better makeup, and, for the first time, really expensive lingerie. In return, he took her to dinner when he could. Her dinners were nicer because she could afford it. Just like she could afford the mountain getaway - - he bought some groceries and the alcohol. She could afford the nicer clothes she liked seeing him wear, which he would have never bought himself because he wasn't as materialistic as she. But even that didn't really matter. Sissy just wanted more time with Dave.

So, after only four months of dating, Sissy and Dave decided to move in together. However, her apartment was too small, and his dorm was, well, a dorm. The two of them decided to buy a house, because it would be cheaper than renting. And Sissy finally realized her bank account had dwindled. Dating Dave had inadvertently become her fulltime job. So, it would have to be starter home until she could build her finances up again.

A house just made sense, too. If they left after a year, they could easily sell it to either make a profit or break even. But for Sissy, it would be neutral territory. A place to practice all of the things she only recently wanted with her whole being. Ever since her ovaries kicked her in the butt, she couldn't think of anything but babies. Sissy hid this from Dave even though it made her just want to talk about it twenty-four/seven with him. Besides, her periods were becoming heavier, more painful, and more frequent. What if she were going through early menopause and her time for childbearing was running out? She couldn't scare off the only decent prospect she had since she started looking.

***

One bright, sunny, summer, Sunday afternoon, Sissy grabbed the keys to several houses, and was determined to find something they both could agree on, especially since her ovaries were knocking hard in her empty belly, begging her to "get on with it, already!" Sissy was a woman with a mission, house first, marriage second, and that damn maternal clock stopped third.

And if Dave should decide not to propose? She'd pop the question. And if he should turn her down? She'd be sure to have only her name on the deed and make him pay rent, all the better to kick him out with, should he foolishly decide to turn her down. That was the plan, and whether or not Dave suspected a thing, Sissy cared not. Biology was taking over, and her shrewd business instincts were being held hostage by overpowering levels of estrogen. These babies needed to be born; it was her soul's mission. Or so she told herself.

After looking at a couple of "handy man specials" in crime

ridden neighborhoods, Sissy and her beau pulled into the driveway of what looked to be the ugliest eyesore in Athens.

A faded sea foam green Knox Box with doo-doo brown trim. The red brick underpinning looked as if the green vinyl siding took a crap and smeared it all over to the ground. To complete the look was a rusted single carport filled with cardboard boxes full of painting accessories and opened paint cans. The only endearing aspect to the entire lot was a well maintained flower bed full of peonies in the front yard. Dave was the first to let out a sigh of frustration. Sissy's heart sank and she wondered if they'd ever be able to find anything in their price range. After all, most of Dave's loans were unsubsidized, so he borrowed as little as possible, and didn't work so he could completely focus on his studies and finish quicker.

She refused to be house poor or dependent on another human being, so low mortgage was the game plan.

Sensing Dave's frustration, Sissy pleaded with him, "Can we just see what it looks like on the inside? This neighborhood's better than the others."

Dave just slowly exhaled and got out of the truck.

Sissy unlocked the box on the side entrance and pushed the newly painted door open. Because the occupants were away on their honeymoon and had not found a new house, they had left all of their furniture. The door opened to the living room, which was brightly decorated in deep jewel tones, matching a plaid sofa, but not the dark brown hand-me-down recliner. The coffee table was a whimsical antique and the Oriental rug was surprisingly nice. Even the vent and outlet covers were brass. The ruby red walls and cherry stained hardwood floors were refinished by the semiskilled newlyweds, but all of it looked original to the house, lovingly worn and lived in. Even Dave was impressed.

He walked over to the sofa and plopped down on it. The silly man closed one eye shut and began acting as if he were flipping through channels on the TV, "Man, I never had anything like this when I was in college. Not even the second go around."

Sissy was too busy envisioning toddlers running around to notice Dave's antics, "Do you think they had planned to stay here?"

Dave shrugged, "Looks like it to me. They put a lot of work into it."

Sissy motioned for Dave to move his legs and sat beside him on the couch, "Well, they're desperate to sell. He took a job up north."

Dave stopped flipping through pretend channels and gave Sissy a perplexed look, "Why didn't he get a job here and stay in the house?"

Sissy shrugged and imagined a munchkin sitting in between them, wearing soft baby clothes. She patted the empty spot on the sofa. "Beats me. I'd stay. There's no way I'd sand floors only to move and sell the house below its value."

Dave let out a snicker, "Kids."

The only bathroom was newly painted, too, and adequate. Sissy wanted the tub replaced, but Dave suggested they not invest too much into the house until they saw what the neighborhood would be like. Sissy felt exhilarated and hopeful . . . maybe Dave would not return to Flemming after all.

The guest bedroom was painted a bright, glaring pink with pure white trim. A flower print bedspread covered the bed and a white painted chest covered in hand painted flowers sat daintily in the room on industrial grade carpet. Dave hated the cheap carpeting, "We could finish the job on sanding the floors. I mean, if a couple of kids can do it, we can too, right?"

Sissy just quickly turned her back and nodded in the affirmative; she desperately wanted to hide her wide toothy grin.

The next room was small and currently being used as a study. The walls were painted what Dave thought was supposed to be Confederate blue and the room itself was covered in handmade model boats and airplanes ranging from various periods of history. Civil War books lined the bookshelves. Handmade curtains with antique airplanes covered the windows. Dave loved the study and seemed to audibly salivate.

Sissy teased him, "I don't know. It's too manly. They definitely didn't plan on having kids in this house."

Dave was oblivious to Sissy's hint and just answered without thinking, "This would have been a good size for a nursery. And I didn't say anything about that god awful pink color." Sissy could sense that Dave had already territorially pissed on the study and to hint at taking it away might have proved to be a deal breaker.

The biggest bedroom was last on the hall. The walls of this bedroom brooded back at Sissy and Dave. Sissy didn't like the dark, green-black wall color, but Dave loved it. He called it "relaxing."

Lastly, Sissy wandered into the kitchen, which led to the front yard. The kitchen was huge, or at least, huge to Sissy, who preferred dining out to cooking. Her idea of baking had always involved a tube of pre-made synthetic tasting cookie dough and a dull knife, just for safety's sake, and a warped cookie sheet her mother had given her in college. Still, all of the appliances were staying, and if she ever *wanted* to learn how to cook, she could definitely do it in the sprawling kitchen and its loads of counter space and spacious cabinetry.

Dave had commandeered the house showing and was still visibly excited about the house, "Let's see what the yards look like."

Dave unbolted all of the locks and politely opened the outside kitchen door for Sissy and held his hands for her to exit first. Immediately upon stepping out of the kitchen, they were met by a tall crap-brown concrete wall with decorative open spaces filled with seashells. The wall stood just four feet from the house, creating a narrow privacy cranny. An old lounge chair and a bottle of forgotten tanning lotion kept company with a rusted-out Weber grill. Concrete stepping stones did not completely cover the ground, but made a strange design, making it difficult to walk.

Dave saw Sissy's disappointment with the entrance and tried to make light of the situation, "Maybe they thought we'd like to finish the patio ourselves," he chuckled. Sissy only grunted.

Around the wall was the front flower bed full of large pink peonies, supported by tomato cages. A healthy line of border plants made a lovely dark green and purple petal border around the peonies. However, a strange straight line of plucked peony petals lined the yard from the paved driveway all the way around to the back of the house, which Dave followed like a curious little child.

Dave motioned his hand for Sissy to follow him, "This is weird. They end at the fence by this big, old, fig tree."

Sissy shrugged, "I told you strange things happen around

me."

Dave looked over at Sissy and put his hand to his chin, "Why would somebody go to the trouble to line the front of the house with rose petals?"

Sissy stared at the gnarled fig tree and blandly corrected him, "Peonies."

Dave kicked at a petal on the ground, "Pee on *knees*?"

Sissy shook her head, "That's what they're called, 'peonies.'"

Dave picked up another petal and sniffed it, "Oh, well. They're too pretty to tear up like this, you know?"

Sissy squinted her eyes at the fig tree and tried to see if she could read any sort of energy from it, "Well, we won't have to tear them up if you don't want to." She could sense nothing from the tree, but the petals left her feeling suspicious. Maybe the "bargain" was too good to be true. Sissy decided to put such things out of her mind. Being around Dave gave her the safest feeling in the whole world, as if just his presence were enough to keep her safe from *everything*.

Dave handed the petal to Sissy and started walking to the front yard, "I like the house. It's all ugly on the outside, like an anti-theft device, and all nice on the inside, which is all that really matters."

Sissy pointed to the house with a look of repugnance, "I'm getting rid of that ugly vomit green vinyl siding and shit brown trim."

Dave's eyes opened widely, "That's even better. And when we get ready to sell, our repairs will increase the value of the house."

Sissy looked around at the neighborhood, "I hate to say it, but I wonder if any exterior improvements would be appreciated by this crowd."

Dave just walked over to the frowning realtor and put his arms around her shoulders, "Are you kidding? They wouldn't even notice."

"Until the property taxes increased."

Dave grabbed Sissy and snuggled her into his side, "Or ours stayed the same and we'd have the best looking house in the neighborhood."

Sissy was not amused, "Whoo-hoo."

Dave used his weight to swivel Sissy around. Normally she hated any sort of pulling or tugging, even if it were playful. But when Dave did it, she enjoyed it. He felt manly to her and solid when he did it. Dave didn't let go of his hold on Sissy and walked forward, "Come on. Let's look at the back yard and the shed."

The junky carport led to a gate that held the most undesirable back yard Sissy had ever seen. The yard was level for a few feet before it plummeted to the adjacent back yard in a red-clay mudslide. Grass grew in pathetic little spurts of tender tufts and huge dog prints holding mashed brown grass sprigs dotted the upper part of the yard. A tangle of ivy that appeared to be a few feet deep matted over itself, rolling down the slope of the back half of the yard.

However, Dave didn't seem to care and took a seat in a brown painted swing and patted his hand on the bench to signal for Sissy to sit beside him. Sissy hesitated. Dave just goofily grinned, making the realtor's estrogen driven heart melt. Squishing into mud produced by midmorning summer showers, the realtor daintily stepped across the yard and felt her feet trying to slide out from beneath her. Once secure in the frame of the swing and Dave's outstretched arm, Sissy checked her new loafers for damage.

Dave gave Sissy a tender squeeze, "You didn't grow up in the country, did you?"

Sissy didn't look up from her loafers and began inspecting her jeans, "Oh, how could you tell?"

Dave took a deep breath, "Well, the yard needs some work, but I can do it."

Sissy put her hand over her forehead and looked over the width of the yard around them, "The yard needs to be leveled with a bomb and put out of its misery."

Dave dug the tip of his tennis shoe into the clay, "Nah. You've got no vision, woman."

Sissy shrugged and let Dave hold her with his heavy arm around her shoulder, "Hey, as long as it's your project, and I don't have to get involved."

The couple sat in the swing and lightly pushed the ground with their feet. The pecan trees produced a dark shade and made for an otherwise peaceful atmosphere.

Dave tried to sell the house, "I don't hear any scary noises like car alarms going off or gunfire."

Sissy sarcastically replied, "Yeah, car alarms and gunfire, scary. Well, to be honest, the students have gone home for the summer and the natives are probably all sleeping off a nice middle-class-blue-collar drunk."

Dave snickered, "After all of that liquor I saw you throw

back last night, you're one to talk."

Sissy looked over at him and playfully said, "Maybe."

Dave stopped the swing from moving, took a deep breath and paused before saying, "I like the house, Sissy. I'll make it look better. Even the yard."

Sissy didn't want to answer. The adjacent fig tree made her wonder and the deliberately placed peony petals were odd. Sissy wanted to stall. She looked around and saw a tiny shed, "Let's look at the shed. You know, I always said you could tell a lot about a house by its shed."

Dave bought the lie, "Really?"

"No, but let's look at the shed anyway."

Dave stepped heavily into the mud like a true country boy and held up Sissy, who skidded and almost made them both fall. The shed had a concrete pathway, but it led out to a dog pen in the middle of the level part of the yard. There was a lock on the door, but it wasn't pushed shut completely, so the couple undid the lock and ushered themselves into the dark, dank shed. Sissy felt a very cold spot inside and it made her shiver.

Dave grabbed her arm, thinking she was going to slip and fall again, "You've got goose bumps. You're not afraid of a little ol' shed are you?"

Sissy rubbed her arms, "Remind me to tell you a story about a little ol' shed some time." Sissy grabbed Dave's arm and felt her missing right middle finger wrap around his arm with the rest of her fingers. That "ghost finger" had become a "ghost alarm" and immediately she knew something was amiss, "I don't like this place. I want to leave."

Dave acted as if he didn't hear her and reached in the dark

for a light switch. Once he found it, he turned on the light, "Did you say something?"

Sissy was mad because she knew he had intentionally ignored her, but before she could retort, she saw a pentagram painted in red spray paint on the far wall of the shed and pointed, "That's rather ominous looking."

Dave looked at it and turned around, making a bad Dracula impersonation complete with fake Transylvanian accent, "Ah, ha! That explains it! They were Say-tan-ists!"

Sissy pushed the silly man away, "This shed is really cold for a June afternoon."

"So? Maybe it's well insulated."

"Who insulates a shed? And why aren't they using this? I mean, it'd help make the car shed look a lot better. If I were their realtor, I'd make them clean up that car port and sell for a lot more money."

"Well, thank God you're not, because now we can afford the place."

Sissy felt for her missing finger and touched the stub. She scratched her arm with her right hand and felt her missing finger scrape her skin, "I don't like the shed."

Dave put his hands on Sissy's shoulders as if he were anchoring her there, "So, you'll never have to use it, then."

Despite Dave's weight on her shoulders, Sissy felt as if she were being pushed out of the shed and quickly dislodged his grip and stepped out onto the concrete path.

Dave held out his hands in slight frustration, "Where are you going?"

Sissy wrung her face with her hands and then pointed

inside, "I don't like the shed."

Dave huffed. He tapped his foot and angrily said, "Fine, then, let's go. We're never going to find a place. I'll just go back to my dorm, all alone, and you'll go back to your tiny apartment, all alone."

Sissy quickly walked to her car and waited for Dave, because he said "let's go," so she figured he would be following right behind her. After a few minutes, Sissy began to worry and went back to the shed to look for him. Inside the shed, she found Dave cleaning cobwebs from around the boards with his bare hands, "Stop that! What are you doing?"

Dave just looked blankly at Sissy, "Huh?"

Sissy pulled his arm down and touched his face, "You're going to get bit by a black widow or something."

Dave picked the cobwebs from between his fingers and shuddered, "God, I hate spiders. What the hell was I thinking?"

"I don't like this shed."

"Well, the first thing I'm going to do is cover up that damn hexagram thing with some paint and put up some spider traps."

"Let's go. Please."

"Yeah, okay, but I really like the house. It would make a great investment property. A great first house until the kids got big."

And with that, Sissy was sold.

## Chapter 32: Cut It Out

A month later the papers were all signed and contracts bound. Sissy owned a 1940s Knox Box with foam green vinyl siding and "shit brown" trim on a quarter acre of land, more and more of which sat in the neighbor's back yard after each good rain. A few of Dave's strapping, young, twenty-something buddies from school helped him move all of their things within a weekend. The shed still gave Sissy the creeps and she tried dropping hints that Dave should just tear it down in addition to the other upgrades. All of the bedroom floors needed to have their industrial grade carpet taken up and floors refinished. And in their free time (which was somewhere between work, school, sex, and socializing, but not always in that order), Sissy and Dave visited various building supply places, home improvement stores, and independent contractors, pricing the cost of new vinyl siding.

The house was spacious and homey feeling. The neighbors were quiet and kept to themselves. But, whether out on the town or shopping or chatting with the semi-social neighbors, everyone Dave and Sissy met thought they were married, or at least should be.

Sissy was enamored with Dave, her job, the new house, and life in general, even the pain from her biological clock that woke her at night seemed less frustrating. Then the duo actually started working on the house itself.

One weekend, Sissy and Dave painted the bathroom and put up a new shower curtain. All the while discussing taking up the carpet, sanding floors, and putting in new linoleum in the kitchen. Later that night, Dave was studying and downing a cold beer in his armchair, as usual, when he walked into the back of the house and didn't return. Not hearing any water run from the bathroom, Sissy became curious and looked for him. In the pink bedroom, Sissy found Dave tearing up the carpet like a fiend, cutting with a large knife he used out in the yard to cut back vines and tall woody weeds. The floor was a mess and Dave looked obsessed, which frightened Sissy a little, "Economics get to you?"

A stern eye glared up at Sissy, "It's not economics. It's agro-economics. I'd already taken economics back when I was a freshman."

Dave's response was completely uncalled for. Still, Sissy didn't want a fight, so she congenially asked, "Does that give you a good reason to tear up the carpet?"

Dave didn't bother to acknowledge Sissy, rather he continued to cut away at the carpet, "I don't like this carpet. I never have. It's cheap and uncomfortable to walk on. I'm sick of looking at it."

Under her breath Sissy muttered, "Or something." If Dave heard her, he wasn't going to waste his time with her. Not one to like being ignored, Sissy tried to change the overall mood of the conversation with a show in interest, "How does the floor look underneath?"

Dave's severity didn't let up an inch, "I can't tell. There's this awful black pad in the way."

Hoping that optimism and good moods are contagious, Sissy offered a suggestion, "Pull it up?"

Dave wasn't giving in any. His bad mood was as stubborn as he was, "I can't. It's glued. Every last damn inch of it is glued."

Feigning empathy, Sissy tried to console her boyfriend, "Oh, my."

Dave merely muttered with scathing sarcasm, "No kidding."

"Well, shouldn't you be studying? I mean, that's . . . "

With no warning, Dave yelled out, "I'm sick of this carpet! Have you heard a single fucking thing I've had to say?"

Sissy was shocked. Unable to feel anger because her feelings had gone temporarily numb, Sissy backed out of the room as one would from a cornered animal. In a soft, submissive voice, Sissy said, "Okay, fine. Just don't yell, okay? Do whatever it is you've got to do."

Sissy returned to the living room, stayed up a couple more hours, and browsed through Dave's agro-economics book, while finishing off his beer, channel surfing, and feeling quite hurt. Not being familiar with relationships, she didn't know how to approach Dave about her feelings. The more she flipped through the channels, the angrier she became. Rather than confront Dave for his rude behavior, Sissy decided to send her message by ignoring him and went to bed without speaking to him.

Early the next morning, Sissy awoke in an empty bed. She always rose before Dave, who didn't have classes until eleven in the morning. Curiosity filled the realtor, who began to imagine where on earth he could be and what on earth he could be doing. Her imagination ranged from scenarios of him making her breakfast in an attempt to apologize for his irrational behavior the night before, to him leaving in the middle of the night because he was secretly seeing someone else.

Racing against her heart to throw on one of her many

casual dress suits, Sissy stormed out of her bedroom and headed straight for the kitchen. There was no sign of Dave. Perhaps he had fallen asleep on the couch, so she checked the living room, but no Dave. Maybe he was in the bathroom. Nope. So, her suspicions about the other woman were being confirmed more and more! But when she looked out of the kitchen window while making coffee, Dave's car was still in the carport. So, at least he was in the house.

Sissy walked down the hall and tried to open the door to the pink room, but it wouldn't budge. Recognizing that Dave was the obstacle, Sissy called out his name in a gruff voice and flapped the door over and over again against the man's sleeping body.

Finally, Dave awoke and in a groggy, confused tone asked, "Huh? What? Sissy?"

"Yeah, Dave, it's me. Roll away from the door, Son, roll away from the door."
Sissy began pulling the door toward her and pushing it into Dave over and over again to be playful.

Dave was most inappreciative of his wake-up call, "Damn, you're beating me with it. Stop! Stop!"

However, Sissy was enjoying herself, "Roll away from the door, Dave."

"Okay, give me a minute. Stop hitting me with the door, dammit, Sissy!"

"Just making sure you're awake," Sissy giggled even though she was still mad about his behavior the night before and since she might not get an apology out of him, she figured she could make him suffer a little. The door completely opened, and Dave stood up, holding his back and rubbing his neck. The scene inside of the room was frightening, "You spent the whole night tearing up the carpet and scraping that black stuff . . . ?"

Dave just groaned, "Yeah, I guess. I feel like I used a butter knife."

"Looks like you sprouted claws and used the floor for a sharpener."

"I'm too sore to go to class."

Sissy was confused, "Why'd you do this? I would've helped you. And we could've gotten the right tools."

Dave's tone showed his personal confusion, "I don't know. It was just one of those things."

Sissy was not ready to accept "one of those things" and felt hurt by his flippancy. Did he not remember how badly he behaved the night before? Sissy decided he needed a reminder, "Well, maybe . . . but you still acted like a complete asshole last night."

The look on Dave's face showed that he felt as if he were being attacked, "How?"

Not wanting to hurt the man's feelings, Sissy said softly under her voice, "Yelling at me."

A completely different Dave, rather, the original, good ol' Dave looked up at Sissy with apologetic eyes. He tenderly reached his hand out to Sissy and touched her on her shoulder, "I'm sorry. I don't remember doing that. I don't remember hardly anything past surfing between the news and pop music TV."

Sissy felt as if she were going to cry, "But you did and now you're going to miss a day of lecture."

Dave stretched out his back, arms in the air. After popping his neck, he sniffed his armpits, "It was just . . . (sniff) . . . one of those things. I can't explain it. God, I am beat. I need to sleep in the bed."

The look on Sissy's face was one of disgust and surprise, "Even so, you should apologize."

Dave winced. Apparently, he stank. He farted. Loudly. Pulling at his groin, Dave asked, "I did. But, what are you upset about? Me tearing up some ugly carpet?"

Between the conversation and Dave's caveman antics, Sissy was appalled, "No! For yelling at me!"

Dave let out a distinct fart and fanned it away. He said in a nonchalant manner, "Now *you're* yelling."

"EWWW!!!" Sissy screeched before storming off to the bathroom to put on her make-up. Her anger from the night before was doubled and she contemplated throwing Dave out on his ear. After the mess he made in the guest bedroom and the way he acted, Sissy felt that he more than deserved it. Still, she didn't want him to go. He kept her from being lonely and gave her something to do. Besides, she told herself, he didn't always act like that. Something had just gotten into him. Sissy snickered as she thought to herself, *Thought that sorta thing only happened to me.*

When Sissy got home from work, the house smelled like muscle-rub ointment. An empty pizza box sat wide open beside the garbage can, and a scattered line of empty beer cans led the way to the bedroom. Apparently, Dave did not leave the house all day and had decided to eat and drink his pain away while soaking in a muscle ointment bath.

"Are you trying to seduce me with that attractive litter of beer cans, because I'd prefer rose petals." Sissy stood in the doorway and looked over at her boyfriend. She wanted everything to go back to what it was just a few weeks before when they playfully bantered back and forth, laughed, and made love.

Dave lay in bed with his arm over his head. It would not have surprised Sissy if he had a hangover, "It's not funny Sissy, I'm in pain. I think I pulled every muscle in my body."

Sissy walked over to Dave and slapped him on his side, "Hey! That's my side of the bed."

Dave didn't budge, "I feel more comfortable on this side of the bed. I think it's your mattress."

Swapping sides of the bed without asking was just a veritable sacrilege. It was probably written down somewhere in the Live-In Bible, "Thou shalt not swap sides of the bed without asking." Sissy was mad, "That's a new mattress. I like sleeping on this side!"

Dave kept his arm over his head, but pointed toward the wall, "Well, the extension cord was easier to plug in on this side."

First the bed, and now her beloved heating pad? Dave was treading treacherous water. Taking a deep breath to steady her nerves, Sissy asked, "Are you using my heating pad? You better not get that smelly-rub-stuff on my new heating pad. I'm going to need it tonight. You know that."

Dave rolled onto his side and wrapped the covers around his head like a gypsy. In a whiny voice he said, "Go get a new one. I need it and I'm not moving. I don't think I can. Oh! I hurt so bad."

"It's your own fault. At least you could have put the pizza box and your beer cans in the garbage."

"I'm sorry. Please don't yell at me. I don't feel good."

"I'm leaving."

Dave responded with a loud snore.

Sissy stupidly waited for Dave to make a real reply, but the man was truly out cold.

The alcohol had finally taken effect and he was momentarily in a drunken sleep, safe from the aches of his body and the pain of his nagging girlfriend. Sissy went to the mall and fell into her old habit of trying to pick up men in the bookstore. Unfortunately, there weren't any worth picking up, even though a few months earlier she would have thought otherwise. After shopping and browsing for a couple of hours in various stores, Sissy decided to go find herself a new heating pad, because if Dave really were in as much pain as he complained of, she knew she wouldn't be getting hers back.

Stopping in the mall's pharmacy, because she didn't feel like driving all the way to the local Big-Mart, Sissy looked high and low for a heating pad, but couldn't find one. Finally, she decided to ask the pharmacist, who turned out to be a fatherly looking elderly man who moved with a slow hobble and proved to have a penchant for prying.

Sissy asked the pharmacist, "Got any heating pads?"

"Yes. We keep them back here to save shelf space. You know, you could find one a lot cheaper at Big-Mart."

"Yeah, I know, but I don't want to go to the trouble of Big-Mart traffic."

"Mind me asking what you need it for?"

"No, I get these pains in my lower abdomen at night, and this helps. Plus, my boyfriend's got mine."

"Mmm. You might want to get that checked."

"I think it's just my biological clock going haywire on me. It'll be alright."

"Like, I said, you might wanna get that checked. Could be anything from cysts to cancer. How's your period been lately?"

Sissy felt her face turn a deep, deep red, "It's been . . . you know? I think I'll call my doctor tomorrow."

The pharmacist chuckled, "I didn't mean to get in your business. Just my daughter had surgery not too long ago for that sort of thing. If it had gone unchecked, she wouldn't've been able to have kids. Lucky thing she . . ."

Sissy didn't want to hear anymore and cut the man off, "Yeah, well, thanks for the advice. I'll call tomorrow."

Sissy paid an exorbitant fee for the convenience of not having to fight traffic and drove home. It was late and she hoped Dave would be up, worrying about her. Instead, Sissy came home to a Dave who was in much better spirits, having metabolized the alcohol he imbibed, and watching TV in the living room with white splotches of muscle ointment around his ears. He grinned at her momentarily and went back to flipping through the channels.

Sissy was irked at the sight, but was in need of conversation, "Well, I got my heating pad."

Dave didn't look at Sissy, but continued flipping through the channels, "Huh? Oh, yeah. Good."

"Went by the mall," Sissy said, hoping to pull a conversation from Dave.

"I wish I'd a known you were headed out that way, I would've sent you to the movie store; there's nothing on TV."

"Mmmm." So much for being worried about. At least she was needed . . . as a gopher. Sissy audibly stomped to the bathroom and started her bath. A strange smell emanated from the tub. A rotten smell that she had not ever noticed before. The water ran hot and steam began to permeate the room and fog the mirror as Sissy took off her make-up. Without testing the water, the distraught woman *sploshed* into the tub and felt the scalding hot water tingle her legs and turn her skin a glowing red. Sissy loved it. If she could have turned her tiny little tub into a Jacuzzi full of scalding hot water and submerged every inch of herself, she would have. *This is just what I need. Stupid man. You'd think he was having his period or something.*

Easing down into the deep end of the shallow tub, Sissy found the fiberglass to be stone cold, as if none of the heat from the water could warm it. Her bottom was freezing, but her feet were so hot she had to hang them over the side of the tub to cool. This was unpleasant to say the least. Still, the realtor was determined to enjoy a steaming hot bath, and so she turned herself around and sat at the opposite end of the tub. Her hinny was warm, but the spout poked her in the back, which then made her feet cold. Dave opened the bathroom door and found Sissy in this awkward position.

"What are you doing?" Dave said in a sarcastic tone. Sissy thought that if Dave had the balls to add the word, "Weirdo," she would have minded his barging in through the bathroom door less.

"Trying to enjoy my bath. Did you drop something down the drain?"

"What?"

"The tub drain. Did . . . you . . . drop . . . something? Like a dead mouse?" Sissy knew she was just reacting to his tone and didn't enjoy being sarcastic with him. Instead, she felt as if she were potentially poking a sleeping dog in speaking to him in this manner.

In an angry and intimidating tone Dave boomed, "No. Why?" Tension swelled the air and seemed to compete for space in the steam filled bathroom.

Sissy sassed back, "Because it smells."

"Probably some of your hair and all of that feminine shit you use festering in there." Normally, Dave could care less if Sissy had her panty hose and bras drying in the tub. Now he was using the archaic macho term "feminine shit?" Perhaps his true feelings were starting to show.

Sissy just grunted and turned herself back around to the cold spot, and hung her feet over the side, again.

"Why were you sitting like that?" Dave meanly laughed.

"Because this end is cold," Sissy did not want him in the bathroom with her anymore.

"I don't know why. I mean, you only can see the steam coming off of your red feet. Get out of there." The tone of Dave's voice was not his usual easy going tone, but reminded her more of a fatherly, instructional tone. Hell, her own father would not speak to her in this manner. Hell, her own father would not let another man speak to her like this, either.

"Why?"

"You're gonna hurt yourself. Let that water cool a little."

"No. I like it like this. The real problem is that this end of the tub won't make my butt look like my feet."

"You want that?"

"It helps my sides."

"Go to the doctor," Dave said curtly.

Sissy would not have minded this response, except he said it not out of concern for her well-being, but rather out of frustration, as if he were tired of hearing her complain.

"What do you want, Dave?" Sissy was hurt by his intrusion and impatience.

"Huh?"

"Why are you in here bothering me?"

"Oh, I came in here for something, but I forgot. Why are you being so pissy?"

Sissy just turned her head and ignored Dave, who got the hint, made an angry face, and slammed the door shut. The deep end of the tub wouldn't warm, so Sissy got out and toweled off. Looking in the fogged, full length mirror, Sissy could see that her rear end was the same bright pink as her scalded feet, which stung in the cooler air. Bending over, Sissy rubbed her feet and found them hot to the touch. Sissy wondered what her fanny felt like, so she put her hands on her cheeks, which were cool in spots and hot in others, but red all over. The mystery of her hot/cold butt confused her, so she decided to go to bed.

When Sissy passed the study on the way to her bed, she found Dave carving away at the carpeting with the same dogged determination as the night before. Both his behavior over the course of last night and the bathroom scene really pissed her off, and to find him at it again, just made her want to explode. "What in the hell are you doing, Dave?"

Dave stopped what he was doing momentarily and looked up at his girlfriend with fiendish eyes, "Don't you talk to me that way. Don't you curse me. Not when I'm working on your house."

Sissy's first instinct was to back off, but she was determined to stand her ground, "You've already missed one day of class. I thought you were in unbearable pain, anyway."

Dave went back to cutting the carpet, "I'm better now. Let me work."

"You better go to class tomorrow."

Dave grunted his acknowledgement and slashed wildly at the carpet with the yard knife.

Sissy felt a little scared, "I could get you some scissors."

"Don't you think I tried that already! Nothing will cut this tough carpet but this knife. Now quit distracting me before I cut myself."

Without a hint of sarcasm, for she felt none, Sissy simply said, "Sorry." For some reason, despite her independent nature and somewhat strong personality, Sissy felt cowed.

Without looking up from his work, Dave curtly demanded, "Go to bed or something."

## Chapter 33: Or Something

Sissy shut the door behind herself and went to bed. Remembering that Dave now preferred her side of the bed, she politely conceded and laid down on his side by the window. The glow from the streetlight beamed through the closed vertical blinds, creating a striped pattern on the bed like a zebra skin comforter. The light's stripes bothered Sissy; she didn't want to touch them; she didn't want them to touch her. Her feelings were so hurt that she felt apathetic toward the pain aching in her side and pulled her knees up into her chest like a helpless child. Slowly, she fell asleep to the sound of carpet ripping and what she assumed to be the fig tree's branch tapping on her window. When she awoke, she thought she had only been asleep a few minutes. Dave was sitting up in bed beside her.

Groggily, Sissy asked, "What time is it?"

Dave asked in his "normal Dave" voice, "Three o'clock. Shhh. Don't you hear it?"

Sissy listened. Sure enough, she realized that a loud sound from over her head had awaken her, "What is that?"

Dave reached over and touched Sissy's arm, "I don't know. It sounds like somebody's kicking a bunch of empty boxes around up there." Dave was shaken, but his voice sounded like his old self and his energy was calm, level. None of that bossy monotone cold heartedness that Sissy had recently become all but too accustomed.

"Squirrels?" Sissy jokingly asked, but then a loud sliding sound, as of something heavy being pushed across their gritty attic floor, disproved her theory.

Dave said in a hushed tone, "I never knew a squirrel to do

that." The kicking of boxes resumed.

"Go check on it." Sissy nudged Dave, who nudged back.

"I really don't want to. Let's wait. Maybe it'll just go away." Dave lay back down and pulled Sissy toward him. They spooned so perfectly together. She felt so cozy and safe, despite the frightening sounds over head in the attic, she didn't dispute him. It felt like decades since he had been, well, himself. In a moment, Sissy drifted back to sleep to be re-awaken by Dave, who said, "Sissy?"

"Mmm."

"Thanks for giving me your side of the bed. I don't like that one."

Sissy felt herself floundering in a sleepy consciousness, "Yeah. Me neither." The pain in her pelvis pinged and the creepy sensation of the streetlight on her legs made her reluctantly roll over and pull her knees back into her chest.

The next morning, Sissy woke, but felt as if she had not slept at all. Dave was not in bed. Without a second guess, the sleepy woman walked to the study, expecting to find him there in much the same position as she had found him in the guest bedroom the morning before. But, she was wrong.

When she swung the study door open with a sudden force, she almost fell through the entrance. Dave was not in the study at all. Looking down the hall, Sissy saw the bathroom light on and the door wide open, but there were none of the familiar "Dave-getting-ready-in-the-morning" smells of acrid Athens water, melting soap, and shaving cream.

There weren't any breakfast smells either, much to Sissy's dismay. After all, he had never cooked for her before, why did she expect him to cook her breakfast, of all things? The "other woman scenario" jealously popped back into her head, which she literally wiped away by waving her hand in the air as if shooing a fly. Rationally, she knew he seemed to really care for her, except when he got on a tear, literally. At the very least, he was getting free rent; why ruin a cheap thing? Walking into the living room, Sissy heard the familiar sound of Dave's rattle-trap snoring reverberating against the upholstery of her white leather couch.

Sissy lovingly bent over the back of the couch to look at her lover sleeping like a little boy, cramped on the couch with his knees tucked up, covered by his offering to the living room decor, a duck print throw, which barely covered his oversized body. She didn't even mind that he was slobbering all over her couch in his sleep. Suddenly, Dave woke up and let out a frightened yell, his body contorted in such a spasm, Sissy knew she had genuinely frightened him.

"Don't do that! You scared me."

"Sorry, you just looked so cute."

"Cute. Hmph. You'd think after all that craziness you went through last night, you'd call in sick this morning."

Sissy smoothed his hair on his head and cooed, "What are you talking about?"

Dave looked up at her in confusion, "You're not tired?"

"Yeah, but those boxes, or whatever it was."

"No. I'm talking about after that. You went nuts on me last night."

Sissy withdrew her hand and felt like she were being falsely accused, "How so?"

"First you nearly yanked the blinds off of the wall, pulling on them and yelling at the only decent next door neighbors we've got. Then you started beating the bed, yelling at the lights on the comforter to go away and stop bothering you. Ran around the house, tightening all of the blinds, pulling the curtains shut, and turning on all of the lights. Nuts."

Sissy put her arms around herself even though she did not feel cold, "I don't remember any of that."

Dave rolled over in the couch as if he were hiding his head and said into the couch, "If it was sleep walking, I never knew it could seem so awake . . . and loud. Just insane."

Sissy rubbed his arm, not to comfort him so much as to feel connected to something in this moment, "What was I yelling?"

Dave lifted his head out of the couch, "Something about how they need to stop talking about you. Stop . . . laughing at you. Go away! Some schizophrenic crap."

Sissy continued rubbing his arm, but was staring at the hardwoods beneath her feet, "And what'd you do?"

Dave grabbed her hand to hold it tenderly, "I turned off the lights after you, but that sent you into a frenzy. Talking about how 'they' could only bother you through 'their' light. You had to make 'their' light disappear with 'our' lights. Crazy. Scared me. I hid my knife, you had me so worried."

Sissy let Dave hold her hand. She liked the heat that was emanating off of his hand, "I have no idea about any of that. I really don't like the window side of the bed, or the light that comes through the window. I just remember my sides hurting and me pulling up my knees. Nothing else."

Dave rolled back over on his other side, "I left the bathroom light on for you. That seemed to make it a little better.

Crazy woman. I'm getting a hotel room, you do that again."

The word, "hotel room," created an intense sudden anger in Sissy, who snarled out, "And I suppose you could call your other woman to spend the night with you."

Dave stared at Sissy with a look of absolute confusion on his face and threw his hands up in the air, "God, what are you talking about, now?"

Sissy honestly didn't know, so she played it off as a joke and giggled, "Just messing with you."

Dave snatched the little bit of blanket he had covering his feet up over his head and tightly rolled over, "You go to work now. Scaring the baby. Not nice."

Sissy was genuinely tickled, "Go get in the bed. I reset the alarm clock for you."

Dave nodded "no" with his blanket covered face, "Not until you leave. You might still be crazy."

Sissy left for work and thought about what Dave said. If she weren't so tired, she would have discredited his entire story. Being in real estate, she knew she could easily leave the office to look up past deeds and ownership on her property at the courthouse, downtown. After all, having been possessed once in her life already, she was more than aware that there might still be previous tenants staying in her new home. Perhaps if she could just get a better idea of who they may have been, she could figure out why Dave and she were behaving so strangely.

## Chapter 34: A Little Help Here

The deeds were not in the courthouse, but were in another building two blocks away, an actual "Office of Deeds." Walking through downtown Athens, Sissy decided she'd have to pay Mimi a visit and ask for her thoughts on the situation. At the very least, the Goth could sell her some sort of herbal remedy guaranteed to get rid of evil spirits, or as Sissy saw it, most likely just stink up the house.

The deed office proved to be unorganized and unfruitful. And worse, it stank. The odor was something Sissy could not place, a strange mixture of scents: dust, citrus, and a putrid musk. The office was an unpleasant environment that made research difficult. All Sissy could find were property lines and the names of the two previous owners, whom she already knew about, but records prior to that were missing. It seemed as if the property disappeared altogether. The last thing Sissy wanted to do was ask the clerk, an androgynous type who looked as if breathing were an inconvenience, for help.

With no other alternative, Sissy approached the tall desk that separated the clerk from the rest of the room, "I'm having a little trouble. I can't find some records on my house."

Immediately the emotionless clerk retorted, "They must be lost."

Sissy put her hands on her hips in an attempt to intimidate the androgynous person, "Lost? A fifty year old house with forty-five years of missing records, lost?"

A tuxedo cat jumped onto the clerk's desk and sprayed a wet mist into the air from his buttocks. The clerk picked up a can of citrus air spray and spritzed the air. The cat was offended and pawed the aerosol can in retaliation. The clerk addressed the cat, "There was a fire. That's how we got this lovely office, thirty years ago."

Sissy took a step back and turned her head in disgust. She put her hand over her mouth and asked, "A fire? No back up records?"

The cat purred and lifted its tail to spray the air, again, but the clerk thumped the cat on one of its prominent balls. Letting out a cry of pain, the cat jumped from the desk and ran under a table, where it licked itself in consolation. The next installment of chemical warfare had been temporarily terminated.

The deeds clerk blankly stared back at Sissy with no reply.

"Never mind. I'm so sorry I came in here and bothered you. Really. Please, go back to sucking on the government tit by all means," Sissy exited the cramped space as quickly as possible. She hated being mean to people, but lately, it took very little to send her over the edge.

Sissy walked and thought to herself. She knew that the house was owned by a college student's father, a Mr. Mulberry, and before him, a Mr. Praither, had owned the home for a marginal number of years. No, whoever was bothering Sissy and Dave had a strong attachment to the house, which would have more than likely been the result of living in the house for many years. Somewhat daunted, Sissy left the Office of (some) Deeds, and headed for Mimi's.

When Sissy walked the three blocks to Mimi's bar, she found a sign taped on the door that read, "Closed for Vacation. Will Return on 7/30."

Sissy couldn't believe it and inadvertently yelled out, "Two weeks! Who takes a two week vacation in July?"

Unfortunately, a pair of preppy looking college students who were walking by overhead the frustrated woman. The girl, a bouncy cheerleaderly sort, leaned over to her beau, a thick necked, football player type, and giggled, "Lush."

Sissy flicked the couple a bird, but they were oblivious, having returned to their self-absorbed bubble before being fired upon.

On the way back to her car, Sissy found an independently owned bookstore called "Ophelia's Corner," which advertised a specialty in the occult, women's literature, and alternative lifestyles. Sissy decided that the owner would have an idea as of to where Mimi had gone and how the realtor could get in touch with her. In her heterosexually egocentric mind, all women of alternative lifestyles went to the exact same places, knew one another, and were close friends. Surely, they'd know exactly where Mimi was and how she could get in touch with her. Normally, Sissy wouldn't dream of bothering someone while on vacation, but this was different. Whatever was haunting her could potentially ruin the only serious relationship she had ever had in her entire life!

The thought sent shooting pains through her abdomen, and she felt herself start her period. Wearing a light beige suit, Sissy ran into the store and turned bright red, well, her face did.

The inside of the store was tidy and highly specialized, divided into only three subjects: the occult, women's literature, and alternative lifestyles. At the far end of the store stood a fragile looking woman behind a long glass case filled with books opened to their inside covers, showing they had been signed by their authors. Behind the display case was a glass bead curtain through which filtered a bright yellow light and sounds of nature set against a beat and synthesizers. The fragile woman turned out to be a pale hippy-looking, earth-mother-sort with long frizzy, uncut, brown hair, a long chain of amethysts around her neck, John Lennon glasses, and a purple tie-dyed broomstick dress that showed only her unshaven ankles and well-worn Birkenstocks. After a moment's hesitation, the woman tore herself away from her open book and smiled politely, but looked confusedly at Sissy, "May I help you?"

Sissy stammered, "Yyyess. I . . . I need a book or something, and oh, God, I hate to say this, but a feminine pad or tampon or something. I'll pay you. This is a REAL emergency."

The woman looked around Sissy and pointed in the direction of a pharmacy that sat about two more blocks away.

"No, I know there's 'Mitchell's,' but I really need something, *now*. I've never had anything happen like this before. I'll buy like a hundred dollars worth of stuff if you'll just . . . "

The woman suspiciously eyed Sissy, walked over to the front door, and locked the two of them in the otherwise empty store. Sissy thought to herself, *God she thinks I'm trying to run a scam on her - - I got my accomplice outside waiting to pounce on the cash register as soon as her back's turned.* Then, without saying a word, the hippy woman walked to the back of the store through a glass bead curtain and emerged with a brand of feminine pad Sissy had never seen before: a gray, mottled fat pad that looked to be made from recycled paper and had a green label wrapped around it that read, "Bio-organic," all the way around.

Without making a face, even though Sissy wanted to ask, "What is *this?*" the embarrassed woman took the pad and followed the hippy's pointing finger that lead to the left of the store through a hall labeled "EXIT."

The bookstore's bathroom turned out to be a veritable shrine filled with crystals, lit candles, and incense. A large mirror was hand decorated with gold painted plaster-of-Paris embedded with fake jewels. The light in the bathroom was shrouded with scarves, which filtered the overhead light, creating a very moody atmosphere. Sissy almost felt as if she should worship at the altar before using the throne, but the trickling sensation prompted her to carry out her urgent duties. When Sissy finished, she jokingly left a two dollar tip and borrowed a squirt of lavender scented, "organic," hand lotion.

Emerging from the bathroom, Sissy regained her composure and found the fragile woman in the "women's literature" section talking to a larger woman with very short hair and a white tailored shirt paired with dark jeans, who seemed vaguely familiar. Then it dawned on Sissy: she and the larger woman had met at Mimi's one night months before she met Dave, and Sissy had accepted a dance from her, never thinking they'd actually run into one another under similar circumstances again. Now, Sissy felt somewhat embarrassed and wondered how she should act.

Nervously and awkwardly, Sissy tip-toed up to the pair of women and nervously cleared her throat. They looked up at the realtor and stared. Sissy just stared back for a moment, and realized that she wasn't saying anything, when she really should, and forced a response, "Hi. Don't mean to bother you, but I was wondering if you knew where Mimi went, and if I could get in touch with her."

The long haired woman looked confused and walked away, disappearing behind the curtain. The larger woman rolled her eyes, "Is that the bar owner down the street?"

Sissy sweetly nodded in the affirmative.

The woman crossed her arms and said in a deep voice, "No. Am I supposed to?"

Sissy felt extremely embarrassed and stuttered, "Uh, well, well, I guess not. Actually."

"Do you want to buy something?" The large woman was most intimidating and did not seem to recognize Sissy at all.

"Umm, I think we know each other. Dancing?"

The large woman eyed Sissy up and down and did not seem to care, "At the bar? Is that why you think I know Mimi?"

"Yes, I guess so."

"Well, I got me a gal, so, I hope you don't mind. If that's what you're really . . ."

Sissy felt the blood rush to her face, and knew she must be a deep crimson color, "Uh, no. I actually need a book, or something."

The large woman laughed at Sissy, "What on?"

"It's embarrassing. To me."

The large woman took a more masculine stance with her feet spread apart. She looked enormous. In a voice hinting at double entendre, the woman said, "Either you need this . . . book . . . or you don't."

"Okay. Fine. I think my house is haunted and I need to find out how to . . . fix it."

"Good God, that's Virginia's area." The large woman turned in the direction of the beaded curtain and yelled through it, "Virginia! One of your kind is out here; I'm goin' to lunch!"

Virginia, the hippy woman, emerged from the beaded curtain room and acted as if this kind of behavior was a normal occurrence, and answered in a raspy, hushed voice, "Get me a salad, Sheila."

Sheila smirked and skulked off before muttering, "Damn salad muncher," and left the building.

Sissy stood face to face with Virginia, who acted as if her customer were wasting her time, "What do you need? I don't have any more . . ."

"No. Thank you, though. I've never . . . anyway, I . . . well," and Sissy went back to staring, hoping Virginia could read her mind and miraculously pull a magic book out of her extremely wrinkled dress.

Virginia's hushed voice grew impatient, "You need?"

"I think my house is haunted and I need to get rid of it."

"Call a real estate agent," Virginia was visibly annoyed. Apparently, begging for a pad had put Sissy permanently on the wrong foot.

"No, I *am* a real estate agent. I need to learn how to get rid of whatever's making my house haunted."

"The occults. Over there." Virginia acted as if Sissy had a plague, a nasty, undesirable, tabooed, plague.

"Do you suggest anything?"

"No. Do I look like I could suggest anything?" Virginia stared at Sissy, making her feel stupid.

"Well . . . I . . . You seem to be all into that crystal stuff."

"I channel positive energy. You, apparently have channeled something negative, being as it has driven you to seek out something to 'get rid of it.' I don't have any suggestions for your situation. Sorry."

Sissy walked through the section labeled "The Occults," but couldn't find anything but astrology and numerology. The bright book jackets made everything look the same. For some reason, she was having problems concentrating and reluctantly called, "Virginia? Virginia? I need some help."

Virginia walked over to Sissy and waited.

Feeling very self-conscious, Sissy made herself tell the agitated woman, "I can't find anything but these books about birth dates. I need something for spirits and stuff."

Virginia took two steps to Sissy's left and waved her hands in front of a wide display of books that covered all sorts of magical subjects, none of which Sissy had ever heard of before. Virginia promptly walked away, leaving Sissy to stare blankly at the catalogue before her.

Sissy decided to grab a handful of books and browse through their indexes. However, the books she found all assumed their readers were well versed in the supernatural or occult arts. The more she looked, the more bogged down in jargon she became. Some of the pictures gave Sissy the shivers, pictures of demonic looking creatures and symbols like the one in her own shed behind the house. The more she tried to educate herself, the more frightened she became. Suddenly, an onslaught of intense emotion flooded the realtor, who began to sob. Never, never before in Sissy's entire life had she actually lost control over her emotions in a public area. Where was all of this coming from?

Sissy had no idea; all she knew was, she needed to cry until she couldn't cry anymore, right there, right then.

Virginia heard the pathetic sobbing and found Sissy sitting on the floor, slumped over an open book, her chin touching her chest, slobber wetting her shirt, "What's wrong?" the waif whispered in a horrified tone.

Sissy looked up at the sliver of a woman and cried harder than before, "I . . . I don't know. I . . . I . . . usually don't . . . don't act like this!"

"Is it your house stressing you?" the woman seemed to feel sorry for her customer.

Unable to speak, Sissy just nodded her head, "Yes."

Virginia put her hands on her hips and appeared to be momentarily lost in thought, "I know there's a book with remedies for clearing bad energy. Are you good with herbs?"

Sissy looked away from Virginia in shame and hunched her shoulders to say she didn't know.

"Well, if you're not familiar with how to really use plants, it won't help. Do you know what's causing the problems?"

Virginia handed Sissy an organic tissue from one of the many folds of her flowing gown. Sissy gratefully took it and dabbed her running nose, and waited for her chest to stop convulsing, "I'm psychic, but I didn't feel anything before we bought the house."

"Now, you feel things?"

"Yeah, we don't act like ourselves. It's just there's. See this symbol?" Sissy pointed to a pentagram in the book. Virginia looked and feigned concern with a fake smile. Sissy closed her eyes to avoid looking at Virginia's faked empathy, "This is in my shed. It's cold and I don't like it."

"Probably kids. They'll vandalize anything with pentagrams and anarchy symbols. Have you tried communicating with this energy?"

Sissy shook her head, "No."

"Why not start off with an Ouija board?"

"Those scare me. I've heard bad things about them."

"Try the board. Maybe you can tell it to just go away."

"You think it'll listen?"

Virginia replied in a motherly tone, "Sure."

"Where can I get one?"

Suddenly Virginia became nice and helpful, "We sell them." She obviously wanted to get Sissy out of the store as quickly as possible.

Sissy lumbered off of the floor and Virginia went to the other side of the bookcase and handed the weepy eyed woman a board. Sissy gratefully took it and made her way toward the register. On the way, she stopped by the "Self-Help" section and picked up a few books on relationships, even if they were about alternative ones. She knew she could NEVER be caught dead in the "Self-Help" aisle at the mall. If a woman were even caught looking at that aisle, she would be permanently branded "desperate." Perhaps this was the only safe way to avoid that label. Well, from strangers who mattered to her anyhow.

After her pathetic little crying scene, Sissy told herself, *What the hell?* and marched up to the register with her strange assortment of goods, just as Sheila came walking in with two white sacks of food, "Finally sold one of those things? I thought you didn't like 'em."

Virginia looked mortified, "Sheila, she needs to communicate with an entity that is bothering her. I'm in favor of all communication that has a positive motivation. You know that."

Sheila just huffed, pushed her way through the glass beaded curtain, and disappeared into the back of the store.

After taking Sissy's money and shoving her goods into a thin, transparent, white plastic bag, Virginia gave her customer one last fake smile, thanked her for her business, and wished her luck.

Before Sissy could reply, the waif-like woman had re-absorbed herself into her opened book, and either did not hear, or had pretended not to hear Sissy's apologies for her unusual behavior. Sissy was left awkwardly holding her sack until she realized she did not have to be excused to leave the store.

Walking back to her SUV proved to be awkward and embarrassing. The Ouija board's black, bold, archaic lettering showed through the plastic bag, making Sissy feel as if the entire world were watching, thinking that she were some kind of nutcase. Once inside her SUV, Sissy had an unexplainable desire to take the day off and just go home. Perhaps it was her hormones. Perhaps it was that god-awful uncomfortable pad that felt as if it were a little too earth-friendly, biodegrading right in her panties.

Normally, Sissy would never take a day off from work for the simple reason of "felt like it." Most of the time, no matter how restless she was, she'd force herself to work the clock and get something done. Anything. Re-organize her files. Re-organize her desk. Re-organize her purse. Assort her pens by color and pencils by length. Anything. But, today she had an excuse.

Barb had already told her once not to break down in tears in the office. It was only two o'clock and already she had broken down into convulsive sobs in front of strangers while sitting on the floor of a user-unfriendly bookstore. Sissy's justification for calling into the office was an unclean track record in the hysterics department.

Barb just snickered, "It's that damn man, isn't it? Go home and work it out of your system, but no maternity leave. Ya' hear?"

## Chapter 35:  Smells Like . . .

Once at home, Sissy longed for a hot bath.  Her sides were aching, again.  Dave's car was gone; hopefully, he was in class today.  As she turned the knob to the front door, she heard the TV, some sort of manly historic documentary; the airplane gunfire came barraging through the walls of the sea foam siding.  Dave was all too aware that leaving the TV on was one of Sissy's (many) pet peeves.  Still, he would absentmindedly leave the TV or the radio on and deny the whole thing.  Dave's lying rubbed Sissy the wrong way and caused many a heated argument.

The key stuck in the door, adding to the realtor's aggravation, "Damn key.  Stupid man.  Bitchy women.  Shitty day!"  Then Sissy lost it and yelled at the door in full voice, "Give me my goddamn key back!"  When the realtor turned the key, it came out of the lock in a smooth, single action, which only pissed her off more, so she kicked the door to "punish" it for making her wait.

Inside the house, all was calm, peaceful, and dead silent.  The TV was not on, as expected.  In fact, the house seemed to have an altogether "other" appearance, somehow.  Was it the light from outside?  The emptiness?  No, the house *felt* different, as if it weren't her home at all.  There was a strange sheen in the very air itself that sat upon her furniture and made it seem foreign.

The first thing Sissy did was turn on all of the lights and the TV, which was tuned to a pop music station, making a war documentary seem highly unlikely.  The walk to the bathroom seemed longer than usual, the hall stretching on forever.  Then that all too familiar stench hit her.

Not wanting to sit in a stink bath, Sissy went to the kitchen and found Dave's toolbox, from which she extracted a pair of needle nose pliers and a pair of plastic gloves. If something had fallen into the drain and died, she didn't want it to touch her skin. Marching dutifully back to the bathroom and cursing Dave for not upholding his manly duties of getting the smell out of the bath drain, Sissy turned the corner of the hall and stopped dead in her tracks.

There, through the bright red painted drywall, was a face. It wasn't supposed to be a face but was a plaster patch that now resembled a kind of face. The entire wall wavered and was uneven, but one small section bubbled out in the shape of a round head, in which sat two small bulges for eyes, and a strange bulging line that sufficed for a devilish smile. The patch scared Sissy, so she forced herself to poke it with her pliers and quickly walked on to the bathroom, should it decide to somehow poke back.

The smell in the bathroom was still present, much to Sissy's dismay. Sliding on her gloves, and leaning over the tub, the realtor put her independent nature to use and prodded the tub drain like a pro. Gobs of long, blonde hair came out of the drain in jellied mats. Red strings, like ones from a sweater, hung in the shallow teeth of her pliers. Dried, wetted, and re-dried gummy plugs of mold came out as big as pressed flowers. Finally, she poked and prodded until she could get nothing else out. It was a fruitful experience that filled the palm of Sissy's gloved hand, and made a deep "thud" when she emptied her plastic covered palm into the trash. However, the endeavor only left the bathroom smelling worse than before. Sissy grimaced, "Don't tell me all of that shit was plugging up that stink!"

Daunted, the tired woman decided to forgo the bath and trudged her way to her bed.

A consuming exhaustion overcame Sissy, forcing her to lie down and rest before taking off her clothes. The lethargy was so intense, she found it difficult to remove her clothing, and had to take a break between each article. Finally stripped, Sissy crawled into bed wearing only her underwear. Just thinking about finding a gown and having to go through the rigor of putting it on made the realtor ache.

"Am I coming down with the flu?" Sissy asked out loud and snuggled into her cool pillow.

Not long after falling into a deep sleep, footsteps awoke the slumbering woman.

"Dave, is that you?" Sissy lazily called out, but there was no reply. The footsteps ceased.

"Ah, hell, whoever you are, whatever you are, go away! Leave me alone!" Sissy yelled, not caring if the neighbors heard. The house was silent again, as if a vacuum had sucked all of the life out of the house. "That's right, damn it," the realtor dreamily murmured and quickly found her snuggly place in her dank pillow.

Sleep, heavy, and hard, like the sleep that comes as a gift after a hard day of strenuous labor took over Sissy, who dreamed nothing but the darkness from her eyelids. Two hours passed and then a hard slap on the wall overhead startled Sissy awake, "What the?" A dark sheen covered the atmosphere of the room, darkening the bright summer light that filtered through the blinds. "That was not nice, now leave me alone!"

Sissy tried to go back to sleep the second time but found it nearly impossible. Her comfy place in her pillow was gone and no matter how much she fluffed and adjusted, she couldn't find it again. The smell from the bathroom was penetrating the air of the bedroom, making sleep even more difficult.

Sissy sat up on Dave's side of the bed, and found that despite all of her rest, she was even more tired than before. Her arms were heavy and hard to lift, not tingly when they fall asleep, but heavy like wearing weights. Her legs felt achy, as if she had been lifting weights.

"I am getting the flu," Sissy felt her head, but it was cool to the touch. "No fever. Unless I ran one earlier." She rubbed her hand across her pillow but found it dry and warm.
"I need some tea. Hot tea." Sissy threw on Dave's robe because the tie on hers was missing.

The kitchen was bright and cheery, unlike the rest of the house, which seemed to cast an almost palpable darkness. Sissy filled her favorite tea kettle full of water and waited for it to whistle a reply. Inhaling deeply, the realtor noticed that the air in the kitchen was easier to breathe. It didn't smell like the bathroom, whose foul odor had filled the rest of the house with an unsanitary dankness.

"Ah, sanctuary," she sighed and rubbed her arms, which were still not a hundred percent. A key rattling at the door jingled Sissy out of a momentary lapse. Dave walked in and seemed surprised to see Sissy sitting at the kitchen table.

"What are you doing home?" he chuffed in an annoyed tone.

"Nice to see you, too," Sissy rebuffed. She could tell he was in one of his moods, again.

"You know that's not what I meant," he said as he

rummaged through the fridge, clinking bottles and sloshing the milk.

"Well, I've had an eventful day," Sissy was hoping to pique Dave's curiosity so that he would show some interest in her mysterious break from work.

"You look like hell. Gettin' sick?" Dave didn't even bother to poke his head out of the fridge, making his statement on her looks that much more annoying. Even worse, he seemed to ignore her invitation to inquire into her day altogether.

"If I'm lucky," Sissy turned her body away from Dave in a frustrated, quick manner because she hoped her terse statement and body language would prompt Dave to see that she was being evasive, and he needed to be more attentive.

"What's for dinner?" Dave asked with a piece of cheese dangling from his mouth. Sissy's evasiveness was completely missed. Dave pulled out an ancient can of slimming diet drink from the fridge and began audibly shaking it. Sissy knew he hated those things and was, now, intentionally trying to make her mad.

"I dunno, you tell me," Sissy turned her head to the man and cocked her brow. She was beyond the state of feminine hurt from having her little ploy of seeking his sympathy deterred and was now ready to fight.

"Delivery?" Dave grinned goofily and put the diet drink back in the fridge and drank from the milk jug after sloshing it until it was bubbly.

Sissy squinched her eyes shut and tried to remain calm. "You're not as dumb as you look," she said with a forced grin, all of her teeth showing. Sissy still wanted her feelings known, but for now just wished he would leave her alone in the kitchen.

"I try," Dave smiled an annoyed smile and grabbed a beer from the fridge. Then he lightly walked into the living room, where he sat in his ugly recliner and channel surfed until finding a war documentary on television. The sound of machine gun fire filled the serenity of the kitchen.

Finally, the kettle whistled and blew steam, signaling Sissy to get up from her chair and steep her tea. With tea kettle in one hand and her favorite dainty floral print cup and saucer in the other, Sissy walked into the living room, ready to take the remote from Dave, but he looked so enthralled with his program that Sissy decided to be nice, despite his previous bad behavior and her ornery inclinations.

"Think I'm gettin' the flu," if she couldn't have the remote, she could at least have a piece of his attention.

"Weird time of year for that, isn't it?" Dave said to the television with a forced tone of interest.

"Not for a town full of weirdos," Sissy took a sip of her tea and coughed a pitiful cough, even though coughing was not one of her symptoms, yet.

"True." Dave channel surfed again, knowing Sissy preferred to be the one to surf. Again, he came across the war documentary and stopped. Even though the volume was loud enough to reach the kitchen, he turned up the volume even more, making the sound of the machine gun fire charge into Sissy's chest. She wondered if he were trying to drown her out.

"I thought I heard this exact program on when I came home at two this afternoon," she yelled over the television.

Without yelling, Dave over-calmly said, "I did NOT leave the damn TV on, if that's what you're gettin' at." Perhaps he was trying to prove that Sissy's louder tone was superfluous. Perhaps he didn't even care if she could hear him.

"No, no. You didn't. It was off, but I heard these war sounds through the door, like it was on," Sissy got off of the couch and manually turned the television down.

Dave hunched his shoulders, telling her he didn't know and didn't care. "They're running an all day deal, where they're showing all airplane shows."

"A marathon?" Sissy said with a snobby air, because she hated when he couldn't remember the words for things, and she knew he especially hated when she filled in the words for him.

"Umm," Dave grunted. Yep, she had definitely gotten a direct hit with that one.

"But the TV was off. When I turned it on, it was on another station," maybe he'd get the hint and talk to her.

"Weird," was all he said. Then again, maybe not.

"What about the smell?" she really, really wanted to talk.

"What smell?" Dave said as if he were taking personal offense. Finally, Sissy had hit upon a subject that may elicit more than just a one word response.

"You didn't smell that smell when you walked in the door?" Sissy turned her body towards his recliner.

"No. I don't smell anything now, either," Dave moved his thumb to turn the volume back up, but Sissy gave him "the look," and he turned it one notch down at the last minute.

"Me either. I thought it was because I was used to it," Sissy sat back in the couch and scuffed her feet on the floor.

"What's it supposed to smell like?" he asked the television.

"What?" she pretended to not be listening to him and took a long sip from her pretty little cup.

"The smell. It smells like?"

"Oh, it smells like the smell from the bathtub, which I pulled all sorts of lovelies from this afternoon, thank you very much," Sissy said with a bit of irritation, hoping Dave would at least acknowledge that she had been asking him to poke around in that drain for days now.

"You used your hands?" he laughed in disbelief.

"Pliers and gloves," Sissy was beginning to not feel like talking. His laughter was hurtful.

"Didn't make the smell go away?" he seemed all too pleased that her attempt at fixing the drain had gone awry.

"Made it worse," she said in a low tone to his robe and fidgeted with the tie.

"Eww. Sounds nasty." He was truly happy that she was unsuccessful in fixing the drain!

"What're you going to do about it?" Sissy put her hands on her hips and stared at Dave.

"Me?" Dave asked as if accused. Sissy was still staring him down, so he shrugged, "I could call a plumber, I guess. I'm sure they get, 'Hey, could you come over, my tub stinks?,' all the time."

"I just don't like a bathroom that doesn't make you feel clean."

"It'll go away. Needs time to air out," Dave ignored her perturbed facial gesture and turned up the volume.

Sissy drank all of her tea and felt bloated. More so than before. Her body was achy and the noise from the TV was aversive. "Goin' to bed," she said in a tone so intentionally low, she hoped he would have to ask to repeat her question, which she could then yell at him.

"Mmm." Apparently, Dave had played this game before.

"Do me a favor, get my package out of the truck for me," Sissy yelled out. If he didn't get her stuff, it wasn't because he didn't hear her.

"Mmm," Dave wasn't going to acknowledge her outburst.

Sissy stomped off to the bedroom, thinking to herself, *Perpetual bachelor? More like perpetual bastard. Doesn't care that I'm sick. Have to take the day off from work and he just drinks his damn beer and watches TV. Made me leave my own living room!*

The bedroom was no longer bright, as an encroaching storm had overcast the sun. It was only six o'clock. Sissy wasn't sleepy. Didn't want to read. The lights outside had come on and made those stripes of shadow and light fall across the bed. Lying on her back made her sides hurt. Lying on her sides made her back hurt. From her bed, Sissy heard Dave turn the television down. "Asshole," she murmured to herself and sat up in bed with her arms folded.

The dark green walls made the room look like a cave with almost day-glow white trim shinning against the darkness. Bright white closet doors looked more like cleaned teeth than sliding doors. "The mouth of the cave," Sissy snickered and thought about Freudian symbols. Dave's voice ordering pizza over the telephone averted her attention. *Wonder if he'll even let me know the pizza's here. Probably eat it all, too, the bastard.* Then the television's volume increased to an almost deafening level. *Is he deaf?  God, it's like living with an eighty year old man after fifty years of marriage!*  Sissy inhaled and was about to shout over the volume of the television when she heard a loud thud from under the house.  The surprise literally took the wind out of her sails.

## Chapter 36: Looks Like Last Time

"That you, Sissy?" Dave yelled from the living room.

"NO!" Sissy yelled back.

"It came from your part of the house!"

"Well, it wasn't . . ."

"HUH?" Dave interrupted Sissy.

Sissy huffed and got out of bed and threw Dave's robe back on. As she tied the belt tight on the oversized robe, Sissy felt that all too familiar throb shoot from the nub of her missing finger. Dave walked into the bedroom as another thud sounded from beneath the house.

This thud was so hard, Sissy could feel it beneath her feet, "It wasn't me, Dave," she said in a normal tone.

Dave stood in the darkness and put his index finger to his lips for Sissy to be quiet. Another thud sounded.

"It sounds like it's making its way toward the wall," Sissy whispered, pointing to the far wall, against which the bed sat. After pointing, she felt a little silly. The room was dark and filled with a filtered, dirty twilight. Maybe he could see her, maybe not.

Dave nodded. The light from behind him made him look like a modern day Frankenstein, big and bulky. Ominous. "That's where the door to the crawl space is."

"Did you shut it?" Sissy was still talking in whispers, fixed to the side of the bed.

"I put a lock on it," Dave whispered back. His voice showed that he was a little frightened by the noises. Airplanes loudly zoomed and buzzed in the background, but Dave's and Sissy's quiet voices carried as if they were competing with total silence. Dave remained in the threshold, his arms held out by his sides, as if he were on a ship and may have to brace himself in the doorway.

"Damn, Dave, you locked an animal under the house! It could die under there and stink up the place!" Sissy yelled in a hushed whisper. The thuds stopped. After Sissy's declaration, the heavy wooden door to the crawl space began to violently jar. Whatever was in the crawl space wanted out and sounded like it was using hands.

"I think it's your attic squirrels, Sissy," Dave said with a barely audible forced, frightened chuckle.

"I really don't think squirrels can do that," she whispered back, fear shaking her voice. The jarring got louder and louder. The thing under the house was banging against the door and jarring it until it was partially slamming against the house. Scratching, as of with long nails against wood, sounded beneath their feet. The thudding began, again. Sissy could feel the thing frantically beating the bottom of the house in all directions from beneath the bedroom floor. Finally, the noises stopped altogether. Dave relaxed in the doorway and let out a deep sigh. Sissy sat on Dave's side of the bed, her robe gaping wide open.

"Whatever . . ." but Sissy was cut short.

The noises came back more violently than before. "Whatever" had apparently needed a rest. Now it was back to focusing on the crawl space door, pushing and thrusting against it. The "Whatever" was so loud, it drowned out the television from the living room. Dave put his hands over his ears. Sissy looked to him and knew that if something had to be done, she'd have to do it.

"God, what is it, Sissy?" Dave said out loud.

Sissy just ignored him and picked up the phone on the night stand, dialing 911.

Dave finally walked into the bedroom and sat next to Sissy on the bed, "Who're you calling?"

"The police. We've got somebody under the house, and I'm not letting them out."

Finally, after a moment's pause, Sissy got a dispatcher, "Yes, I need to report an emergency. I think I've got someone locked in the crawl space under my house. You can't hear them banging on the crawl space door?" There was a pause as Sissy waited, "Okay." Sissy held the phone's receiver against the wall. Through the receiver, Sissy could feel the vibrations of the pounding, which had intensified during her phone call. She gave them her address and asked, "You sure you can't hear that? It's deafening! Okay. We'll be here." She hung up the phone and put her hands over her face.

"What . . . what?" Dave poked her.

"They're sending a car over to check it out. I can't even hear the TV over this!" Sissy put her head on Dave's shoulder.

Dave sympathetically rubbed her hair, "The police will get whoever's under there out. I bet we won't even have to see who it is." Dave pulled Sissy off of the bed and led her into the living room. The doorbell rang, making him yell out loud. "That was fast," he laughed to Sissy. His face was bright red.

Sissy looked at Dave with a look of exasperation on her face, "I think it's your pizza."

"I forgot all about that."

Dave opened the door and saw a recessive looking teenage boy holding two pizzas on the side stoop. Dave apologized, "Sorry about the noise."

"I don't care how loud you watch TV, dude," the kid said in a bored manner.

"You mean, you don't hear . . ." the noise stopped. The kid waited for Dave to finish his sentence, but the large man turned to Sissy, who was busy trying to find the "mute" button on the remote. Finally, she found it, and the entire house was silent.

"Mister, I gotta haul major ass, or I'm gonna have to pay for the pizzas I got in the car, so . . ." The boy trailed off his words with an indifferent look upon his face.

"Oh yeah, Son, sorry," and Dave pulled a twenty dollar bill out of his pocket. The kid opened the pouch on his smock to make change, but Dave waved him away, snatched the pizzas out of the kid's hands, and shut the door in the grinning delivery boy's face. Dave swirled around on his heels like an ice skater, "Think it's resting, again?"

Sissy held Dave's robe tightly across her chest, "I don't care. I just wish the police would get here."

Dave opened the boxes on the coffee table, "Want some? I got all meat for me and a Hawaiian for you. It is your favorite, right?"

"Yeah. Thanks. That was nice. You need a plate?" Sissy knew she and Dave were acting as if nothing had happened.

"Nah. Not unless you want one. Less dishes for . . . me to do, ya' know?" Dave stared at his box of pizza, proving he was really freaked out. Normally the man could inhale pizza like a tornado over a trailer park.

An official, hard knock on the door signaled to the couple that the cavalry had arrived. Sissy answered the door, allowing

Dave time to get his bearings straight and consume his food.

"Did you all call about a crawl space?" the larger of the two officers with a pot belly shaped like a Jack 'o Lantern's head asked in a dead serious, authoritative deep voice that made his whiskers ruffle. The two men smelled like a new car and stood with their legs slightly apart and hands on their hips, typical "I'm an authority" stance. The smaller, younger one (sans Jack o' Belly) was slightly behind the larger one, rubbing his hand across his nose like a little kid. As intimidating as their stance and official the bigger one's tone, the smaller one just didn't seem that capable.

Sissy felt her heart sink and hoped they wouldn't get her or Dave killed in a botched extraction of a wild, crazed person from beneath their house, "Yes. Please. The pounding was really loud. It scratched on the floor."

The big officer asked, "Sure you ain't got yourselves an animal?"

Sissy pointed toward the far end of the house, "I don't know, but it sounded like it was using hands, not paws, to try to force the door open."

The big officer paused with his hand to his right ear, "I don't hear anything, now, ma'am."

"Maybe it's tired."

"We'll take a look, if you . . ." the older officer took a step forward, forcing Sissy out of her own doorway. He looked around Sissy to see Dave, who was completely absorbed in the silent version of his television program, stuffing his face with pizza, sitting Indian style in his ugly recliner.

Sissy was truly embarrassed and knew the officer wanted Dave, not her, to show them to the crawl space door. The woman thought to herself as she watched Dave, who was unaware, or didn't care, that he was being watched, *Regression, thy name is Dave.*

". . . or your husband could show us to the door," the officer finished his sentence.

When Dave didn't respond, the officer put his black, patent, shiny, boat sized foot into the living room entrance and shifted his body just enough to make the various appendages of his belt jingle in that dreaded metallic fashion that only a policeman can do. The large man never took his hands off of his hips the whole time.

Dave finally looked up, "What? You got it taken care of, Sissy, or do you need me?"
He was valiantly trying to save face and had carefully planted both of his feet on the floor, making a sincere effort to put his pizza back down in its crate.

Sissy smiled. By now she was fearing the police might be thinking they were crazy, drug addicts, or God-knows-what. Sissy addressed Dave to try to show they were not crazy, drug addicts, or God-knows-what, "Yes, thank you for offering your services, Dave. Officer . . ."

"Michaels, and Thurber, ma'am," the officer pointed to the smaller man behind himself.

Sissy finished his sentence, addressing Dave, " . . . would like your help in locating the crawl space outside. Which is LOCKED, right?"

Dave quickly picked up his pizza, taking one last bite, "Oh, yeah, there's the key."
Dave pointed to the key rack where his large mass of keys dangled

by a metal ring.

Sissy squinched her mouth and fired her eyes at Dave, trying to signal him to take the officers outside. Dave looked confused at first, but got the hint. In an instant, Dave put on his "manly-man" voice and said, "I'll take 'em outside, Sissy. You wait here."

Officer Michaels stepped completely back onto the door stoop upon hearing Dave's commitment to the venture. Sissy tightened her robe, embarrassed that the robe and her underwear was all she had on. Up to this point, all she could think about was the strange noise under the house and had completely forgotten that she was not dressed for company. Unless, of course, she were auditioning as a spousal abuse victim on one of those police reality shows. Still, it seemed a little late to attempt to put on a full set of clothes. Sissy went to her favorite spot on the couch and opened her box of pizza, which looked as cold as it felt in her mouth.

In a few minutes, Sissy saw flashlights show through the vertical blinds of the wide window on the outside wall of the living room wall and heard the crawl space door reluctantly open with a stiff creak. Someone knocked on the little wooden door, and a young man's voice gruffly called out beneath the house, "Anybody in there? It's the police, come out with your hands up!"

There was no reply.

Manly murmurs made a muffled sound through the wall. Someone walked past the window, opened the creaking door to the shed, and walked back to the crawl space. Then a raking noise beneath the house showed that the officers were at least exploring the outer perimeter of the crawl space. Finally, Dave came through the side door to the living room, Officers Michaels and Thurber following.

"Ma'am, you were the one to make the call?" asked Officer Michaels.

Sissy nodded, and put down her third piece of pizza.

"Well, it's real dark and we couldn't find any sign of anybody underneath your house," Michaels motioned to Thurber, who handed him a clipboard with papers and a pen. "You can fill out a report, or I can file it as a false alarm. Whatever you want to do."

Dave sat next to Sissy on the couch. He put his arm around Sissy and explained to her, "There was nothing. There weren't even any footprints or handprints. Nothing. It didn't look as if anybody had been under the house."

Thurber came around beside Michaels, "All there was, was a couple of leaves and gumballs. I raked around, hoping to find some footprints, but they weren't none."

Michaels inhaled deeply and situated his belt, "We don't think anything's under your house. We flashed our lights around and could see about everything under there. There really wasn't anywhere to hide."

That was the last thing Sissy wanted to hear, "I don't know. Let me fill out a report, I mean, what if somebody's under there and they die?"

The officers looked at each other as if they were sharing a moment that Sissy couldn't interpret, but the two men never offered a reply. Michaels handed Sissy the paperwork, who filled it out with pen in one hand and robe tightly closed at the breast with the other. Dave looked over her shoulder and watched as she filled out the report. When all was complete, the woman handed the clipboard over to Michaels, who gave it back to Thurber, who began to peruse it.

"Now, ma'am, if you feel the need to call us for any reason concerning this crawl space, call this number, and tell the clerk you're calling regarding this here case number," Michaels said in a less gruff voice, handing Sissy a card with the number to the police station on one side and a handwritten case number on the back.

Sissy took the card and looked at it, "Thank you. I feel better. I don't know what it was. Kinda' scary, you know?"

Thurber finished looking at Sissy's paperwork, "It's good," he said to Michaels.

"Call us if you need us," and the two men moseyed out of the door with that confident swagger that must be a part of every policeman's training.

Sissy and Dave sat in silence, until they heard the police car's engine start up and its wheels roll out of the driveway.

Sissy threw her hands up in the air in disbelief, "Well, what the hell was that racket? I heard it. You heard it. So, what the . . .?"

Dave got up from the couch and took a seat in his recliner, "I don't know. But did you see the look they gave each other when you said something about somebody dying under the house?"

Sissy played with the belt of Dave's robe, "Yeah, they think I'm a loon. Partially nude loon."

Dave laughed, "I forgot you were in my robe! Don't worry, they've probably seen worse. But, I mean, they looked at each other as if you hit on something."

"What?"

Dave picked up the remote, but put it back down, "I bet this

254

isn't the first time they've had to check on our crawl space."

"What makes you say that?"

Dave leaned toward Sissy, "They checked and said something about, 'Looks like last time. Nothin' here.'"

Sissy threw out her hands in disbelief, "'Looks like last time?' You sure they said that?"

"Yeah."

"So, we've got some sort of pissed off ghost?"

Dave picked up the remote, again. Apparently, he was growing bored with their conversation. "Maybe. Anything's possible."

Sissy held up her right hand with the finger missing at Dave, "Oh, you have NO idea."

Dave shuddered, "I don't want to know, knowin' you."

"You thirsty?" Sissy asked Dave. Dave nodded and twiddled his empty beer can.

Sissy just rolled her eyes and walked into the kitchen. What she saw there shocked her. "DAVE! Come in here!"

Dave came running into the kitchen, "What, what?"

"Look at this!" and Sissy pointed to the white surfaces of the washer and dryer, on top of which sat a bright, pink, dried residue.

"Good grief, Sissy, I thought there was somebody in here with you! What's wrong, now?"

"No, LOOK. You see it?"

Dave leaned closer to the washer and dryer, "You spill something?"

"No, I just saw it."

Dave pointed his finger at the substance and asked in an

annoyed manner, "Well, what do you think it is, Sissy?"

Sissy gave an annoyed shrug back at Dave, "I don't know."

Dave leaned back away from the pink splattered appliances, "Will it come off?"

Sissy licked her finger and was about to rub it, but Dave grabbed her wrist, "Don't touch it, woman. We don't know what it is, yet. I'll get you a sponge." Dave gave Sissy the raggedy sponge they used to wipe the floor. Sissy scrubbed the washer and dryer. After a little elbow grease, the pink residue came off. Dave walked around the kitchen, "It's on top of the stove and the cabinet and the microwave."

Sissy walked around the kitchen, "So anything white?"

Dave leaned closely over the table, careful not to touch it, "Might be on top of the table and the sink, but they're so dark, I can't tell."

"Weird." Sissy threw up her hands in frustration, "As if having to listen to all of that noise wasn't bad enough, now I have to clean up some sort of neon ectoplasm."

"At least it's a pretty pink. Not a scary green or gross black or something. Could be worse."

Sissy lowered her shoulders in defeat, "Yeah, like a ghost taking a dump all over my kitchen appliances?"

Dave grinned and said playfully, "There you go. See, there's a bright side."

The rest of the night passed without incident. Even the smell from the tub was less than it had been earlier that afternoon. Dave was proud of his prediction that the tub just needed "airing." The rest of the night crept by without event, as did the next several months, until the couple had completely dismissed the strange occurrence beneath their bedroom floor.  Life was good, again.


Until . . .

## Chapter 37: I Think We Have Ghosts

One Saturday night, Sissy sat up straight in bed, pulled the blinds open, and screamed through them, "Stop talking about me! Stop looking at me! Leave me alone! Go away!"

Sissy tried to lie back down, but immediately sprang up on her knees to commence screaming through the blinds, "I can hear you! Leave me alone!"

Dave woke up with a yell, "What! What!"

Sissy stood up in the middle of the bed and tried looking through the blinds at other angles, "They're out there. I know they are. I can't see them, but I can hear them."

"Who?"

"If I knew who, I'd tell you. But it's them, again! They won't stop talking about me!"

Dave rolled over in the bed, "I haven't heard anything."

Sissy steadied herself in the bed by putting her hands against the wall, "They won't let me sleep, and they're telling lies. Nothing but lies."

"Like what?"

"I can't make out all of it, but they're being mean to me. Telling lies. Calling me names."

Dave sat up and acted as if he were tearing at his hair, "God, Sissy! I'm tired! You were dreaming!"

Sissy remained immovable from the wall, pointing to her chest, "So, why do I still hear them?"

Dave reached over and leaned toward Sissy and said in an angry tone, "Because you're insane?"

Sissy lifted her right leg and put her right hand on her

mouth, "That's what they said! You DID hear them! *You're* lying to me!"

Dave flopped back into his pillow and threw his hands over his face, "No, Sissy, I was joking with you. You're sleepwalking or something. Like last time."

Sissy shook her head back and forth rapidly, the sensation proved to herself that she was feeling, attached to the moment, "No, I know what's going on. This is different. This is real."

"Real freakin' weird is what it is, Sissy. Go to bed. Nobody's talking about you. If they are, I'll beat them up . . . in the morning, okay?"

Sissy's heart beat fast in her chest and then, without notice, she felt calm. The urgency of the moment passed. "Fine. You go back to sleep. I'm gonna make myself some tea."

Dave rolled over in bed and fell asleep, following orders a little faster than Sissy wanted. Sissy hesitated to see if she heard anything, but everything was quiet. The idea of sleepwalking or talking in her sleep was embarrassing. Maybe some warm tea would calm her nerves and make her realize she was dreaming.

The curtain-less kitchen windows let in the full moonlight without any intrusion. The room was so bright, Sissy didn't have to turn on any lights. In just a matter of minutes, the kettle was warming, and Sissy was slowly nodding off to sleep on the stool she kept by the tiny table in the center of the room. Leaves rattling outside woke the dozing woman. The tea kettle started to whistle, so Sissy took it off of the eye before the kettle woke Dave. To make her insomnia even worse, her scar on her right hand was hurting. The ghost finger felt stiff, and she would have given anything to pop her missing finger.

She was pouring herself a cup of tea when she heard the leaves, again, but this time, it sounded like someone walking in her yard. The sound froze Sissy. With a force of will, the terrified woman turned her head toward the window by the stove, dreading what she might see. Nothing was there. She told herself it was probably a cat. Taking a sip of warm tea, Sissy sat down on her stool. Then she heard the voices.

Anger overcame any feelings of fear. Sissy quietly put her tea on the table and tiptoed across the linoleum. This time there wouldn't be any stupid blinds to get in her way. Crouching to avoid detection, Sissy raised her nose over the front door window ledge by the stove and peaked outside into the front yard. Nothing. Between the full moon and the bright streetlamp, the front lawn was completely illuminated. Had anyone been out there, they would have nowhere to hide, except immediately behind the brown wall to their patio. But that was made impossible by all of the flowers in the front flower bed. The peonies were no longer in bloom, but the azaleas were thick and overgrown.

Sissy crouched back down and walked over to the second window, which overlooked the side yard. Nothing. The fall wind blew a few dried leaves across the driveway, but that was not the sound she heard. That was not the crunching sound of someone walking on leaves. A harder breeze briefly kicked up, making the leaves in the neighboring trees "shush." That was not the sound she heard, either. That was nothing like the voices. Something *had* to be there.

Sissy tried the third window, looking into the carport. Despite the shelter, light still managed to show every ugly detail of her junky carport. Like the previous owners, their shed in the backyard was empty, while their carport was filled to maximum capacity. Dave had promised to move the clutter to the shelter out back, but "never got around to it." Sissy made a quick inventory. Boxes. Cans. Recycling. Trash cans. Mops. Brooms. Buckets. More boxes. Her SUV. His hatchback subcompact. Nothing out of its place. The only place to hide was between Sissy's truck in the carport and Dave's tiny car on the grass beside it.

Sissy wondered to herself, trying to find logic so as to counteract her feelings, *Why would someone want to hide between our cars? How would someone know she wasn't still in bed on the other end of the house? How would someone know to follow her around to the kitchen? Why would anyone want to talk about her, anyway?*

Just to be on the safe side, Sissy walked into the living room and flicked on the carport light. Let them know she was onto them. Maybe they'd feel she was holding all of the cards now, and they were the ones being stalked.

By the time Sissy made it back to her tea, it was cold. At this point, Sissy was too tired to bother sipping tea and just wanted to go back to bed. Just wanted to go back to sleep. Sissy was walking through the living room to make her way to the hall, when she saw in her periphery a dark figure run past the window by the side door. The sight made her heart fall into her stomach. Someone *was* there! As quietly as she could, Sissy ran into the bedroom and woke Dave.

"Dave! Dave! Wake-up! I saw someone run past our window into the backyard!"

Dave sat straight up in bed, "You what?"

In a hushed voice, Sissy yelled, "I saw someone run into

the backyard through the window by the living room door. I heard someone walking and the voices and . . ."

Dave grabbed his head, "You're sure?"

Sissy shook him, "Yes! I was wide awake! Go, do something!"

Dave let out a sigh, "This is getting old. I really don't want you to be crazy, but, I really don't want to have to deal with somebody in the middle of the night, either."

Sissy pleaded with him, "Could you go? You can prove me wrong, and I'll apologize for being crazy."

"You admit you're wrong? Fine." Dave got out of bed and put on a t-shirt to go with his pajama bottoms. Quietly, he slid the closet doors open and grabbed his gun off of the closet shelf. "You stay in here. If you hear anything, don't check on me, just call the police."

Sissy let out a squeal of fear.

"Shhh. Now, remember, don't get in the way, just call the police."

Sissy sat in bed and looked at the light's stripes, which lie across her bed. That creepy feeling came over her, again. *The light. It's in the light. Their light.* The thoughts bounced in the scared woman's mind, intensifying the fear she was already feeling. *Get out of the light. It can see you through the light.* Sissy's heartbeat hard in her chest. These thoughts were not generated by her mind. They were coming from somewhere else. Still, she felt that what the thoughts were telling her was true. True but partial, as if she were not privileged to more information, making her feel even more fearful.

She pulled her legs up to her chest, out of the light.

Everything was silent. Too silent. Nothing to do but wait.

Sissy thought to herself, *Dave said to call the police if I heard anything. He didn't say what to do if I heard nothing. If I check on him outside, he might shoot me by accident. This is awful. Absolutely awful.*

After what felt like hours, the living room door opened, and the familiar tread of Dave's feet walked heavily through the living room toward the hall. Different scenarios ran through Sissy's mind, *What if Dave's not alone and he's being held at gunpoint with his own gun? What if it's not Dave, but someone else? What if Dave saw nothing and he's really mad?*
*What if he saw someone, but they got away?*

Finally, Dave appeared in the bedroom. He was silent. Sissy watched as he put his gun back on the closet shelf and smooth the bed where the light's stripes were. Uncharacteristically, Dave didn't bother to take his t-shirt off, but left it on and crawled into bed.

Sissy put her hands at her mouth and nudged Dave with her elbow, "Well, what'd you see?"

Dave lay next to her as if he were frozen, "I'll tell you in the morning."

Sissy's mind momentarily went black with fear, "Why?!?"

With the same emotionless tone and frozen posture, Dave said, "Just, don't worry about it now, okay?"

Sissy's heart pounded, but then she realized, "But you saw something? I'm not crazy?"

"Shhh. Go to sleep." Dave tenderly reached out for Sissy and pulled her to him.

The warmth of his embrace made Sissy feel secure and warm,

again. If this was his way of shutting her up, she liked it.

The next morning the snoozing couple woke to the sound of breakfast cooking in their kitchen. A radio was playing gospel music on a crackling A.M. station, bacon fried in a pan, and dishes clinked as a table was being set. Sissy and Dave rolled over and looked at one another. The sounds were amusing. The smell was convincing. And then it all disappeared. Sissy waited for Dave to speak first, wanting his take on the situation.

Dave sat up in bed, pulled Sissy to him, and put his arm around her, "I never thought I'd say this, but I think we have ghosts."

Sissy feigned surprise and put her hands to her mouth, "No!" She felt her missing finger touch her skin.

"Mm-hmm. I also remember you bought an Ouija board a few months ago."

Sissy didn't say anything.

Dave got up and walked toward the closet in which the Ouija board sat, still in its original wrapping, "I think we should take it out back and burn it."

Sissy felt falsely accused, "But I've never even used the thing!"

Dave threw up his arms in exasperation and spun around toward her, "Why'd you buy it, then?"

Sissy felt cornered by Dave's over reaction, so she said in a cowed voice, "Because I thought our house was haunted."

Dave looked genuinely confused, "Before this morning?"

"Yeah."

Dave sat on the edge of the bed and grabbed her feet, "What gave you that idea?"

Sissy sighed, "We've been acting so weird lately. Your obsession with the carpet. Me screaming about the light. Something's gotten hold of us, and I just wanted to find out what it was."

Dave crossed his arms in front of himself, as if he were protecting his space from Sissy, "Those things are evil. I heard they cause crap like this to happen."

Sissy remembered Sheila's comment to Virginia in the store, but played on Virginia's words to fake herself into believing they were true, "The lady who sold it to me said it was useful for communicating with spirits. I could ask it what it wanted and try to get it to go away."

Dave lowered his head and snickered, "I bet she has some beach front property in Montana she'd like to sell you."

Sissy looked at him confusedly, "I thought it was Arizona."

Dave leaned in close to Sissy and said as if she were a child, "Oh, but you'd just LOVE Montana."

Sissy leaned over and slapped Dave on the arm, "That's not nice. I was trying to make things better, and you're calling me stupid."

Dave rubbed his arm and pretended to be hurt, "I'd never call you stupid. I'd just pick on you."

Sissy let out a huff of anger.

"I'm kidding! Why do you have to take everything so personally?"

Sissy grabbed Dave and snuggled into him, "Let's see if they left anything for us for breakfast."

Dave snuggled back, "Probably have more of that pink crap all over it."

"Might be tasty," Sissy pulled on Dave's face and kissed his lips.

"Taste like chicken?" he laughed at her.

"As long as it smells like bacon."

After making love past the normal breakfast hour, Sissy and Dave slowly made their way into the kitchen where they were, in fact, greeted by pink stains all over their countertops and appliances.

"Woman, clean up this here kitchen and make me my breakfast!," Dave said, mimicking a bowlegged cowboy with his hand down the front of his pants.

Sissy threw a damp sponge at her cowboy, who caught it and held it like a football player going for a long pass. In a thick Southern accent, Sissy exclaimed, "My hero!" and locked her hands under her chin and batted her eyes like a southern belle.

Dave's next impersonation was that of a police officer, thumbs in the sides of his pajama bottoms, swaggering his hips, "Don't worry ma'am, I'll take it from here." To Sissy's amazement, Dave actually started scrubbing away at the pink residue while she started breakfast.

The couple's mood remained light as they ate their bacon, eggs, and toast on the dining room table. Even the house had a contented air wafting through it. Then Sissy thought about the intruder she'd seen the night before.

Sissy cut into her eggs, "So, what'd you see outside last night?"

Dave took a swig of his orange juice, "Do we have to talk about that now?"

Sissy watched the yolk ooze out of its thin bubble, "Why

not?"

"Cause it's . . . I don't know."

"Weird? Like hearing and smelling breakfast cooking and finding pink stuff all over our kitchen?"

Dave looked toward the back of the house as if he were making sure no one could listen in on their conversation, "It was weirder."

Sissy did not want Dave to duck out of this conversation. She decided to make a joke, to ease his tension, "A drunk student jumping the back fence in the buff?"

Dave put his palms against the side of the table as if he were bracing himself, "I don't want to talk about it."

Sissy didn't care about how he felt about "it" and whatever "it" was. She wanted to know, and she wanted to know *right now*, "Well, I want to know because it scared the B'Jesus out of me."

To her amazement, Dave continued the conversation. He looked into his plate like a trauma victim, "I looked all around outside, and I thought I saw something looking through our bedroom window."

Sissy pushed her plate away and put her elbow on the table, "Which one?"

Dave darted his eyes over at Sissy without ever moving his head, "The one that overlooks your side of the bed."

Sissy huffed in relief, "That's crazy. There's a slope on that side of the house. They'd have to be nine feet tall or standing on a ladder."

Dave swallowed hard, "Hovering."

Sissy sat up straight, "Are you sure?"

Dave turned toward Sissy, "Wearing a cloak like some kind

of Druid, monk thing."

Sissy put her hand on Dave's wide shoulder, flabbergasted at his explanation of the previous night's events, "Hovering, wearing a cloak like a monk?"

Dave took a deep breath and blew it out, "Looking in through the window."

Sissy could feel fear emanating from his body through her hand, "Sure it wasn't that gnarly fig tree or a shadow?"

Dave lowered his head as if he were ashamed, "It turned and looked at me. But it had no face or hands or feet. Just this floating cloak looking at me. Felt . . . cold."

Sissy didn't like feeling Dave's fear. It made him seem . . . less somehow. She removed her hand, "You think that's what I hear at night sometimes? That thing talking to me?"

Dave watched Sissy remove her hand as if he knew she did not want to touch him, "Don't know, but I feel crazy talking about it. If I could make it go away, I would, you know."

Sissy let out a deep sigh. She felt the need to tell him about her experiences with the paranormal to help him feel better, "Well, I don't think you're crazy. I'm . . . kind of psychic."

Dave paused for a moment, then let out a guffaw, "That's why you need an Ouija board? I thought psychics knew everything."

Sissy felt offended, "Apparently not. I get pieces of some things. Stories from others. Been possessed once."

"Possessed? By a demon? Head spin around?" Dave chuckled and spun his index finger in the air.

Sissy turned her head in embarrassment, "No. I got possessed by a murdered woman who wanted me to help her."

Dave shook his head and raised his brows, "This is too much. Are you sure you're not making this stuff happen?"

"Why would I want to make anything like this happen? It scares me."

Dave raised his eyebrows, "Can we even figure out what 'it' is?"

Sissy rubbed the nub where her middle finger was missing, "I tried to find the history on the house, but a fat chunk of papers was missing." She looked at the ugly, bulging scar, "How come you've never asked me about my finger?"

"My uncle lost his finger when he was a little boy helping load hay. He never talked about it, and you were never supposed to, either. Just used to it, I guess."

Sissy's nub was starting to throb, "Oh, well, that's nice. It is kind of a long story, anyway. Not good breakfast conversation."

Dave nonchalantly shrugged, "That's fine. But, what about the breakfast sounds this morning?"

"Might be more than one ghost. Could be several. Remember the noises coming from the crawl space?"

"You really think somebody might've died under the house?"

Sissy reached out and touched Dave's shoulder again. His reverence for her finger, her "deformity" as she saw it, put any feelings of his lessening to rest. She had even more respect for him than before. "I don't have a clue. May have died. May have been buried. May have been bad energy left behind from some freak accident."

The conversation lulled for a moment.

Dave scratched his chin, "How do we make it go away?"

"That's why I bought the Ouija board. The woman said I could contact it, or them, and ask them to go away."

Dave grabbed his fork and put it on his plate, "I guess. I still think those things are evil."

Sissy shrugged, "Probably right. I'll take it back if you want."

"Keep it. I mean. Those things are just toys, right? It's not like you'd go to hell for using one or anything."

# Chapter 38:  I'm Here

After breakfast, the couple decided to spend the day in bed, making love and sleeping, sleeping some more and making love. They rose for lunch and went back to their bedroom. They rose for a quick drink and went back to their bedroom. They rose for a snack and went back to their bedroom. They rose for dinner and went back to their bedroom. They rose for another drink and went back. Then a night toddy and went back to their bedroom; this time to actually sleep.

About three o'clock in the morning, Sissy awoke to whispers. It wasn't the dreaded voice from the night before that sent her into paranoid rages. It wasn't the sound of thoughts infiltrating her head, telling her about "their light." These whispers she'd never heard before. They were different. Dreamy.

A small, unobtrusive voice barely squeaked out a pathetic plea, "I'm here."

Sissy rolled over and saw that her bed was not butt up to the sidewall below the window but was three feet away from it. Different sheets, thick sheets for allergies, covered her bed and the musty odor of sickly old people and their aging things filled the room. None of this bothered her. At the moment, she found it absolutely normal. Her response seemed absolutely normal to her, as well, "I know you're here, Little Mouse."

Little Mouse shyly responded, "It's his eyes. Don't let it devour his eyes."

Sissy looked over the side of the bed, but didn't see anything there, "Quit teasing. Where are you?"

"I'm *here*," came the still little voice.

Sissy stared into the light filtered darkness, "I can't see you. Are you sure you're there?"

Little Mouse whispered, "Yes, I wait here. For you."

Sissy rolled over in bed, "Go away and let me sleep."

Little Mouse whispered in a pleading tone, "I can't leave. The eyes will be the death of you."

Not of her own volition, she asked, "They watch me?"

Little Mouse rustled as if it were moving closer to Sissy, "They fear you. They want you."

"They can't have me." Her response was not of her own making. Yet, she could feel her own consciousness creeping into her head, competing for room in the conversation. Sissy began to feel as if she were telegraphing an ongoing conversation that she merely spat out of her mouth like a radio. The more her consciousness invaded, the more the conversation became confusing. She knew there was a natural response that would keep her safe, but her own consciousness was pushing it away, making her ability to be safe from "it" uncertain.

Little Mouse barely whispered out, "Don't take another serving from his plate. It will be the death of you."

After Little Mouse finished his obtuse statement, Sissy felt another voice talk to her from the dark shadows of her room. It did not speak out loud but broke into her thoughts. It was the voice that warned her about "their light." The Thought quietly bounced in her brain, *Don't believe it.*

Sissy still felt as if she were in control and everything was normal, "I want to ask you to leave, Little Mouse."

In a deeper, more authoritative tone, Little Mouse replied, "I will save you."

The Thought interjected a warning that spread through her body in the sensation of fear, *You know what he really is. He is no mouse. Do not say what he really is. Do not tell him what he wants to hear.*

Sissy stared into the darkness by her bed. A cherry nightstand stood dark and massive beside her bed, white doilies glowed in the void-like darkness. Upon the stand sat a pretentious lamp outlined in tassels and scrolled iron work. Medicine bottles stood sentinel around the lamp like tiny soldiers defending a fort. Sissy reached out to the darkness and saw that she was wearing a bed jacket, silky and white, glowing with a silvery sheen against the darkness.

Her nails were long and yellowed; her hand was shriveled and so pale it, too, glowed against the darkness. Sissy put her hands up to her face, and felt deep wrinkles and loose, thin skin against her withered fingertips. All of her fingers were accounted for. The middle finger of her right hand throbbed intensely. What was so strange about that finger? She knew she knew the answer but couldn't remember why it was hurting her. Sissy instinctively reached out to the darkness, not knowing what she was reaching for. The deep emptiness beside her bed felt cold and terrifying. Quickly she pulled back her hand in fear.

The Thought told her, *Do not show it fear. Do not give it your fear.*

Sissy tried to obey and addressed Little Mouse with confidence, "I want you to leave."

In a deep, dark tone Little Mouse sarcastically chuckled. It's voice grew deeper, more confident. It asked, "Do you know what I am?"

Sissy tried to warm the chill off of her hand and answered in a weak voice, "Yes."

The Thought interjected, *Do not tell him what he wants to hear! Do not tell him! Make him stay a mouse! You can trap the mouse!*

Little Mouse seemed to be aware of The Thought's cognizance in Sissy's mind. No longer pathetic, Little Mouse no longer whispered, but demanded in an angry, loud voice, "Tell me what I am!"

Sissy held her hand to her chest and started to cry, "I cannot."

Little Mouse said in its original, whispered, shy voice, pleading to Sissy, "Tell me. You know what I am. Tell me what I am. I feel so small. So lonely."

The Thought bounced in Sissy's mind, but her fear scattered it, making The Thought's message confusing. She could not connect with it. All she could feel was the intense fear that pinned her to the spot, making her unable to look away from the darkness, which was swirling at the base of the nightstand. The swirling was starting to create a form, a darker darkness that emanated coldness and fear.

Little Mouse snickered with disdain. It seemed to enjoy Sissy's pain. In a strong, angry tone it asked Sissy, "Who will protect you?"

Sissy remembered there was someone who would protect her. Who was it? Slowly the memory of Dave crept into her mind. The realtor reached over to Dave's side of the bed and felt his sleeping body beneath the sheets. Sissy confidently told Little Mouse, "He will. He will protect me."

Little Mouse did not hesitate to respond, "Not if he isn't there."

Sissy tried to find Dave's hand, but everywhere she grasped on Dave's body, that place disappeared. Frantically, Sissy looked behind herself and saw that Dave was not there. No one was there. She was alone with Little Mouse and the feeling gave her absolute terror, "I'm not alone. He is here!"

A deep grumbling voice, as if a wild animal were speaking, "He is here. For now. I *will have* your eyes. I will devour them and eat your soul."

Sissy's eyesight began to blur, the room darkened even more. She thought she was going blind. Begging Little Mouse, Sissy pleaded through her tears, "Stop it, please."

Little Mouse paused before answering. The pleasure it felt in causing Sissy pain was palpable. In a calm, controlled voice it asked, "What am I? Tell me what I am."

Sissy blurted out in a fearful whisper, "Demon."

The darkness dissipated and the dream room seemed to brighten. Sissy's consciousness began to recognize that the setting in the room did not belong to her. It was someone else's. Whose? Sissy looked at the bed jacket and tore it off, throwing it onto the foot of the bed.

The jacket separated into two pieces and shrank into two little white orbs. Despite her desire to not look, Sissy acted not of her own will. She leaned over and picked up the orbs. They were eyes, human eyes sitting in the palm of her hand. Before Sissy had time to try to comprehend her feelings about the eyes, a rough, ragged breathing focused her attention to the side of her bed. There on the floor beside the bed, she saw the demon.

It was black and decaying. The thing was sunk halfway through the floor such that its legs were not on top of the floor but standing beneath it as if the floor had opened up to form a tunnel straight to hell. But its torso was bare and muscular. With long, strong arms, it began lifting itself further up through the floor. Long arms with giant claws on the ends tore through the darkness, reaching, grabbing. Its face was twisted and evil, maniacal. It had no eyes, only sunken features that were human like, emanating chaos, fear, and insanity. Sissy recognized the face and tried to pull away from the side of the bed. Suddenly, Sissy smelled smoke, as from a large fire. The thing pulled itself up the side of the bed with one hand and grabbed Sissy's wrist with the other, making her spill the eyes onto the floor. The eyes melted and bubbled into the wood floor of the alternative universe's bedroom. In a guttural voice filled with hate, the demon asked her in a strange cadence, almost like rhyming, "Do you still feel sorry for me? Pity? Was I ever truly human? No! Human in form only, never human in sum. Hell will swallow you whole and I will have your eyes. I will have your soul!"

Sissy couldn't think. Terror made her unable to scream. Her heart pounded heavy in her chest. She couldn't find her voice. The only sound she could utter was an involuntary cough from choking. The room was filling with smoke. A fire. Her chest was tight. She couldn't breathe. The demon began to shake the frightened woman. Sissy imperceptibly shook her head "no."

The demon was empowered. In control. Its anger was abated by a sense of triumph. Arrogantly it asked, "Do you still think *you* can save *me*?" It laughed and pulled on her arm, trying to drag her off of the bed.

Sissy felt the demon's nails dig into her flesh and its strong grip squeezed her wrist. She tried to speak, but her mouth opened with no words coming forth. Simultaneously focused and consumed by fear, Sissy tried again and again to make the words come out of her mouth, but there was nothing. Each time she tried to speak, her chest tightened and burned, as if the smoke were filling her lungs. Her mind cried out to God. Finally, she was able to find her voice and let out a scream filled with terror and desperation. The same scream shared by all creatures who know they are about to be devoured and all hope of escape is lost.

Dave sat up straight in bed. His panicked yelps responded to Sissy's screams.

Dave kicked off the covers and ran to the closet to grab his gun, sleep sat heavily upon his lids. After fumbling through the darkness, Dave regained his consciousness and turned on the light. He saw that Sissy was completely awake, struggling against something, her arm tightly wedged between the bed and the wall. Her screams made Dave want to hide for his own safety and run to her rescue at the same time. Finally, he called out to the pinned woman, "Sissy! Sissy! Wake up! You're dreaming! Wake up!" His pleas went unheard. Dave ran to the side of the bed and pulled the mattress away from the wall. As if freeing her arm from an immovable position, Sissy yanked her arm to her side with a strong force, waking her from a wide-eyed dream.

"Dave?" Sissy asked, tears streaming down her face.

"Yeah. You okay?" he asked as he put his arm around her.

"No. It was awful." Sissy buried her head in Dave's shoulder. He could feel her body tremble in what felt like an infinite number of tiny little spasms.

"It was just a dream. Just a very bad dream." He stroked her hair and felt angry.

Anger at whatever had caused her fear and anger at the innate sense of helplessness he felt to truly help her.

Sissy sobbed, "No. It wasn't. It was horrible. It . . . it grabbed hold of me. It wants us."

"To do what?"

"No, it wants to kill us."

Dave felt his heart race and hoped Sissy's trembling would prevent her feeling his heart pound beneath his chest. His temples pulsed and his vision blurred. This was the most afraid he'd ever been in his life. Somehow, he knew she was right. What about, he didn't know. But she was right. Not wanting to upset his lover further, he just held her tight and kissed her on top of her head. Sissy lay on Dave's shoulder until she bawled herself back to sleep, completely overcome by exhaustion. Dave held her close and never let go of her throughout the rest of the night.

Dave couldn't sleep anymore that night. Sissy slept soundly, as if nothing had happened. He was somewhat envious of her slumber but had no desire to earn it the way she had. What could he do? Nothing. He could only sit and watch. He could not protect her from the entity that had made its presence known. All he could do was sit and watch.

## Chapter 39: Donut Holes

The next morning, Sissy awoke to her alarm clock blaring out an inappropriately upbeat tune about love and sunshine. The previous night's events were erased from her mind. She felt satisfyingly refreshed. A good, deep sleep. Sissy went through her morning routine to find that she had started her period, again. The sight filled Sissy with frustration, "Am I going through menopause already? This is the third time in two months!" The sound of her voice was embarrassing. She didn't want to awaken Dave, especially from something as silly as talking to herself about her period.

Suddenly, Dave knocked on the bathroom door, "Sissy, you okay in there?"

Sissy chuckled, "Yes. I'm fine."

Dave uncharacteristically responded with a tone of meekness, "Good. Just checking. Okay?"

***

That day at the office started out particularly uneventful. Business was slow. Sissy had a couple of house showings scheduled, but both clients cancelled. No one called for appointments, showings, appraisals, anything. It was the second week of August, a very dry and hot August. Everything was suffering, from businesses to the dying grass and shedding trees. School would be starting in September, bringing with it the annual influx of college students. Barb assured a restless Sissy that the procrastinating college students would be in town in one more week.

Then the agency would have about ten thousand students looking for everything from affordable slum housing to overpriced apartments. In another month, kids would be sick of the overcrowded dorms, desperate for somewhere else to live. More work than she'd have time to handle. The beginning of "The Feast Cycle," Barb called it.

Sissy was warming a donut in the microwave when she heard a mouse trap snap shut. The sound startled her. As she stood in front of the microwave, impatiently counting down the time with the digital numbers, the initial shock deepened to a more sinister fear. The memory of a voice telling her, "You can trap a mouse," slowly swam into her consciousness. The message was silly in and of itself. What was causing her fear? She couldn't remember.

Barb walked into the kitchenette and looked behind the fridge, "Hot dang! I caught the little bastard!"

Sissy poured herself a cup of coffee, "And I thought it was just a mouse."

Barb held up the still twitching little beast with a maniacal gleam in her eyes, "A donut pilfering mouse! He's gotten into every box I've bought this week! And my loaf of pumpernickel. Peed on the emergency roll of toilet tissue. You know how annoying that is in an office full of women? Die, you little bastard, die!"

Sissy took her warm, gleaming donut out of the microwave and examined it closely. Sure enough, there was a small, circular chunk missing out of the delicious smelling pastry.
"So, I guess it would be a bad thing if I ate this donut with the mouse bite in it."

Barb dangled the trap in the air, "What's the worst thing

that could happen? Rabies? Black Plague?"

"I cooked it in the microwave for fifteen seconds."

Barb showed no fear toward the mouse as Sissy had assumed she would. Rather, Barb inquisitively and shamelessly poked the dead mouse with a long fingernail, "I'm sure that's plenty of time to nuke some bacteria and viruses. Mouse saliva. Mouse urine. Mouse droppings. Oh, yeah, it's *good*."

Sissy stared at the dead mouse with its bulging black eyes, "Little bastard. I had my mouth all set for that donut!"

Barb walked over to the trash can and threw the trap and its prey away, "Looks like one of us needs to make a donut run."

Sissy's face brightened, "Oh, let me. I'm *dying*. Everybody else has something to do." Sissy gave Barb "the praying hands" and said, "I'll bring you back something special."

Barb turned the faucet on full force and cupped her hands beneath the liquid soap dispenser, "Soap me."

Sissy did as she was told.

"More."

Sissy gave the liquid soap dispenser several good whacks, "That enough or should I give you a good dousing of Bug Be Gone?"

Scrubbing her hands in thick, white lather, "No, that won't be necessary. But I dooooo want you to get me a Bavarian filled donut with whipped cream, not that fake chocolate crap on top, and a diet Coke."

Sissy looked at Barb with a quieted snicker.

"Oh, hush. It's not my fault that artificial sweetener is addictive."

***

Sissy loved donuts but hated the way donut shops smelled. Heavy grease, lard, too much sugar. Just breathing the air could cause a person to gain ten pounds. The best donuts in town were only two blocks away in an unappetizing and dated store front reminiscent of the seventies. Brown, orange, and hot pink decorated the torn canopy outside and the carved-up Formica tables and countertops inside. The dark brown cobblestone floor was buried beneath twenty years of ground-in dirt. Pictures of past employees of the month were plastered in a sludgy mixture of grease residue and decades of dust. Despite the overall grunginess, the business managed to get a ninety on its health code inspections.

With an air of complete indifference, a pimply faced twenty-something year old asked, "Can I help you?"

"Yes, I'd like a dozen donuts. And a Bavarian cream filled donut with real chocolate and whipped cream on top."

"Anything else?"

"Let me look while you get that," Sissy walked the length of the counter until she came across the powdered donut holes. The hair on the back of her neck stood on end as she couldn't help but to think that they looked very much like eyeballs. The thought had never occurred to her before.

The boy mouth-breathed. Mouth-breath saliva stuck to his lips, "Made up your mind, yet?"

Sissy poked at the "eyeball" donuts from behind the safety of the glass with her car keys "Yeah, that's all. Ya' ever notice that these powdered donut holes look like eyeballs?"

The boy huffed a phlegm-sounding laugh, "No, that's sick."

Sissy grimaced at the scrawny boy with the oily sheen. As

if it weren't bad enough, he worked in a donut shop and couldn't gain weight if he tried, and he had to be blatantly rude as well. He probably didn't even like donuts. Sissy paid the boy and drove back to work.

With nothing better to do, Sissy decided she'd try sending Dave an e-mail. Not computer illiterate, but not computer savvy, the realtor felt a little intimidated and decided to erase her message. What if it should go out to everybody in the office? Then everyone she worked with would know she didn't have a lot of business and had nothing better to do than play on the computer. How embarrassing! Suddenly, her wrist began to hurt. The muscles in her fingers clenched and her hand tingled as if the circulation had been cut off. Sissy had never experienced carpal tunnel syndrome before, but was aware she didn't have it now either.

Suddenly, the bad dream came back to her. The conversation with Little Mouse.
The beast that materialized from the swirling darkness. Its message. Its hatred. Sissy rubbed her wrist and, for the first time in her life, felt afraid to go home. She needed to talk to someone. Someone who'd understand. Mimi.

When the human brain is besieged by anxiety, time seems to come to a standstill.
The rest of the day went by so slowly, it was painful, unbearable, despite the fact that the phone rang off the hook and she was lucky enough to be the only other person on site. Just as Barb had predicted, business picked up. Now, though, Sissy didn't care that at ten o'clock that morning she had nothing and at three o'clock her calendar was practically full. All she wanted to do was make a

mad dash downtown and find Mimi.

Finally, five o'clock made its grand entrance with the suspense of a spoiled diva waiting to hear her audience grow impatient. Within minutes, Sissy had her SUV parked, meter running, and bottom planted firmly at Mimi's bar. Mimi's female associates were busy wiping down the bar and all of its gadgets and appliances that give a real bar its fabulous mystique.

## Chapter 40:  While You Were Away

A shorter, younger version of Mimi approached Sissy.  The girl had obviously spent many an hour perfecting the simulation of her idol:  dyed black hair, pale base, crimson lips, thick eyeliner, and silver jewelry accessorizing a black lace dress, paired with a clunky pair of knee high combat boots.  The girl awkwardly pushed her limp bangs behind her conspicuously large ears.  Sissy accidentally stared, which did not go unnoticed by the girl.  In self-defense, the barmaid played off her self-consciousness with the over confident facade of an amateur.

In a forced tone of superiority, the girl asked, "What can I get you?"

Sissy smiled and thought to herself, *So service here is some kind of a privilege?  I should be grateful you acknowledged me?* Rather than respond in this manner, Sissy got down to business, "I'm here to see Mimi.  Is she in?"

The girl rolled her eyes, "Yeah.  She's upstairs in the shop."

Sissy chuckled confrontationally at the barmaid's attitude, "Thank you.  I feel I should leave you a tip for putting you through the harassment of waiting on me."  Sissy reached in her purse and pulled out a penny.  She placed it on the countertop and slid it toward the girl, who abruptly turned and walked away.

To Sissy's relief, the old rusty stairs leading up to the shop had been replaced with new, shiny, galvanized ones.  Other surprises awaited inside.  The old, hidden liquor parlor was completely renovated.  The interior walls were painted purple with silver stars and mystic symbols.  A crimson carpet lined the floor with a border of gold. A marble countertop with copper bowls and crucibles, much like those found in an alchemist's lab, waited at the far end of the room. There was even a miniature Zen rock garden sitting on the counter. Shelves of books and strange bottles lined the walls. In the middle of the room sat a couple of tables and chairs with laminated placemat/menus. Mimi's shop was also a cafe. Interesting.

Sissy wondered to herself, *So, what's on the menu? Eye of newt? Bat wings? Boil, boil, toil and something, cauldron burn and something, something. What play was that?*

Sissy walked over to the nearest table and read the menu. Herbal teas. Medicinal drinks. Organic muffins. There were old English style pies and tarts filled with such strange ingredients as rhubarb and horseradish. Each item had a list of physical, mental, and spiritual benefits under it. Addressing no one in particular, Sissy said aloud, "Yummy. I can drink licorice tea for PMS. All at the low, low price of three bucks."

Mimi emerged through a curtain made from indie print chiffon scarves. A smirk was on her face, "So, how much tip did you leave Brittany?"

Sissy pocketed the menu, "A penny. She was being snide."

Mimi leaned onto the cold marble countertop, "I'd fire her, but she worships me.
Pays her rent on time, too." Mimi pointed overhead to the loft.

Sissy nodded, "Good decision . . . I bet she'd stalk you."

"No doubt. I'll tell my shadow to serve you anything you want, free of charge as penance."

"Actually, I'm here to see you."

Mimi cocked her head to one side, "Really? What about?"

"I've got a bit of a problem and I don't know who else to talk to about it."

Mimi grinned from ear to ear, "I'm flattered. A kind of guru, I am, hmmm?"

"We'll see. Should I be polite and ask about your vacation, first?"

Mimi ran a black fingernail through the sand of the rock garden, "No. I'll just tell you. You know Talon moved to California, which lasted all of two weeks before working with Daddy's garbage-slash-trucking business lost its flavor. So, he moved back here and decided to form a rock band, living off of the money from selling the bar, which his dad let him have. Lucky bastard. Anyway, he begged for me to take him back. I did. He wanted to 'party like a rock star' and go on tour. Hence the 'vacation.' Two weeks doing the local circuit thing. God! It sucked. Talon was getting pissy because he started to figure out I leech off of him, so I had to play nice and follow his suck-rock band around until they ran their entire pathetic little circuit."

"How often you gonna have to do that?"

"Hopefully, never. They split up."

With an air of flippancy, Sissy sighed, "Such is the life of sex, drugs, and rock 'n roll."

"I wish. That would've made it interesting. Stupid drummer decided to become a priest."

"Bad trip?"

"No, on the very last day of the tour, idiot spilled his beer on an amp and nearly electrocuted himself. Said he saw God. Why he couldn't have done that like the second day on tour, I'll never know."

Sissy watched Mimi's spindly finger draw dots in the sand. Trying to sound like her old self and not freak Mimi out, Sissy said with a forced up-beat tone, "Well, if it's any consolation I bought a haunted house that makes me afraid to go home."

Mimi stopped swirling her finger in the sand and looked up, "That does suck."

Sissy wanted to play down the situation, not show her true feelings, "Yeah, bad dreams. Cold spots. Voices. Even Dave's seen stuff."

Mimi raked her nails deep into the sand as if it were someone's back, "Sissy's got a man! Use him and throw him away, baby!"

The unexpected outburst made Sissy feel a little self-conscious, "I actually kind of like him."

Mimi shrugged and went back to playing in her garden, "That's no good. Screw the ones you like. Screw over the ones that like you." Mimi winked at Sissy and went back to playing in the sand.

Sissy felt semi-offended, "You should make a poster of that." The realtor let out a deep sigh and forced herself to continue the conversation, "*Anyway* . . . my house is going to kill me if I don't do something fast."

This bit of information seemed to pique Mimi's interest. At least it caught her attention long enough to make her stop playing in the sand, "That's not good. Did you go through the house before you bought it?"

Sissy was bursting with anxiety, "Of course. I'm a realtor, for Christ's sakes! There wasn't anything there when we toured it. Seemed normal. No energy whatsoever."

Mimi stood erect and dusted off her hands, "Nothing weird at all?"

"The shed made me uncomfortable, but it's a shed. What woman cares about a creepy old shed?"

"Nothing else?"

Sissy sat and thought for a moment, "Well . . . there was this neat little row of pink flower petals lining the front of the house. They went all the way to the back like a neat little path."

"What kind of flowers?"

"Peonies. There were some in the front flower bed."

Mimi cocked her head, "Were? None there now?"

Sissy wondered where the conversation was heading, "No, too hot, I guess."

"Too bad, you could just make another path of petals."

"I don't think so. This thing has really gained momentum."

"Getting stronger?"

"Yeah. Stuff bumping, well, pounding on the crawl space door and under the house.
I think there's more than one - - some make us feel at ease, comfortable and others make us feel like we're losing our minds. Sometimes there's pink residue all over the kitchen appliances after strange things happen." Sissy raised her arms in the air for emphasis, "Oh, my God, and this nightmare I had."

Mimi pushed her hair behind her ears, "Who says it was a nightmare? Might have been the room remembering something. Or you were actually contacted."

Sissy shook her head in affirmation and agreed, "Well, it *was* real to me at the time."

Mimi nodded her head, thinking over the issue at hand,

"Pink petals. Pink residue. What feeling do you get from that?"

"Not scary, if that's what you mean. Why?"

"Could be a protection color. Pink have any significance to you?"

Sissy goofily grinned and felt her face blush, "A guy with bright pink sun block on his nose kept me from drowning when I was little. You could say I have a strange affection for the color."

Mimi snapped her fingers, "Okay, so pink *is* your protection color. Something is trying to protect you with that color. Anything bad happens in the future, I'd run to the kitchen."

Sissy pointed to Mimi as the thought struck her, "There's a bright pink room, but it's creepy."

Mimi's voice gushed with enthusiasm, "Maybe pink is the good entity's protection color and the other owners picked up on it. That room may be filled with too much bad energy for the color to matter."

Sissy scuffed her foot on the floor and vaguely remembered tripping over a champagne bottle there, "We can't just camp out in the kitchen. Maybe I should take a big, fat loss on the house and pray it'll sell quickly."

Sissy's comment momentarily dampened Mimi's momentum. Mimi shook her head, "Not yet. On a bright note, something wants you there if it gave you a pink petal line of protection around the house."

"I can't spend all of my money on pink flowers."

"If the painted room doesn't work, you throwing flowers around wouldn't either. It's got to come from the good entity."

Sissy pulled a chair from the counter and sat down, "Why can't the good get rid of the bad and leave me out of it?"

"Maybe it would like to. Maybe it needs your help. Who knows?"

"I sure as hell don't." In a quieted voice of embarrassment, Sissy said, "I bought an Ouija board."

Mimi laughed and poured a handful of sand onto the lunch counter, "From who? A toy store?"

"The gals at Ophelia's Corner."

"Oh, yeah, that shop down from here. You tried your board yet?"

Sissy still felt embarrassed, "No. I'm kind of scared of it."

"Those things can be tricky. Don't ever use it by yourself."

Sissy seized the opportunity, "So, that means you'll come over and use it with me?"

Mimi had a pernicious look on her face, "What about your man? He won't help?"

Sissy waved off the question, "Dave? Nooo. He wanted me to throw it away."

"This guy sounds like a real stick-in-the-mud." Mimi blew the sand down with the counter with an inaudible puff, "No offense."

"None taken. He just thinks it's evil. All of the things that've been happening around the house have got his nerves rattled, too. He actually followed me to the bathroom this morning. Asked if I was alright."

Mimi shrugged, "That was nice. You said you don't want to go home. What would you say is the worst thing that's happened so far?"

"That dream last night. Or whatever it was."

"Remember much?"

Sissy rubbed her arm, "Yeah. Something about I was asleep, but then I woke up and saw that the room was different. The bed was moved. Furniture was different. Then this thing that I thought was a mouse started talking to me."

Mimi huffed, "More like a rat."

"It started out really meek and sweet sounding."

Mimi joined Sissy in doodling in the thin scatter of sand, "What'd it want?"

"To tell me it was there. Warned me about eyes. Something about eyes. Eating eyes?"

Mimi squinched her face, "Nasty. So, I take that it didn't stay a mouse?"

"Let me tell you what happened next. I smelled lots of smoke. Then this voice *inside* my head came to me." Sissy put her hands up by her ears to emphasize her point.

"Not your voice, though?"

Sissy paused and made herself relive that moment to try to fully describe it, "No. This voice started talking to me, but not through my ears. Just . . . in my mind."

"Did it sound like the mouse?"

"No. I've heard it before. It warns me about 'the light' and not to get in 'their light.' Tells me to move out of 'their light.' Sounds confusing when I say it, but when it talks to me, it makes sense."

"What did it tell you last night?"

"It warned me not to trust the mouse. That I knew what it really was."

Mimi picked sand out from beneath her nails, "What was the mouse, then?"

"A demon. It came from up out of the floor by the side of my bed. Grabbed me by my wrist so hard. I woke up, or I was already awake, but I came to, screaming."

"What'd the demon look like?"

"A twisted, hateful man. Muscular. No legs, though."

Mimi shook her head, "This is weird."

Sissy sat up in her seat, put her hands in her lap and said with a sound of defeat, "That's your verdict?"

Mimi put her hand on Sissy's arm and pulled her hand quickly away, "No, I never said that. You've got some sort of vindictive spirit in your house. I know what I said earlier, but you might want to sell your house, if that's an option. I don't know that it can be gotten rid of from the sound of things."

Sissy put her head in her hands, "God! I can't afford to sell it!" Sissy let out an angry huff and yelled, "Well, it's my house! Why can't I get rid of it?"

"It may be spiritually integrated into the structure itself."

Sissy stared at Mimi for a moment and then asked, "What?!?"

"Could be an angry burn victim. Particles, energy, permeated . . . never mind. Has the house ever been in a fire?"

Sissy thought back to the cat at the Deeds Office, "Don't know. I looked up its history, but several decades on the house were missing."

Mimi wiped the sand off of the countertop, "There was a fire at the Deeds Office years ago."

"So I've heard."

"You said the demon was beside your bed in the dream. Where would it have been in real life?"

"Under my side of the bed."

"Ooh, that gave me chills. How often do you hear voices?"

"All the damn time! They drive me crazy! Say the worst things about me."

"Dave ever hear them?"

"No. But he did see a cloaked figure hovering above the ground by our bedroom window."

Mimi poured the remaining collected sand back into its garden, "Where is the window?"

"Right beside my bed."

All of a sudden the information seemed to sink into Mimi's brain, "Cloaked figure? What, like a Druid?"

Sissy shrugged, "That's what Dave said."

A glint sparkled in Mimi's eyes, "Staring through your window?"

"It looked at him, too. Didn't have a face or limbs. Just a darkness. Said it made him feel cold."

Mimi patted Sissy's arm again but did not pull away as if she were repulsed this time, "They all do. Take energy from their environment, making it cold. Doesn't mean it's evil."

"Why would it want to stare at me?"

"Could have been keeping watch over that demon in your room. If it is a demon. It could be somebody who thinks they're a demon. Some sort of lost soul."

"It did ask me if I still thought I could save him."

Mimi clapped her hands over the garden, "Well, that settles it. I think it's really a person. Somebody who either did something really bad or thinks they did. A twisted mind, tortured soul kind of thing."

Sissy put her head on her folded arms and muffled into the table, "Great. So what do I do?"

Mimi grinned, "Let's talk to him and find out."

Sissy sat up with a serious look on her face, "I don't know, Mimi. The more I remember, the less I want to go through anything like that again." Sissy looked at her hand and rubbed her wrist, "My wrist still hurts."

Mimi rubbed Sissy's wrist with her index and middle finger, producing a soft, warm heat, "I'll bring some stuff over from the store for cleansing and protection. Trust me. I'm good at this type stuff."

Sissy looked down at her wrist in amazement, "I guess."

Mimi pulled a small order pad and a chewed-up pencil from behind the counter, "Where do you live?"

"108 Haven Way."

Mimi scribbled the address, "There's an old family cemetery in a backyard on Haven Way."

"Backyard of somebody's house?"

"Yeah. But it was a family. Not like that movie where the whole subdivision was built on top of one."

"Surely this spirit wouldn't be from that."

Mimi tapped her pencil on the notepad, "Nah. Just kind of coincidental. As psychic as you are, they may visit, but I don't think they'd be harmful."

"So, I'm a ghost magnet?"

Mimi replied matter-of-factly, "Best get used to it."

Sissy suddenly realized that once her conversation with Mimi were over, she'd have to go home sometime that night. That thought frightened her. With a sense of urgency in her voice, Sissy asked, "When are you coming over?"

Mimi inhaled deeply, "How's about tonight?"

"Fine by me. Dave will just have to get over it."

"We could do it some other time."

Sissy felt a little relief. Just having someone else there than Dave and herself made her feel better. She wanted Mimi there, feeling as if the strange woman could help her, "No. He's got things he could do. If not, I'll tell him to find something or give us a hand."

Mimi smiled amusedly and loudly tore the address from the pad, "Literally. I close in about thirty minutes. See you in about an hour?"

"I'll see you then."

## Chapter 41:  Doing It on the Dining Room Table Was
## NO Fun

Sissy pulled into the driveway and found Dave pacing their front yard with his hands on his hips, staring at his feet, obviously agitated.

Dave ran over to Sissy's SUV and motioned for her to roll the window down, "Where have you been?"

"What do you mean?"

"You're late.  You're never this late.  I was worried."

Sissy felt confused, as if she had forgotten something, "Late for what?"

Dave opened her door for her as if to hurry her out of her car, "You're normally home by now."

Sissy stepped out of her car and looked at her watch, "It's all of five forty-five.  I haven't been gone *that* long."

Dave was breathing heavily, "Where were you?"

Sissy was getting angry at this unwarranted invasion of her privacy, "Visiting a friend, who will be coming over here in a few minutes.  What does the house look like?"

Dave pointed at the house, "I've got to pick up my beer cans."  With a sudden tone of aggression he asked, "What *friend* is this?"

"The woman who owns Jade. Mimi is going to try to help me with the things going bump in the night."

Dave sounded unimpressed and sarcastically asked, "The one that owns the lesbo bar downtown?"

Sissy grinned, trying to make it seem like a normal situation, "One in the same."

Dave had a serious look on his face, "Can I leave you two alone together?"

Sissy rolled her eyes in frustration, "Oh, good grief. She's got a live-in boyfriend."

"That really doesn't mean anything anymore."

"Yes, Dave, Mr. Macho-Man, you can leave us alone together. And if you go into that *other* scenario, I'll make you sleep in the pink bedroom for a week."

Dave grinned like a sneaky little boy who'd just gotten caught with his hand in the cookie jar, "What other 'scenario?' I don't have a clue as to what you're talking about."

"Good. Keep it that way. Outta my way, now, I've got some quick sprucing to do before Mimi gets here."

"Fine. 'Spruce' away. What do you want me to do?"

Sissy looked Dave up and down, "Go somewhere. Do something. Stay out of the way. Don't be a pain. Shall I continue?"

Dave faked a kid's voice, "Awe, but I get beat up when I go play outside!"

"Smart ass."

Dave walked into the house and immediately grabbed his wallet, keys, and cap. Apparently, the idea to leave overrode his duty to pick up his own empty beer cans in the living room. Sissy was in the bathroom when the doorbell rang. From the long hall, she could hear Dave answer the door and let Mimi into the house. Then the door shut, and his car revved out of the driveway. Mimi was standing behind the couch, looking around when Sissy entered the room.

Mimi grinned, "This is nice. I really wasn't expecting it to be this nice on the inside."

"We didn't either when we first saw it. What do you think?"

"It's haunted as hell."

Sissy chuckled. Having Mimi with her gave her a sense of security. Sissy just hoped it wasn't a false sense of security coupled with misplaced trust, "Get you a drink?"

Mimi looked at the floor by Dave's recliner and pointed at the cans, "Looks like somebody already drank the place dry. Should he be driving?"

"Some of that is left over from last night."

"I hope so. Otherwise, your man is an alcoholic."

"Dave? Nah."

Mimi rubbed her arms as she looked around, "I'll just have some water. I want to be fully cognizant when we contact your entities."

Sissy pointed at Mimi with one eye closed, "Good idea. Normally I just come right home and have a little something to take the edge off. Probably not a good idea for tonight, huh?"

"No." Mimi walked over to Dave's recliner and began cleaning up the cans. She followed Sissy into the kitchen and threw them away in the garbage.

Sissy was completely embarrassed, "You didn't have to do that."

"I can't stand clutter. Ever since I bought that bar, I especially hate to see empty beer cans lying around."

"I can see that." Sissy found one of her "good" glasses and filled it with ice and water. From the corner of her eye, she watched Mimi walk around the kitchen, dragging her fingers across the tops of the appliances and countertops.

"This is where the pink residue was?"

"Yeah. On two different occasions."

"Which were?"

Sissy watched the faucet run for a moment, letting the rust out of the pipes before filling Mimi's glass, "After we heard banging noises underneath the house. The morning after I heard the voices and Dave saw the cloak, and the morning we both heard breakfast being made."

"Breakfast sounds like an older couple. They might be the voices that get in your head. Is it a female or male voice?"

"Just a voice. Like an androgynous thought."

"Probably both of them acting in tandem."

Sissy handed Mimi her glass of water, "So, they're aware of the demon?"

"Apparently everything you've experienced is."

"I didn't think that could happen."

"Oh, yes. Being as they need energy to manifest, they may even compete for energy."

"Weird."

Mimi nudged Sissy, "You ready to get started?"

Sissy shrugged, "Now's as good a time as any."

"Where do you think we should set up?"

"Set up?"

"Didn't you read the instructions?"

"I haven't even taken it out of the plastic. I'm telling you, I'm afraid of those things."

Mimi laughed, "Scaredy cat. Got any candles?"

Sissy walked over to a cabinet drawer and pulled it open,

"For emergencies."

"Get one and a holder. We also need to dim the lights, but not so much we can't see."

Sissy made herself a glass of water, "Let's do it on the dining room table."

Mimi chuckled beneath her breath, "Like I haven't heard that before."

Sissy huffed and turned flush, "That's not what I meant."

Mimi gapped her mouth open in offense, "It was a joke. This house really gets to you, huh?"

Sissy returned with a candle and the unwrapped Ouija board still captive in its shopping bag. Trying not to show any fear, Sissy made herself take charge and open the box. A small set of instructions with a picture of smiling preteens spilled onto the table, along with the shuttle. Unknowingly, Sissy had bought a board with glow-in-the-dark lettering, which really embarrassed her. How can you have a serious spiritual experience with glow-in-the-dark lettering? Sissy glanced at Mimi and saw the woman's bemused smile on her face.

Mimi raised a skeptical brow at the board, "Glow-in-the-dark lettering. You paid how much for this?"

"More than it's worth. Look at the instructions. They're covered with little kids!"

"That's to make it seem harmless. You're supposed to look at this pamphlet and get the warm fuzzies."

Sissy took a deep breath and unfolded the instruction sheet, "Yeah, a great game for F-cubed night."

"F-cubed?"

"Forced, family, fun."

"Oh, didn't catch that one." Mimi snatched the instructions out of Sissy's hands and held the instructions over her face like a mask, holding each side close to the sides of her face. In a girlish voice she said, "Let's pop some popcorn and get in our jammies!"

Sissy played along, "And after we contact the dead, we can have a pillow fight!"

Both women yelled, "Yah!!!"

Sissy was feeling better just having Mimi there. She slid a piece of ice up her glass and chewed it up, "You're the guru. You set the damn thing up."

Mimi opened the board and positioned the shuttle in the middle between the "yes" and "no." Then she lit the candle in its holder and turned out the lights. Twilight spilled in through the kitchen and living room windows, giving the room an eerie glow. Immediately the board lit up.

Sissy cocked her brow and sat back in her chair, "Doesn't glow paint have to be exposed to light for so long before it can glow?"

Mimi looked suspiciously at the board, "Yeah. Typically."

"Do we really want to do this?"

"Shit. I forgot the cleansing and protection herbs."

"They work?"

"Supposed to. *I* believe they do."

Sissy was feeling daunted, "Well, I've never really had much faith in things that are 'supposed to' work."

"Then they wouldn't have worked at all, anyway."

Sissy talked around another piece of ice, "Mmmm. You still haven't told me whether or not we should do this."

"Let's give it a try and stop if things get too weird."

Sissy sat her glass down and leaned over to look at the board, "Fine. After I've been through, you could probably talk me into believing in Santa Claus if I thought it'd make this stuff go away."

Mimi looked at Sissy with a serious expression, "Now, we have to clear our minds. Take this seriously. No joking. The spirits get angry if you tease them. There is one spirit guide assigned to each board. Some spirits are good, others not. Some are smart, others not. Some tell the truth, or as much as they know of it, and others will intentionally lie. That's what makes these boards so dangerous. Focus on your questions and be open to whatever the shuttle guides us to. It might not make sense . . . it might be in code. These things require patience and practice."

"So there's a good chance this might not work at all."

Mimi took a sip of water, "It might not work the way you want it to, but it'll work."

"That's not encouraging."

Mimi shut her eyes, "Shh. Clear your mind."

Sissy mimicked Mimi and shut her eyes, too, "Okay. Clear."

"Put your index and middle finger on the shuttle beside mine. Lightly. It has to move."

Sissy held out her left hand and put her fingers next to Mimi's. Despite her innate skepticism, she felt the shuttle vibrate. Either that, or her nerves were really bad, "Mimi, I think I can feel it!"

"Yeah. Me, too. Ask it a question. Start with 'yes' and 'no' questions."

Sissy felt self-conscious and scenes from old black and

white movies popped in her head. She wanted to make a sarcastic comment because the situation was getting too serious for her. Mimi was being really serious, which was something she really hadn't expected. After inhaling and exhaling loudly, Sissy found the courage to speak to the board, "Are you there?"

The shuttle did nothing. Sissy's heart began to sink. Now she wished the board would work because her curiosity was getting the better of her. Finally, she felt the shuttle bump forward, then it slowly moved, grating its way across the cardboard toward "yes."

Mimi looked up at Sissy and smiled. Mimi asked the next question, "Are you old?"

The shuttle didn't move. They waited. Still it didn't move. They waited some more. Nothing. Mimi spoke out loud, "I'll take that as a yes."

Sissy looked at Mimi, "I think it's working." Sissy addressed the board, "Is there something under my house?"

Mimi looked at Sissy with a giddy expression as the shuttle slid further into the word "yes," but then turned and continued to "no."

Sissy was glad the room was dark. The heat from her face flushing was fogging her thoughts.

Mimi took her turn. This time she moved the shuttle back to the center of the board, "Is it evil?"

Again, the shuttle slid from "yes" and then to "no."

Sissy took her turn, "How can we get rid of it?"

The shuttle made a grating meandering line to the letter "F" and then it paused. After what felt like a lifetime to Sissy, the shuttle began to grate across the board to "I," "N," "D," "P," "I," "E," "C," "E," "S."

Sissy let out an audible whimper and whispered to Mimi, "What is *that* supposed to mean?"

Mimi ignored Sissy and asked the board, "Can we ask it to leave?"

Rather than head toward the "yes" or "no" section of the board, the shuttle headed toward "T," "H," "E," "M."

Mimi restated her question, "Should we ask them to leave?"

The shuttle grated to "no." Before Sissy could ask her question, the shuttle continued to the letters, "F," "I," "N," "D."

Sissy whispered to Mimi, "Find what? This isn't making any sense to me. I need more information."

Mimi looked at Sissy and cocked her head to the side in impatience, "Give it time. We just started."

"I don't have all night. Dave'll give me hell forever if he comes home and finds us doing this."

Mimi cocked her head, "We need to ask better questions."

Sissy inhaled and exhaled loudly, "What is the demon?"

The shuttle grated, "P," "I," "E," "C," "E."

Sissy impatiently blurted out, "A piece of what?"

"T," "H," "E," "M."

Mimi asked the next question, "Will they hurt Sissy?"

The shuttle raced to "no." But it hit upon the word for only a second before it raced to the top of the board, grating across to "yes."

Mimi whispered to Sissy, "I think that's enough for one night. This is starting to freak me out."

Sissy stared at the board, "I don't think I could take my fingers off of this thing if I wanted to. They feel heavy, like they're being forced to stay put."

Mimi took her fingers off of the shuttle, "Try now."

Sissy tried, but the shuttle began to move, "I'm not doing that!"

The shuttle made its way across the letters, "I," "A," "M," "H," "E," "R," "E."

Mimi put her hands over her mouth. After clearing her throat, Mimi said in a loud, authoritative voice, "This session is over." She blew on the candle flame, but it wouldn't extinguish. She tried the dining room light, but it wouldn't come on. Mimi walked into the kitchen and turned on the light. Once her eyes adjusted to the fluorescent bulbs, she saw a bright pink residue covering the kitchen appliances in the twilight.

Mimi called out to Sissy, "Are you okay in there?"

Sissy didn't respond.

Mimi walked into the dining room and found Sissy sitting at the dining room table, crying with her eyes shut. The shuttle effortlessly moved through the letters across the top of the board without a sound. Mimi put her hand on Sissy's shoulder, which was cold to the touch. Something was draining her friend's body heat.

"I can't move, Mimi! I don't know what it's saying anymore! There's a voice in my head that's telling me to not show it fear, but I can't help it! I'm scared!"

Mimi licked her fingers and tried pinching out the flame, but it wouldn't extinguish.

The Goth took her seat at the table and put her fingers back on the shuttle beside Sissy's, "It wants to communicate, so let's see what it has to say. Maybe it'll let go if it can say what it wants."

Sissy sniffled and shook her head in the affirmative.

Mimi pressed hard on the shuttle and dragged it back to the center of the board.

She looked around the room and saw darkness swirl in the living room. Mimi talked to the darkness, "Are you about to manifest?"

The shuttle lifted slightly above the board and flew to, "yes."

Sissy took her free hand and wiped her running nose and falling tears, "Oh, God!"

Mimi forced the shuttle back to the middle, again, "What are you?"

"U," "N," "O."

Sissy let out a stress laugh, "Uno? Like Spanish one?"

Mimi nodded "no" in the darkness, "You know."

Sissy was silent.

Mimi asked the spirit, "What is your name?"

The shuttle lifted slightly, "D," "M," "O," "N."

Mimi looked over at Sissy, who had her eyes shut. Mimi told Sissy, "'Demon,' it says." She looked at the darkness, "What do you want here?"

"W," "N," "T," "U," "R," "I," "S."

"I want your eyes," Mimi translated for Sissy.

Sissy snuffled up thick snot and coughed.

"Why are you here?"

"T," "H," "E," "Y," "K," "E," "P," "T," "M," "E."

"They kept me, it says. Who kept you?"

"M," "O," "N," "K," "S."

Mimi turned to Sissy, "'Monks,' it says, Sissy. There aren't any monasteries or nunneries around here. There's a

Catholic church. Why would there be monks here?"

Sissy spoke through her tears, "It's the last name of the people he killed in this house. That's what the voice says. It's trying to tell me more, but he won't let it into my head."

The shuttle silently flew to "yes."

The room became cold. The darkness swelled and undulated, appearing to come closer to the dining area.

Mimi pressed hard against the shuttle to keep it from moving, "Why did you kill them?"

"I," "S."

Mimi looked at Sissy, who now had her eyes open and was wiping away more tears, "'Eyes,' it says. As in the windows to the soul?"

The shuttle spun on its axis around "yes."

Thumping and banging began under the house. A foul odor spewed into the room from the direction of the hall. The room grew even colder. Darkness, once a swirling void, took form, long and slender. Human in form.

Sissy began to hyperventilate, "It's here! It's here with us!"

The human form slumped to the ground and began pulling itself across the floor toward the women.

Mimi grabbed the candle and threw it at the dark figure, which shrank back from the light and disappeared. The letters ceased glowing. The candle extinguished itself on the floor. The dining room light came on. The shuttle did not vibrate. Sissy removed her fingers from the shuttle and held them in her lap. The trauma lingered in her chest, making her visibly shake with each breath. Tears ran down her cheeks. Wiping her left cheek with her right hand, she felt her ghost finger scratch her face.

Mimi watched to her amazement as a red whelp appeared on Sissy's cheek where the missing finger would have touched her cheek. Sympathy overcame Mimi, who got up from the table and grabbed Sissy by the shoulders and put her cheek on the hysterical woman, "Sissy, I'm so sorry! I had no idea it was that bad."

Sissy motioned to her glass of water. Mimi gave it to her, and Sissy slowly sipped from the fogged glass. Mimi continued to rub the realtor, who was visibly shivering as if she were running a fever. But she wasn't. Sissy felt as if she had taken a swim in sub-degree temperatures. A couple of times, Sissy choked on her own snot. Finally, Sissy's breathing began to slow.

When Sissy caught her breath she said, "The Monks were an elderly couple who lived here with their grandson." She shook her head and took another sip of her water, "These impressions. Little pieces of what happened. I don't understand. It was too . . . scattered."

Mimi closed the cardboard Ouija board and packed its goods back into the box, "I'm pissed. That thing has no right. No right. We'll get rid of it."

Sissy sardonically laughed, "I'll lose everything. We have to move."

Mimi smoothed Sissy's hair behind her ears and cupped her cheek in her hand, "No, these things can follow you. Especially if it wants something from you. We need to know what happened."

Sissy looked into Mimi's eyes, which looked dark and angry, "That could take forever! All I ever get is fragments and I can't remember all of it!"

"That's the demon's bad energy. Did the previous owners

leave behind anything when they moved out?"

"Dave said there was some stuff up in the attic."

"Let's go up in the attic."

"I've had enough, Mimi. I feel so tired."

"If we don't figure this out, it will drain your energy on a regular basis. Even the board said there's something here that wants to hurt you. You can't pack up and move out tomorrow. This thing has got to go."

## Chapter 42: Forgive Me, But I Just Want To Bash Your Head In

Sissy took Mimi into the hall and pulled down the attic stairs. Looking around, Mimi saw the plaster patch in the wall that looked like a maniacal face. She felt it with her finger, "Sissy, have you seen this?"

"I try not to. It scares me."

Mimi pushed at the plaster, which pressed under her finger, "Something has got to be inside of it. You should open this patch and look inside."

"Let's go ahead and do it," Sissy lightly pushed the middle of the patch with her hand. The patch sunk back into the wall. Sissy snatched her hand away from the wall and stepped back.

Mimi reached out her hand and pushed the patch in the rest of the way. The patch fell back into the wall, leaving a circular hole. Behind the circle was a pentagram spray painted onto the wood frame behind the sheetrock. Burn marks seared the wood studs, revealing smoke and fire damage. The smoke smelled pungent and strong.

Sissy peeked over Mimi's shoulder, "There was a pentagram in the shed, too. What are they for?"

"Witches of various religions. Amateur Satanists, who get their symbols wrong. It's not the Satanic one, though. This is actually a protection symbol."

"Those things work?"

"It all works in the right hands. For true believers."

Sissy didn't want to think about believing in such things. She hadn't even prayed since she was a little girl, unless her unspoken cry to God counted from the night before. She felt a sense of urgency when she wondered what Dave would say about their little wall renovation, "Let's hurry up and see what's in the attic before Dave gets home."

***

The attic smelled musty and smoky. Despite the heat, the attic felt cool. When Sissy turned on the naked bulb in the attic, the two women could see sear marks in the rafters of the attic.

"This is where the noises first began. Boxes being kicked."

"Somebody might've been looking for something."

"Dave said he put all of the old stuff in the left corner."

Sissy and Mimi had to stoop as they made their way toward the corner. There they found a chipped vase, carpet scraps, and a dented baseball bat. Mimi handed Sissy the vase first.

"Do you get anything from that, Sissy?"

"No. Nothing."

"What about these carpet scraps?"

"Nope."

Mimi handed Sissy the bat.

Sissy examined the heavy wooden bat. It was stained a deep black at the tip, not seared from a fire, but black as if it had been dipped in a stain or varnish. Sissy lightly touched the tip of the bat, "This just feels cold."

"Maybe there's something else up here that Dave didn't see," Mimi walked over to the middle of the attic floor, her back turned to Sissy.

Sissy suddenly got the urge to hit Mimi on the back of the head as hard as she could, "I just felt like using your head for a baseball, Mimi. I'm sorry, but the urge suddenly came over me."

312

Mimi turned around and looked at Sissy, "It's the absorbent wood of the bat. Energy, like memories, are locked in it. That may be what it was used for. Rub your hands over it and see if you can pick up anything else."

"I don't want to hurt you."

"You won't. I won't let you. Even if it means I have to take that away from you and knock you back to reality with it," Mimi smiled.

Sissy scrunched her lips at Mimi and rubbed the bat with her hands. Images came to her mind, a boy. Sissy told Mimi what she saw as the scenes raced through her mind, "A young boy playing a game. About twelve, muscular, big for his age. The Monks' grandson. A strange layer, like a shadow stands over the boy. It's bigger than he is. The size of a man. There's two other boys, neighbors. Younger, smaller, about ten. Walking through woods. Monk boy falls down. The other boys laugh. The shadow steps out and grabs the bat. It hits the boys. Hard. Lots of blood. Kills them. The Monk boy runs home. He didn't do it. A bad man did it. He didn't do it. The man put the bat up here. To hide it. The man . . . this is . . . confusing me, the man . . . is the boy?"

Mimi's mouth dropped open, "He was possessed?"

Sissy dropped the bat with a loud clang on the floor, "What?"

"Or, the boy was schizophrenic? He could've had an older male personality. The bad one. The crazy one."

It sounded good to Sissy, who took the explanation at face value, "What about the pentagrams?"

Mimi put her hand on her hip, "Kid might've dabbled, thinking he was being naughty or some shit."

"Or all of it. What if the demon is the 'bad' multiple personality of the little boy?"

Mimi nodded her head in triumph at solving the mystery, "That's the feeling I get. That feels right."

"The cloaked thing looking in through the window?"

"Could be a symbolic representation of one of the Monks. Like the grandfather. Could be the little boy, or another of his personalities."

"Mimi, I think the kid killed his own grandparents."

"House caught on fire at one time. I get the feeling he did that, too. Sissy, rub your hand on one of the sear marks and see what you get."

Sissy had to walk across the exposed cross beams, careful not to step through the floor. She reached out her hand and felt the sooty charcoal of the damaged wood. "It's hot. But that's it. Maybe we should do this with the hole in the wall downstairs."

***

Downstairs, the house felt unusually cool. The air conditioning was turned on, but not running because the thermostat read, "sixty-one degrees" despite being set to seventy-two degrees.

Mimi rubbed her hands together and blew into them, "I might've released some kind of energy when I pushed through that hole in the wall. Sorry."

Sissy felt angry, but was too appreciative of Mimi's help to stay mad with her, "Well, it's too late to do anything about it, now." Sissy pushed up the attic stairs and closed the attic door with a reverberating bang. "I'm going to stick my hand against that symbol on the wall, and you're going to make sure I don't hurt myself."

Mimi rubbed her nose, which had turned red, "Okay."

Sissy reached into the hole and put her palm flat against the symbol, "The symbol feels cool, but the burn marks behind it literally burn."

Mimi held out her hand with her palm open, "When you said that the room warmed. I don't think the boy or his family had anything to do with the symbols. Somebody else did that. And if the wall feels hot and the symbol feels cool, it was put there to remedy something."

Sissy affirmed, "Like medicinal purposes."

"Yes. Can you see anything below the symbol?"

Sissy looked down, "No. It's too dark. The wall's in the way."

"Can we tear it down and see?"

"You want to put a bigger hole in my wall? Do you know how much that'd cost to fix? This could get expensive. I don't know what I'd tell Dave."

"He'll get over it or kick you out."

"I own the house."

As she picked at the loose plaster, Mimi sarcastically said, "We gotta talk about personal empowerment after we're through with this."

"Okay, I'll tear the rest of the sheetrock down, then what?"

"Feel more of the smoke damage and see what you get."

"See what I get. Great."

## Chapter 43: Don't Say I Never Helped You

Sissy and Mimi pounded at the sheetrock with hammers from Dave's toolbox. The work was loud and slow going. While they were working diligently at the wall, Dave came home. The inebriated man walked into the hall and found the two women sitting on the floor, hitting the wall with the hammers and pulling out chunks of sheetrock.

Dave stared in bewilderment, "When I saw her car in the driveway, this was the last thing I expected. What, what, what are you two doing to the wall?"

Sissy stood up and dusted herself off, "We're trying to see what's inside. We figured out part of the mystery, so we're trying to figure out the rest."

Dave pointed to the wall with a woozy stance, "Inside the wall?"

Sissy looked back at the wall and then at Dave, "We think so."

Dave looked down at his shoes and then up at Sissy, "Shit, I hope so. That's making a hellacious mess."

Sissy grinned at Dave and touched his arm, "I'll clean it up."

Mimi stood up and straightened her dress, "*We'll* clean it up. There's a seriously disturbed presence in this house and we're going to try to get rid of it."

Dave looked confused and steadied himself against the wall, "Fuck it. Sell it. It's not worth this shit."

Sissy explained, "We can't, Dave. It could follow us."

"No. Follow me? She-it. I'm taking a bath."

Sissy picked her hammer back up and turned to Dave as he walked past her, "Could you wait until we're through?"

Dave turned to Sissy with a grin. He fluttered his eyes, pretending to be bashful, "What's the matter, you afraid your friend there will see me neck-ed?"

Sissy looked at Mimi and grinned. She was so happy that Dave was being his old self, "On her behalf, yes. Yes, I am."

Dave threw out his hand as if to playfully wave her away, "That's not nice."

Mimi interjected, "Take your bath. It's nothing I've never seen before. Might even help you sober up. We'll be finished here in a minute."

Dave walked back over to the wall and examined it like a building inspector. Without a word, the drunken man held out his booted foot and kicked the remaining small section of wall in, "There, now don't say I don't do nothin' for you. For the record, I'm just a little tipsy, spent some quality time with my friends since I wasn't welcomed in my own house. Where's my robe?"

"In your closet."

"Don't I get a thank you?"

Mimi and Sissy simultaneously said in an unenthusiastic tone, "Thank you, Dave."

The two women began excavating the hole in the wall, removing the chunks of plaster. Dave started his shower and started to sing, badly and loudly, a tune he made up as he went along.

Sissy felt embarrassed, "He does that when he's had a little too much."

Mimi daintily picked a piece of plaster out of the opening

in the wall, "How often is that?"

"Every other weekend. Day. Every."

"Lucky you."

Once all of the debris was removed, the women saw deep
sear marks in the structure of the wall. Sissy put her hand against
the wall and rubbed her hand against the sooty surface. The room
began to warm. Mimi touched Sissy's arm for moral support. The
realtor's skin had broken out in sweat droplets.

"I feel the heat. The house is burning. A cleansing. The
boy's grandparents are dead. Their eyes are in the shed. All of his
victim's eyes are in the shed. One was tortured under the house.
The man's victims. The boy knows about the man. Inside him.
Tried to kill him.

Set himself on fire in their bedroom. Tried to drag himself to the
bathroom. Found by a fireman. Died on this spot. Where we are."
Sissy pulled her hand back from the wall. It was covered in soot.
Tiny blisters began to whelp on her palm. The realtor took a look
at her hands and ironically chuckled, "Huh, would you look at
that? Burn marks."

Mimi held Sissy's hand and lightly touched the whelps, "I
have never seen anything like this before. Does it hurt?"

Sissy pulled her hand away, "When you touch it. Doesn't
hurt like a real burn, though." The realtor blew on her palms and
watched as the red turned to pink splotches, "I think they're
already starting to go away."

Dave stepped out of the bathroom. Steam poured out of the
room behind him, making him look like a plump robed God
stepping out of the clouds, "Goin' to bed. It's late, ladies. Join me
if you want."

Simultaneously, Mimi and Sissy said, "No."

Dave stomped his way past Sissy and Mimi. With a careless motion, he loudly shut the bedroom door behind himself.

Sissy just sighed with relief, "He'll sleep it off. I apologize for that…"

Mimi cocked her eyebrows and forced a smile, "Wouldn't be the first time, but I just don't dig you like that. Him, I detest. No offense. Anyway, what do you think about your visions? What's the overall picture?"

Sissy shrugged, "I don't know if I can explain it."

"Don't try to explain it. Just talk it out. Like stream of consciousness. Just say whatever comes to you."

Sissy closed her eyes and began rambling, "The boy thinks he left the bad man behind to die in the bedroom. That energy is left . . . in the bedroom. It thinks it's a demon. The grandparents . . . knew he was crazy. Didn't want to put him away. They're the ones in the kitchen. It's the only original structure . . . in its entirety. Their regular routine. The boy's energy thinks he's a guardian. It is his voice that warns me. The man's voice that talks about me. They see themselves as separate entities."

Mimi pursed her lips and nodded her head, "The man was all bad, so the boy thinks he's all good? Something like that?"

"Yeah."

"What about the pink ooze?"

"I don't have a clue."

"You know what I think has got to happen?"

"What?"

"You've got to convince the boy that he's not a saint and

that the bad man is a part of him. Integrate the two and hope that's what the kid needs to move on."

"Play therapist to a dead kid who's still sick in the head? My BA in psychology is useless. Everyone knows that."

"Yes. To helping the child integrate. Not putting your degree down."

"Again, I'm a real estate agent, not a psychologist. Couldn't I just get the house blessed?"

"It could help. But, you've got to be the one to do most of the work. It wants you."

Sissy wiped pieces of plaster off of her sweaty forehead, "Well, I can tell I'm going to sleep good tonight."

Mimi put her hand on Sissy's arm, "You're being sarcastic, right?"

"Oh, yeah."

Mimi began putting the large chunks of plaster into small piles by the wall, "Would you mind having a white witch do a cleansing ritual?"

Sissy helped Mimi, "What about the whole young priest, old priest thing?"

"If you could convince a Catholic priest in this town that your house is haunted, more power to you."

"Oh. Well, sure, I'll take whatever I can get."

Mimi looked up at Sissy with a tone of doubt, "You're not big on faith, are you?"

Sissy let out a big sigh and stared at her missing finger, "I never really thought about it. I used to pray all the time when I was a little girl. But I grew up, ya' know?"

Mimi wiped her brow, "This thing has it out for you, so you

might want to try and have a little faith. In something. Otherwise, you'll always be a victim to these energies and their whims."

Mimi's words scared Sissy, who tried to play off her fear and self-doubts with the comforts of forced humor, "Bring me an old witch and a young witch, woman!"

Mimi rolled her eyes, "How's about Wednesday?"

"At night, I suppose?"

"Yes."

"Full moon. Power of the spirits. Mystical, magical stuff?"

"More like she gets off work at eight."

"Oh."

\*\*\*

Mimi left after setting up the details for the house cleansing. Sissy had a terrible case of insomnia. Anxiety, fear of falling asleep. Anxiety, fear of not getting enough sleep for work. Anxiety, not abated by pacing the kitchen floor.

Dave deeply snored from the bowels of the house, raking her jealous nerves. TV offered no solace. Chocolate turned her stomach. Not wanting to, but finding no other quick solution, Sissy raided the fridge for Dave's stash of "good" beer. Behind an opened, but full, box of diet "Meal-in-a-Can," sat Dave's carefully rationed and beloved imported ale. Dave liked the "cheap stuff" for a buzz and the "good stuff" for the taste, at least that's what he said.

To drink the expensive ale without him would be a sacrilege. In light of his snoring, Sissy relished the profanation.

Sissy held the dark brown drink in her hand and scoffed at her trepidation, "Screw it, to self-empowerment." Once the brew entered her mouth, her anxiety and fears ceased.

The alcohol was like nectar, an answer to prayer. After downing three bottles back-to-back, Sissy forced herself to leave Dave the last one. Sissy knew she was self-medicating, but in light of the situation, felt it all justified. Finally, she felt brave enough to go to bed.

With the window unit cranked as high as it would go, Sissy found her man wrapped in all of the blankets like a cold mummy. Dave slept loudly and deeply. When Sissy leaned over to kiss him, the sleeping man licked his lips, murmured, "You smell good," and rolled over back to sleep.

Sissy wanted to ask Dave to sleep on her side of the bed, but he was sound asleep.

The issue would have to wait. Until the light of six in the morning, the numbing and depressing effects of the alcohol would have to be enough to get her through the night. Sleeping in the kitchen had briefly occurred to her, but the prospect of waking up covered in pink residue was almost as unappealing as waking up to a demon on the side of her bed. While the room spun, Sissy closed her eyes and gave into the animalistic need for sleep.

Normally, Sissy didn't dream when she was sleeping off a drunk, but not all illusions are the result of dreams.

## Chapter 44:  You Should Leave

A scuttling noise woke Sissy from the deep darkness of her inebriated sleep.

Once awake, Sissy realized the noise was the sound of a mouse darting about in her untidy room, rummaging through scattered paper and tearing at the carpet. After such a wonderful, unconscious level of sleep, the annoyance of being awaken was more than she could stand.

The angry woman sat up in bed, ready to go to the kitchen and set a trap for her little night visitor. Then she saw "it" staring at her.

In the corner of the room, at the foot of her side of the bed, sat the demon who had visited her just one night before. The thing leaned against the closet door as if it were out of breath. Its twisted, evil face now shined pale and glowing against the darkness. An exposed torso of muscle and masculine chest hair. Long arms that hung by its side, weary in posture. Hands that ended in claws. No legs, just a trailing pile of cinders. When Sissy saw it, she shuddered, unable to scream. The thing smiled in the twilight; the bars of light from the vertical blinds made it look as if it were in some sort of neon jail cell. Obviously, the creature was pleased with itself, but what were its intentions?

The creature whispered in a deep, animalistic voice to Sissy, "I've caught your little mouse."

Sissy, feeling a sudden show of bravado, angrily whispered back, "Where is it? Show me, Asshole."

The creature cockily scoffed and knocked upon the closet door with its knuckle, "In here. Do you want it?"

Sissy pulled the covers over her breasts, "No, I want both

of you to go away and leave us alone." As she held the covers tight in her fists, she felt the sheets encase the ghost finger. Her nub was sore and throbbing against the cotton sheets.

The creature rocked its head against the closet door in a fatigued manner, "We can't leave. They keep us here, and here we'll stay. With them. And so will you. Forever."

Sissy was angry. Her anger fueled her courage, "Like a family? Is that what you're getting at?"

The demon chuckled, "A collection."

"What is that supposed to mean?"

The demon continued to rock its head back and forth across the closet door, "You will stay here. We will have you."

Sissy wanted the thing to leave, "Who *are* you?"

The monster exhaled a phlegmy sigh, "I am the thing he cannot be."

That was not the answer Sissy had expected, "And just what the hell is that?"

The creature stopped rocking his head, "He never told me."

Sissy sarcastically snipped at the demon, "Perhaps you should tell him."

The creature resumed rocking its head and chuckled, "He does not know me."

"He blamed you for the death of his grandparents. He knows you well enough."

"He thinks he killed me."

Sissy wadded her bed sheet in her hands. Slowly, feelings of anxiety were beginning to replace her drunken courage, "I know. Why are you here?"

Rocking its head, the creature absentmindedly responded,

"I am always here. Why are you here?"

Sissy held her ground, "I own this house. It's mine, now. You and the boy need to leave." After Sissy uttered these words, a dark shadow flew by the window, rapping against the panes.

The creature looked at the window, "He is always here. He watches you. Do not anger him."

Sissy was confused. At first she thought Little Mouse was the alternate personality of the little boy. Now it sounded as if the boy were outside her window. So who was Little Mouse? A third identity? Perhaps the creature would tell her. Sissy asked the demon, "Who is Little Mouse?"

The creature cupped its face in its hands and inhaled deeply, "A pathetic little thing. Do you want to see it?"

Sissy tore at the sheet. She was becoming overwhelmed with frustration, "A name. I need a name. Who is the mouse?"

The creature snarled, its teeth were sharp and angular, "Names? We have no names. We are not so fortunate." Suddenly the creature sniffed the air, "You have angered them. They will catch you in the light if I cannot catch you in the dark." In a deliberate manner, the demon stared directly into Sissy's face, "Thank you for entertaining me and giving me such exquisite attention. Give me your eyes."

Every fiber in Sissy's body told her to lift her hands and pry her eyes out with her bare hands. Fear seared through Sissy's body. Voices began to whisper in quick fragments that filled her mind, confusing themselves with her own thoughts. The bed sheet was becoming damp from the sweat of her palms as she fought off this dark compulsion.

Feigning courage, Sissy spouted, "I am not afraid of a little boy or some split personality from his imagination. You are *not* a demon. He is just a sick little boy who needs to be punished for the evil things he's done."

Within an instant, the demon was not sitting in the corner any longer, but was breathing right in Sissy's face, inches from her nose, "Could you not feel me if I were not real?"

Sissy's heart beat so hard, her eyesight wavered with each beat of her pulse.

Fear choked her ability to speak. Fear held her to the spot, making her unable to move, unable to think.

The creature exhaled a hot, fiery breath into Sissy's face, choking her. Sitting up on the nubs of its missing legs, it held out its hands, pressing its thumbs against the frightened woman's eyes, "He does not know God hates such as we are."

Sissy could feel its strong fingers cradle the back of her head in its tight grasp. The sharp claws dug into the thin flesh of her eyelids. From the closet came a furious scratching sound; the mouse wanted out. Sissy could hear the closet door slowly open. A little boy stepped out of the closet and walked over to the foot of the bed, putting his hands on Sissy's feet.

The boy spoke in a tiny little whisper, "I am here."

From outside, something banged against the window, yelling at the inhabitants within, "Put her in the light! She must not ever leave; she knows too much!"

The creature lightly caressed the perimeter of Sissy's closed eyes with its thumb claw, breathing in her face, quietly laughing, "Do not trust false symbols. Do not trust misgiven names. Do not trust in men who cower like boys. Do not trust girls masquerading as women. Do not go blind seeking faith. Your eyes are my redemption. I won't have such notions dim your light."

While the demon cradled Sissy's head, the boy lightly tugged at Sissy's toes, pleading, "Tell me what I am." At the same time the boy spoke, breakfast cooked in the kitchen. Bacon fried, plates clanked. A radio played a far away, familiar tune. Suddenly, from the hall came a rushing sound. Someone was frantically running up and down the hall, panicking. The heavy footsteps trod from the bathroom, down to the bedroom door, someone began to scream in hysteria, "Quick! Quick! I think he killed her! I think he killed her!" As Sissy listened, she realized the voice belonged to an older man. The grandfather.

Still the demon held her face and breathed searing air upon her eyes, "Your eyes belong to me. Let me show what you so desperately wish to see."

Sissy's eyesight went dark.

The little boy at the foot of Sissy's bed whimpered as he tugged at her foot, "Don't make me go in there."

From the bathroom, Sissy could hear an older woman's voice begin to moan like a wounded animal, "What did you do? What did you do? What did you do?"

The little boy began to cry. Kneeling down, he put his head on the foot of Sissy's bed, "Don't make me go in there."

The creature tightened its grip on Sissy's head and nuzzled her face. She could feel and smell burnt flesh. She felt nauseous and completely petrified. Pain seared Sissy's cheek. Burning heat seared through her flesh. Sissy saw a light through the darkness:

*It was the bathroom light. Morning. The grandmother*

*held a limp little girl draped in a pink bath towel. The girl couldn't have been older than a year. Her mouth was blue. Her eyes were open and covered in the lifeless film of the dead. The little boy shook his head but was too afraid to speak. Perhaps the boy was eight. Perhaps he was younger. A skinny, pathetic little thing, clothes covered in water. His hands were slimy with soap. Pink soap. The girl glistened in the bathroom light, her hair still matted with soap bubbles.*

*The grandmother screamed at the small boy, "You killed her! Damon! Look at her, look at what you did! You drowned the baby!"*

*The boy cried with his hands over his mouth, "I didn't mean to! I'm sorry! I couldn't catch her! She was too slippery. She's okay, she's not dead!"*

*The grandmother shoved the dead girl in the boy's crying face, "You killed her!"*

*The boy whaled, "No, no, it was an accident! I didn't. She slipped."*

Sissy transported like ether, watching the events from above:

*The grandmother placed the dead child into the bathroom, tossing the boy in with her, "If you didn't kill her, then bring her back. You are never leaving until you bring her back!"*

*The boy cried harder. To stop making noise, he stuffed his fists into his mouth. His sister lay against the wall, lifeless. Her eyes wide open, staring at him. He walked over to her to close her eyes, but stopped. He didn't want to get soap in them.*

*Slowly, the bathroom doorknob began to turn and the door creaked open. The boy tried to shut it, but the door continued to open until it softly hit the doorstop on the bathroom wall. There in the doorway stood the demon, holding the baby sister's eyes in the palm of its hand.*

The vision stopped. Sissy was back in bed, the demon pressing hard against the woman's eyes. Tears poured down the woman's cheeks, but she wasn't crying. The pain was creating the tears. Even though Sissy could not see him, she felt the little boy stand at the foot of her bed, silently weeping.

The child put his hands back upon Sissy's feet, "Tell me what I am."

Sissy swallowed hard and found the courage to speak, "You are a little boy who had an accident. Your grandparents were wrong to leave you alone with a slippery baby in the tub. It's not your fault. You are no demon. There is no demon. Your grandparents were bad, not you."

The sounds, the smells, the sensations, everything disappeared into a vacuum. The house sat eerily quiet. Sissy opened her eyes but found them difficult to see through. Everything was watery, as if her eyes were filled with a thick ooze. The entities were gone, all of them.

## Chapter 45: Sore Eyes and a Pain In The Neck

The alarm clock went off. A DJ's voice pierced the too normal silence, scaring Sissy so badly she jumped in the bed.

Dave rolled over and held his head with his hands, "Oh, God, my head! Sissy get me something from the kitchen, will ya'? Oh, my head!" Dave lurched upright, heaving, "Oh, no, I'm gonna be sick. Oh, Jesus. Oh, no." The man shot up out of the bed and trod heavily down to the bathroom, where he immediately vomited. To Sissy's dismay, she didn't hear it land in the toilet . . . but rather heard it splatter on the floor. *Great he missed. Oh, he better clean that mess up or else I'm gonna . . .*

Sissy opened her eyes as wide as she could muster, but found her eyesight was not improving. Though she found it hard to see, her eyes did not hurt. Rather, Sissy felt an enormous pressure sitting heavily upon the corners of her eyes. Feeling her way down the hall, Sissy made her way to the bathroom, where she stood in the doorway, inhaling Dave's vomit.

Dave looked up at Sissy, "Could you get me some . . . good, God, what happened to your face?"

Sissy tried to frown, but moving her eyebrows hurt her face, "I'm having a hard time seeing this morning. I had some bad dreams."

Dave spat, the sound echoed in the toilet bowl, "Dreams don't do that. You look like complete shit."

Sissy walked into the bathroom but found the bathroom light painful. She looked into the mirror and made out a blurry outline of her face. Her eyes were swollen and matted almost completely shut.

Dave put his hand upon Sissy's leg, "Could you go to the kitchen and get me something for my head? I'm having a bad time here."

"I don't know if I can see to find my way to the kitchen. I'm having a hard time, too."

Dave put his arm on the rim of the toilet bowl and rested his head upon his arm. In an exasperated voice, the man forced out, "If you'll just get me something for my fucking head, I swear I'll take you to the doctor."

Sissy ran the sink and splashed water upon her face. The crusts on her eyes turned to a gooey mush. Then her eyes began to itch. When she rubbed them, her eyes burned.
Dave reached onto the shelf of the toilet and handed her a washcloth. Sissy ran the water until it turned warm and saturated the cloth. The warm water soothed the itching and burning of her eyes. Finally, she could see well enough to make the trek to the kitchen.

Inside the kitchen, Sissy found a terrible mess. Through the watery blurriness of her eyesight, she could discern that everything was covered in pink residue. From the bathroom, Dave moaned, dry heaved, and vomited.

The kitchen cabinet where she kept all of the medicine was covered in pink residue. Rather than reach for a cloth with which to open the door, Sissy grabbed a hold of the handle and slung the drawer open. The pink residue did not feel sticky, and it disappeared upon contact. Sissy muttered under her breath, "Finally, something is getting better," and rummaged through the door until she found the powdered aspirin.

Dave moaned and groaned in pain from the bathroom.

Sissy decided she needed some, too, and tossed a packet back. Slowly, she made her way around the kitchen, making him a glass of water and feeling her way back to the bathroom.

Dave took the aspirin with a grimace and audible sound of disgust from the powder sticking to his tongue. After several groans and more grimaces, the man motioned for Sissy to help him off of the floor, muttering, "Take me back to bed. When I get up, I'll take you to the doctor. My head is killing me."

Sissy called Barb and told her to take her appointments for her. Next, she called the doctor for an appointment. When she explained to the nurse what was wrong, the woman told her to come to the doctor's office immediately. Sissy tried to explain that she needed someone to drive her because her boyfriend was sleeping off a migraine. The nurse snapped at Sissy, "Let him sleep if you want, but if it were my face, I'd make him sleep it off in the office while I got some medical attention."

Sheepishly, Sissy hung up the phone and walked into the bedroom, "Dave?"

Dave let out a half snore, "Huh, huh?"

"The nurse says I should go to the doctor's now."

"Tell her I've got a migraine. When it's gone, I'll take you."

"I did. She still wants me to go now."

"You can't drive yourself?"

Sissy was so hurt, she was silent. When Dave started to snore, again, Sissy loudly answered in an angry tone, "No, I can't take myself. I can't hardly see my eyes are so swollen."

Dave grabbed his head, "Fine! I've got a terrible headache, but your eyes are obviously messed up, so let *me* take *you* to the doctor!"

Sissy shrank from his anger, "No, Dave, you just sleep, try to get better."

"No, no! I'm up now. I'll never get any peace until you get to the doctor. All I wanted was a half hour, but God knows, you can't wait. *You* need medical attention, right now."

"Dave, just go back to bed, I'll take care of it myself."

"Oh, no, I told you I was up! I'm up. We're going to the doctor."

Sissy was so hurt, she left the room and sat on the couch. When she felt herself cry, her eyes began to burn intensely. No tears would come out. The sensation was so strange, it scared her, making her want to cry more, which only created a vicious cycle.

Dave emerged from the hall, stretched, yawned, and held his head with his hands to steady himself. When he looked at Sissy, he cocked his eyebrows, "What's wrong with you? I said I'd take you to the doctor."

Sissy just sniffled and shook her head, "Nothing."

"Whatever. Are you ready?"

Sissy shook her head in the affirmative.

"Well, what are you waiting for? Let's go."

# Chapter 46: Hello, I'm The Patient?

By the time Sissy made it to the doctor's office, her eyes had matted over, again. Dave had to help her into the office, which he did with the care and concern of a true gentleman, despite his all-too-obvious pain. The nurses were impressed, remarking how gentle and sweet he was. One nurse even brought Dave a cup of water for all of his strenuous effort. In a wheelchair, Sissy was taken right in to see the doctor. Dave stayed behind in the waiting area and made himself as comfortable as he could, given his circumstances. Nurse Walters also brought him the TV remote. The last image Sissy had of the waiting area was a blurry vision of Dave lying down in the loveseat, learning how to work the remote from the attentive nurse, who had a second cup of water in hand and her cleavage in Dave's face.

***

After what felt like an endless amount of time had passed, Sissy's nurse finally walked into the room, "I see your boyfriend found the will to get to the doctor's?" Her voice was the one from the phone for the appointment.

Sissy forced a grin and tried to say in an ambiguous voice, "Yeah, he's a real gem."

The nurse sarcastically grinned, "Aren't they all?"

Sissy just politely chuckled but wanted to cry. By this time, she was all too aware that if she did, her face would hurt, so she tried to focus on staying mad at Dave, rather than feel sorry for her situation.

The nurse walked over to Sissy and held a small pen light to the sick woman's eyes, but decided not to use it, "Dear God.

What was on fire? I might need to check your lungs for smoke damage."

Sissy pulled her face away from the nurse, "What do you mean?"

"Well, the doctor hasn't seen you yet, but I'd bet he's gonna tell you this is the result of exposure to smoke. Your ducts are severely clogged and irritated."

"I haven't been around any smoke."

"Camp fire? Burning leaves?"

Sissy shook her head "no."

"Cigarettes?"

"No. No smoke. My house has smoke damage in the framework, but I didn't smell anything. It's all been repaired or replaced or covered up."

"I don't think that would be enough to cause this serious amount of damage. Either you played poker all night at the Deer Lodge, or you almost died in a burning house."

"Could it be an allergy?"

"Yeah, a smoke allergy. Did you rub your face in something smoky?"

The forgotten memory of the demon rubbing its face against hers came back to Sissy and made her shudder, "Uh, no, no. This is just one of those weird things, you know?"

The nurse just raised her brows, "Hmm."

The thought of having to return to work worried Sissy, "How long am I going to have to live with this?"

"Typically, the doctor prescribes a cream, so it depends on how you react to it. Could be a couple of days, could be a week, but you'll feel some relief within a couple of hours."

Sissy rubbed the scar on her nub. The ghost finger was bothering her again.

The nurse grabbed Sissy's right hand and examined the nub, "What happened here?"

"Long story. The scar is hurting me, but the doctor said it'd take a while to heal."

The nurse lightly rubbed her fingertip across the scar, "This thing is hard. It shouldn't be hurting you anymore. I'll make a note for the doctor to look at it."

"NO! I mean, that's alright. I think it hurts because I miss it so much. You know?"

The nurse scowled, "Whatever you say."

A light knock and the doctor entered the room. After a quick greeting, he put his thumbs next to Sissy's eyes, "What'd you catch on fire?"

Sissy put her hands over her eyes, "I think we've been through this already. Can I just get the cream and go? This is not pleasant."

The doctor shrugged his shoulders, wrote a few notes in Sissy's file, and prescribed her an antibiotic cream for her infected eyes.

*** 

The nurse wheeled Sissy out to the waiting area, where she found Dave completely relaxed on the loveseat. Someone had gotten the man a throw blanket for his legs. If she could have driven, she would have left him there. Sadly, she knew it would be hours before he caught on that she left him, and then she'd just have to go to the trouble to pick him up.

In a calm voice Sissy said, "Dave, I'm ready."

Dave sat up and looked at Sissy with concern, "So soon? You could have taken your time."

"Well, it really wasn't up to me. I need to get some medicine as soon as possible, so . . ."

Dave sat up and stretched, "I'm so glad you're okay. Let me take you to get your medicine."

"Thank you."

Dave dutifully wheeled Sissy out to the car and took the chair back inside, where he thanked the nurses profusely for their attentiveness. Sissy felt like she had the old Dave back. She remembered their good times and why she wanted to cohabitate. He was the sweetest person . . . before the house. If she had never set foot in that house . . .

Dave came back to the car and drove Sissy to the pharmacy. When he pulled into the parking lot, he waited for Sissy. Sissy waited for him.

After what felt like a Mexican stand-off, Dave gruffly inquired, "Aren't you going to get your medicine? I thought you said you needed it."

"I do, but I was hoping you'd get if for me."

"Fine. Where's the prescription?"

Sissy handed it to him.

"I'll probably need your insurance card, too. But, they may not want to take it from me. Insurance fraud and that sort of thing."

Sissy's patience with the situation was exhausted, "Look, if you don't want to go inside and get me some medicine, fine. I'll do it myself. I can't see, but I'll do it myself."

Dave backed off, "No, no. I was just concerned is all. If

you think they'll take it from me, then, fine."

"Yes, Dave. My name is on both the prescription and the card. If they want to be anal, I'm just here . . . in the damn car in the damn parking lot!"

"Why are you shouting at me? You know I've got a headache."

In a tone of frustrated restraint, Sissy uttered through her clenched teeth, "Sorry, just get my medicine, please."

***

After an hour and a half, Dave emerged from the pharmacy, triumphant, "That is one slow pharmacy. Took forever. Here, go ahead and put this stuff on, you need it."

The ride back to the house was silent. Sissy was so angry, she could burst. Dave was oblivious or making a convincing show of it. Once inside, Dave gathered his books and started out the door.

Sissy was hurt, "Where are you going?"

"Got my books, looks like I'm headed off to class."

"I thought you had a migraine."

"It's a little better. If I miss any more lectures, I'll have to take the course over again. See you later, hope you get to feeling better. Don't worry about supper, I'll find myself something."

Dave left so quickly, Sissy was left with her mouth open, ready to ask him to bring something home for her to eat. Sissy tried not to think about the pains she had to go through for a trip to the doctor versus the almost overt enthusiasm he showed in going to class.

The cream felt cool against her eyes, though extremely gunky. If she tried, she could open her eyes enough to see through the gunk and walk around. Sissy said to herself in a sarcastic voice, "I think I will have that last beer. The last thing he needs is more alcohol in his system. The jerk. I should kick him out. I can't take anymore of this." Immediately her ovaries pinged, and she knew she would never have a chance to meet someone new. If she stood a chance to be a mom, this was it.

Sissy took a deep breath and uttered out loud, "I have to keep him" as she walked into the kitchen, which was pink residue free. Even better, the last beer was still in the fridge, and ice cold. Sissy looked in the freezer and found Dave's special frozen mug and poured the last of the good import beer into the frosty mug. "This is so good, it's sinful. I hope he gets pissed off. I will laugh in his face. What's he gonna do, leave? Where's he gonna go? He has to keep *me*."

Sissy got her favorite chenille throw and settled into the couch. The house was quiet. Cognizant energy free. She was alone with her throw, her couch, her beer, and the remote. A thought occurred to Sissy, *I want that old Dave back. I saw a glimmer of him today. If I can just get rid of this demonic influence, I can have my Dave back. My Dave. I will have my happy family if it's the last thing I do.*

# Chapter 47: Recipes Are Just Spells for the Initiated

Around eight thirty, a knock came at the door. Sissy opened the door, not knowing who to expect. There on her door stoop stood Mimi and a blonde-headed woman in business attire, her name tag, "Paula," from the clothing store she worked at still pinned to her collar.

Mimi smiled, but the smile quickly dropped, "What happened to you?"

Sissy ignored the question and congenially invited the women inside, "Come in, Mimi, and uh, Paula."

The two women stepped in. Paula shivered and rubbed her hands.

Mimi took Sissy by the hands, "What happened to your face?"

"Long story. I wasn't expecting you until tomorrow night."

"I know, but Paula wanted to meet you first to get an idea of what she might need to bring for the cleansing."

"Oh, that's fine. What does she need to know?"

Mimi gripped Sissy's hands, "I want to know what happened to your face before anything else."

Sissy blinked and the gunk went into her eyes more, "I had another visitation after you left last night. I think I know who we need to get rid of."

Mimi looked over at Paula, who was staring at Sissy, "Great, but what happened?"

"It's embarrassing."

Mimi walked Sissy over to the couch, "Have a little faith. Nothing that happens to you would surprise me."

Sissy remembered the demon's words. Doubt settled upon

her heart, but she pushed it away, "Fine, the demon personality visited me, threatened me, held my head in its hands, and almost gouged my eyes out. Oh, yeah, and it breathed in my face this smoky dragon breath and rubbed its face on mine. The doctor said I have an infection of the eyes from smoke exposure."

Paula wasn't listening but was gathering Sissy's blanket around her shoulders for warmth, "This house is full of bad energy. It's trying to drain me. I don't know how long I can stay here."

Mimi turned to Paula, "As long as it damn takes. This thing is going to hurt my friend if we can't get rid of it."

Sissy sat on the couch and turned off the TV, "That's just it. It can't leave until the grandparents do. They're keeping all of those personalities here. A real couple of sadistic sons-a-bitches."

Mimi stood behind Sissy and rubbed Sissy's scalp in a motherly fashion, "I thought the grandparents were the helpless victims. The good guys."

"Hardly. Had a sort of vision. They're the ones that created all of these lost personalities. They've somehow convinced the main personality that it can't leave. Some sort of prolonged punishment. It's awful."

Paula seemed agitated, "I don't want to be here. You need to find somebody else, Mimi."

Mimi grabbed Paula by the arm, "No, I don't. Quit being a child and tell us what we need to do."

Paula flapped the blanket and rocked from side to side. Her teeth were chattering, "I need more people. We'll form a circle. Say a couple of cleansing spells. Leave behind some icons. But, if she's not into it, it won't work."

Mimi let go of Paula, "When can all of this come

together?"

Paula shrugged, "Tomorrow?"

Mimi looked at Sissy and resumed rubbing Sissy's scalp, "Will you be okay through the night?"

Sissy shrugged, "I guess. If it's that bad, I could see about getting a hotel. To be honest, I'm not sure I'm comfortable with spells, rituals and stuff. Dave might get mad."

Paula suggested, "The three of us could say a protection prayer that should last at least one night. If you want. I mean, spells are no different than following a recipe. You want a cake? You follow the recipe. You want a house exorcism? Follow the recipe. If you don't want it . . ."

Sissy just closed her eyes, which wasn't hard considering how swollen they were, "No, I'm open to trying anything. Mimi, if you could just stay for a bit and rub my head, that'd suit just as well."

Mimi laughed, "Look, that's Dave's job, and I am not afraid to tell him." Mimi saw Sissy's distress, "Since Dave's not here for whatever reason, I'll rub your head for a little while, but then I gotta go babysit my employees, make sure the little shits don't rob me blind. Do you want to say the prayer or not?"

Sissy exhaled a sigh of relaxation, "Sure. I gotta have some faith, right?"

Paula and Mimi cleared the coffee table from the living room. The three women sat in the middle of the room, held hands, and were about to start the prayer when Dave came into the living room.

In a sarcastic tone, Dave laughed, "Well, what do we have here?"

Sissy was annoyed by his intrusion, "We were praying you wouldn't come home drunk, again. Looks like the prayer worked."

Dave frowned and in an angry tone, huffed, "What are you trying to say?"

Sissy turned her head away from the man, "Oh, nothing. Could you leave? Or do something that won't bother us for like fifteen minutes?"

Dave was obviously angry and did not attempt to hide it, "Sure. What did you have in mind, oh, my queen?"

"How's about you get me something to eat, since that's what I was going to ask you to do before you rushed out the door this afternoon."

"And what do you want? Don't say 'anything,' because I wouldn't have asked if I didn't want to know."

"A tuna melt from Ralph's."

"That's it?"

"That's it. Can you handle it?"

Dave didn't respond but headed out the door in an angry stomp.

Mimi smiled at Sissy, "After we're done with you, you might have the balls to kick him out and find one that'll behave."

Sissy just shook her head, "It's not him. It's the house." To deflect, Sissy said in a tone mimicking a priest, "Let us pray."

Paula started the prayer. It was unlike anything Sissy had ever heard before. Not a Christian prayer, but references to Mother Earth and "She." Still, if it would prevent another nighttime encounter with whatever lurked in her bedroom, Sissy was ready to buy into it hook, line, and sinker.

Paula paused and finally addressed Sissy, "You can look

up, now. We're through."

Sissy felt her cheeks flush with embarrassment, "Oh. I didn't know."

Mimi put her hands in her lap, "So, what'd you think? Feel better?"

Sissy inhaled, "You know, I do. I wasn't really expecting anything, but I do."

Paula took the chenille blanket off of her shoulders and looked around, "The room is warming. I think the presence has retreated for tonight. We'll come back tomorrow and do the best we can to take care of the rest of it for you."

After saying her goodbyes, and ushering the two women out of the door, Sissy found herself alone in the house. When would Dave be home? She hoped soon.

***

Two hours passed before Dave returned home. He handed Sissy her tuna melt in a greased-through bag.

Sissy was irked, "Dave, this is cold! How long did you have my sandwich before you brought it home to me?"

"Well, I got the sandwich and then I figured I'd give you some more time to be with your friends. I mean, I came home last night and that weird girl was still here. You said that wouldn't take long, too, and she was here all night. I wanted to give you your space since you seemed so mad at me for some reason."

"The whole point of a melt is for it to be *hot*. I don't even know if this is still safe to eat."

"It hasn't been that long. Besides, you're on an antibiotic already."

"But that's topical! You know what? Never mind. Just

never mind. Thank you for the sandwich and giving me some space. Alright?" Sissy hated insincere apologies and was hoping Dave would perceive that she was trying to pacify him.

Dave sneered back at Sissy, "I'm going to take a bath and go to bed. You kept me up all night, whimpering in your sleep and breathing in my face. You gotta stop all of that."

"That's what I'm trying to do, Dave. That's what all of this is about."

"Whatever, Sissy."

"Goodnight, Dave," and under her breath she muttered, "Asshole."

That night passed without a bump, thump, scuttle, or rap on the window. Sissy slept well enough. The gooey medication itched, making her want to wipe her eyes. To avoid rubbing the medication off on her pillows, she had to sleep on her back. Sissy hated falling asleep on her back. Still, it was nice to just lie in bed, taking in the darkness of the night, and not feeling potential harm in it, not feeling afraid.

## Chapter 48: If You Can't Stand the Heat

The next morning, Sissy awoke to the alarm clock. She felt rested, making her realize that it had been a long time since she had gotten a good night's sleep. Still, her eyes were crusted and the goo was dry. Sissy had to feel her way to the bathroom and grasp around the linen closet for a soft washcloth. After washing her face and freeing her eyes from the brown crusts, Sissy could see that some of the swelling had gone down. Now she could open her eyes wide enough to see in front of herself. If she drove slowly enough, she could safely drive herself to work. Sissy couldn't wait to get to work.

***

When Sissy got into the office, Barb was sitting at Sissy's desk, writing down a few notes on Sissy's desk calendar. Barb held up her finger for Sissy to wait and finished her phone call. When Barb looked up at Sissy, the smile on her face disappeared, "Good, Lord, Sissy, what happened to you?"

"The doctor says my eyes are infected."

"Wasn't that mouse-bitten donut, was it?"

"No. It's kind of a mystery. I've got ointment. My eyes actually look better today than they did yesterday."

"Which is still not good enough for work. You just take yourself back home and wait for that mess to heal."

"I'm fine, really."

"Sissy, you'll scare our clients! I'll handle the rest of your appointments for the next couple of days. You just focus on gettin' better. Can't have my best seller gettin' worse on me!"

Sissy knew better. Barb was up to something, "What's

your percentage?"

"I'm takin' three percent of your five if I sell anything for you. Just one percent if you get back and sell something I've already shown."

Barb was going to make a killing off of Sissy's business. Sissy unenthusiastically replied, "Oh, well, then. Three of my five, as long as I get better, right?"

Barb opened her mouth as if she were shocked and hurt, "Hey, you still get at least two percent just for sittin' on your butt at home with that man of yours waiting on you hand and foot! Wish I had it that good."

Sissy was surprised, she expected worse. Still, the idea of someone thinking Dave would wait on her "hand and foot" brought out irony from the darkest depths of her soul, "Mmm. Yeah, well, he's just caring and attentive like that."

"Now, don't tell me he's not taking good care of you."

Sissy just painfully raised her eyebrows and looked away.

"Well, tell him I said he better take good care of you. I need you back here at work, looking like a normal person." Barb got up from Sissy's desk and rubbed her associate's shoulder. "Don't worry about a thing, Sissy, I've got it all taken care of. You'll be back in the swing of things by Saturday. Those properties won't move between now and then, honey."

***

Sissy slowly made her way back home. The ointment was starting to dry and mat her eyelashes together. Finally, after straining her eyes into a cluster headache, Sissy made it home. The house was quiet. Sissy walked in and got goose bumps. The realtor turned down the air, thinking that she was cold. When

Sissy walked into the kitchen to make herself breakfast, she found Dave sitting at the kitchen table, eating cereal, and reading a textbook.

"What're you doing home?" Dave asked with a mouth full of cereal, milk dripping down his chin.

The question peeved Sissy, who responded with a scathing, "Oh, and it's *so* good to see you, too, honey."

"Are you still mad at me?"

Sissy just grunted.

"Why? I took you to the doctor and I got your medicine for you. I gave you space. I brought you food like you asked."

"Could it possibly be your attitude?"

"What attitude? I'm just trying to deal with holes in the walls, freaky chicks at all hours of the night, being unwanted, and putting your needs ahead of mine."

"WHAT?!? First of all, this is *my* house and if I wanted to gut every wall, I could. I don't need your permission for the kind of friends . . .," Sissy was more than ready to finish her tirade when Dave interrupted her.

"Wait, wait, wait. This isn't about me caring about the house or any of the other. You're just freaking me out, is all."

"How so?"

"I thought you were," and Dave paused, not wanting to say the first thing that came to his mind.

Sissy planted both hands firmly on the wobbly breakfast table, and said in a low, deliberate voice, "Yes, I'm waiting."

Dave sat back in his chair and blurted out, "Normal."

Dave's response made Sissy's blood pressure surge. The angry woman flailed her hands in the air and boomed out, "Well, who the hell is?"

In response to Sissy's anger, Dave responded with a cool, "I'm perfectly normal. You don't see me having cultist rituals in the middle of the living room floor! Why didn't you tell me you were into . . . witchery type shit?"

"I am not! Who else is going to help us? Do you have any better ideas for how to deal with this shit? Mimi is my friend and all she wants to do is protect us! Yeah, but I'm the only one with problems here. The one causing the problems, right? Like you're a saint. I see you come home and down a twelve pack every night, coming home late so drunk you spend the next morning puking on the bathroom floor."

"I cleaned it up."

"It shouldn't have been there in the first place! You're in your late thirties for crying out loud! Grow up! At this age, it's called alcoholism, not a good time!"

Dave shoved the last spoonful of cereal into his mouth and picked up his heavy books under his arm, "I need to study. All I wanted to know was why you were home so early."

Sissy crossed her arms and pouted, "Barb sent me home because of my face."

Dave laughed and walked toward the dining room, "Well, I wouldn't want to be around you, much less buy a house from you."

Sissy felt as if she had lost this battle and was ready for Dave to leave so she could throw herself a pity party, "Thanks. I figured as much."

Dave closed his eyes and shook his head in frustration, "What? Oh, now, don't take *that* the wrong way!"

Sissy decided to let her hurt show and pitifully said, "How

else am I supposed to take it?"

Dave took a step toward Sissy but stopped when he glanced at the clock on the kitchen wall above Sissy's head, "However you want to, dear. I said I didn't mean it that way, but, whatever. I've got to go."

Sissy turned her back to Dave, "Don't bother coming home early tonight, I'm having the house cleansed and I don't need your negative vibes messing up everything."

Dave propped his books on his hip, "Don't worry, I've gotten used to not being wanted around here."

"Not wanted? I'm trying to make the things-that-go-bump-in-the-night go away, and you always come in with that judgmental look on your face and that condescending tone in your voice." Sissy felt tears start to swell up in her swollen face, so she tried to focus on staying angry.

Dave stepped back into the kitchen, "I'm a good Christian man, and I'm trying to be open minded about your little experiments with witch . . . ism."

Sissy laughed, "'Witchism'? That's a good one. Oh, and I had no idea you placed so much value on Christianity. Being as you go to church every Sunday, abstain from premarital sex, and lead by such a caring and gentle example."

Dave put his books back under his arm and stepped back into the dining room, "At least I don't play with the devil's toys and invite witches over to the house to go chasing after ghosts. I think you call 'em all out. You *are* the one who's making all of this happen."

Sissy felt embarrassed at Dave's accusations, "Sure, blame it all on me. If you only knew half of the things I knew, you'd shit yourself."

Dave sat his books on the dining room table and waved his arms in anger, "I don't want to know what all you're talking about in the middle of the night, ranting and raving. I think you should consider yourself lucky to have a man who'd put up with that crap! Even my friends think I'm crazy for putting up with you."

Embarrassment quickly turned into a deep, seething, rage, "Lucky? For you to put up with . . . Nobody's making you stay. If this is all so stressful on *you,* maybe you should cut your losses before you wake up with a face full of infection!"

Dave's face turned slightly pale, all sarcasm disappeared, replaced by a sincere respectfulness, "You scare me. I don't know what's going on. I just don't want to be here sometimes."

Sissy was deeply hurt. Her eyes throbbed. Her temples throbbed. "Well, don't. Stay out as late as you like. You can even wake up and puke on the bathroom floor, as long as you clean it up. And you know what I'll call you?"

Dave tried to inject a little humor to diffuse Sissy, "A drunk?"

Sissy wasn't willing to let go so easily, and used her sense of humor to prove how mad she really was, "Oh, yes. That, too. But, I was thinking more of 'paying roommate.'"

That one must've stung, because Dave dropped the "let's-not-be-angry" routine, "Who says I'd ever pay to stay in this hell hole with you?"

Sissy felt her nostrils flare as she threw her arms up, as if to advertise herself, "Oh, but if it's free!"

"What are you trying to say?"

Sissy turned her back to Dave, "I don't know."

Dave leaned over the table and spoke in a quiet, cool voice, "You know what? I don't care. I really don't. Don't wait up for me tonight. Okay?"

Sissy hunched her shoulders and walked over to the stove, pretending to check that the knobs were all off.

Dave grabbed his books and walked out the door, slamming it behind him. The last thing Sissy heard was Dave's wheels spin out in the driveway and onto the pavement. She looked out the kitchen window and saw black tire marks on the pavement.

Suddenly, Sissy felt very tired. The thought of breakfast turned her stomach. All she wanted to do was lie down on the couch and rest. At first, she thought her fatigue was from the pain in her face and the fight with Dave. Then books started falling off of their shelves in the study. So much for Paula's blessing. Maybe eight-thirty would come soon.

Sissy thought the best thing to do was ignore the sounds coming from the study.

Then, she heard the same heavy object fall on the floor three times. Curiosity got the better of Sissy. She literally tip-toed into the study. There she found the books on their shelves, not the floor. But, Dave's heirloom wooden clock was lying on the floor. Sissy picked it up and examined it. On the left side, there were two fresh nicks in the wood. The clock was stained a dark mahogany, but the nicks were a bright, unvarnished red. Apparently, someone found the clock interesting and was having a look at it. Sissy just put the clock back on the floor and figured she'd pretend to not know what happened to it when Dave got home.

Sissy settled back on the couch and got a sudden desire to

read. Normally Sissy read magazines, did her paperwork, and watched TV, but she had an uncanny desire to read a novel and drink coffee. However, the woman knew her eyes were still throbbing from the strain she put on them while driving. To read would be asking for a migraine. So, she surfed through the channels and curled up in Dave's duck themed chenille blanket. Footsteps trod up and down the hall.

Sissy was too tired to deal with more of the supernatural, especially since it seemed to be causing problems between herself and Dave. Sissy yelled at the noises, "Go away! Go the FUCK AWAY!"

The footsteps stopped.

Sissy walked to the bathroom where she applied a second coating of antibiotic to her tear ducts. That old familiar dank dead smell began to emanate from the tub drain. Sissy flipped the stopper and covered the drain with a large wad of tissue followed by a full bottle of shampoo. The smell continued to heighten.

Sissy looked up at the ceiling and shouted, "Oh, stop it! Just stop it! I'm sick and tired of all your crap! Leave me alone!"

The angry woman stormed out of the smelly bathroom and barged into the study.

Once in the study, Sissy grabbed the nearest large book and went into the living room. On the couch, she fluffed her decorative couch pillow, cozied up in the blanket, and opened the book over her face, making an impromptu mask. Despite the "house settling" and other light noises, Sissy drifted off to sleep.

## Chapter 49: There's More Than Skeletons Hiding in the Closet

Sissy dreamed: *she was the little boy, carrying a sack of groceries. Not exactly groceries, but decorations and food for a party. Excitement filled her heart, or the boy's heart, as he waited for his grandmother to unlock the side door. The TV was on. A war documentary was on a public station, as the blasts of large cannons and guns blared through the closed door.*

*The grandmother muttered to herself, "Wonder what your grandfather's doing home at this time of day." Then to the boy, she asked, "How are we supposed to surprise him if he's already here?"*

*The boy hunched his shoulders to say he didn't know.*

*The grandmother swatted the boy across the back of his head, "Don't hunch your shoulders at me! Show some respect. Answer me."*

*The boy was so used to these swats, he didn't even try to rub his head, "I'm sorry. Maybe I can get these groceries into the kitchen without him seeing them!"*

*"What am I supposed to say when he asks what you're doing home from school and I'm not at work?"*

*The boy looked up at his grandmother, "I'm sick and you had to get off work to take care of me?"*

*The woman laughed, "That's a good one. You're always the spittin' image of health. Like he'd believe that!"*

*The boy faked a cough and sniffled, then he turned around and smiled at his grandmother.*

*The woman frowned at the boy with a look of contempt,*

*"Get on in that house and quit tryin' to be cute. You ain't cute. I'll figure out something."*

*The grandmother unlocked the door and the boy lightly tiptoed to the kitchen.*

*He was so excited about surprising his grandfather for his birthday, the boy wanted to run and shove all of the goods away in the kitchen cabinets. But he knew if he ran in the house, he'd have to spend time in the closet. He didn't want to miss his grandfather's birthday party, so he kept his enthusiasm restrained.*

*After putting her cardigan in the closet, the grandmother walked to the back of the house, calling, "John? John? You here?"*

*The boy engaged himself, quickly putting the decorations in the cabinets and the party food hid safely away in the fridge. He listened to his grandmother call for his grandfather and wondered what kind of a mood his grandfather would be in. Would he be angry? Was he home because he was sick? Suddenly, he heard his grandmother let out a yell from her bedroom.*

*The boy left the sack on the kitchen counter to run to her rescue.*

*Inside the bedroom, the boy saw his grandmother standing at the foot of the bed with her hands over her mouth. She was stuck to the spot. The boy tugged at her pants pocket to get her attention. The woman ignored him.*

*Suddenly, the grandfather roared from the bed to his shocked wife, "Get the boy out of here, Genevieve! Don't let him see!"*

*But, it was too late. The boy saw. His grandfather, John, was in bed with another woman. At first the boy didn't recognize the woman, who had the sheets pulled up to her nose. Then, the boy realized she was the mother of his two friends who lived through the woods.*

*They used to play baseball together on the weekends until the demon got them. The boy always thought their mother was pretty, until now. Now she was the ugliest person he had ever seen. Her hair was a mess. Her face was a mess. She was sniveling and crying. The room smelled. The smell was probably her fault, too. Even worse, she was ugly because she made Grandma cry.*

*Genevieve slapped the boy's hand away from her pants pocket and walked out of the bedroom. The boy didn't know what to do. He felt ashamed. He wanted to run, but he was panicked, glued to the floor. Couldn't someone tell him what to do?*

*The grandfather had a look of hatred upon his face, reached over his side of the bed, and threw a heavy shoe at the boy, "What're you looking at? What are you a pervert? Go get your grandmother! NOW!"*

*The boy didn't feel the shoe hit him, and he barely comprehended the man's words. Finally, the old man was getting out of bed, dragging the sheet with him. The boy's survival instincts took over and he ran out of the room. He ran to the kitchen, but his grandmother wasn't there. She wasn't sitting in her favorite chair. She wasn't in the house at all. Her car was gone from the driveway. He was left alone with John and Mrs. Ruis. What was he to do? The boy ran to his room and hid in his closet.*

*From the closet, the boy could hear the grandfather yell to Mrs. Ruis, "Get out! Get out you damn whore! Get out!"*

*The boy stifled a fearful whimper, hoping his grandfather would think he had left with his grandmother and not look for him.*

*Not in his closet.*

*The grandfather stomped through the house, drunk and stumbling, "Genevieve? Genevieve? You here, Gal? You here? It ain't what it looked like! She . . . she tempted me, Genny! It ain't my fault!"*

*The boy heard John's heavy footsteps plod down the hall, throwing open the bathroom door with a loud crash, "You in here? Genny, get out here and talk to me!" John swung the door wide open to the boy's room, "Where's the boy, Genevieve? What've you done with him? What're you going to do to him, Genevieve?"*

*The boy felt his heart beat hard in his chest. Fear made the blood pulse so hard in his temples, his eyesight blurred. If only he could stop breathing! He was breathing too hard.*

*Too loud. John would hear him. John would find him, and what then? From the darkness of the closet came a pair of glowing red eyes. The demon was back. What would it do to John?*

*The boy tucked his head into his knees and tried to hold his breath until he knew John was gone. John had to leave, soon, or it would get him. The demon would get him, and it'd be the boy's fault.*

*"Boy, get out in the light where I can see you!"*

*Ferociously, John swung the closet door open so hard the knob imbedded itself in the sheetrock. Seizing the boy by his shirt collar, John demanded, "What're you doing in there? Huh? You think you saw something? You ain't seen nothin', you hear me? Nothing. Tell your grandmother you ain't seen nothing."*

*The boy began to cry, "Please, grandpa, you need to leave before it gets you!"*

*John shook the boy, tearing his shirt, "What gets me? I already married your grandma, that's punishment enough!" John laughed in the boy's face, his breath was pungent with alcohol.*

*The boy looked up at his grandfather, "I don't want it to hurt you! Let me go!"*

*John held fast to the boy, "Let you go? Where?" The boy pushed John, who lost his footing and stumbled back onto the footboard of the boy's bed. John loosened his grip on the boy's collar. The boy rolled over the catty-cornered mattress and looked in horror at his grandfather, who had a wooden shard from the bed stuck through his right shoulder by his neck.*

*The boy walked over to try to help his grandfather, but the old man swatted him away. The old man did not seem to feel pain, but was consumed with anger, "Look, look, what you made me do! You did this! You did this to me! This is all your fault! Goddamn your mother! Damon, you are nothing but a whole demon! Get away from me!"*

*The boy watched in horror as the demon emerged from the closet. To his amazement, his grandfather didn't see it, but kept his gaze frozen in horror upon his grandson. The demon grabbed another long, wooden shard of the broken footboard and pulled it loose from the splinters that held it loosely to the rest of the footboard. The demon walked up to the old man and shoved it right through his heart. Then the demon held the old man's head in its large palms and pushed its index fingers into the sides of the old man's eyes. In terror, the boy ran out of the house and down the street . . . in his mind.*

*The grandmother returned with a gun, which she dropped when she saw her grandson gouging out her husband's eyes with his bare hands. Genevieve put her hands up to her face and screamed, "What have you done! Get away from him!"*

358

*Genevieve ran over to her husband, falling on her knees to try to pry the wood stakes out of his body. She looked back at the boy, who saw her drop the gun. More importantly, the demon saw her drop the gun. The demon picked up the gun and pointed it in her face.*

*Genevieve laughed, "I can see you, I know what the hell you are. You can't do it."*

*The boy-demon held the gun steady at her forehead, "Since your mother left, you're stuck with us forever. I'm your only family. You've got nowhere else to go. You can't . . . " As the woman reached to take the gun away from the boy, he pulled the trigger. Dropping the gun to the ground, the demon grasped the woman's head in the palms of his hands . . . and began to extract her eyes with its bare hands.*

*Everything faded away into a blur of sobs and tears.*

Sissy knew she was dreaming, now. She was not the little boy. In the regions of her brain that control semi-consciousness, Sissy told herself that she did not want to dream anymore, she wanted to sleep. Just sleep. Just sleep. Just sleep.

Darkness. Like sleep. But out of the darkness came a pair of red glowing eyes. The demon was coming to visit her, again. Sissy told herself to wake-up, but her body would not respond. She told herself she was just dreaming, but her brain would not take control of the dream. Desperately, she screamed at her body to wake-up, for her eyes to open, for the dream to end, but she was trapped. In terror, she stood as a bodiless consciousness in the darkness, watching as the demon approached.

# Chapter 50: Have A Little Faith

Sissy woke on the couch. The light from outside shone brightly through the naked windows. Something was wrong. What was it, though? Sissy looked at the windows, again. They now had opened blinds on them. Something was still wrong. "I left those blinds closed, why are they open?" she asked herself out loud. The blinds shut themselves tight, and a swirling darkness formed. Now she had no doubt she was still asleep, unable to awaken.

"Do you wish me to leave?" the darkness asked Sissy.

"I want your grandparents to leave. They're evil, terrible people. Then you can go, too," Sissy hoped she was being visited by one of the less harmful personalities.

"Eyes. Living eyes. For her," responded the darkness.

"I won't give . . .," Sissy tried to speak, but her mind became muddled.

Many voices swirled in her mind all at once, echoing, "There is a thin veil . . .veil . . veil
. . . between this life and the next. Only a small moment . . . moment . . . moment . . . in time determines the difference between happiness . . . happiness . . . happiness . . . happiness . . . anguish . . . anguish . . . anguish. People think they have control . . . control . . .control.
They control nothing . . . nothing . . . nothing. Do you agree . . . agree . . . agree?"

Sissy listened and thought it sounded reasonable. In a soft, dreamy voice, she responded, "I suppose."

"I can show you . . . show you . . . show you. Do you wish

to see . . . to see . . . to see?"

A warm feeling came over the woman. Safety, security. Nothing could go wrong. In the far reaches of her mind, her instincts were trying to tell her to say "no," but they weren't loud enough. Not persuasive enough. Not like the warmth. It was so comforting, of course she wanted to see. Let it show her. Anything, anything at all for that warm, fuzzy feeling.

As soon as Sissy thought the word, "yes," the feeling disappeared. The room became cold. Sissy awoke in reality, her breath stolen from her chest. Taking a loud, hard breath, the woman sat up on her couch. Her chest hurt. Her arms felt as if they were made of lead. She was too tired to try to remember her dreams. The images bounced in her mind but didn't make sense anymore. All she knew was, she had made a terrible mistake.

***

An eternity passed before eight-thirty arrived. The doorbell rang. Sissy answered it and found her driveway full of oddly dressed women, all with flowing long hair and flowing long dresses with silver jewelry. They actually fit Sissy's idea of what a coven of witches in Athens would look like. However, Sissy was surprised at how comforting she found their stereotypical images to be. They did seem to come dressed for the occasion. A dark-headed woman made her way through the small crowd. It was Mimi, who immediately hugged Sissy upon reaching her.

"Are you okay?" Mimi was genuinely worried.

Sissy felt her heart beat faster with anxiety, "This has got to work. There is no other option. I had another dream."

Mimi walked into the house, motioning for the others to stay put as she partially closed the door, "What happened?"

"I'm not sure, but something about it wants . . . eyes . . . before it'll leave."

"Again with the eyes? This thing is obsessed."

"They're for the girl, the baby girl that drowned in the tub. Somehow, I think I got tricked into agreeing to let it do . . . something."

"You agreed for the evil personality to have your eyes?"

"I was tricked, somehow. It talked to me. No, they talked to me. The voices, they were so loving. Soothing. I felt as if nothing . . . could hurt me."

Mimi loosened her grip on the door, "This is awful. Your life could seriously be in danger." Mimi took the realtor's chin in her hand, "Let us try to help, okay?"

The women came inside and made their introductions. Upon closer examination, all were decked out in black nail polish, Celtic jewelry, long flowing gowns of velvet, and dark, Gothic make-up. Sissy felt as if she had just invited a coven of vampires into her home.

Paula lingered outside the longest, bringing up the rear in a reluctant manner.

She walked over to Sissy and handed her a bracelet with a Celtic symbol on it, "This means protection. All we can do is try to make your home clean and, therefore, unpleasant for your unwanted visitor."

Sissy put the bracelet on her left wrist, "Thank you, it's beautiful. How much do I owe you?"

Paula smiled, "It's a gift so as to charge its protection abilities. We need to channel all of the good karma into this environment that we can."

Sissy wasn't expecting that answer and just responded, "Oh. Okay. Thank you, again."

Mimi and the other women rearranged Sissy's living room, clearing the center for all six women to sit Indian style. Sissy joined them in the circle.

Paula flipped her hair over her shoulder, "No, Sissy, you are the seventh. You sit in the middle, and we will cleanse you and your home."

Sissy did as she was told and watched as the other women held hands and bowed their heads. Sissy bowed her head, too, though she didn't know why she should or even if she was supposed to.

Unlike the prayer for protection, this prayer had several parts to it with each woman participating. As with the prayer, Sissy found the jargon and mannerisms hard to follow. Paula started the process, babbling something about calling on the cleansing element of water and praising its goodness and asking for its help. Then Paula took a vial from one of the folds of her dress and opened it. She dabbed a dot on herself and passed it around the circle.

Each woman dabbed a drop on herself, until it came to Sissy. Mimi took the vial and dropped several drops on Sissy's head and made a circle of drops around Sissy on the wooden floor. Each woman had a physical or spiritual property she called upon, with a symbol that was passed around the circle, shared, and encircled around Sissy - - her favorites were the olive oil on her forehead and the nip of cinnamon alcohol.

No strange sounds issued from the house. The house didn't settle. Footsteps did not trod. The bathroom did not smell. The cleansing seemed to be working. Sissy had her hopes up. She hoped that just having hope would be enough faith to make the spells and their charms work.

Finally, the cleansing was over. Sissy felt relieved. Each woman took her turn out of the circle by holding Sissy's left hand, kissing her on the top of her head, and saying, "May you pass this circle in safety," before stepping outside the circle. Each woman was sincere, which comforted Sissy more. Finally, Mimi's turn came, and she blessed her friend, tears in her eyes.

After the cleansing, the women introduced one another and lit white candles and long sticks of aromatic incense in the living room. Each woman wanted to know Sissy's thoughts on each of the symbols, and if she felt it was working. Sissy felt warm, much like the sensation she had felt in her dream earlier that day. There was much discussion over the validity of the symbols. Praise and support filled the conversation. A positive air filled the home, dispersing the negative atmosphere of Sissy's fight with Dave from earlier that day. After a couple of hours passed, the women rearranged Sissy's living room (for positive chi), said their goodbyes and left. Sissy felt safe. But, Mimi lingered behind.

Mimi watched with Sissy on the stoop as the women got in their cars and left, "I don't want to leave you here alone. If you and Dave get into a fight, it could feed that thing."

Sissy looked surprised. She wondered to herself, *Isn't everything supposed to be okay now? Permanently?* Rather than ask Mimi that question and potentially be told something she didn't want to hear, Sissy calmly responded, "I don't have anywhere else to go.
Dave will be home sometime late tonight."

Mimi grabbed Sissy by the arm and theatrically tugged on her, "Come stay with me, at Talon's. Dave should come, too. We have a spare bedroom. I put fresh linens on it just for you . . . and Dave."

Sissy pulled her arm out of Mimi's tight grasp and steadied the worried woman, "But you said these things can follow you."

"I think this thing wants to hurt you here. Please, stay with me."

"I thought you said you have to have faith. I believe the cleansing works."

"So do I, but I would just feel better if I could keep an eye on you until that thing has time to dissipate."

Sissy didn't like the sound of that. And it was killing her spiritual high, "As much energy is in this house? That could take weeks!"

"Just one night. So I won't feel guilty."

"How is any of this your fault?"

"I wanted you to enhance your skills. I never thought you'd encounter something like this. Look at you, it hurt your eyes. It wants to kill. It tricks you. I . . . I feel somewhat responsible. If you hadn't gone through the bar . . ."

"Fine, Mimi, if it'll make you feel better, I'll stay over at your place tonight. Can we wait for Dave to come home?"

Mimi smiled with relief, "Yes. I'll stay and you can follow me home."

Sissy packed a bag for herself and one for Dave. She hoped he would come home before the wee hours of the night. Finally, Dave pulled into the driveway, and to Sissy's shock, it was only ten o'clock.

Sissy greeted Dave at the door, but he pushed her out of the way and ran down the hall with his hand cupped tightly over his mouth. The bathroom door crashed open, and Dave violently vomited into the toilet. Mimi looked at Sissy and nervously picked up a magazine. Sissy went to the bathroom to see about Dave.

"What's wrong, Dave?"

"Oh, man, we did tequila shots, again. I got the worm." Dave put his head back into the toilet and vomited several times in a row.

"I don't think you have the worm anymore."

"I have never had a hangover before passing out before. Oh, man, I feel sick."

"I don't think we should stay here tonight."

Dave dry heaved and groaned, "I'm not leaving. Too sick to get back in a car. Didn't barely make it here."

"There's something really evil in this house. Mimi wants us to stay with her for the night."

"I'm not leaving! Oh, my head. Oh, God, I never thought I'd drink something'd make me want to die!" Dave dry heaved twice, then vomited into the toilet. This time he was puking stomach bile.

Sissy visibly grimaced, "We need to leave. The thing that's been bothering me has gotten violent. It hurt my eyes. That's what's wrong with my face. It wants to . . ."

"To what, Sissy? What?" Dave rested his face against the cool linoleum.

Sissy demurely responded, "Hurt us."

"Those damn witches have you brainwashed. I can't take it anymore. I can't."

"Dave, please, give me some time. This will all go away."

"I'm staying here with my toilet. Go wherever the hell you want, just leave me be! Leave me be, goddammit!"

Sissy let out a sorrowful sigh, "I'll leave you directions to her house. If you get scared, I already have your things packed, and I'm taking them with me. If you don't come, I'll assume everything's alright."

"If you loved me, you'd stay here and take care of me. I'm sick, Sissy."

"I can't, Dave. This thing is real to me, and I know it wants to hurt me. Please, come with us."

"No! Aw, God, my head! Just go! There ain't nothing here. Your damn witch friends got you brainwashed, so go with them. We will talk tomorrow."

Sissy turned her back to Dave, "I'm leaving. If you don't come by tonight, I'll check on you before work tomorrow morning."

"Whatever. Just leave me a wet washcloth before you go."

Sissy dutifully fulfilled Dave's request, "I wish you'd . . ."

Dave lifted his arm into the air and snatched the cloth out of Sissy's hands, "Go away!"

Sissy rubbed her hand, even though Dave had not hurt it. Tear drops slowly trickled down her cheeks, "I don't want you to get hurt."

Dave scowled at Sissy, "Stay or get the hell out."

Sissy walked into the living room and looked for a pen and paper, "He's not coming with us. I'm going to leave directions to your house and a little note."

Mimi put the magazine down on the table, "It's 2430 Smith

Way, one street over from the organic grocery store and Good Faith House. A white house with black trim. One red car, one green car, and your SUV parked out front."

Sissy wrote down Mimi's directions and added her personal note:

*Dave,*

*I'm sorry you're not feeling well, but I've got to stay at Mimi's tonight. If you want, you can come over later and stay in the guest bedroom with me. Don't worry about waking anyone, we're expecting you. If you decide to stay here, I'll check on you before work in the morning.*

*God Bless, Much Love,*

*Sissy*

## Chapter 51: Welcome to The Normal Room

Sissy followed Mimi in her green Honda over to her house on the "hippie" side of town. The house was an older home, possibly from the turn of the century. Hopefully, it wasn't haunted, too.

Mimi got out of her car and waited for Sissy to get out of hers, "I hope you like the room. We call it our 'normal' room."

Sissy forced a snicker. She was very worried about Dave and considered going back, but the fear wouldn't let her. Somehow being around Mimi had a calming effect on her.

Sissy went inside Mimi and Talon's house and found it decorated in much the same way their studio apartment had been, only much more upscale and grown-up. Walls painted with purple and crimson harlequin diamonds. Polished cherry wood floors. Brass accents.

Sleek, black leather furniture with sharp clean lines, upon which sat that damned white cat. Candles of every shape and size on every available space. A cabinet full of antique books and exotic porcelain figures of harlequin clowns and lustful masks. Tapestries hung on the walls. The windows were covered in black crushed velvet curtains decorated with intricate bead work. A giant chandelier of aged brass covered in a woven ivy filigree helped the room reach its pentacle. Apparently, Mimi's bar had afforded her the ability to indulge herself. That and renting out her loft in conjunction with free rent from Talon.

The guest bedroom truly did prove to be "the normal room," especially in comparison to the living room. The bed was covered in a red, white, and blue quilt with the white sheets folded down and about a dozen lacy pillows covering the headboard. The bed, matching side tables, chest-of-drawers, and stand-alone mirror were oak, as was the floor. The curtains were blue, coordinated to the quilt in that matchy-matchy style from a catalogue. The valances on top were ruffled with a deliberate "designer-but-not" look to them. Even the lamps were . . . ordinary, oak bases with white cloth shades and brass accents. Folk art painted pictures of cats adorned the walls. Sissy never took Mimi to be one of those "cat people" types. The entire room was confusing, like stumbling into a hidden panic room in your grandmother's basement.

Sissy dropped her bags on the floor and let out a sigh, "I think I smell apple pie baking."

Mimi laughed, "That's the potpourri. Horrid isn't it? Talon's mom doesn't like our decorating, so we gave her a room for when she visits. She decorated it. I just keep the door shut."

Sissy liked the explanation and settled into bed. After listening to the house settle, sleep invaded Sissy's eyes. Nothing but a sleep, a sleep as wholesome as the red, white, and blue quilt under which she slept, besieged her. Apple pie filled her nostrils. A warm, kind hand reached out of her dreams, and stroked her head while she slept.

The next morning, Sissy woke early, only to find herself alone. Despite her peaceful rest, Sissy felt very worried about Dave and wondered what exactly she'd find when she arrived at her house. And yet, deep down inside, Sissy knew. She knew she was too aware of what awaited her at home. The feeling was nauseating. Mimi was waiting on Sissy when she walked out of "the normal room."

"I made you some herbal tea. It's good for infections and

inflammation. Hey, your face looks better, already."

"Thanks, can I take it with me? I've got to see about Dave."

"Tell me one thing. Did you sleep well?"

"I did. Did you come in and rub my head while I slept? It was weird at first, but very comforting."

Mimi's ivory face turned bright red, "Actually, that was our ghost. We just call her 'Gramms.'"

Sissy took a big gulp of the earthy tea and sputtered out, "Oh, that's fair. You get Aunt Bea for a ghost and I have an escapee from the lower depths of hell."

"After your experiences lately, I didn't want to tell you. I was afraid you wouldn't stay. I don't think she'd let any harm come to you, which is another reason I wanted you to stay here."

"Fighting ghosts with ghosts. That's different. But whatever works. I gotta get going."

"Do you want to call? I mean, what if something bad has happened? You could become, like, a prime suspect. Get the police to go with you, or something."

"Jesus, I never thought of that. What should I say? I can't tell them I stayed with you because my house is haunted."

"Tell them you and Dave had a fight. He was supposed to come over when he was less mad, a neutral territory kind of thing. But since he didn't show, you're worried he might still be mad. Hint at domestic violence if you have to, but don't go in that house alone."

"I take it you've been thinking about this a little, huh?"

Mimi looked down, "Yeah."

"You go with me?"

"Then we'd both be suspects. Maybe. I just think . . ."

"No, you're making sense. I really hadn't thought it out that far. Jesus Mimi, I can't stand the thought of . . ."

"Just call the police. I'll feel better."

## Chapter 52: Dave Wellness Check

The police met Sissy at Mimi's house and escorted her over to see Dave. Once at home, Sissy found the house filled with the smell that only Athen's water can produce. To Sissy's relief, the bathtub was running, which had to mean that Dave was going through his normal routine.

Sissy's thoughts raced as the police followed her inside the house, *He can be mad. He can be angry. He can even pack his things and leave. Yes, he can pack up and leave. As long as he's okay. Please let him be okay. Please let him be okay.*

Standing in the living room, Sissy called out to Dave. But no one answered. She looked at the two policemen with a panicked sadness in her eyes.

Officer Marks, a confident man with a slight build and well-manicured brown mustache gently asked her, "Ma'am, he's not answering. I hear the water running. Do you think you'll be okay?"

"He was really drunk when he came home last night. He's probably hung over. I'm just afraid. I'd feel better if you'd just check the house for me."

"What's his name?"

"Dave." Just saying his name made Sissy feel all alone. Despite her desire to keep a poker face, Sissy started to cry. The swelling in her face had gone down enough to allow tears to trickle out for the first time. The other policeman, Officer Watts, motioned for her to sit on the couch. Sissy sat as if the couch no longer belonged to her and she were visiting unfamiliar relatives: straight backed, feet planted firmly in front of her, hands on her lap, scared to swallow or make a noise.

Officer Marks walked over to the hall entrance and knocked on the hall wall with his knuckles as he poked his head into the hallway, "Dave? I'm Officer . . . What the . . .?!? Watts, call 911 now!" Marks ran down the hall. Squishy footsteps followed by sloshing sounds.

Officer Watts, a middle-aged man with a round gut and dark features, stepped into the hall, his back facing Sissy. Officer Watts tensed up and froze. The big bellied man walked over to Sissy in a manner that oozed a badly portrayed act of calm, "Uh, ma'am, we need you to come outside with me for a moment." Watts grabbed Sissy with one hand and his radio with the other, immediately asking for medical assistance.

Sissy's heart raced, tears streamed down her face, "Oh, God! What's wrong?
What's happened to Dave? Is he okay? Is he hurt? Oh, God! What's happened?"

Before Sissy knew it, life as it existed in a near perimeter around her body came to an almost dead standstill. People and things raced around outside her bubble in an unfathomable blur of questions, directions, and sirens. The slowest, longest sight that burned a horrifying impression on her brain was that of Dave's dead body being wheeled out to the ambulance, the white sheet covering his face. After that moment, Sissy found she could not remember what he looked like without a photograph. Dave, for her, became a lifeless body beneath a white sheet that would ride out of her life forever.

*** 

It would be days before Sissy would learn what Officer

Marks saw. The door to the bathroom had been opened so violently the doorknob was embedded in the sheetrock. All the policemen needed to do was look straight down the hall to see the man's dead body floating in the bathtub, with the water still running. The coroner found Dave's blood alcohol level to be toxic. The investigation concluded that Dave had most likely drowned by slipping into a coma while bathing.

Sissy stuck to her story of being scared to be at home alone with him. She felt awful for doing it, but the demon possessed house, though truthful, was not an option. The women from Mimi's coven said they were there that night for an intervention. Talon's home camera's proved that Sissy was at Mimi's house when Dave died. Sissy's grief and trauma were so overwhelming, she moved into Mimi's "normal room."

## Chapter 53: Suck it Up, Buttercup

Days after Dave's death, Sissy got the invitation to Dave's funeral in her post office box. Not wanting anything to do with the haunted hovel she bought less than a year before, Sissy hired Barb to sell the house for her. Barb was more than understanding, blaming the house on "too many memories of Dave." If only she knew . . .

The funeral invitation was hand-written and very warm, but Sissy was unsure of whether she should attend the funeral or not. Though comforting, moving into Mimi's ultimately felt like defeat. Complicating Sissy's life even more - - Mimi worried that the presence in Sissy's house would leave an evil imprint on her furniture and other belongings, so Sissy agreed to hire an auctioneer to hold an estate sale for her. Sissy's life was filled with shock and sudden, catastrophic change.

The funeral was scheduled on the following Tuesday back in Flemming, over three hours away from Athens, which would mean taking time off from work and being unable to oversee the appraisal of her belongings. However, Barb was more than a little persuasive in helping Sissy decide whether or not to attend the funeral.

"Damn it, Sissy, if you don't go to that poor man's funeral, you're fired!"

Sissy rubbed her face with her hands, "It's just so . . ."

Barb threw her hands up in the air, "Sad? That's the whole point, Sissy! If I didn't know any better, I'd say you're having difficulty grieving. You might want to get some counseling when you get back from the funeral."

"I haven't agreed to go, yet."

"Yes, you have."

Sissy lightly banged her head on Barb's desk, "*No*, I haven't. I don't know his family.

I never met them. What if they think badly of me?"

"You're going. Take the rest of the week off."

Sissy looked up and dryly smiled, "I'll take the rest of the week off, no problem."

Barb pursed her lips and pointed a crimson fingernail at Sissy, "To go to that boy's funeral. I'll call those people myself and find out if you went to that funeral."

"You don't even know who they are."

"I have my ways. Besides, not going to your live-in boyfriend's funeral is like . . .

like . . . just asking to send yourself to hell! The man had a drinking problem. I've been clean for the past twelve years. If I had known, I would have invited him to my meetings."

Sissy cocked her brow at the angry woman, "Wait. Did you just say I'd go to hell for not attending his funeral? Oh, but living in sin?"

"Ya'll were gonna get married. Things just came up."

"Like he died?"

"Are you making jokes, now?" Barb had an abhorred look on her face, "I'm giving you the number of my therapist. He's really good. When my second husband left me for another woman, I had grieving issues, too. Making jokes, laughing it off, and one day I just broke down and cried in the middle of traffic at five points. Held traffic up on all sides until a policeman came and pulled me out of my car. Bastard wrote me up a ticket. Two hundred damn dollars. When I appealed on account of mental anguish, the judge made me pay *and* sentenced me to two months of therapy. Best thing ever happened to me."

Sissy took the sticky backed note from Barb's hand and sarcastically asked, "Did it work?"

"Sissy, if I call you a bitch, I mean it in the most loving way possible, because I know you're still in shock."

"But, of course."

With her hands planted firmly on her hips, Barb turned her back to Sissy, "Go to that funeral, and I'll have your house sold in thirty days with enough profit to help you buy another house."

## Chapter 54: You're One of Us, Now. Sorta.

The ride to Flemming was lonely. Beyond lonely, it was so painful that Sissy had to pull off on the side of the road and cry uncontrollably at her steering wheel. A bucolic drive that would normally have taken three hours, stretched itself out into five hellish hours of tears, sobs, and long stints of "Why? God, why?" The occasional car would whiz by, and once, a deer skittishly came close to Sissy's car before darting back into the woods from which it came.

The glaring orange lights of the Flemming "Hunker Home" cafe were a welcome sight. Even though grief had stolen her appetite, Sissy felt she might benefit from a bite to eat and getting reacquainted with the sights and sounds of the locals. Sissy also realized she felt oddly compelled to "bum a smoke," despite the fact she had never smoked in her life.

Once inside the restaurant, the smell of hamburger grease and cigarette smoke brought back a strange nostalgia for the cliquish little town that never really accepted her and never really rejected her, either. A sign above the counter read, "Save Booths for More than One Person, Please." Sissy huffed at the sign's feigned politeness and sat in the middle of a booth by the window. The grieving woman grabbed a menu from behind the napkin dispenser and pried its sticky leaves open. About the time she was perusing the side items, she had an epiphany. For the first time, Sissy realized she had seriously been thinking about marrying Dave and moving back to Flemming with him.

Suddenly, she knew that thoughts of settling into the small town, having children, being content with a rigorous routine of "nothing much," and fading into the periphery as a working mom had been brewing in her subconscious a little more strongly than she had allowed herself to admit. Now what of her plans? Now what of her future? Sissy knew she couldn't live the rest of her life in "the normal room." Everything she had known for the past year had suddenly become utterly fruitless.

"Futile," Sissy accidentally said out loud.

"Ma'am?" a scrawny waitress with a bad home perm and hopeless, sunken eyes asked.

"Oh, am I ordering?" Sissy looked up at the waitress, "Donna," for an answer.

Donna snickered with an air of superiority, "I guess, lady."

Sissy knew she should be offended but couldn't muster the strength to care. At the moment she felt numb, utterly numb, "Right. I'll just have some hash browns with cheese and a cup of grapefruit juice."

Donna stared at her pad and tapped it impatiently with her "Bank of Flemming" pen, "Out of grapefruit juice."

Again, Sissy knew she should be offended and say something to defend herself, but she was unable to care. Maybe coming back to Flemming was nothing more than a big mistake. Sissy let out a loud sigh of defeat, "Decaf?"

"Alright. Is that all?"

"I'm not really hungry," Sissy looked up at the waitress and handed the menu to her.

The waitress pointed at the napkin dispenser where three other menus waited. Sissy felt her face turn red, "Oh, right," and she placed her menu with the others.

A group of four drunken men dressed from head to toe in

camouflage walked into the restaurant and took a seat behind Sissy. Donna walked over to the men, who snickered at her approach.

A loud, overly confident voice ordered, "I want the special with a Coke and a slice of pie."

Donna puffed in frustration, "What kind of pie?"

The man chuckled, "What kind of pie? What ya' got?"

Donna reluctantly responded, "Cream and . . ."

"*Cream* pie? What kind of an establishment is this?" The male voice laughed, and his cronies boisterously followed suit.

Another higher pitched male voice with a very country accent asked, "Hey, wasn't you Donna Tucker in high school?"

"Yeah, you're Rory, right?"

"Uh-huh. If I remember correctly, Walter Crumbley knocked-you-up senior year."

Donna didn't respond. Her silence was painful and made Sissy feel almost glad she had allowed the waitress a moment of superiority. But the waitress held her ground and nonchalantly said, "Yeah. That's me. Can I get you something?"

Rory laughed, "Nah, I think Walter beat me to it!" The men laughed. To her amazement, Sissy heard one man slap the other on the back.

Donna raised her voice, "Look, I ain't got to take this. Either you order and leave me alone or I'm gonna have y'all leave."

Rory's voice was full of mocked apology, "I don't mean nothin,' Donna. My brother died is all. I'm just tryin' to blow off some steam. You understand."

Donna didn't respond.

Rory continued, "Aw-right, den. I'll have what Terry's having. Sounds good to me." The rest of the men mumbled in concurrence.

Terry re-started the conversation, "Man, I can't believe Dave died! It's just not real."

Rory added, "I remember how we used to drink every weekend out in the field behind Daddy's house. Party with a keg. Just get tore up, but nothing like that."

A third voice responded, "Who'd thought he'd end up drowned in a bathtub?"

Terry's voice added, "They said he drank himself into a coma and then drowned."

The unnamed third voice said, "Wasn't he living with some ole' gal he met up in Athens?"

Rory responded, "Momma said she invited her to the funeral. Name's Sissy, or Missy, or something. Woman called, said she'd be here."

Terry asked, "Was it his house?"

"Dave? Naw, it was her house."

The third voice asked in an excited tone, "You don't reckon she had something to do with it? Ya' know, some of that . . . foul play?"

Rory laughed, "I reckon anything's possible. I mean, who'd've thought Dave'd actually get serious enough with some gal to move in with her?" All of the men laughed, and then a sad silence followed.

Donna scuffed her feet on the floor as she brought Sissy's food to her, "Anything else, ma'am?"

Sissy felt a lump in her throat and a mischievous spark in

her chest, "Call me Sissy, Donna."

Donna frowned, "Why?"

"Well, I know your name. I think it's only fair I know yours."

Donna shrugged her shoulders, "O-Kay," and walked off.

Just as Sissy had suspected, the men behind her began to whisper to each other, "Did you hear that? She said her name's Sissy. You don't reckon that's Dave's Sissy?"

Sissy smiled into her coffee, took a big swig, and turned around in her booth, "As a matter of fact, gentlemen, I was Dave's Sissy. We lived together until he had an unfortunate accident. I already explained everything to the police, but if you would like to hear it first hand, I've got the time."

The men just stared at Sissy as if she had held them at gunpoint with a banana and told them to take her to their leader. Finally, Rory spoke up, "Mama's been wanting to meet you. She was wanting you to spend the night at her house so you wouldn't have to spend money on a hotel room. She forgot to tell you that when you called."

"I've already made reservations, but that was nice of her to think of me."

"My name's Rory. I'm Dave's baby brother. Mama'd really like to meet you, if you had time tonight."

"That's alright, I'm tired."

"Lemme call her." Rory walked over to the counter and motioned to Donna, who put the restaurant's phone on the countertop. Rory leaned against the counter with his feet crossed, all while motioning for Sissy to stay seated and then gave her the confident country boy wink'n nod of "I got everything under control."

Rory held his index finger in the air to denote he was accomplishing his self-imposed task, "Nanna? Get Mama. Yeah, get Mama. Mama? Mama. Yeah, it's Rory. I'm here at the Hunker. I said . . . I SAID, I'm here at the Hunker Home. Yeah, I can pick you up something. What you want? Huh? They got cream pie, I think. Yeah, cream. Diet Coke? Aw-right. Naw, I's calling to tell you Sissy's here in the restaurant with me right now. Sissy. Yeah, Dave's Sissy. Here. Right now. You coming? Here? Right now? Still want me to order? I can. Sure? Aw-right. We'll see ya. Yeah, I'll keep her here for ya.' I'll . . . bye."

Sissy stared at Rory as if he were holding her hostage with a banana, telling her to take him to her leader, "I really just want to go check in at the hotel and go to bed."

Rory reached over the counter and gave the phone back to Donna. Bending over, grinning as if he were quite pleased with himself, Rory snapped his fingers and pointed with both hands at Sissy, "Mama's on the way. You leave now, and she'll be pissed at you for a long while."

Sissy just smiled, "Gee, thanks. I guess I'll wait here. How long is this gonna take?"

Rory resumed his seat at the table and gave another wink'n nod to Sissy, "Not long."

Sissy felt extremely awkward. Somehow, and she was not sure how, this redneck man had turned the tables on her and taken control of her life for at least the next hour. This wasn't how she had planned the situation to turn out at all. Minutes passed before a woman with short, gray hair wearing faded mom jeans and a plain white t-shirt with white canvas tennis shoes burst through the doors, "Where is she?"

Sissy looked up from her empty plate, "Mrs. Howard?"

The woman walked frantically over to Sissy's booth, "Are you Sissy?"

Sissy felt her face turn red, "Yes, ma'am. How do you do?" The moment those words left her lips, Sissy wished she could hit the "back" button and smash "delete."

"I'm not good, Sissy, not good at all. My oldest boy is dead, and nothing's making any sense." Mrs. Howard sat down opposite of Sissy, "What happened? How did he die?"

Sissy swallowed hard and felt the tears swell up in her eyes.

Mrs. Howard reached out and held Sissy's hands, "I know about the police report and the argument. I even found out about the hole in the wall. I never knew Dave to be a violent man, and I just want you to know it was the alcohol. Did he hurt you?"

Sissy's mind raced, until she realized Mrs. Howard was referencing her fabrication about the need for a police escort the day of Dave's death, "No, ma'am. We just had a really bad argument, you know, about his drinking. I wanted him to . . ." Sissy broke down as she heard herself lie.

"It's alright, honey. It's alright." Mrs. Howard's eyes filled with tears, "I raised him better than all of that. I did. His daddy's been sober for over ten years. He knew better than all of that. I just want to know . . .," Mrs. Howard put her hand over her face and waived her other hand in the air, "do you have any idea why his eyes won't close?"

Sissy felt her chest burn and her mind go blank, "I . . . I don't know."

Mrs. Howard looked up, "Of course you don't. Why did I

ask you that question?

I'm sorry. It's just . . . Bonnie can't get his eyes to shut and nobody knows why. I hoped . . .

I don't know. I'm sorry. You didn't have to know that. I bet I've upset you. Did I upset you?" Mrs. Howard reached across the table and put her hand on Sissy's arm.

Sissy was confused and comforted all at the same time, so she just let herself cry with a woman she had never met before. The two women sobbed until Mrs. Howard wiped her tears and called Donna over to their table.

Donna sauntered up, unaffected by the women's bereavement, "What can I get you?"

Mrs. Howard sniffled, "I'll have a burger, fries, and a diet Coke to go. And, put her tab on mine. I'm paying."

Sissy wiped her eyes, "You don't have to do that."

"It's alright. You're staying at my house tonight, so you can follow me to my house."

"I've already made reservations."

"I won't hear of it." Mrs. Howard patted Sissy on the hand and sniffled, "I would like to get to know the woman who Dave was gonna marry before she gets on with her life."

Sissy froze in her seat and felt herself ask a thousand questions at one time in her mind; fortunately, nothing came out. She felt a half stupid, half shocked look surface on her face.

Mrs. Howard looked down at her own wedding ring and wound it around her finger, "Yeah, he asked me if I still had Granny Mae's diamond ring a couple of months ago. I told him I did. Asked him why. Then he told me about you. About y'all. I don't like livin' in sin, but you was takin' good care of him it

sounded like, so I told him he could have it after I met you.
I didn't know . . .," Mrs. Howard broke down in tears, again.

Sissy's grief lifted as she witnessed the sorrow of Dave's
mother, "I had no idea, Mrs. Howard."

"Well, it's alright. I at least want to show it to you before
you go back to Athens. He had his demons, but he was a good
boy."

Donna arrived with Mrs. Howard's to-go box and
delicately put the check on the table. Sissy grabbed the check
before Mrs. Howard had a chance to.

"Sissy, I said I'd take care of it."

"It's the least I can do. Is your house far? I kind of need
gas."

Mrs. Howard smiled and motioned for the woman to follow
her, "We'll both get gas at the station up the road. The night
manager is a friend of the family. I bet she'd like to meet you."

*** 

After the two women got gas, Sissy followed behind Mrs.
Howard for about two blocks until they came upon a prim little
white house with dark green shutters. A fat mottled cat stretched
itself and stuck its curled tongue out at the women in the porch
light. Sissy stepped out of her SUV and smelled the crisp air. Fall
was in full swing in South Georgia. Perhaps they'd have a winter
this year. Sissy missed wearing just long sleeved shirts and jeans
in the winter. The thought of having to go back to Athens, that
dismal little rainy town - - cold and lonely little rainy town - - was
more than she could bear. Somewhere close by someone was
drying clothes with an aromatic fabric softener. The atmosphere
surrounding Mrs. Howard's home was one of family, love, and

security. Sissy wondered if she could keep in touch with the Howards when she felt lonely or nostalgic.

"I set up Anna's old room for you. That's my middle child. You met Rory, my youngest, back at the restaurant. Anna lives about three blocks over in a nice old house. She wants to sell it, though. You're a realtor, right?"

"Yeah, I used to sell houses around here, as a matter of fact. Who's selling her house for her?"

"Nobody, yet. She wants to get it appraised. I told her to hire Rob, but they've never liked one another."

"Anything wrong with it?"

"The house? No. Nothing wrong with the house that I know of. Then on the other hand . . . that whole family's been acting strange, lately. I don't know what's going on over there. My granddaughter . . . well, you'll see for yourself at the funeral tomorrow."

Sissy followed Mrs. Howard into the house through the back entrance. A familiar scent wafted into Sissy's nose - - baked apple pie potpourri. Sissy looked around and felt as if she had stepped into the whole house version of Mimi's single "normal room." The back entrance led into the kitchen, which had oak countertops and apple decorations everywhere. The linoleum was a dark green and white checkerboard pattern. Matching dark green checks were sponge painted onto the walls. A fake pie cooler had doors covered in punched tin. Folk-art dolls hung from every available shelf space. Bright white appliances gleamed, from the oversized fridge, the oversized stove, to a large industrial sized mixer, and eight slotted toaster on the countertops. Mrs. Howard grabbed a TV tray from a stand beside the pie cooler and walked into the living room.

The living room was just as Sissy imagined it'd be. There was oversized oak furniture everywhere. All of the wood pieces matched: the end tables, TV stand, magazine racks, coffee table, built-in bookcase, and a hat rack in the corner by the front door. Mrs. Howard's furniture was a jewel tone plaid, with the reds and greens complimenting the colors in her kitchen. The walls were beige, as was the carpet.

An older man sat in an overstuffed, big man's plaid recliner, which hummed and vibrated. Upon closer inspection, Sissy saw he was asleep, the remote control propped on his fat belly. An empty tumbler with half melted ice cubes and a brown watery residue sat beside him on the end table.

Mrs. Howard walked over to the man, "Earl? Earl! Go on to bed, now."

Earl startled awake and rubbed his face, "Tammy? I'm not asleep. Resting my eyes." Earl picked up the remote and started channel surfing.

Sissy stood in the threshold between the kitchen and the living room, not knowing how to act.

Tammy smiled at Sissy and motioned for her to take a seat on the loveseat, "Earl, Dave's lady friend, Sissy, is here. She's gonna spend the night in Anna's old room. Why don't you go on to bed and let us talk. Girl talk."

Earl yawned and stretched, reminiscent of the mottled cat on the front door stoop, "OH! Ahhh." The old man took a disinterested look at Sissy, "Nice to meet you. I'm going to bed, now." Earl flipped the arm of his chair over, revealing a set of dials and switches. He fiddled with the knobs and the chair stopped vibrating. He flipped over the other arm, held out the remote, turned off the TV, and put the remote in a holder inside of the chair, "I reckon ya'll want the TV off?"

Tammy nodded, "Good night, Earl. I'll be up directly."

Earl slowly swaggered down the hall and disappeared into the darkness. Tammy looked at Sissy, tears in her eyes, "He hasn't touched a drop for years. Now, after the accident . . . it's alright for him to have a little something." Tammy set up her TV tray and opened the Styrofoam box, "I can't eat all of this. You can have half, if you want."

Sissy shook her head, "I already ate. My appetite's been off. You know."

Tammy opened her plastic fork and knife and began sawing into her burger, cutting it up into bite sized pieces, "Granny Mae's diamond is in the third book from the left. Tales of Tomorrow. Go get it."

Sissy turned her head to see what Tammy was looking at. Against the beige wall was a sturdy oak bookcase as tall as the wall it stood against. Books and dust catchers decoratively filled its shelves. Once she found the requested book, Sissy quickly did as she was told.

The book, which looked to be about three hundred pages long and quite sizable, was not heavy at all. She held it out to Tammy, but the woman did not take it.

"You open it, my hands are greasy from eating these French fries."

Sissy opened the book and discovered the reason it felt lighter than it looked. Inside, the book was hollowed out. A navy blue velvet box sat in the middle.

"Open it. Take a look at it."

Sissy opened the box and saw a large rectangular diamond ring. The band was wide and gold, with a smaller diamond on each side of the large center diamond. Sissy's first thought was, *It's so gaudy.* The thought made her feel guilty, "I like it; I would have loved it. Thank you for showing me this."

"Altogether, that there's a three carat diamond ring. Fit for a queen. Dave wanted you to have it. He said you have a missing finger. I was kind of worried, but he said it was on your right hand, anyway."

"Yeah, it's a long story. Farming when I was a little girl," Sissy heard the lie slip out of her mouth before she could stop it. Hopefully, Tammy would be like Dave and not ask too many questions about it.

"Oh, yeah. Earl's brother done the same thing. I understand, Gal." Suddenly, a pernicious gleam sparkled in Tammy's eye, "Wanna know how this here ring ended up in our humble little family?"

Sissy held the ring in the light and watched the prisms reflect on Tammy's TV tray, "Sure."

Tammy wiped her hands on her thin "Hunker Home" napkin and closed her to-go box, "My grandfather was a gambler. They said he had gambled up and down every part, south of the Mason-Dixon line. Then he met my grandmother, Granny Mae, back when he was making his way to the old casino in Albany. Supposedly, it was love at first sight. Well, my great-grandfather was a preacher, so marrying off his only daughter to a gambler was not in the question. My grandfather became a Christian, got baptized in the creek behind Great-Grandpa's church, and made a life change.

Pappy and Granny Mae finally got permission to court, but Pappy couldn't find work at first. He was so poor, Great-Grandpa set him up on a circuit with the church members to work in exchange for room and board. Finally, Pappy got work as a field hand for Oak View Plantation on the other side of Flemming. So they set him up in one of the sheds on the plantation.

He saved up his money, which he kept in an old cigar box under his box springs in the shed. Well, he kept most of it in the cigar box. A little of it he kept in his shoe, kinda like a savings account, I guess. Pappy was saving up his money to buy Granny Mae a ring. Back then, you didn't have to have a ring, but he wanted to prove to Great-Grandpa that he was a responsible young man, and could make an honest living.

Anyway, the shed caught fire while he was gone to work one day, and it burned up everything, including his ring money. Well to hear it told, Pappy took off right then and there. He didn't come back for several weeks. Great-Grandpa thought he'd skipped town and wasn't coming back. Told Granny Mae he was just a crook and always would be. Stuff like that. Then, out of the blue, Pappy came back to Granny Mae with this here diamond. Great-Grandpa swore up and down Pappy had gone gamblin' and won it cheatin' at cards or some mess. Pappy said he didn't win it gamblin,' but that he had gone off to look for more work to make back the money that'd gotten burned and he came across this man who was bein' robbed," Tammy coughed and took a big sip of her diet Coke.

"Anyway, Pappy said he saved the man's life and gotten stabbed in the shoulder in the process. As re-payment, the man took Pappy in, nursed him back to health, and asked him how he could repay him. Pappy said he had worked hard, gone without eating some days, just to buy Granny Mae a ring, but the money burned up in a fire. The next thing Pappy knew, the man had called his wife into the room with him and told her to take off her ring. She did. That man gave Pappy her ring. Pappy refused. Pappy asked him for work, instead. The man said he didn't have any work, but that Pappy could spend one more night in the big house.

The next morning, Pappy got ready to leave, and the man's wife packed some food for Pappy to be on his way. Around noon, Pappy got hungry and unpacked the little picnic he had with him, and low and behold in the middle of a loaf of cornbread was the ring. Pappy said he ate and thought about returning that big ole ring but couldn't bring himself to do it. He even got the urge to go gamble with it and see if he could use it to get more money and keep it at the same time. But his Christian ways got the best of him and he decided to take it as a sign from God that he should marry Granny Mae. It took some doin', but Great-Grandpa finally relented and they was married that June."

Sissy put the ring back in its velvet box, "That is such a lovely story. So who was the rich man?"

"Pappy never did say. Said he promised to keep it a secret."

"And he kept it a secret his whole life?"

"Yeah, Pappy never was too good at remembering names. Especially ones he made up."

"You mean?"

"The whole thing is a damned lie! Pappy took that money in his shoe and went gambling. Got stabbed when he was caught cheating at cards. BUT, he got out with his life and that there ring!" Tammy laughed, but tears fell from her eyes.

Sissy inhaled and exhaled slowly. It was a lot of information to take in at one time, personal information that made her feel as if she were caught between worlds, that of stranger and family member. Still, she felt she had to say something, to connect to this poor woman who had just lost her son to an element she would never understand, "That is just . . . unbelievable. I'm glad I came over. The ring is lovely. I can't believe Dave was going to ask me to marry him with this precious family heirloom. I loved him so much. I'll miss him dearly."

Tammy patted Sissy on the leg, sniffled, and got up, "I'm going to bed, now. Come on with me, and I'll show you to Anna's room."

Sissy followed Tammy down the hall where family portraits from perhaps every generation were hung. Earl's snoring seemed so loud, Sissy wondered if the pictures ever vibrated themselves off of the wall. Tammy rubbed her nose and pointed at a black and white photograph of a stiff looking couple in an elaborate antique frame, "That's Pappy and Granny Mae right there." Sissy didn't have time to get a good look, but followed Tammy to Anna's room.

Once inside, Sissy found herself in a room that made her feel time warped. Apparently, Anna had moved out and not bothered to take any of her teenage or childhood memorabilia with her. There were pictures of the woman as a teenager, hair teased and crimped. There were pictures of her as a pre-teen, with long stringy hair and gawky thick glasses. There were pictures of her as a little girl with white stockings, black Mary Janes, and a starched handmade dress. Teddy bears of every size and color lined the walls of the room. Pillows that spelled out her name and initials covered the bed. A cork board covered with old messages and signatures of "best friends" looked like it was decorated yesterday except for the fine line of dust all around it. In fact, the room smelled of flowery perfume and dust. Sissy felt like an intruder, that any minute the teen version of Anna would come barreling through the door, demanding to know who was sleeping in her bed.

"I left the room pretty much the way Anna left it the day she eloped. We didn't speak for a long time afterwards. Then Deborah came along. That girl . . . anyway, I hope you have a pleasant night's sleep. Maybe Earl won't wake you too much. You oughta' try lying next to him. Then again, preferably not, huh?" Tammy let out a forced laugh, "I'm rattling on. See you in the morning."

Sissy pulled down the covers, turned out the lights, and closed her eyes. Throughout the night she thought she smelled Athens water and aftershave, and felt a gentle hand rub her back in her sleep.

The next morning, Sissy awoke to the sounds and smells of breakfast being made.
A hung-over Earl stumbled through the hall, complaining about not being used to drinking anymore and asking where the aspirin was. Sissy dressed for the funeral and joined the family for breakfast. A somber mood seemed to have overcome the safe little home.

Sissy rode with the Howards to the funeral home. Nothing could prepare the realtor for her own grief and that of people whom she'd never met before. Suddenly, it occurred to her that there was a large part of Dave that she had never known and would never really know thereafter. A deep sense of loss, loss of what was, and what might have been overcame her. Tears welled in her eyes.

Earl gave Sissy a spare handkerchief from his hip pocket with a fatherly smile, "I figured one of you women would break down and cry, so I brought extra." The old man tapped at his breast in a joking manner, "This one here's mine, so don't go snottin' that one up all at one time."

The comment was so absurd, Sissy let out an unexpected guffaw, sending snot bubbles flying out of her nose. Earl turned his back, as if he hadn't seen. Sissy couldn't help but to think what a great family they would've been to marry into.

Tammy walked off and immediately came back with a young slender woman's arm in her clutches, "Sissy, I wanted you to meet Anna."

Sissy dabbed her eyes with her handkerchief, "I hear you have a house for sale?"

Anna gave Sissy a dirty look.

Tammy laughed nervously, "Sissy's a realtor who used to sell houses here in town before moving up to Athens. I told her you were wanting your house appraised. That's all."

Anna smiled, but her eyes were filled with anger, "I didn't understand what you were talking about. Sissy, is it?"

Sissy smiled back, "If you wanted, I could appraise your house for you. Just to give you something to compare with your actual realtor later on." Sissy had no idea why she just emotionally vomited up that information. Was she trying to get along with the sister-in-law she'd never have? Her emotions would not allow her mind to think clearly, and she felt like a fool for offering to do something for someone she didn't know. Someone who appeared to be so disagreeable. Then again, they were meeting for the first time at a funeral. And, not just any funeral, but that of a brother and future fiancée, whose death was altogether beyond explanation.

Anna rolled back on her high heel, "For free?"

Sissy laughed in a submissive tone, "Of course. We would've been family, after all." Every time Sissy opened her mouth, she just wanted to punch herself in the gut and get it over with. Why couldn't she just be herself in this woman's presence?

Before Sissy could continue her track of self-loathing, a young girl of about twelve or so came running up to Anna, tugging on her dress sleeve, "Momma! Grandpa's teasing me like I'm five years old again, and he won't stop!" Apparently, this was Deborah.

Deborah was a gaunt, disturbed version of Anna's pre-teen picture in her old room at Tammy and Earl's house. Anna grabbed the girl by her wrists and whispered in her ear. Upon closer inspection, Sissy saw that the girl's fingertips were covered in fresh, bright red scabs and rubbed calluses. Some of the girl's fingernails were broken and split. Her eyes were sunken and dark, as if she had not been sleeping well. Her clavicle and the bones in her wrists stuck out, as if she had not been eating well, either.

Deborah pulled her bony wrists out of Anna's grasp, "I wanna go home. I wanna go home, now!"

Anna snatched at Deborah's hand, but the girl dodged her, "I am not taking you home. Look at your hands, just look at them! I swear to God, you peel on that door one more time . . ."

Tammy grabbed a hold of Sissy's wrist with one hand, and put her arm around Anna's thin waist with the other, "Anna, have a little respect, honey. Deborah, if you don't like your grandpa pickin' on you, stay here by us."

Deborah stood patiently by her mother, hands behind her back, foot digging at the chipped marble of the sanctuary and said in a far away voice, "Yes, ma'am."

Anna flashed her mother a look filled with contempt, "You have no idea what that daughter of mine has put me through. She won't eat. She won't sleep. All she wants to do is pick the paint off of that damn door!"

Tammy leaned in closer to her daughter, "We're here for your brother's funeral, not to discuss your problems. I told you, make Wayne take the door down and get rid of it."

Anna snarled back, "I told you he won't get rid of it! I've asked and I've begged, but he won't get rid of it!"

"Get rid of it yourself. If he comes home to a gaping hole in the wall, he'll have to go out and get a new door."

"I've tried! The stupid hinges are rusted stuck. It won't even open! I told him it was a fire hazard, but he wants that door for some damn reason. I *need help*, Mama."

Tammy took her arm off of Anna's waist, "I told you what a hell it was for me and your father back when his mama wouldn't let our business be our business. This is a simple problem, and you can handle it as a family." Anna stared Tammy down, who stared right back, "It's just a door, Anna. Really."

Anna looked at Sissy, who was having a hard time looking as if she weren't listening. The skinny woman let out a faked chuckle, "I know you didn't come here to listen to my *petty* problems, but if you could just come by later this afternoon or before you leave and appraise the house for me, I'd appreciate it."

Sissy faked a startled look, as if she had not been listening. The movement was absurd, she knew, but it was the most comfortable of all the reactions she could think of, "How's about four-ish? I don't think it's too dark by then, is it?"

Anna put her arm around Deborah's shoulders, "No, I'll see you then. Maybe my little obsessive-compulsive-disorder right here won't send you away screaming."

***

The funeral was sad. The preacher was charismatic. The eulogy was heart-felt. The men sniffled stoically. The women cried to the point of competition, and Sissy sat in the midst of it all, wondering when she'd wake up from this sad, sad, nightmare. The ride back with the Howards was deathly silent. Everyone seemed cried out, but knew they weren't. For the time being shock had replaced grief, and all welcomed its numbing effects.

## Chapter 55: I've Got a Door to Pick With You

Four o'clock rolled around just when it seemed time had ceased to be. Sissy got directions to Anna's house from Tammy and headed out. When Sissy got to the home, dark clouds were filling the sky. It would rain. Sissy tried to stop herself from thinking, *It'll rain on Dave and his tiny little house in the earth.* But the thought reverberated in her head until the only way she could release it was to say the words out loud.

Anna was waiting in a rocking chair on a front porch that buckled so badly it undulated. The skinny woman rocked with a vengeance, the chair's rails hitting the bowed wood boards, throwing off her rhythm. To say the least, she didn't look comfortable.

Before Sissy had time to stare at the woman jarring back and forth upon the porch, a tall man dressed in camouflage barreled out the front door, slammed it, almost knocked over Sissy as he crossed the front lawn and into his truck, slamming that door. He spun out of the driveway, towing a fishing boat behind him. Sissy didn't recognize the man and supposed that was Anna's husband.

"Nice house! Looks real big. How old is it?" Sissy shouted as she walked across the front lawn. From the look of things, Sissy gathered that now was not the time for polite conversation as it would only bring about a long story that she had no interest in hearing.

Quite frankly, she'd had enough of long stories to last her a long time. Perhaps if she could quickly assess the house, she would have time to leave for Athens before it got dark.

Anna, not one to take hints, explained, "That was Wayne. Goin' fishing. Again. We talked about the door, again. He just got mad, like always, and took off with his boat, like always, and won't be back until late tonight, like always. That's that story, in case you were wondering. About the house, it's about two thousand five hundred square feet. The records on it were lost in a fire."

"Isn't that always the case? My house had the same thing happen. To its records, I mean."

Anna stared at Sissy as if she had just interrupted an important speech, "Anyway, it's supposed to be about a hundred years old. The roof's only five years old. New paint on the inside. No structural damage. Had some sort of gas line, old well, some hole in the ground covered when we bought the thing. Glass in the windows is original. Some are cracked.
Just fixed a rotten sash in the dining room. Kitchen's got all new appliances. They'd stay. Attic's not floored all the way, but it's got this weird little box you crawl up into to get to it, so I've never used it. Wayne says it's scary, so nothing of ours is up there. Any other questions?"

"How much land is it on?"

"Three quarters of an acre. Just put in a chain link fence out back. Wayne says he's taking it down if we sell the place. I'll see about that."

"Not much grass in your front yard, but I'd call it landscaped because of the azalea bushes and dogwoods."

"Wayne's momma likes to park right beside the front porch. Killed all of the grass. I told him to tell her not to park there, but he won't do it. That man . . ."

"Well, let's take a look inside, shall we?" Sissy took a big step forward, leaving Anna mid-sentence.

The home was very nice. Plaster walls, hardwood floors "with lots of character" (translation, "not restored") and high, ten foot ceilings throughout the house gave it a feeling of grandeur. To Sissy's surprise, Anna actually had good taste and seemed to have done her homework in historically accurate colors and decorations.

"The furniture is reproductions. If a buyer was interested, they could stay," Anna said as she rubbed her hand over a baroque style velvet couch.

"So you want two different appraisals?"

Anna shrugged, "I guess. What do you mean?"

Sissy sighed as she tried to hide her impatience, "One for a furnished home and one for an unfurnished home?"

Anna glared at Sissy, "Yeah."

Sissy invited herself into the dining room and took a quick inventory. At this point, she realized she had nothing to gain from being exceptionally nice to this woman. There was no way she could possibly be Anna's realtor, and memories of selling NO houses for months in Flemming came crashing upon her like waves of bad consciousness.

If anything, this was a mission of mercy somehow wheedled out of her by a confession of promised marriage from a mother in-law she'd never have. Once out of the huge dining room, Sissy whizzed through the kitchen, took a quick glance out the backdoor, and peered through an open side entrance into the laundry room, where she was stopped dead in her tracks.

In the laundry room was the infamous door that had been

such a hot topic at the funeral earlier that day. And there, just as Anna had described, was Deborah obsessively picking away at the peeling paint on the door. The sight was so strange that it literally drew the reluctant realtor into the room, until she found herself standing beside Deborah, staring at the girl.

Deborah seemed oblivious to Sissy's presence until the preteen spouted, "He wants out. He promises that if I help him get out, he'll forget everything and leave me *alone*."

Sissy was startled at this revelation, but not surprised. A sense of relief came over the woman as she realized she was finally getting used to such situations. A decade earlier and she would have thought the girl needed counseling. The past few months proved the girl might, in fact, just need some empathy. Therefore, Sissy had no problem calmly asking the girl, "Who wants out?"

The girl just shrugged, "I don't know. But he's stuck in this door. I can finally start to see him. Can you?"

Sissy stared at the door and just saw white paint cracking off in long slivers. With a shift in focus, Sissy saw that the gray wood underneath the paint was water stained. "Where did this door come from, Deborah?"

"I don't know. Momma hates it because it's old and ugly, 'Brings down the value of the house.' Daddy won't get rid of it, because he found it and brought it home like some sort of trophy. What kind of crazoid is proud of an old door?"

"Will peeling the door get the man out of the door?"

"How else can I get him out? He won't leave me alone about it. The sooner I finish, the sooner he'll go away."

"What do you mean he won't leave you alone?"

"He yells at me all the time, begging me to let him out.

He's 'trapped inside.' He gets really crazy at night when I'm sleeping. But, the worst is when it rains. He cries for help a lot. Then he makes this nasty coughing sound and chokes. Then I wake up with *my* chest burning and I feel like I'm . . . floating away. I hate it. If I could just get this man out of the door . . ."

Anna walked into the room behind the two women, "Good God, Deborah, give it a rest. There is no 'man.' You are embarrassing me."

Sissy stepped back beside Anna, and then she saw it. Behind the paint on the bare gray wood, the water stains undulated in dark and light hues. In the middle of the door, the hues were the darkest, forming the outline of a person. Sissy looked at Anna, "You don't see the outline of a man in the door?"

Anna glared at Sissy, "I suppose you do?"

Sissy was tired of trying to be nice. She felt her standard snarky ways quickly return, "Yeah, I do. And, for another thing, your daughter's not crazy." Sissy took a small step toward the door, wondering if she should touch it, "How did your husband get this door?"

Anna cocked her brow, "He came home with it awhile back during the flood."

Sissy wanted to sarcastically ask Anna if she were sure her husband's name weren't Noah, but she knew better. "The flood" was a reference to a natural catastrophe that hit Albany in the summer of '94. It was all over the news, even in Athens. Sissy walked up to the door and put her right palm flat upon it. She dug her nails into the wood and felt her ghost finger join the others in scratching the surface of the wood. Something was definitely about to happen.

Darkness and the sensation of drowning engulfed Sissy, until she found her way out of it, into the larger consciousness.

## Chapter 56: A Pilfering We Will Go

Sissy's mind floated its way to a rainy night: *Wayne was navigating his small fishing boat in the flood water.* At first Sissy thought she might be watching him boat the Flint River, but as her sight became sharper, she saw the sides of flood swamped houses stick out of the rising water.

*Why are you here?* Sissy asked, but there came no response.

*Onward Wayne boated, rowing through the water, taking breaks to shine a flashlight into the darkness. Within a few minutes, Wayne was beside a house he seemed to recognize. Only a few inches of the front door stuck out above the floodwater.*

*"You in there Snoops?" Wayne yelled as he pounded on the top of the door from his boat.*

*A voice helplessly called out, "Yes! God, yes! Help me! I can't get the door open!"*

*Wayne let out a laugh, "Bet you wish you hadn't put them bars on those windows now, huh?"*

*Snoops became frantic from within, "Wayne? That you, Wayne? Oh, God, let me out, Wayne! You gotta help me!"*

*"What, and then have you owe me?"*

*"With my life, Wayne. Just get me out! I'm gonna die in here!"*

*"I don't want your life, Snoops. It ain't worth a damn."*

*"Anything you want, Wayne. Get me out! The water's rising!"*

*"You know I already have to sell everything I own to pay you back! Been borrowin'. Next I'll be beggin'. Already lost my*

*dignity. 'Bout to lose my pride soon as Anna finds out.*

*A man can't never get his pride back from a woman like that."*

"You said you could pay when you sat at that table!  How was I supposed to know?"

"You cheated me.  You didn't give me a fair game, Snoops."

"I never cheated you.  I swear!  Let me out and I'll give you back all of the money you lost to me!"

"You, you owe me!"

"I owe you!  I do!  Let me out!  Let me make it up to you!"

"Oh, you're already making it up to me!  I'd say in a little while, I'll be paid in full."

"Don't go, Wayne!  Let me out!  Please, Wayne!  Please!"

Wayne pulled his oars through the black water.  The rain pelted down harder, drowning out Snoops' cries for help.  Further into the darkness, Wayne boated his way to 4th Street and flashed his light upon the second stories of "The Abbot's Luxury Condos," which were now abandoned.  He shined his light until he found what he was looking for, a lowered ladder hanging from a balcony.  Fumbling through a tangle of rope that had twisted around a large, double bladed axe in the bottom of the boat, Wayne finally found the anchor and threw it over the side.  The rope was slack, so Wayne wound the excess on a hook on the side of the boat.  After a bit of maneuvering, Wayne pulled himself onto the ladder, which gave him easy access into an opened sliding glass door.

With flashlight in hand, Wayne pilfered his way through the condominium.  A cookie jar sitting unobtrusively on a kitchen countertop yielded a nice bounty of three hundred dollars and *some loose change. After trashing the place, Wayne made his way back, jar in hand, to his small boat. Wayne then contemplated rowing to the next abandoned building.*

*The water was rising, and the boat was collecting water at a rate faster than Wayne had anticipated. He realized he had lost track of time and did not hear how hard the rain was falling. The thief decided to call it a night and get back to his truck before his strength abandoned him in the small aluminum boat. Using the street signs for markers, Wayne rowed way his back to Snoops' home. No part of the door was sticking out of the water; it had become completely submerged. Wayne knocked hard against the roof above the door, but the shingles squished beneath his gloved hand.*

*Wayne leaned over toward the submerged door and yelled, "Snoops? You still alive?"*

*No answer came back. The rain, which had covered everything in a continuous sheet of heavy drops that hit as hard as spiked darts, took a respite from its terrestrial targets. The rain had momentarily stopped. Wayne turned his left ear toward the house and heard something knock against the door. He shined his light into the water and saw that the knocking was making ripples.*

*"I reckon you want out, ya' old bastard." Wayne stripped himself of his raincoat and heavy boots. After dropping his anchor overboard, Wayne grabbed his axe and raised himself onto the roof. A small, decorative, gabled window that promised a second story, but gave none, gleamed back in Wayne's face. The man smashed through the window and crawled inside where he pulled himself through several inches of water. Wayne was in Snoops' attic. There was no way Snoops could be rescued if the attic were*

*full of water. Wayne decided to go back to his boat and home with the knowledge that his debts were no more.*

*Suddenly, Wayne felt the attic floor give way and disintegrate beneath him. This unexpected turn of events startled the man, who dropped his flashlight into the murky depths below. Wayne looked into the darkness and saw nothing but the eerie glow of his sunken flashlight peering up at him through the black water. Terror seized the thief, who clung to a nearby ceiling rafter for dear life. He was unable to see and too frightened to move. He felt his mind begin to swim with panic. The irony of drowning in a drowned man's house to whom he owed money and repaid with murder sunk into Wayne with the force of the Old Testament God's wrath.*

*Wayne laughed. He laughed at his luck. He laughed at his lack of luck. He laughed at his fear. He laughed at the possibility of his own death. He laughed because he didn't know what else to do alone in the darkness with the rising water. He laughed until he didn't care.*

*He laughed until he was angry and refused to die. The image of his dead, bloated body floating only inches from Snoops' dead, bloated body only intensified his swelling anger.*

*Wayne let go of the rafter and plunged himself into the flooded main story. The water was pitch black and the flashlight beam was blinding. Wayne felt his hands and legs bump into furniture. A lamp swooshed around an unseen end table. A Styrofoam plate floated between the ray of light and Wayne's vision. Finally, Wayne made his way to the flashlight, which had landed upon what felt like a braided rug. His flashlight in hand, Wayne made his way back up to the hole in the roof. But he* couldn't find it. Debris covered the skim of the water, making the roof look like an obscure undulating puzzle. His lungs began to burn, and once again he felt panic begin to reintroduce itself.

Keeping his bearings, Wayne made his way to the front door, which he found impossible to open. The doorknob would turn, but the dead bolt was locked and the key wasn't in the hole. Feeling through the water, Wayne made out the long cylinders of the hinges of the door and prized them apart with the tips of his fingers until he thought his fingernails would burst from the pressure. The first cylinder came out, and then the second. Lifting up on the door, Wayne felt it swish open until he was able to squeeze himself through the narrow opening. Finally, after what felt like an eternity, Wayne burst through the floodwater and felt the rain hit his face.

After taking a giant breath, Wayne exclaimed, "Jesus, Snoops, you liked to have killed me!"

Wayne proceeded to pull himself up onto the roof and lower himself back into the safety of his small boat. Secured in his water logged boat, Wayne began to pull the anchor's rope, only to soon realize it was caught on something. "Damn it, bet it's caught on a bush or something." Wayne tugged on the anchor, but it wouldn't budge.

The boat was now filled with so much water, it covered Wayne's ankles. The man grabbed an oar and knocked it around in the water, until it caught on something large and heavy. Dragging the oar across the unseen impediment, the hapless thief cursed his existence under his breath. Finally, the weight lifted from the anchor. As the thief was pulling the rope, he felt something large thud against the side of his boat. Wayne grabbed his flashlight to see what it was. To his horror, Wayne discovered Snoops' drowned body floating face up.

"Holy!" Wayne fell over backwards in the boat, capsizing the tiny vessel. All of the craft's contents emptied like an opened purse, including the cookie jar full of money. Abject fear and the relentless rain made Wayne unable to pull himself onto the slippery side of the boat.

The thief was stranded, floating in the water. Warnings of snakes and being swept into unseen hazards blared in his mind. But, a tiny beam of light made its way through the rain splashed water. Once again, the man dove into the murky depths. Grabbing his flashlight, Wayne swept the ground with the light, searching for the lost jar and its stolen bounty. It was gone. The light's rays could not penetrate the darkness far enough to make the effort fruitful.

The thief once again made his way to the surface but bumped his head into Snoops' floating body. The man pushed the corpse away and took a breath of air, "Damn it, Snoops! You made your point, already. Now, get!"

Wayne flashed his light into the darkness looking for something to cling to.
Wispy branches stuck out of the water like strands of teased hair. Nothing that could hold a big man against the rising tide. Then he saw it. A door slowly floating into the darkness toward the abandoned apartments. Not just any door, though. Snoops' door. The locked door that probably had a key lying patiently on the floor just in front of it, dropped in a moment of bad nerves, or hanging on a nail, forgotten in a moment of terror.

Wayne realized that Snoops died from panicking. And, the

*door that killed its owner would be the door that saved its intruder. Wayne swam over to the door, propped himself on top of it, and kicked his legs. It worked. The door held the soaked man's weight. After much exertion, the thief made his way to dry land. On a bridge overlooking the swollen river bank, Wayne saw his truck waiting patiently with an empty trailer.*

*"Lost my boat. Lost my loot. But I got a door and my life. Screw it, I'm going home." Wayne dragged the door up the tall embankment and loaded it into the back of his truck. He pulled the truck further up the embankment. Exhausted, the man fell asleep in the cabin of his truck.*

*When Wayne awoke, it was early dawn. The sun was just beginning to rise. The rain had stopped. Wayne took a moment to look at the beauty of the sun's rays as they reflected off of the calm water when he saw his capsized boat stranded on the bank.*

*"Hot damn!" Wayne let out a yell of joy when he pulled the stranded vessel onto the shore. "Had to pawn you and buy you back for twice what you was worth. Lost you to the flood. Now I get to drag you back to my truck. I promise I will never let you outta my sight again!"*

*A darkness not of night, but like that of stolen dreams, engulfed the man as he labored over the aluminum craft, pulling it up the embankment to be joined once again to his truck's barren trailer.*

*Darkness*, until Sissy's consciousness found its way to Wayne's home. *Christmas time. Christmas time of this year . . .*

\*\*\*

*A giant Christmas tree towered beside the long dining room table. Beautiful presents waited patiently on the floor in a* pile so tall they stacked up to the middle boughs of the tree. White lights reflected off of the freshly buffed wood floor. Nighttime darkened the window panes that surrounded the tree and all of its glory.

Deborah ran with heavy footsteps across the room, rattling the China on the table, "I did it! I let him out! All of the paint is off the door, Momma! He can get out, now!"

Anna stood on a step ladder, hanging long strands of wired ribbon in spiraling ringlets down the sides of the tall tree, "What are you talking about? That stupid door? I swear, I'm having you committed on the first of the year."

"No Momma, I can stop because I finally finished. All of the paint is gone and he can get out now."

"Well, hallelujah. If only I knew what in the world you were talking about."

Deborah made little skipping motions, "Come see, you can finally see him. I'll show you."

"Only if you promise that once I take a look at that stupid door, you'll never talk about it again."

"I promise, just come see before he goes."

"And I can paint it, now that all the paint's peeled off?"

"Yeah, come on, hurry!"

Anna followed Deborah into the washroom where she let out a loud gasp. There, waiting patiently in front of her eyes with no thick paint chips obstructing her view stood the undeniable outline of a man's body. In a hushed, awed tone, Anna exclaimed, "I'd never believe it if I hadn't seen it with my own eyes." Anna yelled at the top of her lungs, "Wayne! Wayne! Get in here, now! Right now, Wayne!"

*Wayne's heavy steps thudded through the house, until they stopped at the threshold of the washroom, "What do you . . . oh, my God! Do you see what I see?"*

*Deborah grinned, "It's that man I've been telling y'all about. I finally let him out. He's gonna leave now."*

*Wayne crossed his arms and turned his back, "That is just the grain of the wood playing tricks on our eyes. It looks like something because our imaginations are making it look like that." Wayne turned around and pointed at Deborah, who was still feeling quite proud of herself, "That, and you, you little . . . you've been driving us crazy talking about some man stuck in that door! If you hadn't been running your mouth about a man, we wouldn't be seeing one right now!"*

*Wayne's words were harsh, making Deborah cry, "That's not true! I knew he was there before anybody else did! It's real, and it's all your fault!" Deborah ran past her father who stood staring at the door in shock.*

*Anna bit her nails, "You're getting rid of that thing tonight. You hear me? I want it gone!"*

*"Anna, I ain't got nothing to replace it! You want a big hole in the wall all night? With the presents?"*

*"First thing in the morning, or I will move back in with my momma."*

*"First thing in the morning, then."*

*"I'm going to bed. It's late, and I . . . what's that smell?"*

*"Smell?" Wayne sniffed the air like a primate in search of prey. "I think it's smoke. You cookin' something?"*

*Before Anna could answer, Deborah let out a blood curdling scream from the other side of the house, "The presents are on fire!"*

Wayne and Anna ran into the dining room where they were confronted with a blazing fire.

Deborah was in tears, *"I threw water on them, trying to get the fire out, but it spread! Don't be mad at me! Don't be mad!"*

Wayne threw his hands in the air, *"She made an electrical fire! The lights are on fire! We can't put that out by ourselves, the flames could be inside the walls!"*

Anna grabbed Deborah by the arm, *"Everybody outside. We'll get the Coopers to call the fire department."* Anna tried to open the front door, but it wouldn't open, *"Wayne, the front door's stuck. It won't budge! It's not locked, but it won't open!"*

Wayne ran to the back door, *"This one's stuck, too!"*

*"What are we going to do?"* Anna yelled.

*"Break the windows!"* Wayne grabbed a dining room chair and smashed it into the window. The chair ricocheted off of the panes. Glass shattered, falling away in strips, leaving a pattern of steadfast glass that resembled bars.

Anna shielded Deborah from the fire with her own body, *"Why isn't the glass breaking, Wayne? What's going on?"*

*"I don't know. The glass won't break,"* Wayne choked on the thickening smoke.

Deborah held her hand over her mouth, *"It's that man, isn't it, Daddy? You did that to him. You made him get stuck in that door!"*

*"I don't know what you're talking about! Now, get out of the way, or you're gonna get hit!"* Wayne picked up the massive dining room chair with a rush of adrenaline. The chair bounced off of the next window, which broke in strips, just as the first.

Darkness once again filled Sissy's consciousness until she saw billowing smoke turn violently away from a heavy downpour of water. *Fire engines roared in the darkness.*

*Bodies came into focus. Not charred remains, but dead, bloated bodies surrounded by smoldering ash.*

***

*Darkness, drowning, floating . . . the noise of water draining.*

***

Sissy came to, her palm still planted firmly on the door, "I know what's wrong."

Anna pulled her daughter away from the door, "You know what's wrong just by putting your hand up on that door for all of a second?"

"A second? Really? I thought . . . anyway. You gotta get rid of this door."

In Anna's usual sarcastic tone, she blasted Sissy, "No kidding. I've been telling Wayne that for months now, but he won't listen."

Sissy retorted, "You tell Wayne that Snoops will have payback for what Wayne did to him. You tell Wayne that he'll lose more than a cookie jar with three hundred dollars in it if he doesn't get rid of that door. You tell Wayne to get that door off of that wall, even if he has to cut off the entire wall with it. Then you tell Wayne to throw it back into the Flint River and tell Snoops he's real sorry."

Anna pulled her daughter away from Sissy and held her as if to protect her from the "deranged" realtor. Anna asked Sissy,

"What are you talking about?"

"Wayne knows."

"And if he doesn't get rid of it, which he won't?"

"Snoops is gonna see to it that all of you drown in a fire. Yeah, drown in a fire. Now, I don't feel like giving you an appraisal on your house. The realtor who sells your house is supposed to do that for free anyway. Even if you decide NOT to sell your house. I loved your brother. I like your momma. I even like your daddy. But I don't like you. So, if you don't mind, I've got to be getting back to Athens, because I got a crap load of work to get caught up on and my own haunted house to deal with."

# Chapter 57: Going Home

Without further explanation, Sissy walked out on Anna, who was so angry the veins popped out on the sides of her neck. If the woman were yelling at her, Sissy didn't hear it. The realtor was quite proud of herself. Finally, some good had come of her strange powers. Well, the potential for good. It wasn't her fault if her advice went unheeded. Anyway, Sissy knew what her purpose was. Not only could she sell houses, but maybe she could "cure" them, too. Except for maybe her own house. That house wasn't sick, it was terminally ill. Perhaps she could find a nice couple who were about as psychic as a fence post. People with such strength in their rationale that "voices" would eventually die with the "wind" and the "bumps-in-the-night" would "settle" with the house.

Sissy chuckled with a deepened sense of irony, "Like the Bozemans in the Rawlins Mansion. They really thought the sounds were coming from rednecks *outside* of the house and not residual energy *inside* the house. They survived in that house eight whole years before having enough! Maybe I can sell my house to people like that if I can't fix it."

A dark mood overcame Sissy as she thought about the idea of selling the house to other people. Her heart beat hard in her chest as she imagined the house occupied by a young couple with children. Or worse, babies. After all, wasn't that why she bought the house? Sissy hit her steering wheel in anger, "No, I will fix it. I will find a way, and I will make sure no one else is harmed in that house and send that demon back to hell. For Dave."

Silence filled the cabin of Sissy's SUV. *Oh, Dave. Dave. Dave. Dave. What can I do? How am I going to fix it?* Slowly, that familiar throb began in Sissy's missing finger.

Smiling, Sissy dug in her nails and watched as her ghost finger scraped the leather of the steering wheel. Despite the windows being rolled up and the air conditioning turned off, a cool draft raised the hair on the back of her neck. A draft that carried the familiar scent of Athens' water, soap, and aftershave through the car every now and again . . .

To Be Continued.

## About The Author

Soul'd is based on the people and places that I love the most. You see, I was born and raised in Georgia, a place that holds mysteries and magic for me to this day. If you prod a true Southerner hard enough, they will share a paranormal experience or a family secret that either led to generational riches or ruin. Interesting people and forbidden stories lurk in every swamp, abandoned house, and inherited 100 acre wood where I grew up, or at least that's what I believe. Soul'd is more or less an amalgamation of those stories I collected over the years with enough creative liberties taken to protect the hapless. Any similarities to anyone or event is purely happen stance.

www.ingramcontent.com/pod-product-compliance
Lightning Source LLC
Chambersburg PA
CBHW070616260626
47161CB00007B/2453